For h...

[handwritten signature]

[handwritten signature]

Paul Wilson

London, May 2014

The Alphabet Game

HERTFORDSHIRE PRESS

Published in United Kingdom
Hertfordshire Press © 2014

Suite 125, 43 Bedford Street
Covent Garden, London
WC2 9HA United Kingdom
www.hertfordshirepress.com

The Alphabet Game by Paul Wilson

Author profile picture copyright - David Lamyman

*British Library Catalogue in Publication Data
A catalogue record for this book is available from the British Library
Library of Congress in Publication Data
A catalogue record for this book has been requested*

ISBN 978-0-9927873-2-5

The Alphabet Game

Paul Wilson

London, May 2014

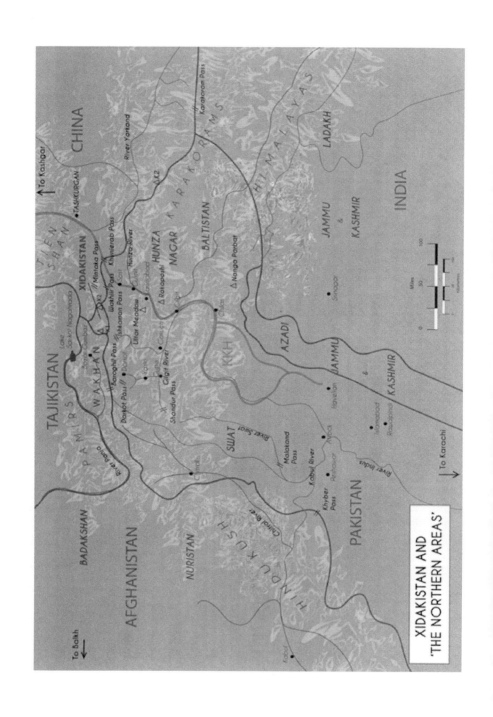

XIDAKISTAN AND
'THE NORTHERN AREAS'

'A good traveller has no fixed plans.'

Lao Tzu, father of Taoist philosophy

The Laws of the Game

Not all games play by the rules. Rugby and football, for example. That such games have no rules to play by, may come as something of a surprise.

Graham placed his pen down on his notebook and remembered the first time he had learnt this – the hard way. Uncle Ray's garden during the school holidays, and his cousin Jos' teasing was once again bordering on bullying.

'Bet you five knuckle raps you don't know how many rules there are in rugger.'

'Get lost.'

'Alright, football, then.'

'I said "get lost".'

Jos was at the posh school, Graham the local comp down the road.

'Chicken!'

Graham kept his fists tight to his chest.

'Tell you what,' Jos egged on, 'I'll give you two either way.'

Graham had hesitated, thought long and hard, and hesitated again.

'Twelve.'

'None. Idiot.' Jos primed his raw pack of playing cards at an angle and forced Graham to hold out a fist. 'Football has laws, not rules.' Strike one. 'Like all proper sports.' Strike two. 'Rules are meant to be broken.'

The laws for The Alphabet Game were drawn up one port-soaked night in 1873, under the watchful eyes of Lord Grey and Edward Ellice. Or at least those of their portraits, hanging on an oak-panelled wall. The wall stood on the now-imaginary dividing line between 104 and 105 Pall Mall, that monumental conjugation of Portland stone better known as The Reform Club. Jules Verne's 'Around the World in Eighty Days' *was about to enter the literary canon, and amidst all the fanfare, excitement amongst members was rising to levels not seen for decades, some said since '32 itself.*

Lieutenant-Colonel Sir Hugh Broadbent-Holmes, a veteran of many a cock-up in India, quickly made his way to the smoking room. There, he had been tipped off, a first folio of Verne's eagerly-anticipated work lay waiting, accidentally left by fellow member Woodman. Woodman, it so happened, had been charged with proofreading the manuscript prior to publication (in translation, of course, French being so passé).

Sir Hugh, cigar fuming, began theatrically recounting Fogg's exploits to his old sparring-partner, 'Badger' Bingham, as he arrived for post-prandials. In his more active days Badger had been the theatrical one, gallivanting up from his tea plantations in Ceylon to couch a stay at Sir Hugh's summerhouse in Muree.

Soon the knight of the realm was dressaging his way around both the billiard table and a gathering crowd of listeners, skilfully flaunting his loot to all, yet ensuring none but himself enjoyed a full 'gander'. As Fogg's ports were called, members' ports were poured. With the narrative reaching its climax, and Verne's hero lamenting his apparent failure, Broadbent-Holmes challenged his audience to guess the number of foreign lands this consummate voyager had racked up during his adventure. Badger, never one to answer the question, wagered that whatever the number, he himself had chalked more. Bingham and Broadbent-Holmes had often sat for hours on the veranda outpointing one another on anything from tiger-bagging to prize tomatoes. Sir Hugh bit the bait, Fogg was forgotten, and horns were locked. As Badger totted up his collection, so Broadbent-Holmes began countering with his, tit for tat.

'What about Phileas?' came the cries from the cheap seats. 'Finish the story!' But to no avail.

Sir Hugh was triumphantly reeling off his thirtieth 'cap' when Amos 'Filthy' Fenshaw, the notorious cotton magnate from Stalybridge, and well-known land-lubber, called time on his vow of silence at the far fireplace, and unceremoniously joined the fray. Unimpressed by all this 'foreign' talk, he poo-pooed his fellow members' and Fogg's achievements as an (ungrammatical) waste of both time, energy and money. There was nothing in the world worth having that wasn't available in this, **his**, 'Green and Pleasant Land', he declared. Before either protagonist could repost, the floor was usurped by 'Natter' Jack Kavanagh, as ubiquitous as he was vociferous. The ex-slave-trader, and once self-styled 'King of Montserrat', launched a vitriolic tirade exhorting Fenshaw to scuttle back to his dark satanic mills post haste, and laid down a marker of forty two for 'the highest number of countries visited by a Reform Club member'. This, he was keen to point out, was almost four times the number of Flash-in-the-pan Fogg, who, it transpired, had only managed a surprisingly paltry eleven.

The chaises longues huffed and the Chesterfields scrunched, as scores were tallied and tallies were scored. At an appropriate juncture, the now-discarded manuscript was discreetly returned to its rightful owner by Johnson, a junior butler as alert to a misplaced umbrella as a possible gratuity.

Finally, to no one's great wonder, Lord Caernarfon, the staunchest Welsh nationalist never to have stepped foot in the principality, took it upon himself to raise a point of order. The land of his fathers may have consistently proven too great an ask, yet the peer had been around the larger 'block' a few times (he secretly fancied himself for a half-century) and regularly enjoyed deprecating himself as a 'sedan-chair traveller'.

'My objection is this: what, or more precisely, "where" constitutes a cap? If any old mumbo-jumbo land counts, we'll still be here next Tuesday.'

'Objection sustained.' Broadbent-Holmes nodded, mindful of the too many times he had been outflanked by Badger. 'We need a Rule Book.'

'Rules?' Bingham riposted. 'Rules are for tiddlywinks.' The collected members could but agree.

The topic for the remainder of the evening's conversation was well and truly fixed. Badger's group made a start on a 'Set of Laws' worthy of their new endeavour, while Sir Hugh and Lord Caernarfon began compiling a suitable list of 'Proper' countries. It was as both tasks neared a conclusion that young Ambrose, a noted puzzler from Ipswich, made a secondary suggestion: rather than ask members to collect caps 'ad infinitum', should there not be a defined criterion, a goal, a holy grail which the victor must attain, as there was for Fogg? Encouraged by the warmth of his audience's response Ambrose offered a thought which had tickled him from the off: couldn't a competition be designed whereby success was measured not just by the numerical 'quantity' of countries visited, but also some esoteric 'quality'? Such as their geographical position. Surely an expedition to Borneo should have a greater value than, say, a ferry ride to Belgium; a collection spread across the Seven Seas must be worth more than a bagatelle picked up on the Grand Tour.

'Geographical?' mused Sir Hugh. 'Excellent suggestion.'

Badger ordered a refill. Broadbent-Holmes needed bringing down a peg or two. As Johnson poured, a discreet suggestion landed in Mr Bingham's ear.

'Or "alphabetical", of course.' Bingham sounded his nonchalant best.

'Letters and Numbers, eh? Now there's an idea,' Kavanagh applauded. Natterjack was on his feet, and thinking. Ambrose could be sent off in search of all the countries beginning with A; Bingham would round up the Bs; Caernarfon the Cs, and so on. However, once Broadbent-Holmes was informed he would have to account for both barrels of his name, the black ball made its customary appearance.

As the members' sobriety levels waned, the complexity of the conundrums waxed until somehow, with the last drops of 'The Glorious Twelfth' (and final) decanter beckoning, a solution so simple it was almost perfect precipitated itself from the coils of smoke. Its message was 'The Game' and, with Johnson suitably rewarded, the matter was swiftly settled. The winner would be the first member to go 'Around the World in the Alphabet'. Or as Bingham extrapolated: 'to visit one or more "proper" countries for each and every alphabetical letter.'

Behind the doors of neighbouring 106 Pall Mall, another copy of Verne's manuscript was being pored over. For decades members of the Travellers Club (est. 1819) had taken great delight in reminding 'those next door' of their seniority in the Pall Mall pecking order, and none more so than Sir Arthur Lampbourne KBE.

'Poppycock. Can't be done, I don't care what Verne or his Morning Chronicle says. It's quite obvious this man has never set foot outside Europe. Why, I'll wager he's never been east of the Alps. The man's a charlatan.'

'Surely, Sir, it's an interesting idea nonetheless?' ventured young Toby Barnes. 'Shouldn't we be supporting it from the traveller's point of view?'

'Traveller?' The old whiskers roared. 'This Fogg's no traveller. Burton, Livingstone, that's travelling. Look what the blockhead has to say here, at Suez: "The thought of going ashore to see the town never occurred".'

Toby sheepishly fingered the bottom of his waistcoat.

'Never occurred to him!' Sir Arthur gruffed. 'Phileas Fogg? Phileas Frog more like. Typical French. He even takes a Baedeker with him in case he gets lost!'

'A Bradshaw, Sir,' the junior member meekly corrected. 'And it says at the beginning that Fogg is an Englishman.'

'Bradshaw, Baedeker, throw them all on the fire. Murray means well, I suppose, but only fools need guide books. Fools and Frenchmen.'

'My uncle went on one of Thomas Cook's tours last year, and he took a Baedeker. He said it came in jolly handy.'

13

'Cook? Don't get me started on that weasel. An insult to his family and a slur on the name of Captain James.' Sir Arthur broke off into a coughing fit. 'And what's more, that timetable of his is all wrong.'

Toby shrank back into his seat.

'Travel Professionals!' Lampbourne almost spat the latter noun in disgust. 'It was always thus, of course. What was it Marinus of Tyre said? "They concern themselves only with their own trade, care little for exploration and are often given to boastful exaggeration".'

The younger man excused himself and retreated to the library, as Lampbourne's mind wandered out loud.

'Around the world, indeed. Look!' Sir Arthur threw the map at the front of Verne's latest offering on the table, in full view of his imaginary audience. 'The man hasn't even left the northern hemisphere.' The knight consoled himself with another whisky. One for the road. 'In eighty days?' He demanded of the empty room. 'Sounds like the sort of parlour game those buffoons next door would play.'

Graham stopped again. He had put this section to bed five weeks ago, but now he was having second thoughts. Maybe his editor, a deceptively-earnest young woman by the name of Anne, would worry potential readers might mistake his satire for snobbery. Maybe, and this was the fear that troubled Graham most, Anne herself would associate him with Badger Bingham or worse still, Sir Arthur Lampbourne. Graham read on warily.

The next morning, Bingham, Broadbent-Holmes, Kavanagh and Caernarfon reconvened in the first-floor saloon, and duly appointed themselves The Game's Masters. Next, they posted a memorandum on the club notice board as way of confirmation. It offered twenty thousand pounds (matching the sum won by Fogg) to the first intrepid adventurer to champion their 'Alphabet Game'. The four swiftly withdrew their own names from the contest ('in the name of impartiality, you understand'), but the fuse was lit. A dozen tyros were in the midst of vowing to start that very day when an ugly brawl broke out between Lord Caernarfon and a 'new' member from Bristol over whether Wales should count as a 'W'. 'Granted,' this cocky know-it-all piped, 'it was a principality' and 'granted, it was of some (limited) anthropological significance', but a quick look in any history book would prove that, following the Acts of Union of 1536 and 1543, Wales no longer existed as an independent nation. This was not a matter to be trifled with and could only be settled, everyone eventually agreed, by the Royal Geographic Society itself.

*The Game, it turned out, was exactly the sort of challenge The RGS was looking for. On November 1ˢᵗ 1873, in their rather dapper new halls on Savile Row, a full and indisputable set of laws was formally drafted at a hastily convened Extraordinary General Meeting. Law Six stipulated that 'caps' would be awarded for trips to every sovereign realm, independent state or territory, **and principality** 'acknowledged as such by The Crown' (a full list was available upon request from the Society Secretary). Would-be players were relieved to discover that 'A' to 'M' could reasonably be accounted for without straying too far beyond the boundaries of 'civilisation', but it became clear as they worked through the second half of the alphabet that not all the destinations required were to be found in Mr Cook's brochures. Oman, Qatar, Xidakistan and Zululand sounded particularly ominous, and it was unanimously agreed that the winner would need a good deal more than eighty days. Nevertheless, the competition was official and, in return for honorary membership, the four 'Masters' reluctantly handed over total control to The Society (it has never been clarified if the offer to cover the twenty thousand prize money tipped the balance). As head of The Game's new governing body, President Rawlinson declared that the RGS Gold Medal would accompany the members' original wager as a prize.*

By 1888 the record stood at twenty and its holder, Sir 'Harry' Flanaghan, was on his way to Jamaica to notch up number twenty one when his ship went down off Cuba. The next in line, with nineteen, was the great French explorer, Gabriel Bonvalot, much to Sir Arthur Lampbourne's chagrin. So it was with considerable relief that a certain Francis Younghusband, freshly elected as the Royal Geographic Society's youngest-ever member, announced at his inauguration ceremony that he would win The Game for Blighty. Not only that, he would do so before the end of the century. The Times dedicated a full page to the story, and Younghusband/ Youngmember quips filled the air. Throughout the Empire, excitement surrounding this precocious youth's daring replaced dismay over the fate of Stoddart and Connolly as the preferred topic at Tiffin. Even the impending threat of a Russian invasion of India was forgotten as Younghusband built on the fourteen caps he had already amassed. Within eight months he had drawn level with Bonvalot, by then on twenty two.

It was at this point that Colonel Algernon Durand, Britain's political officer in the North Indian outpost of Gilgit and himself a keen player, declared that 'The Game has begun'. Some commentators, alas, mistook him to be referring to The Great Game and so it has gone down in History, but he was, of course, proclaiming that the two greatest explorers of the age were now neck and neck, and had declared their intention to head to Xidakistan. There they duly ventured in 1891 but Younghusband broke into the lead as he bagged Oman and Qatar on his return in '92. With his passage booked to southern Africa for 1893 and the King of Zululand preparing a hero's welcome, Younghusband seemed to have the game there for the taking. His ambitions were rudely checked by a diplomatic sleight-of-hand as unusual as it was unexpected.

On the orders of Queen Victoria and the Empire, the valley that encompassed Xidakistan, along with the rest of the remote mountainous area that made up the Pamir Gap, was ceded to Afghanistan. The new enclave was to be known as the Wakhan Corridor and the only 'X' on the ledger had disappeared. Even more saddening for Game players, one of their own had been forced to redraw the boundaries: another Durand, this time Sir Henry, Foreign Secretary of India. Younghusband wrote to the RGS arguing that Xidakistan had been a separate state when he had visited, just as it had been for Bonvalot, but at a second Game-instigated EGM, The Society ordered Xidakistan to be struck from the list and play suspended. In 1897, as defeated Zululand was absorbed into British Natal, the RGS President (now two letters short) was left with little choice but to call time on the whole affair.

That is not to say enthusiastic travellers ceased playing on a social basis, and for the next half century scores were bandied about like batting averages. In the 1960s, spurred on by the independence movements of Zambia and Zimbabwe, hopes were even raised that The Game could be revived in full. The RGS was approached by the grandsons of Bingham, Broadbent-Homes, Kavanagh, and Caernarfon, but, on advice from the Foreign Office, any formal resumption of The Game was deemed inappropriate. Bowed but unbroken, the young men took their cause back to where it all started, the Reform Club. Finally, in 1969, as Armstrong was pushing the case for a new 'M' to be added to the list, The Game had a new guardian. A second gold medal was struck and this, together with life membership, was offered as the prize. Law Six was rewritten based on 'member states of the United Nations' and Law Nine was added, stating that passport stamps would be required as proof of travel. Wales was out but a suitable replacement had emerged in Western Samoa, which left only 'X'.

One apparent solution was stumbled upon by Natterjack's progeny, in an Atlas of The Orient, Past and Present. *The central cartouche displayed the Tibetan Plateau under its newly-established name, 'Xizang'. If only, Kavanagh argued, 'the roof of the world' could be released from the tyrannous grip of Communist China, The Game would have its winner. Letters of support were eagerly penned to the Dalai Lama (accompanied by promises of spectacular donations to his Free Tibet campaign), but each one was politely rebuffed by his slightly-baffled holiness. Jetsun Jamphel Ngawang Lobsang Yeshi Yenzin Gyatso dutifully explained that 'Xizang' was the unwelcome Mandarin moniker imposed by Beijing, and that once emancipation had been secured, the label would be quickly dropped. Perhaps, His Holiness suggested, if Reform Club members really didn't like the name Tibet, they could use the ancient diminutive, 'Bod'? Many of his 'more traditional' followers did.*

So the prize was still unclaimed in 1997, when hopes suffered a further blow. Western Samoa announced the decision to drop its occidental prefix, and 'W' was once again stranded. Yet the Lords of Caernarfon are nothing if not a stubborn breed. Caught up in the fever of the new millennium, the forty-third, and present, incumbent established the Campaign for Real and Autonomous Countries (largely backed by other 'CRACkers' from the Anglo side of the Severn Bridge). This only-ever-so-slightly-motley crew declared that a country's eligibility should be based not on the list of nations recognised by the UN, 'a bureaucratic lapdog to American imperialism', but on that of FIFA, 'guardian of the world's other beautiful game'. At a hastily convened AG EGM, their motion was carried. Law Six was amended once more, and Wales was back on the list. 'X', however, remained as elusive as ever.'

For the second time that morning Graham stretched out for his mug, forgot he was holding a pen and began wiping coffee from his trousers. The Game had inevitably led his thoughts to Sarah.

Ruff Guides

Graham's abiding memory of the summer of 1985 wasn't Geldof's Live Aid, Gorbachev's Glasnost, or Thatcher's crushing of the miners' strike. It was Ibn Al Ahmar's *Calat Alhambra*, the crowning glory of Ottoman Spain. More specifically, it was a stone cornice by the fountain in the Court of the Lion, Graham self-consciously fiddling with his reflection in the water, Sarah gently mocking his inner nerd. He should have been a million miles away (well, fifty at least), floating with Jos in an ice-cream-cone-shaped swimming pool, listening to *I Want To Know What Love Is* on Uncle Ray's Walkman, or sampling the delights of the Harry's Bar *Miss Marbella Wet-T-Shirt Competition*. But Graham had had a change of heart.

Stepping down from the bus he couldn't help looking round to see if the girl who had boarded at Malaga, was also alighting. He feared he was out of luck. She had been sound asleep through most of the journey, and hadn't looked like moving as he made his way down the aisle. Graham was hardly what his mother's sister's son would call a 'player', but away from his peers' gaze he felt the pressure lift, if only slightly. To his delight two slim ankles and a pair of bronzed calves appeared at the top of the bus' steps, just when it seemed the doors were destined to snap shut. They were followed by two screwed up eyes and a jumble of hands in search of sunglasses. His sleeping beauty looked younger that he did, which was slightly perturbing as Graham's baby face had been the bane of his life. However, the crimson culottes and loose linen blouse suggested more gap-year backpacker (without the backpack) than sixth-former escaping her parents' timeshare. Graham set off from the main road and, instead of taking the longer tarmac route to the palace entrance, headed up an old track through the trees. Encouragement followed.

The pines protected them from the worst of the sun, but as Graham reached the foot of the palace walls, he was happy to stop and glug from his supply of water. He surveyed the dusty plain below long enough for his fellow scrambler to catch up. As she stepped onto his rock, he held out his bottle and mumbled something about 'drinking in' the view. Sarah had her own.

'They say this is the best vista in Granada, an "earthly depiction of Paradise in Heaven".' Graham still had the feeling one of his friends might be watching. 'But they forget to mention the stream of 'Day-Glo' buses.'

'Who's "They"?'

Graham ducked his head sheepishly and fiddled with the bottle top.

'You know. The guidebooks.'

'Oh.' Sarah turned and began to climb on her own towards the palace entrance. 'I don't have a guidebook,' she called over her shoulder. Not triumphant, just matter of fact.

Graham latched onto her shadow and followed it through the ticket booth into the large courtyard. Sarah gave no indication that he could accompany her but neither was there a signal to the contrary, so he tagged along a couple of yards behind. It wasn't until, an hour later, when they arrived at the stone cornice by the fountain that Graham plucked up enough courage to reopen the conversation.

'You're not missing much,' he confided.

Sarah gave him a puzzled look.

'The guidebooks,' Graham's head ducked again. '*Small World* are alright for maps and stuff, but even they're a bit bollocks.'

University had only done so much to refine Graham's vocabulary. He bit his tongue in an attempt to take it back.

'I see.'

Graham could tell Sarah wasn't going to make this easy. No doubt over the last fortnight she had been chatted up by every Daz, Baz and Gaz in Malaga. Why, on today of all days, had he decided to wear his football top?

'I mean, it says here that this colonnade was built in the fourteenth century by Al Ahmar.' Maybe that would take her mind off his sartorial inelegance. 'When it's obvious it's not even of Nasrid design.'

'Oh, quite obvious.' Sarah stifled a giggle.

Graham scurried back into his shell and would have remained there for good if she had not added 'but I know what you mean.'

Sarah sat down, so Graham sat down. His eyes stuck with her fingers as she stroked the water's shiny surface.

'I prefer all the reflections in the pools.' Sarah said.

'It makes you want to dive in,' Graham over-eagerly chimed.

'You'd better take your shirt off first. You wouldn't want to get *that* wet!' Sarah's Malaga training had sharpened her ripostes.

19

Graham blushed into the club badge on his royal blue jersey.

'Who on earth are Macclesfield Town, anyway?'

'Macc,' Graham mumbled. 'The Silkmen,' he added as way of explanation.

'Which division are they in?' Sarah knew enough about football not to know.

'Doesn't matter,' he surrendered, before summoning up enough courage to give it one last go. 'Where are *you* from?'

'Doesn't matter,' Sarah teased. 'You want to get some lunch? I'm starving.'

Graham was as confused as he was delighted. 'Sure.'

They walked up to the café, and Graham offered to get the refreshments while Sarah commandeered an umbrella for their table.

He returned with two bottles of water (Sarah didn't drink Coke, not even diet) and a sour look on his face.

'I don't believe it. The café closed half an hour ago.' Graham threw down his *Small World* in disgust. 'It says in the book they're open all day.'

Sarah sucked on her tongue. Since she had been woken on the bus by Graham's increasingly-loud, but still broken, Spanish (he must have asked half the passengers to tell him when it his stop), Sarah had been trying to decide whether her new travelling companion was endearingly overzealous or annoyingly pedantic.

'I mean, it's all very well telling us how many men died building this place but what's the use if you can't even buy a sandwich? It was all I could do to persuade the guy to sell us two bottles of water. And they were a pound each.'

This last grumble pushed her into the endearing camp for good.

'Don't you mean peseta?'

'No, they were two hundred pesetas. I did the conversion to keep track in my budget.'

Sarah hid a smirk.

'I pinched some bananas from the hotel this morning,' she offered as way of compensation. 'We can share.'

Graham retrieved his guidebook, turned to the blank pages at the back which he had allocated to his finances, started writing, thought twice, and felt doubly embarrassed.

'Sorry for making fun of your shirt.' Sarah reconciled. She cited a, thus far, summer from hell with two sex-crazed schoolmates in her defence: between them Amanda and Gayle seemed to have scored with all the replica kits in the league. Graham similarly relived the disaster that had been his last fortnight: he was supposed to be celebrating an end to his three years in Edinburgh, but essentially all he had done was watch Jos crash and burn with every other female in the complex.

Bananas were digested over a stroll around the palace's perimeter and as they returned to the entrance, Graham felt almost optimistic. He had even found out that Sarah's parents were about to move to less than an hour's drive from his Mum's.

'I'll just check what time the buses leave,' he offered, feeling the need to give himself a bit of thinking time.

Sarah willingly allowed her eyes to watch him disappear, but somehow wasn't surprised to see him come storming back into view.

'You're not going to believe this.'

Sarah dug her thumbnail into her palm to suppress a snigger.

'It's not funny.' Graham had seen. 'The last bus for Marbella went at four.'

Sarah gave a fake gasp.

'But the guidebook,' Graham saw himself reflected in her eyes. Was he really that bad? 'It says the last one doesn't leave until 7.25.' He collapsed onto a yellow plastic chair and pulled his shirt over his head in mock despair.

'Oh my God,' Sarah reached out for Graham's hand, like a pretend damsel in distress. 'What are we going to do?'

Graham pulled himself up, and made to withdraw his paw.

'It's alright for you. There are buses to Malaga 'til nine.'

'There you go, then.' Sarah clamped her hands shut on the last of his fingers and reeled in the rest. 'You catch a bus with me to Malaga, we'll find something besides bananas to eat, and you make your way on to Marbella later.'

Graham couldn't persuade his eyes to meet Sarah's but he was soaking up her smile.

'There's a spare bed at our place,' Sarah tempted. 'If you want.'

'How long are you staying?' Graham knew that wasn't what she'd meant but awkwardness has a nasty habit.

'The whole summer.' Sarah decided to play soft.

Graham looked more shocked than surprised. 'You're going to spend the whole summer in Malaga?'

'Why?' Sarah snapped, springing back into her earlier defensive mode. 'What have you got planned that's so special?'

'Three more days of watching Jos in action, then back home looking for a job,' Graham thought to himself.

'Actually, I'm thinking of touring round a bit.' Graham improvised as quickly as he could. 'You know, Barcelona, Seville, Madrid. I might even do that pilgrimage walk up to Santiago Del Campostella.' Had Graham been aware of his linguistic faux-pas he might not have sounded so blasé, but as it was he bolstered himself with the fact that Santiago *De Compostela* had been part of at least one of his plans for the summer.

Sarah felt a pang of the same envy that had been shadowing her throughout her stay, but managed to stick to her guns.

'Ticking boxes, you mean. Typical male!'

'What do you mean "typical male"?' Graham hit back. Sarah wasn't like any of the women in his family.

'You know exactly what I mean. Scoring points. You can't expect to see what a country's really like just by going where your guidebook tells you to. You won't even scratch the surface.' Sarah re-organised her thoughts. 'You'll never stay anywhere long enough to find out what it's really like. You'll never meet any of the local people.'

Graham was getting the feeling Sarah had rehearsed this speech before.

'You can't even speak Spanish.'

Perhaps she hadn't been so sound asleep on the bus.

'Marco Polo didn't speak any languages but that didn't stop him travelling across half the known world.' Graham hadn't been that serious about his 'grand tour' but now it was being attacked he felt it his duty to defend. He ignored the small voice at the back of his head reminding him that his ticket home was for Saturday, non-transferable.

'Is that who you think you are?' The usual softness of Sarah's North Country accent had vanished. 'Some modern-day *Marco Polo*? Don't tell me you've got one of those little leather books for keeping notes in.'

Graham blushed. His black Moleskine lay dutifully on his bedside table. 'There's nothing wrong with keeping a diary.'

'Oh, so now we're Samuel Pepys as well, are we?'

'Look, all I'm saying is that I want to travel around Spain. By train if possible.' Graham wasn't sure where that bit came from. 'And see as much of it as I can.'

Sarah didn't appear convinced.

'Of course I don't think I'm Marco Polo.' Graham began to plead. 'But I want to travel. Is that such a crime?'

'No, but it still depends on what you mean by travelling?' Sarah wasn't going to concede defeat easily.

'Well,' Graham nervously racked his brain, 'Syed Manzurul Islam says in his *Ethics of Travel* that there are two types of traveller: the "Sedentary" - who travels at high speed but in fact is not travelling at all, just changing "locales". And the "Nomadic" - who follows a more supple line, which brings about a more open encounter.' Graham had written this on the inside cover of his notebook.

Sarah pulled a face. 'You are joking?'

'What?' It made sense to Graham.

'Wait! I get it.' Sarah was nodding furiously. 'You fancy yourself as a guidebook writer. Don't you?'

'No.' Graham never had a very subtle side-step.

'I bet you do! I bet you're planning on writing a special little guidebook for your special little holiday.'

Graham squirmed. It was not his number one recurring daydream but it was close enough.

'That's it, isn't it? You want to have your own book. *Spain by Train*. With your picture on the jacket sleeve.'

Sarah was enjoying herself too much. Graham turned away.

'Well?'

A Robert Louis Stevenson quote offered itself as a comeback, but for once Graham refused to fall back on someone else's words. 'Not necessarily.'

Sarah raised her eyebrows as high as they would go, prompting a long silence.

'You're not playing that stupid Alphabet Game as well, are you?'

23

This time Graham flipped. He'd never actually heard of The Game, but wishing he had, he did what any self-respecting not-very-good-at-talking-to-women twenty-one-year-old male would do: lie.

'As a matter of fact, I am.'

This time, Sarah rolled her eyes. In her mind, The Alphabet Game had been designed *by* little boys *for* little boys.

'Almost finished it, if you must know.' Graham grabbed his things together and looked with relief to see their bus pulling up to the kerb.

Having taken a separate seat, Graham promised himself to cross-check every Alphabet Game reference he could find when he got home. He pulled out his map of Spain and ostentatiously marked a possible route for his new trip. At Malaga station his day-mate attempted a reconciliation, via an offer of fish and chips, but Graham defiantly declared his lack of hunger, and sulked around the concourse looking for a connection to Marbella.

Back at the pool, a six-pack of San Miguel and an fight with Jos later, Graham summoned enough heart to give the imaginary itinerary a shot. After years of aimless application, he finally packed his bag with a purpose.

*   *   *

Six months on, the Formica furniture in Jos' open-plan office was as out of date as it had ever been, but at least his suits were moving with the times. The plastic ashtrays were full and the glossy magazines were open, but the place was empty. It was five thirty-two and everyone had shot to The Cock at the sound of the 'factory whistle'. Jos cursed his digestive system as he emerged from the lav to a chorus of twenty seven ringing phones. His name would be the last one chalked up for pool, again. There was a chance he wouldn't get a game all night.

'Rammington McBride!' Jos barked, diving across his team's bank of desks and reeling in one of the phones. Switchboard were long gone.

'Jos? How you doing? It's Graham.'

'Well, well, well, the wanderer returns.' Jos slid into his seat and started scrawling down his 'closes' for the next day. 'Where you been all my life?' Leaning over, he dropped the logbook onto his manager's desk.

Graham's Iberian adventure hadn't gone strictly according to plan, but the semblance of a guidebook was now sitting proudly on his mother's kitchen table. He gave Jos a loose version of the trip.

'Almost sounds like fun.' Jos began toying with his matador key ring, picked up at the airport, and started to think of Mandy, the Essex girl sitting next to him on the plane home. Why, oh, why, hadn't he got her number? 'So what happened to the chick?'

Before their argument poolside, Graham had somewhat embellished his relationship with Sarah. In fact, he had rewritten the whole journey-back-to-Malaga bit and given it a romantic ending.

'Sarah?' Graham hesitated. 'Oh, you know, it was great. But she had to come back early to start uni.'

Jos span round on the leatherette swivel chair he had won as December's 'Salesman of the Month'.

'So how can I help?'

The problem was that Graham's semblance of a guidebook had been sitting proudly on his mother's kitchen table for three months now. And no publisher had shown even a glimmer of interest.

'Well, truth be told, it's turning out to be a little bit harder than I expected.'

'And now you want some advice from your old cousin, eh?' Jos kicked back off the side wall but one of the chair's wheels got tangled in a mess of wires under his desk. As he crashed into a heap, his phone line tore out of its socket.

Graham was surprised that Jos had understood the situation so quickly, but had to wait patiently while Jos reconnected the lead.

'You still there?' Jos crackled.

'Yep.'

'Yeah. Just had to sort something out with my seccy.' Jos loosened his tie and undid his top button. 'So where were we?'

'About my ...'

'Yeah, no probs, I've got the answer. If she's in her first year that probably means she's got her own room in halls. Now you could jump straight out with it, and say you're coming down to stay, but she might think you're being a bit forward. What I'd do is say you're coming down to stay with me, and then, when you've got her pissed, suggest staying over at hers.'

'Jos that's …' Graham was speechless.

'Genius?' Jos gave his newly-righted chair a celebratory twirl. 'Yeah, I know.'

'Jos, you're an utter moron.' Graham groaned.

'Hey, hang on there, Don Quixote. It's not my fault if you spent two months on holiday with a bird and didn't manage to get laid.'

Graham took a deep breath.

'This is not about Sarah, Jos. It's about the book.'

'What book?'

'My travel guide. *Spain by Train*. The one I've just spent the last three months trying to get published.'

A light flickered dimly on Jos' register. He lit a cigarette.

Graham knew he should have known it would be a waste of time, but now it was out in the open he felt he might as well continue. 'I need to get it professionally laid out and printed. And your mum just told my mum that you'd got some high-flying job in publishing.'

Jos had fed his mother this line to tart up the reality of commission-only advertising sales.

'Well, yeah, I have.' Jos' ability to do his job depended on pulling at least some sort of wool over the other person's eyes. But it was a skill that required plenty of practice. 'It's just it's not that simple.'

'I know. I know. But I was thinking, what with your gift of the gab, you could put the word around and see what the score was.'

Graham knew well enough that Jos' ego could rarely resist a massage.

'I'll see what I can do.'

'I'll give you ten percent of any money we make.' Jos' ego often equated to his wallet.

'Twenty.'

'Fifteen.'

'Done.' There wasn't much Jos wouldn't do for fifteen percent.

'The Kid' had only been with Rammington McBride for three months but the impact he'd made had been sufficient to earn himself his own soubriquet. It also meant Jos was on first name terms with Barry, owner and MD.

There was a bookshop on the other side of Highbury Corner and Jos nearly fell over at the prices some of the travel guides were charging, *Small World* in particular.

'Where were you when I was selling cars?' he sang to himself as he headed back across the roundabout to The Cock. Inside, he spurned the pool table and made his way through to the 'red room', where the production and admin guys hung out. He bought Sean and Tabs a couple of drinks and began pumping them for info. After a bit of number-crunching, Jos was kicking himself. It not only appeared childishly simple to publish something yourself, it seemed remarkably cheap. Sure there were some technical details but Sean could handle those.

'No wonder Rammington always looks so smug.' 'The Kid' chuckled to himself.

'But there's also distribution, don't forget.' Tabs sipped her Bailey's. 'It's all about distribution these days.'

'Leave that to me.' Jos stacked his figures into his shiny leather briefcase. 'Here's a tenner for the next round. Gotta shoot.'

He strode out of the pub and jumped in a cab to Antonia's pad, stopping only to buy a knocked-off bottle of Bolly to celebrate.

With Jos 'on the case', Graham now set about his second quest. He didn't have much to go on, but before the row at The Alhambra, Sarah had definitely mentioned UCL, and he was sure he had seen Sarah's surname written on a 'This book belongs to......' sticker inside her copy of *For Whom The Bell Tolls*.

Graham put on the most serious voice he could muster and picked up the phone.

'Yes, good morning. This is John Fletcher from the Euston branch of NatWest.'

'Mornin'.' Porter Reeves was already bored and it was only two weeks into term.

'I'm just checking the details for one of our customers. Ms Sarah Kennedy. She opened a student account with us over Christmas, and has stated UCL as her university. Can I just check that's correct?'

The porter fingered his way through the register to 'K'.

'Sarah Kennedy. Yep.'

'That's Sarah with an "h"?' Graham smiled at his sudden forethought.

'With an "h", yep.'

'But she's put for her address, "Halls of Residence". Is that right?'

'Yeah, she's in Gower Street. Blackmore Hall.'

'Right. Yes, I see now. She's put that at the bottom of her form.' Graham couldn't believe how well this was going. 'Is that number 12 or number 17?' Graham held his breath.

'Can't give out numbers.' Young Reeves chewed his gum.

'Sure,' Graham tried to sound officious. 'Of course you can't. That's fine. But if we send her statements to Blackmore Hall, she'll get them there, won't she?'

'Should do. They all get put in their pigeon holes.'

Graham replaced the receiver softly and looked at the parcel in front of him. It had taken Graham quite a long time to pluck up the courage to put pen to paper but finally it was ready. Inside was a complete photocopy of his guide, an apology note for his behaviour that fateful day, and an invitation.

'Please send comments and suggestions on what I've done, and maybe even put together some ideas for the blank pages that are the Malaga chapter?!'

He wasn't quite sure why he was going to all this trouble, particularly the bit about letting her write her own chapter but it seemed to make sense.

*　　　　　　　*　　　　　　　*

'Have a seat.' Barry Rammington sat at the head of the boardroom table, his lunch spread out before him.

As Jos took the chair directly opposite, Rammington began masticating on his chicken nuggets.

'Thanks, boss.' Jos opened with a smile. 'I've got this idea and I was wondering if you could give me a bit of advice.'

It took roughly three minutes to outline the plan.

'Nah.' Barry used a third serviette to wipe the barbeque sauce from his fingers. 'Not for me. Nice idea, don't get me wrong. Always money in travel: like babies, and weddings. But not the sort of money I'm interested in.'

Jos didn't respond.

'Those boys don't allow advertisin', ye see.' Barry moved on to his fries. 'No ads, no deals. No deals, no meals.'

Jos had been rather hoping his boss might buy into his venture, as some sort of silent partner. Barry Rammington might not have been the most sophisticated businessman in London but his ability to sniff out a pound note was unquestioned. If Barry wasn't biting, Jos realised, he had a problem. 'The Kid' made his excuses and traipsed back downstairs. As all calls were recorded, he couldn't risk ringing Graham from his desk, so instead, he slipped out the back door and headed for the nearest phone box.

'Good afternoon, may I speak to Mr Graham Ruff?' Jos never tired of winding Graham up. 'This is Chief Constable Moncur of the Metropolitan Police.'

'Hello, can I help you?' Graham didn't recognise Jos' Scottish brogue and began to panic. What was the punishment for impersonating a NatWest employee?

'Baah! It's me, G. Jos. We're on!' Always be positive. Jos shot the cuffs on his Thomas Pink shirt despite the confines of the phone box. With the money he'd make out of this, he promised, he'd buy himself one of those new mobile phones.

'Yeeeessss!' Graham whooped, slamming his fist down on the hall table. 'I knew you could do it.'

'All you need is five grand.' Jos held his breath.

'Five grand?' Graham gulped.

'Up front. Think of it as an investment.' In reality, Jos reckoned he could do it for three, and not pay the bulk until after publication.

'An investment? I thought you said your boss…'

'I did. But that was until I ran the figures, and realised just what a business opportunity we've got here.'

'Business opportunity?' Graham stopped himself short of saying all he really wanted was a book with his name on the cover.

'Yeah. Don't you see?' Looking out of the phone box onto the litter-strewn pavement, Jos was relieved Graham couldn't. 'Screw the corporates. We set up our own thing. Independent. Shake things up.' Jos had recently read an interview with Alan Sugar.

He waited for as long as he could. 'So what do you think?'

'It's a lot of money, Jos.'

'Christ, Graham. I've just got you the sale of the century and now you're playing chicken.' Jos made his voice sound all hurt. 'Thanks a bunch, man. Remind me not to do you any favours in the future.'

'Don't be like that, Jos. I'm just saying it's a lot of money. Maybe I can ask mum.' Graham thought again. 'No, that won't work.'

You're damn right it won't, Jos cheered to himself.

'There was one other idea I had.' Again, Jos paused a few seconds, hoping this time Graham would sweat.

'*I* could put up the money for you.' Jos let the offer sink in. 'But I'd need more than fifteen percent.'

'Go on.' Graham's initial enthusiasm was returning.

'We split the company fifty/fifty, but I get a bonus once we're in the black.' Jos clenched his fist and jabbed – he was now officially a BUSINESSMAN.

'You get half?' Graham choked the word out.

'Plus bonus.'

'No way. I've bust my arse on this'

'Alright. Sixty/forty to you. But you'll have to allow advertising.'

'I'll give you twenty-five percent.' The fact that the whole project had yet to make a penny seemed to be lost on both of them. 'And no advertising.'

Jos had been prepared to go that low all along. 'Tell you what, I'll accept no advertising if you write me in for a third. A third/two thirds, and you've got yourself a deal. But you're going to have to do a hell of a lot of legwork to get this off the ground.'

That was the least of Graham's worries, but he still wanted to think it over.

'G? Are you still there?' Despite Barry's training, Jos had not mastered the art of silence just yet. 'Alright, call it a flat thirty three percent. You can keep the point three, three recurring. OK?'

'No, it's not "OK".' Graham tried equally hard not to sound too triumphant. 'But it will do.'

'Right then. Get your arse down here to London and I'll show you what's what.' Jos envisaged delegating as his primary role, at least until any real money started coming in. 'You can kip on my sofa. I'll take the rent off your first pay cheque.'

'Thanks,' Graham sneered. But he was happy to be on the move.

'Oh, and one other thing,' Jos remembered. 'If it's going to take off, you'll need a name for these guides. You know, something catchy, like those guys at *Small World*.'

'Already got it.' Graham dreamed back to a long night he had spent in a Bilbao bar playing name games with an English teacher from Grimsby: '"Follow Your Nose".'

'Follow your what?'

'Follow your nose.' Graham's voice rose up an octave. 'You know, like the-'

'I said "catchy", you div.' Jos spammed his forehead. 'Don't worry, I'll think of something.'

Living with Jos in a one-bedroom basement flat in Archway wasn't easy. On several occasions over the next few weeks, Graham came close to sacking it all in, but finally the letter arrived that made it all worthwhile. Not from the printer, the distributor, or even a potential reviewer, but his mother. Amid all the usual updates on the garden and the W.I. was the line he had almost given up on:

'Some post arrived for you yesterday. From the handwriting I think it might be a girl.'

Dutifully enclosed was the real treasure he had been waiting for – a longer than expected epistle from Sarah congratulating him on a 'not bad' first attempt, AND volunteering not only to write the required section on Malaga but to knock the remainder 'into something approaching literary shape'. There was also a phone number and a synopsis of her first two terms of English at UCL. This was all the more encouraging in that Sarah didn't seem to be enjoying student life quite as much as she had been anticipating: 'too many boys pretending to be men, and thinking they know it all – sound familiar?'

The phone number may have been superfluous (Graham had wheedled it out of the porter's lodge long ago), and the lit. crit. a bit tart, but the suggestion of a meet up for lunch was sweet, sweet manna from heaven. Sarah had even shortened his name to 'Gray'!

There was one slight hitch. Having given up hope of ever hearing from his Alhambra friend again, Graham had penned his own Malaga chapter, Sean and Tabs had done the proofreading, and the whole thing had been sent off to 'repro'. The book was going to print the following week.

'You think we should do what?' Jos spluttered over the breakfast table, his mouth full of toast.

Graham picked up the letter as some sort of defence. 'We'll just have to delay going to print,' he began. 'I wasn't happy with it anyway, and Sarah's editing will make a big difference.'

Jos looked at him with undisguised contempt.

Graham tried again. 'As you would say: it'll be "sweet".'

'That's right. Silly me.' Jos snatched his jacket off the back of his chair. 'Except, of course, for the fact that you don't know this bird from Eve, and I've just forked out two grand on a printing slot, which we're now not going to use.'

Graham looked sheepish. So should Jos have. The printing was only costing fifteen hundred, and he hadn't paid a penny yet. Barry had taught him that art early on.

'Is there anything else I need to know about your new Kate Adie/great Lady while we're on the subject?'

Graham winced. There was quite a bit of 'else'.

'No. No, G. Tell me you didn't offer her any money,' Jos pleaded.

Jos pulled himself up to his not-quite six feet and Graham could only raise his hands in self-defence. But his cousin was late for work and the threatened right hand never landed.

'I'm not shelling out another bean on this deal, geddit?' Jos straightened his tie in front of the mirror. 'And you're not cutting into my slice of the pie for someone you once crashed and burned with on the Costa Packet.' Graham had eventually come clean on the exact nature of his relationship with Sarah.

'Alright, alright.' Graham desperately needed some thinking time. 'Keep what's left of your hair on.' Reference to Jos' increasingly-exposed pate was a trusted ploy.

'I'm warning you.'

Graham couldn't really afford to pay Sarah anything either. But in his pre-enactment of their forthcoming rendezvous, lunch had led to dinner, dinner to her place, and her place to him irresistibly proposing they become "partners". Sarah had then coquettishly toyed with the word until, unable to contain herself any longer, he was dragged to bed to 'make guidebooks and guidebabies'.

'Look, speak to the printers. I'm sure they can change the slot.' Nothing was going to dampen Graham's enthusiasm on this day of all days. 'Whatever happens, your share stays the same. Anything Sarah gets will come out of mine.'

Jos slurped down the rest of his tea and, as he pushed past Graham's chair, he stole the freshly made slice of toast and jam from his plate.

'OK, Mr Loverboy, but don't say I didn't warn you.'

*   *   *

Much to everyone's surprise, *A Ruff Guide to Spain* not only came out that spring, it did so to a modicum of not-too-disheartening reviews. In Graham's mind, Sarah's insistence on a two-month postponement, it took her one month just to 'get rid of all the testosterone', more than justified offering her half his share in the company.

Graham spent May battling around London with a box of books in his gran's wicker-basket shopping trolley. In an age when those who ran the bookstore usually owned the bookstore, slowly but surely, it worked. Old Mrs Foyle took fifty. All five hundred copies from the first print run were sold, and a second batch of two thousand was ordered. Sarah ditched her English degree and Graham made her his second offer: to share a small flat near The Angel. Separate bedrooms (at least for the moment), and a lounge that could double as the company office. There they planned a second guide, to Portugal, and the following spring was spent researching. Together.

Xidakistan

Graham finished the bitter-looking dregs in his mug, and as he turned to his notes, felt a quiver run through his shoulders. The last of the trekking expeditions to Concordia were all packed up, the number of Pakistani traders coming back from Kashgar had thinned to a trickle, and the few backpackers that had made it this far were on their way home. It wouldn't be long until Gilgit was closed down for the winter.

The heating and the coffee in the K2 Café may not have been up to much but, with the giant Karakoram Mountains looming all around, you couldn't beat the views. That and the papers in his hands were enough to turn the quiver into a warm glow. *A Ruff Guide to Xidakistan*: Ruff Guides' one hundred and forty second individual country guide. *Small World* may have produced more titles in total but, as Jos was always quick to point out, no other publisher in the world came close in terms of individual country guides. Graham had had some sort of a hand in all of them.

According to the marketing boys, this latest offering was going to be the company's 'most unique and ground-breaking'. Again. But Graham had long since given up reading the media blurbs. He knew that what he was working on really would be unprecedented. Nothing much had been written about the valley kingdom for over one hundred years, and no other guide was in existence, anywhere. For the first time, Graham kept reminding himself, unlike any guidebook writer in the modern era, he would genuinely be starting from scratch, creating something completely original. True, Xidakistan had merited a two-line entry in Small World's *Central Asia* guide, and Explore's *Trekking The Karakoram Highway*, but that was it. In fact, it was such unchartered territory, Pat, his old NGO pal in Kabul, reckoned no Westerner had been up there since Aurel Stein in the twenties. Maybe, Graham toyed, he really could make history.

Graham flicked through the 'Context' chapters he had typed up the night before and gave them a satisfactory nod. The facts may have differed in any particular Ruff Guide but there was a structure and tone to all of them that Graham had spent years honing and streamlining. Some had accused him of being too laborious over individual details, too obsessed with minutiae (Sarah continued to dismiss much of these sections as 'too blokey and boring') but Graham never tired of researching them. These particular pages may have taken more time than most, but that only made them more lovable. He proceeded to proofread.

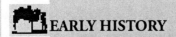

EARLY HISTORY

Xidakistan, 'Land of the Sky', was first recorded in 1837, as the name given to the tiny mountainous region wedged between what is now Afghanistan, Pakistan and The People's Republic of China.

John Woods, the dynamic English explorer, made the log on an expedition in search of the Great Dragon Lake, which he found the following year and re-christened 'Lake Victoria' (now known as Sarikol Nagahrada).

Yet to its inhabitants, the kingdom has always been known as 'The Valley', as Francis Younghusband discovered on his ground-breaking expedition to the country in 1891, and this is the name their descendants continue to use to this day.

Xidakis are, and always have been, largely oblivious to the comings and goings of the outside world. Perhaps it is not surprising, therefore, that so little has been heard of this Pamir state since 1893, when the rest of the world decreed it officially ceased to exist.

Graham turned the page with glee. It all felt right. For once it all read OK, too, and he was reluctant to change a word. This really was it, he thought:

![] THE JADE ROAD

From as far back as the third millennium BC, there is archaeological evidence of merchants struggling across the Taklamakan Desert and up to Xidakistan in search of wondrous stones. In this long-lost age a small 'Jade Road' was forming, linking The Valley and a handful of oases in the Taklamakan Basin to the outside world.

Like the Chinese, western Asian rulers marvelled at jade's texture, colour and, most importantly, its everlasting properties. It was these they took as omens of their own immortality. Thus, as traders took the spoils of the Khotan and Yarkand Rivers to the court of the Chinese Emperor in the east, so the rulers of biblical Mesopotamia paid fortunes for prize specimens to be brought to the west.

The other group to make use of this rudimentary 'highway' was Buddhist priests. Chinese accounts tell us of a series of heroic holy men, who battled against all manner of obstacles to venture into northern India in the pursuit of true enlightenment. Their legacy is the primitive form of Buddhism still practised by all Xidakis, in stark contrast to the Islamic faith of their immediate neighbours.

The first Europeans to travel along The Jade Road were ancient Greeks, prisoners captured by the Persian King, Darius I, at the fall of Miletus in 494BC. They were followed, more victoriously, by none other than Alexander the Great.

In 327BC he conquered Bactria (now Balkh in Afghanistan) and claimed its princess, the irresistible Roxanne, as his bride. From there we are told he led his men up into the Pamir, and the next year he headed down through the valleys of modern-day Pakistan to the Indus River, upon whose banks he wept at the realisation that there was 'no more world to conquer'.

> Exactly which tribes and valleys Alexander and his Greek warriors encountered during this period remains a mystery few expect to solve. However, The White King features in many of The Valley's legends and Xidakis, like their Hunza and Nuristani neighbours, are often striking for their blue or green eyes, straight noses and even curls of ginger hair.

Admittedly, not everyone was going to be quite as excited as he was, but in Graham's mind this was 'big'. He was telling people about a kingdom that had been almost forgotten. A valley that, once it was given the significance it was due, would make experts rethink a whole host of theories and conclusions. A country whose history was bound together with some of antiquity's greatest names:

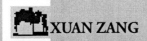 XUAN ZANG

In the sixth century a Buddhist priest left the Chinese Imperial court at Xi'an, bound for northern India. There he hoped to find true copies of Buddha's scriptures to replace the bastardised versions he had repeatedly encountered in China's temples.

Following the Silk Road, he crossed the notorious Taklamakan Desert and found himself at the foot of the Karakoram Mountains. After a week of climbing he reached the small settlement of Tashkurgan, home to a devoutly religious Buddhist sect.

Overwhelmed by Xuan Zang's piety, the priests shared a secret they had been harbouring since the days of Lord Buddha himself: the whereabouts of Anavatapta, the 'Lake without Heart or Trouble'. This is the lake which, according to Buddha's teaching, gave birth to the four great rivers of the world: The Ganga (Ganges), Sindhu (Indus), Vaksu (Oxus) and Sita.

Nineteenth century scholars and explorers presumed the priests took him to the Great Dragon Lake, but in fact they took him over the Mintaka and Wakhjir passes, and up into present-day Xidakistan. This kingdom, the priests said, had once been underwater, and teeming with fish. Until one night, during an incredible storm, crashes of lightning had ruptured the mountain walls surrounding The Valley. Through the fissures, the water had burst out to form the four mighty rivers.

Xuan Zang, with the help of his three disciples: Monkey, Pigsy and Sandy, went on to complete his journey to India and enter Silk Road legend. He was rewarded with true copies of all three original books taken from Buddha's teachings, earning him his nick-name, Tripitaka ('Three Baskets').

Readers of a certain age might remember Tripitaka and his three friends as the heroes of the TV series, *Monkey.*

Graham remembered the first time he had come across the country's name in a footnote in one of his Great Game books:

'Xidakistan: Land of the Sky. Can no longer be found in EB but, prior to WWI, was common place in encyclopaediae and dictionaries alike.'

That had been nearly twenty years ago. Now here he was, finally about to see it all first hand, finally about to write the guidebook to end all guidebooks, finally about to win The Game. He could not help but beam at how close everything suddenly felt.

'*Don't get ahead of yourself, Ruff,*' he inwardly chastised. '*Still a long way to go before the fat lady even starts to gargle.*'

With the café's proprietor, Mr Shah, catnapping once again, and no other customers to be seen, Graham stealthily withdrew a second manuscript from his canvas satchel, *Silkman on the Silk Road.* His 'magnus opus'. He had wanted to include a chapter on Sarah (and Spain) as a sort of introduction, but Anne had warned against it. 'Be personal, but not too personal,' she had said, which seemed to defeat the object in Graham's eyes. Nevertheless, as this was his first sortie into the world of travelogues, he had reluctantly obeyed, and kicked off with *The Alphabet Game* instead.

The remaining reams of A4 fell limp in his hands. He had accepted early on he was no Thesiger or Newby, yet the next eleven chapters of his supposed masterpiece consisted of, at best, ten and a half mildly-amusing tales. True, the episode involving a Bactrian camel on the Golden Road to Samarkand was quite unusual, and the adventure in search of illegal drinking dens in Tehran during Ramadan fairly spectacular, but there was no arm-to-arm combat at the side of a Mujahedeen warlord; no lustful nights spent in an Imperial Harem; and no epic discoveries or ground-breaking conquests. *The Laws of The Game* remained the only chapter he was near satisfied with. Graham looked up to the snow-covered peaks, wished Sarah was there to help, and flicked back to skim over Lord Caernarfon's antics once more. You could always trust The Game he consoled himself. It may have started off as little more than an evening's entertainment, but in a few days' time, he congratulated himself, it might just end up being front page news. And *he* might just be the one to put it there.

Graham slipped the papers back into his bag, returned his attention to proofreading *Xidakistan* and pondered how best to describe the prince.

*   *   *

Prince Hat had been aged thirty when his father, Tah, died. His favourite thirtieth birthday present, given to him by Mr Butt, was a digital clock, which as well as telling the time, displayed the date and the year. This particularly pleased him as now he would know when to be one hundred and forty one, and die like his father. And his father's father, Tah Tah, Xidakistan's most celebrated king.

Hat always knew he would be king. Not because he had been elected or was the eldest son (he had at least two older brothers), but because he was bald. In each generation, one, but only one, member of the Royal family had been born hairless, and remained that way until they died. It was this child, even if it was a little girl, who would become king. He also knew, however, that he would have to wait until the official mourning period was completed before he could be crowned. Tradition dictated that the whole of Xidakistan would grieve until a full cycle of the moon had elapsed. Unperturbed, Hat retired to his chamber and began dictating the invitations for his coronation. It took over eight hours and his scribe's fingers were red-raw from pushing the fountain pen Mr Butt had presented to the prince for his twenty-ninth birthday, but, finally, the last of the missives was complete:

Dear Cousin,

As you are well aware, my father, the great Tah entered Nirvana on the day of the sowing of the rhubarb seeds. It was a sudden, but painless birth at the anointed age of one-hundred and forty-one. We know that he is now at peace with The Enlightened One and will do all in his power to ensure that we too can safely journey to the Western Paradise when our time comes.

As our fathers taught us, so we will celebrate his birth in silence and meditation until the moon has once again grown to her seventh crescent, and we ask you to join in our celebration. On that auspicious night we will be called to the gates of Nirvana, where we will be crowned with the royal turban and cloaked with the imperial fishing net. Thus, we will be anointed 'Tah', and as the sun rises we will return to Xidakistan for my earthly coronation.

It gives me great pleasure to invite you to the ceremony, and to join me in the accompanying feast that will take place in my palace. We hope for the celebrations to last seven suns. On the eighth I will accept all your presents on behalf of my father.

We enclose a royal trout for your pleasure and look forward to seeing you very soon.

Yours in celebration,

Hat of Xidakistan

PS   Please bring a bottle.

The Prince was pleased Mr Butt had told him about the royal 'We'. He finished signing the invitations, wrapped each one, with its trout, in a parcel and instructed his scribe to hand one to the head of every family in The Valley. He then summoned his mischievous Aunt Ta Ta, and quietly asked her to take care of a small pile he had hidden behind his throne. In spite of Mr Butt's objections, the prince was determined that the Maharaja of Punjab, the Queen of England, the Tsar of Russia, the Emperor of the Sun, and the Shah of Afghanistan would be invited, just as they had been for his father's coronation.

The Maharaja's was delivered first but Mr Butt swiftly buried it in his mother's back garden, preventing his deception from being exposed. The next to arrive was the Shah's, by special delivery on the train to the Khyber Pass, but Taliban border officials simply burnt the package without even opening it. The pungent whiff of charred fish may well have proved to be the end of the affair, had the other three suspicious-smelling packages not been intercepted the following week by Scotland Yard, the KGB and Beijing's PSB.

The three agencies themselves were not overly alarmed: the Chinese were already in negotiations with the Xidakis via Mr Butt; the British found a series of ageing documents with reports on Xidakistan from Durand and Younghusband (and put two and two together); and the Russians did what they always did with Central Asian files, now they were no longer a world superpower – locked them in a filing cabinet and threw away the key. It was the US ambassadors in each of the three countries who were agitated, because the Special Intelligence agents they didn't know were spying on them had told the Pentagon about the deliveries. And The Chief was 'on the line'. Xidakistan was back on the political agenda.

'Tell me everything you know,' commanded General Clark Mortimer Martin III with menacing calm. Unaffectionately, he was referred to by his employees as The Chief, and The Chief was surrounded by over a dozen background files, neatly boxed in various colours and, occasionally, languages. On top of the nearest box (mauve) sat his red Priority Line loudspeaker.

'The thing is, General.' Ambassador Theodore Ewing switched to speaker phone so he could continue polishing his nails, 'my people,' his two under-secretaries could take this flak, 'are telling me-'

41

'I don't want "The thing is", Ambassador. I want answers.'

'I'm afraid I don't have any, General.' *Why should he have?* thought Ewing. He was the United States' Ambassador to Great Britain. London. The Queen. Not some 'stinking curry joint halfway up the side of bloody Everest'.

'Who's Hat?'

'I don't know whose hat it is.' Ewing allowed a playful raising of the eyebrows towards his assistants.

The Chief repositioned his red speaker so that it sat on his red box. Sensing a shift, the ambassador retrieved his handset.

'I'd love to help you, General, but in all honesty, I don't know.' The ambassador was in serious danger of being late for lunch. He hadn't asked for any rotting fish to be sent! 'I don't...'

'Thank you for your time, ambassador.'

'I can try and....'

'I said,' General Martin's tone hardened, 'thank you.'

'I do hope you appreciate who you are talking to.' Ewing was beginning to wish he had asked the two under-secretaries to wait outside. He started replaying the grapevine rumours he had heard about The Chief.

'I appreciate everything you could possibly think of, ambassador. And what I particularly appreciate at this moment in time is that what you actually know is of very little concern to anyone. But the Chinese don't know that, and neither do the Russians. So I also appreciate that what you appear to know from now on is critical. Understood?'

'Yes, General.' Ewing realised The Chief had already known everything he knew from the start. Maybe he even knew about the weekends in Paris. 'Apologies, General.'

'Apology accepted.' The Chief, mindful of his Lutheran upbringing, always tried hard to forgive. 'So, what do you know?'

'I don't know, General.' Theodore Ewing surrendered.

'Correct.'

The ambassador wiped his brow, flicked the speaker phone back on, and waved goodbye to his assistants. This particular minister's wife punished him severely for every minute he kept her waiting.

'Now, give me Black.' General Martin could only forgive so far.

Ewing's two under-secretaries looked blank.

'Give you what back, General?' Under-secretary Delaware impersonated the ambassador as best he could.

'Black. Agent Black, for Christ's sake! He's in the office down the hall.'

Graham

The problem with me is I'm a professional layabout. Well not exactly, but that was always my aim. I first encountered this phrase at a talk given by a local author. Mr Littlemore had been invited into our school to 'inspire' the fifth form ahead of our O-levels. Meningitis had swept through our year over the Christmas break and it was thought we deserved a slice of special attention. He wrote children's books mainly, no Tolkien or Rowling but successful enough in his own circles. I think the Head of English had hoped it might help unleash our inner creativity if we could see the potential for a future career. Mr Littlemore had also been struck down as a child, which no doubt was meant to resonate. Unfortunately, when West (Five A) asked him why he had wanted to become an author, 'Professional Layabout' was his phrase of choice. Being a writer, he had imagined, meant receiving payment for getting up when he wanted, jotting down a few ideas as the mood took him, and discussing said ideas with like-minded fellows down the pub. And as it turned out, he explained, he hadn't been far wrong. I was hooked. It was also the first time I remember Jos wishing he could swap schools for the day.

That is not to say I am work-shy. As I keep telling my mother, I regularly burn great vats of midnight oil reading background material or knocking a new guide into shape. I am always working, like Picasso.

Picasso is sitting in a restaurant, having a quiet lunch with friends. A big, noisy group of tourists is eating at a nearby table, and can't stop looking at him. Eventually, one of their number takes the plunge and walks over.

'Wow, are you really <u>the</u> Pablo Picasso?'

'Yes, I am. But, if you don't mind, I'm trying-'

'Yes, yes, sorry, Mr Picasso. Didn't mean to interrupt.'

But the intruder doesn't go away.

'It's just, I was wondering, if by any chance you could, you know, draw me a quick picture?'

'Excuse me?'

'You know, nothing fancy like, just something,' the man produces a pencil from his pocket, 'something simple. On a napkin, say.'

Realising this is the only way he is going to get to finish his meal, Picasso accedes to the request. He quickly sketches the man's face, and holds out the napkin for the taking.

'Thank you. Thank you so much, Mr Picasso. Just wait 'til I tell my wife.'

Picasso suddenly pulls the napkin back into his chest, and raises his eyebrows. The man looks puzzled but then it dawns on him.

'Of course, of course. I'm so sorry. So very rude. What can I offer you in terms of payment?'

'One million dollars.'

'One million dollars? But it took you less than two minutes.'

'That,' Picasso looks down at the drawing in his hand, 'that took me my whole life.'

You see? Just because you enjoy it, doesn't mean it's not hard work. Nevertheless, probably like Mr Picasso (and certainly Mr Littlemore), I've only ever really done what I have ever <u>really</u> wanted to do. And usually at a time of my choosing. When reports came out of Mrs Littlemore leaving her husband amid accusations of alcoholism and philandering, I did try to temper my ways somewhat (particularly on the alcohol front), but deep down 'Professional Layabout' still resonates. Not that I've told Sarah any of this, of course. Except about liking lie-ins.

Graham would never forget the night he first slept with Sarah. But neither would Sarah.

The research trip for Portugal had not quite delivered in terms of the second of Graham's hoped-for 'partnership's, and as the months slipped by, he missed opportunity after opportunity, sober, semi-sober and even blind drunk, to make amends. When the relationship returned from a second trip to Europe as unconsummated as ever, he threw in the towel. Instead he chose to find solace in the reading rooms of the British Library.

At least by the time the Thomas Cook Travel Writing Awards rolled round there was something positive in the air. The recipient of the 'Best Newcomer' category was the worst kept secret in the industry, and Ruff Guides' three partners arrived for the Gala dinner in high spirits. These days, thanks largely to Jos' set, the ceremony is a celebrity affair, held in London's trendiest hotspots amid a sea of glam and glitter, but back in the early years it was still firmly under the auspices of the blazer brigade; Simpson's was the perennial stalwart.

The average age of the faces examining Graham as he entered the dinner hall was at least twice his. He turned to hush his giggling entourage and asked the waiter to be led to their table. Free food and drink was still a novelty, so Jos couldn't help tucking in like a bulldozer. Once the prize had, as expected, been presented and Graham had made his speech of thanks, he too let his hair down, following Sarah onto the top shelf. Soon he couldn't stop jabbering: not only had Ruff Guides scooped Best Newcomer, they had come a close second in the top category, Best Guidebook 1986, to *Small World's* major offering that year: *Madagascar*. By eleven o'clock all three were considerably the wrong side of merry, and some of the older guard were beginning to notice. Graham, sensing goodwill rapidly evaporating, suggested they call it a night, or at least move on to somewhere less public. Sarah jumped at the idea but Jos had latched onto the pretty PR girl from Thomas Cook and refused to budge.

Romantically speaking, Sarah, too, had more or less given up, but seeing Graham on such good form rekindled old flames. Sarah had treated herself to a new evening dress for the occasion and as they negotiated entry into a black cab, she let the iridescent lilac slit fall revealingly open. Graham climbed in. As he dropped into the back seat he felt Sarah's arm slide under the back of his jacket. Graham leaned forward to give their address and her hand squeezed downwards. He turned to face her bashfully.

'Sarah?' he whispered. 'Are you alright?'

Sarah pushed further and used her other hand to pull Graham's Full Windsor loose. 'Come on, Gray, we're supposed to be celebrating.'

Graham's awkwardness was making him angry, and his anger was making him more awkward. His arms and shoulders tensed uncontrollably.

'No, Sarah. Not tonight.'

Sarah snatched her hands back and recoiled into the corner.

'Why not, Graham?' she demanded. 'Why not "tonight"?' Sarah could feel her head spinning but was determined to have it out. 'We've been pitter-patting around for nearly two years now. I really don't understand you, sometimes.'

'I know,' Graham dropped his head. What was wrong with him? Why couldn't he just let go and be happy? 'I really like you Sarah but …'

Sarah flung herself forward and hammered on the glass partition.

'Oh no, Mr Ruff. No way. I don't do *Dear Johns*.'

The cab driver slid the barrier across, he had hardly had chance to change out of first gear.

'Pull over, please.' Sarah tried to choke it all back. 'I'm getting out.'

The cabbie pulled up with a jolt, despite the green light. As Sarah slammed the door shut Graham tugged at the window and managed to slide it half open. His head squeezed through the gap.

'Saz!' He yelled after the low-cut back striding its way down The Strand. 'I didn't mean it like that. I meant it to be nice.'

Silver tassels spun on a stiletto, illuminated by the arc-lights meant for the sponsor's banners. 'Forget it, Graham. Save your preciousness for someone else.'

Graham watched Sarah re-enter and deliberated whether to follow, through a full cycle from green to red and back to green.

'You still want to go to The Angel, son? The meter's running.'

The warmth of the cabbie's tone and the anonymity of the leathery darkness were enough to tip the balance. Graham nodded, reassuring himself that wounds were best licked in private.

Graham heard the front door slam at three o'clock. He was in bed but still wide-awake, tormenting himself over and over. Why was he always clamming up at the merest whiff of emotion? As Sarah's footsteps creaked and tripped their way upstairs in the pitch black Graham scrunched himself up against his pillows. After a period of uncertain silence the landing light clicked on and a white glow silhouetted the ill-fitting bedroom door. Graham dived back under his duvet and braced himself against the intrusion. A soft knuckle tapped lightly against the bare wood panels but he stonewalled.

'Graham?' Despite immense concentration, Sarah's alcohol-debilitated tongue still slurred her whispering. 'Are you asleep?'

As the doorknob rattled Graham lay motionless. On the third attempt, it clicked open but still he didn't budge.

'I know you're awake.' Sarah attempted her baby voice, but any hopes of masking her inebriation were dashed by the crack her shin gave to the end of Graham's cast-iron bed.

'Sorry about tonight, Gray. Really I am.' Sarah lowered her head close enough to Graham's ear for him to feel her humid breath against his neck hairs. 'I didn't mean what I said. I was only trying to be nice too.'

Sarah delicately placed her fingers on his duvet-protected shoulder and waited. Graham twitched but she refused to retract her hand. Both parties remained stock still until Sarah detected an almost imperceptible relaxation of the muscles.

'Don't shut me out, Graham. All I want is for us to be close.'

Graham's back half-turned flat onto the mattress but his head remained averted. 'No, it's my fault. I know I love you but I don't know how to say it. I don't know if I know what "I love you" means. I don't even know what....' Graham descended into a stream of muffled half-words.

'Hush, baby, hush.' Sarah felt a hot tear as she stroked Graham's cheek. 'Come here.' She slowly rolled his head onto her lap and brushed his once-floppy fringe back from his eyes.

Her shoes had already slipped off, and as Graham reached out an arm around her waist, Sarah swung her legs under the duvet. Whispers merged into kisses. Slowly but unsurely pieces of clothing were loosened and lost. By the time the last of the garments fell to the floor the two bodies had drifted into sleep, but in the morning mist more physical displays of affection were silently proffered and received.

As Sarah lay in Graham's arms she shuddered. Not with cold but with the memories of the previous night.

'Gray.' Sarah's voice had a woolly numbness, with an uninvited dry rasp lurking on the 'r'. 'Before we go any further, there's something you need to know.'

The anxiety in Sarah's voice sparked in Graham the panic of no-longer-virgins the world over. Pregnancy, abortion, the pill, even Aids raced across Graham's mind.

'You're not? You've not?' Graham didn't have a clue what he was trying to say.

'No, no, it's nothing like that.' Sarah's giggle turned to dread. 'It's just about last night.'

'I know. I behaved like a prat.' Graham turned Sarah's lips towards his and kissed. 'I'm so glad you came in to see me when you got back.'

Sarah felt herself losing the thread.

'No, Gray. It's something else.' Sarah hesitated. 'Jos.'

'Oh, no. Don't tell me he did something stupid at the awards.'

'No.' Again Sarah hesitated. 'Well, yes. But it was more my fault.'

'Come on then,' Graham smiled his intention to forgive. Sarah was always getting paranoid and fearing the worst. It was probably nothing. 'Spit it out.'

'After the do finished, we shared a cab home.' Sarah stopped again and wished she'd kept her big mouth shut.

'And we had a snog,' she finally spewed out, in a personal best words per second ratio.

'You what?' Suddenly the duvet was on the floor and Graham was sitting bolt upright.

'No, Gray, it wasn't anything like that. It was just a silly snog and it meant nothing.'

Graham continued to stare at the curtains.

'But you know what Jos is like.' Sarah could feel herself fretting. 'He's bound to pretend it's a big deal, so I wanted to warn you.'

Graham felt like pointing out that in his mind 'Sarah getting off with his cousin and then coming to sleep with him' *was* a 'big deal' but there was too much rage locked inside him to speak. Pulling on a pair of trackie bottoms and a shirt, he marched out of the flat, impervious to the fact that he was wearing neither shoes nor socks.

B

Game On

Following his conversations with the ambassadors, General Martin had spoken to his agents inside the US embassies in London, Beijing and Moscow for a second time. He had ordered them to shake down their respective posts, and keep shaking until there was nothing left unshook. Meanwhile back at The Pentagon, he had commanded Lieutenants Smith and Jones to blitz everything and anything they could find on Xidakistan, in particular the 'trout' angle.

With both assignments approaching their conclusion, he summoned the three ambassadors on a conference call, and reiterated the situation, plain and simple:

'If just one of you knows something they're not letting on…'

'Message received, General.' Ambassador Ewing went to yawn but remembered there were eyes everywhere.

'Loud and clear,' chipped in Gilbert, ambassador to China.

'You'll kick our butts so far down the line we'll be ambassadoring polar bears in Antarctica, right, Chief?' Ambassador Humperton wise-cracked.

General Martin didn't have time to point out the niceties of the geographical 'crack' in the ambassador to Russia's attempt to be 'wise'. He consoled himself with the fact that 'Humpty' was tipped to have a 'great fall' in the next round of diplomatic musical chairs.

Six minutes before their twenty-four-hour deadline expired, an exhausted Smith and Jones placed the last of their 'Operation Something Fishy' findings on General Martin's desk.

'So these guys are with the Taliban?' General Martin had finished reading, and directed his question at the space between his two lieutenants' desks. Each of The Chief's box-files sported a newly-arrived fact-file, positioned at exactly ninety degrees. For the second time that week Smith made a break for the fax room, and Jones was left to resignedly assume the Standing Position.

'Well, not really, Sir.' Jones was going to kill Smith.

'Not really? It says here that they've signed a deal with the Taliban.'

'Well, yes, Sir, in a way they have, Sir.'

'So, if they're "with" the Taliban, they're "against" us.' General Martin had been instrumental in the wording of the President's 'you're either with us or against us' speech.

'Not necessarily, Sir. The Taliban are only supporting Xidaki independence as a sort of stop-gap measure against the Northern Alliance. In the long term it will weaken them.'

'The Northern Alliance?'

'No, Sir, the Taliban.'

'Good work, soldier.'

Jones returned to his seat triumphantly.

'Smith!' General Martin hollered, rearranging his collar. Smith ditched his milkshake and poked his head out of the fax room. 'Bring me a map of the area.'

'Actually, Sir.' Smith re-entered the office but headed straight for the cover of the collapsible whiteboard. 'We don't seem to have one.'

'What?'

'Well, I've found something in the back of a *Small World* guide, but it's more Afghanistan than Xidakistan.' Smith pretended to be double-checking the maps cabinet. 'They don't seem to have brought out a Xidakistan guide, yet, Sir.'

'I didn't ask you for excuses, soldier. Strike one.'

'Yes, Sir. Sorry, Sir. I'll try their Tajikistan guide, Sir,' Smith scraped. But a flick of the wrist signalled he was no longer of consequence.

'Jones!'

'Yes, Sir?'

'Get me satellite pictures. I want to see every blade of grass in this place.'

'Yes, Sir.' As Jones' computer screen brought up the bad news, his face dropped. He toyed with the mouse in an attempt to build some inner strength but his response, when it came, was what could only be charitably described as a weak-kneed: 'Sir, the entire area looks like it's been hit by a snowstorm. Not a blade of grass anywhere, Sir.'

'What about the new drones?'

'They haven't been deployed that far north yet, Sir.'

'Jesus H Christ.' General Clark Mortimer Martin III's upbringing hadn't been all Lutheran. 'Is there anybody, anywhere who can tell me about this banana republic?'

'I don't think there are any bananas in Xidakistan, Sir,' Jones frowned. 'Too high up, Sir. Wrong altitude.'

'Smith!'

'There is Butt, Sir.' Smith needed to get back into The Chief's good books, fast.

'But what?' General Martin's facial veins began to bulge.

'No, that's his name, Sir. Zulfiquaar Al Butt.'

'Zulfiquaar?' General Martin could feel his patience being sorely tested.

'It means "crossed swords", Sir.' Smith assisted.

The Chief began one of his famous growls.

Jones sensed Smith's weakness and pounced. 'He's not the sort of Field Intelligence we'd normally use, Sir. Not even for OTB reconnaissance, Sir.....'

'I don't care if he's Commie Castro's cousin, I want him here and I want him here now.'

*   *   *

Zulfiquaar was scared. He was scared because his handlers wouldn't tell him what he had done. In fact his handlers didn't know what he had done, and while Zul didn't know what he had done either, he knew that if the Pentagon's Chief of Special Intelligence wanted to see him, he must know what he had done, and it must have been something pretty bad. Surely it didn't matter to the Pentagon if he had pretended to be the Punjabi Maharaja. But what about his promise to buy Prince Hat a jet fighter for his thirty-first birthday? Or perhaps they knew about his illicit supplies of Marks and Spencer's clothing. Perhaps his brother-in-law working in the packing warehouse in Basildon wasn't really his brother-in-law at all. Maybe, and now Zulfiquaar was really scared, maybe they had uncovered his most heinous crime of all, a secret he hoped no one would ever find out until the day he died. That he had been sent down from Cambridge, without a degree. Whatever the case, Zulfiquaar decided the best plan was to play dumb.

'Sit down, Mr Butt.' General Clark Mortimer Martin III was six inches taller than Zulfiquaar and about sixty pounds heavier. His hair may have gone grey and his belt eased out a notch over the last few years but this patriot still looked capable of ripping a chicken's head off with his bare hands. As any former pupil of Lahore's International Junior High School will tell you, the name Al Butt has been synonymous with yellow belly since the early fifties.

'I said sit down, Mr Butt.' Zulfiquaar was hovering nervously. There must have been over thirty chairs surrounding the oval table and, as General Martin had had his back to Zul since the moment he walked in, there was no logical indication as to where he was supposed to sit. He looked around the large control room for help but both Smith and Jones had disappeared. The Chief began tapping his projector rod against his trouser-pressed thigh with a firm and accelerating beat. He would have caught Zulfiquaar oscillating between yet another two identical backrests but, as General Martin began his slow pirouette, Zul's left eye noticed a tiny gap between table and chair. As the heel of General Martin's right shoe clicked into position, Zulfiquaar straightened his back against the dark blue leather.

'Mr Zulfiquaar Inzaman Mohammed Al Butt…'

'Please, call me Zul,' Zulfiquaar interrupted, with a hopeful smile and a blast on his inhaler.

'Mr Butt.' There was no such smile on The Chief's face. 'You don't know why you're here and when you leave, I can assure you, you will be none the wiser. How long you have to wait before you leave, however, is up to you. And I will give you this piece of advice.'

Zul was all ears.

'Whatever you do,' General Martin warned. 'Don't play dumb.'

Butt's heart sank like a stone.

'Play dumb with me and I'll come down on you so hard you will still be hurting when your god reincarnates you as a piece of bird shit.'

Zul wasn't sure why General Martin thought he was a Buddhist but decided against finding out.

'All I want is answers. Straightforward answers to straightforward questions.' The Chief didn't raise his voice. His rock-hard tone was enough.

'I understand.' Zul exhaled slowly.

'Good. Now, why are you here?'

'I don't know, Mr Sir,' Zul stuttered, 'Mr Chief,' stammered, 'Mr Chief Sir,' and stumbled.

Thwack! The projector rod broke on the edge of the desk, an inch to the right of Zulfiquaar's hand.

'That's your last warning, Mr Butt.'

Zulfiquaar started talking and didn't stop for four hours. By the end, he had described in detail every significant event in the last ten years of his existence. Interspersed amongst this was everything he knew about Xidakistan, right up to the recent pre-independence conference. He even came clean about his plan to help his cousin Jahanghir set up 'X Tours', Xidakistan's first-ever tour operator. Reluctantly, he finished off the account with details of his burgeoning relationship with the prince's Aunt Ta Ta.

'And that was when your men came knocking at my door. And I had to leave my mother to wash my pyjamas.' Zul buried his head in his hands and prayed for clemency.

'Thank you, Mr Butt.' The Chief felt it time to switch to 'good cop'. 'You see, that wasn't so difficult now, was it?'

Zul shook his head.

'So, is there anything else you think I ought to know?'

Uncontrollably, Zulfiquaar started sweating again. He snatched a lungful from his inhaler, but as he looked up to see General Martin offering him a glass of water, he knew the man he was up against was too good. Out came the Punjabi Maharaja embellishment, the Marks and Spencer supplies and finally, after much soul searching, how, thirty years previously, his tutor had caught him red-handed with the exam questions days before his anthropology finals.

'OK, Mr Butt. I'm pretty sure that covers everything.'

'It wasn't my fault. He left them out on his table during the tutorial. I only meant to have a quick look.'

'I said that's all. You will be returned to your country now. But I should point out that we will be monitoring your actions, wherever you go.'

Zul hesitated half way out of his chair.

'And can bring you back here for further questioning quicker than you can say "Republican for President". You understand?'

'Yes, Mr Chief, Sir. One hundred percent.' Zulfiquaar sank back into the blue leather and forced out a smile. 'Yankee doodle dandy,' he added, in the hope that that was the kind of thing General Martin would want to hear.

'Oh and by the way, you are now an employee of the United Sates Army, and will carry out every order I issue you with.' General Martin reached for a document tucked under the various files. 'I have made arrangements for a thousand dollars to be paid into your account every month until the project is complete.'

'Yes, Sir, Mr Chief, Sir.' For the first time in his life Zul found himself pulling a salute. 'Thank you very much, Sir.' Having ploughed almost his entire life's savings into his research, Zulfiquaar suddenly felt much better about all things Stars and Stripes.

'And you'd better have one of these.' The Chief pulled the most advanced satellite phone money could buy from one of his drawers.

'Just one question, Mr Butt.' General Martin stared piercingly into Zulfiquaar's eyes. 'You're sure there's been no Russian involvement in any of this?'

'No, Sir. I mean, yes, Sir. As far as I know, Sir, they don't know anything about it.'

This wasn't strictly true. A listening device hidden amongst General Martin's collection of Civil War memorabilia had just transmitted the entire conversation to a KGB agent posing as a data programmer four storeys above them. Although Zulfiquaar could hardly have been expected to know that. General Martin turned his back and marched out of the automatic sliding panel in the side wall, which Zulfiquaar took as a sign to leave.

Back in his private study, The Chief's face scrunched into a frown. Of course the Ruskies didn't know. Those sly old Chinkies were keeping this one all to themselves. No doubt they already had another of their rubber puppets lined up, someone they could install like they did that fat duck in Korea. Well, they hadn't been up against General Clark Mortimer Martin III that time, had they? Like hell they hadn't.

As Zulfiquaar waited for his flight in the military airbase, he was visited by Jones, who gave him a file which he was to read, memorise and destroy. Most of the notes inside were written in foreign languages on coloured paper. He noticed one document in Arabic and wondered why Jones would want him to memorise an article from the July edition of the Riyadh Gazette's *Homes and Gardens* supplement. At the very back was a single sheet of crisp white paper from The Chief which read: 'Arrange second Xidakistan Independence Conference. Ditch Taliban. Block Chinese.'

Zulfiquaar knew that at this point in the movies, his character would either have eaten the evidence or thrown it onto a raging pyre, but when the guard came to take him to his plane, he simply tucked all the papers under the seat cushion and walked away.

Back in Pakistan he made his way home to his mother's house very slowly. By now it was almost November and the passage to Xidakistan was once again blocked for the winter. He spent the next four and a half months suspended in fright, anticipating the knock on the door which would herald The Chief, come to punish him for his sloth. By the second week in April he could bare it no longer. He kissed his mother goodbye, and set out on one of his cousin Jahanghir's horses. He would open the passes himself if he had to. Five days later, with a severe case of saddle sore, he arrived in Bozai Gumbaz, last stop before The Valley. But here he was met by startling and disturbing news. A Xidaki goat herder had come down the previous week and issued a warning that all foreigners, especially the Maharaja of Punjab, must stay away from Xidakistan. Zul had little choice but to return to Gilgit and pray for a miracle.

*　　　　　　　　*　　　　　　　　*

Although news of the USA preparing to sponsor Xidaki independence was to be kept strictly hush-hush, Pat in Kabul had soon got wind of it, and Graham was the next to know. He had suspended researching the second edition of *A Ruff Guide to Azerbaijan*, and immediately headed for Gilgit. For the second day running, there he was, ensconced in the K2 café, nurturing more notes for his new guide.

The problem was the nurturing was becoming more like wrestling. So little was known about The Valley, and the country was so small, *A Ruff Guide to Xidakistan* was in danger of being not only Graham's 'most unique and ground-breaking' book, but also his shortest. Shorter even than *Liechtenstein*. Graham took an executive decision to add some more boxed texts.

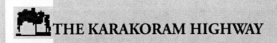

THE KARAKORAM HIGHWAY

The partition of India in 1947 may not in itself have had much of an impact on the daily lives of the people of Xidakistan, but one of its side effects changed their lives forever.

As a fledgling state in a time of climactic change, Pakistan was desperately searching for new, strong partners. When China clashed with India over their border in Ladakh, Pakistan saw a potential ally in its massive neighbour to the north. The only problem was that the two countries were still separated by mountains so enormous that they could only be crossed on foot. A Friendship Highway was therefore proposed, whereby the Pakistanis would build a two-lane road up to the border on one side, and the Chinese would construct a similar thoroughfare on the other.

Work began in 1966 but progress was incredibly slow. In fact, the Pakistani effort fell so far behind schedule that China, with its superior technology and manpower, had to build most of the Pakistani stretch up from Gilgit, as well as their own section down to Kashgar. Rock falls and snow avalanches made the construction work incredibly dangerous and an estimated three men died for every mile of tarmac laid.

The first official crossing was made in 1982, and in 1986 all 800 miles of The KKH (as it is now known), from Havelian to Kashgar, were opened to the public.

Graham thought about adding a footnote here to inform his readers that, serendipitously, the publication of the first ever Ruff Guide coincided with this event almost to the very day, but decided against it. He could already hear Jos back in London complaining about the cost of the extra pages. *'Look at this,'* he felt like saying, holding a couple of leftover leaves of foolscap. *'Look at how much I've red-penned already.'*

(**KKH** cont'd from p000)

The increases in trade, travel and tourism that the KKH has facilitated have been phenomenal. Previously, even the simplest journey from one village to the next had been an ordeal: the old Silk Road path (which can still be seen today) had been scratched out of the sides of the valley walls, and was only wide enough to take a horse, yak or Bactrian camel single file. Now Gilgit, Nagar and the Hunza Valley, together with the access they provide to Nanga Parbat (8125m), Rakaposhi (7790m) and K2 (8611m), are little more than a bus ride away.

Another outcome was much less predictable. During the explosion work in April of 1978, a small team of Chinese workers was trapped in a river gorge, in what is now the Khunjerab National Park. Their route down to Sost was cut off and their path back to the border base was similarly blocked. They had little food and it could have taken weeks to shift the rock falls, so they had little option but to attempt to climb out up one of the two cliff faces. The western wall appeared easier and once at the top they decided to head north, in the hope of reaching the border. Yet the main river is fed by a series of fierce tributaries at this point, and in spring it is often almost impossible to determine which is which. It didn't take long for the men to become completely lost in the maze of ravines.

As the sun was setting the team of workmen finally broke through onto flat land but it was not, as they had hoped, the Khunjerab Pass. It was in fact the Mintaka Pass, a barren stretch many miles to the west of Khunjerab and rarely visited by man.

Nevertheless, there was enough wildlife on the plateau to provide a hearty meal, and the men bedded down for the night, relieved if not wholly unperturbed.

They were understandably surprised to be woken in the morning by the clanging of a sheep bell. As far as they had been told this whole region was only used for grazing in the summer, if at all. The sheep bell, in fact, turned out to be goat bell and the shepherd a Xidaki goat herder, one of the few Xidakis who ever ventured outside of The Valley.

With a minimum of fuss he gathered in his animals, and led the bemused workers back to his homeland. The Xidakis could not understand a word their guests spoke, not even the Uighur members of the team, so the next day the goat herder led them down to Bozai Gumbaz, the nearest Afghan town, and from there they circuitously made their way back to Gilgit.'

Graham was about to take a breather, when an unfamiliar face popped into his field of vision.

'Please excuse me, Sir. I am sorry to interrupt, but I couldn't help noticing your accent.'

Graham smelled a rat. He hadn't said a word.

'Would I be right in saying you are English?' The wiry man in front of Graham was dressed head-to-toe in Marks and Spencer, and nodding his head as though his life depended on it.

'Yes.' Graham sighed. Each version began differently but they all ended with that same promise of a 'special price'. *'If I had a pound for every time....'* Graham muttered to himself. Get ready for the pitch. Heads it's 'Please allow me to be your guide'; tails 'My brother owns a carpet shop'.

'My name is Zulfiquaar Inzaman Mohammed Al Butt. I am very pleased to meet you.'

'Hang on. I've been looking for you,' Graham blurted out in astonishment.

'Indeed you have, and that is why I am here.'

Graham made a mental note to chastise himself severely for his undue cynicism. 'But I've been searching for you all day,' he gawped.

'That is correct. I've been following you.'

Belatedly recognising his rudeness, Graham offered the newcomer a chair. Zulfiquaar, however, chose to crouch next to Graham's seat, his knee-joints cracking on his descent.

'Do you know who I am?' Graham lowered his voice conspiratorially.

'You are Mr Graham Ruff. And you want to go to Xidakistan.'

'That's right.' Graham was nodding in time now. 'And I was told you may be able to help me. Sorry about before, I thought you were a ….' Graham desperately tried to silence the end of his sentence.

'A brother of a carpet seller?' Zul smiled, unoffended. 'No, no. Well at least not for many years.'

Graham looked embarrassed. Zul took a puff of his inhaler. 'I may indeed be able to help you. But, perhaps, you might first be able to assist me. An American has arrived today, staying at the Chinar Inn. I think he could be a spy.'

What Zul had really wanted to say was that an American had arrived that day and Zul was petrified he had been sent by The Chief.

'A spy? Graham's eyebrows arched. 'What does he look like?'

'Plump. A tall, plump man with round glasses and no hair on top.'

Graham was finding it hard not to laugh.

'Does this spy have a name?'

'They call him Mr Pink,' Zulfiquaar whispered. 'A spy's name, correct?'

'In the movies, maybe, Mr Butt, but as things stand it is more likely to be Floyd "Pinks" Housmann.'

'Floyd Housmann?' The Chief had never mentioned that name, but then again The Chief had never mentioned any name. 'Do you think he works for Special Intelligence?'

'Pinks?' Graham was sorely tempted to tell Zul the story but decided to save it for another day. 'No, Mr Housmann works for *Small World.*'

'The guidebooks?'

'Correct. And I suspect he too will be wishing to go to Xidakistan.' Graham added.

'I understand. Thank you, Mr Ruff. I will meet you tomorrow to discuss your travel plans.' Zulfiquaar pulled himself up with the aid of Graham's armchair and turned to go.

'Tell me, Mr Butt. Why did you not think I was a spy?'

'I did. But I spoke with my cousin in Karachi and he told me you are a good man, and an excellent judge of hostel facilities.' Jahanghir Al Butt ran, amongst a host of other enterprises, the second largest guesthouse in Pakistan's commercial capital. In the last edition of *A Ruff Guide to Pakistan,* he had been delighted to see his hostel finally come 'highly-recommended'.

'On his behalf, from this moment forward, please consider me your humble servant. Your wish is my command.'

'That is very kind, Mr Butt.' Graham was a little taken aback.

'Please, call me Zul.'

'Thank you very much, Zul. Perhaps if you see Mr Housmann you can tell him I am staying at the Madina Guest House.' Graham cupped his hand in preparation for a stage whisper. 'By the way, if Pinks asks you to do any favours for him, make sure he pays up front.'

Zulfiquaar appeared not to hear the comment.

'Of course, Mr Ruff. Although I suspect you will soon be able to tell him yourself.'

'He's coming here?'

'Everyone comes to the K2.' With a slight bow of the head, Zul moved towards the blanket curtaining off the kitchen. 'Until tomorrow.'

Graham was determined to look busy when Floyd arrived, and returned to his notebook.

(KKH cont'd from p000)
Little would have become of the incident if it had not been reported to the Pakistani linguist, and amateur anthropologist, Zulfiquaar Al Butt. Butt had been carrying out research for over ten years in an attempt to establish what, if any, common linguistic heritage was shared by the tribes of the region.

It seemed that although virtually every valley had its own dialect, these could all be grouped into one family, Dardic. Each tongue seemed to share as a common root an offshoot of the original Aryan spoken by the inhabitants of the Khiva oasis, in present-day Uzbekistan.

Xidak was the most corrupt of all the forms he had come across but here too, extraordinarily, were traces of the same common core. Excited by his discoveries, Butt was keen to enter The Valley and carry out some studies of his own. His hands were tied, however, as the only viable access to Xidakistan was through Afghanistan, and the whole country was embroiled in the USSR's failed war.

It was only with the retreat of the Russians in the early nineties and the establishment of a regime sympathetic to Pakistan that permission was granted for Butt to investigate.

Research was hampered by the fact that Butt could only stay for the three summer months of each year, through fear of being trapped by the snow. However, by 1996 a working understanding of Xidak had been secured and a broad outline of the history of the kingdom established.

The most significant non-linguistic discovery was that King Tah clearly had little comprehension of any unity between his lands and those of Afghanistan, and even less that he was not in fact his own sovereign.

The boxed text was seemingly going on for ever, and Graham's mind drifted back to Mr Butt. With this last piece of the jigsaw, The Game was almost complete.

The Pinks Guide

An out-of-tune whistling in the car park warned Graham of Floyd's imminent arrival, and the café door duly opened.

'Well, well, well. If it ain't old Ruff himself. Thought I might find you here.'

Graham, pretending to be in the middle of a vital sentence, warded off Floyd with the palm of his hand.

Pinks had little option but to pull up the more substantial of the two armchairs at the coffee table, and order a large cola. Loudly, as neither Floyd's shrill nor the tinkle from the bell had been enough to rouse the proprietor from his habitual slumber.

'Still copying other people's stuff, I see.'

Graham made a feeble effort to cover the pile of old guidebooks spilling out of his satchel.

'Hope there aren't any of mine in there.'

'Ha, ha, Floyd. Just finishing a nice piece of brand new copy. If you must know.' Graham waved his sheets of A4 to prove the point, but his face was already red.

A two-tone buckskin cowboy boot was kicked off, and its swollen left foot unceremoniously planted on the table. 'Haven't you guys heard of computers?'

Ignoring the jibe, Graham took his time tidying up his papers. 'I was wondering when you'd arrive. Did you get lost?'

'"A Fool wanders", G, "a wise man travels".'

Mr Shah hadn't stirred but his eldest son, Mohammed, duly arrived with two cans of local cola and a large glass. Pinks relieved him of the tray, and ordered a large chicken jalfrezi with rice. And a nan bread on the side.

'And bring some poppadoms and chutneys while it's cooking.'

'So you did get lost.' Graham was keen to press home the advantage.

'I could kill those guys at Flashman's. Six days it took them to get me a liquor licence. Six stinkin' days. I could have done it myself in that time and saved myself a hundred bucks.'

'Why didn't you?'

Pinks pretended not to hear, and concentrated on rummaging through his large leather shoulder bag.

'Flashman's? I thought you would have been at The Pearl.'

'Booked out. Again. Every time I come here it's the same. Crammed full of our defence boys selling missiles to the locals, just so they can flog them to that Saudi guy, who'll use them to blow up another one of our embassies. Thank you, Uncle Sam.'

Mohammed emerged bearing a small basket of poppadoms but no chutneys; Pinks sent him back.

'And bring me some crushed ice! My jockstrap's cooler than these cans of horseshit.'

Whilst waiting, Floyd proceeded to mix the cans of the horseshit in equal measure with a clear liquid from his thankfully-found hip flask.

'Don't worry, Pinks, I'm sure there are plenty of our boys keeping them company.'

Mr Shah's son reappeared with ice cubes, using his T-shirt as a makeshift bowl.

'Our guys, your guys, there were even bloody French guys. In my hotel.'

Mohammed proceeded to remove his shirt (careful not to drop any of the ice), wrap up the cubes and stamp on them with his less muddied boot. He presented the crushings for approval.

Floyd stared back in disbelief.

'You're the one who asked for it,' Graham goaded.

Pinks clawed a handful of the cleanest looking crystals into his drink and gave a begrudging 'thank you'. Graham kept his face as straight as Mohammed's.

'What the hell.' Pinks opened his throat to three quarters of the glass, finished it with his second swig, and started topping himself up. Mohammed tied up the remains of the ice and returned to the kitchen.

'Boy that highway sure kills your butt. Still, at least we're here. You having a drink?'

'Sorry, Floyd, had one yesterday.' Graham guessed that the hipflask contained vodka, one of Pinks' many tipples, and ordered an orange juice, no ice, instead.

'Don't tell me you're still doing that "one day on, one day off" baloney. This is good potato juice, G. Russian. Not the shit you're usually lumbered with out here. Borrowed it from the Consul while I was waiting for the license to come through.'

Graham smiled. It had been a while since he'd last witnessed Pinks' practice of 'borrowing'.

'You won't be complaining by the end of the week. I've got four cases with me. Didn't know how long we'd be stuck up here. You think it'll be enough?' Floyd started demolishing the re-served poppadoms (instead of chutneys, they now came with ketchup).

'Enough for what?' Graham acted innocent. Badly.

'Ha, ha.'

'Oh, enough until we find a way to get ourselves up to Xidakistan?' Graham laughed off Floyd's scowl. 'Wouldn't like to say, but things aren't looking particularly good. No one's been up there since Butt in April. If your government boys really are doing something, they're doing it very quietly.'

'Any sign of this Butt?' As Floyd's sleeve wiped red sauce from mouth, his throat made room for more fizz.

'Not a dickybird.' Graham crossed and uncrossed his legs, but Pinks was too engrossed to notice. 'My guess is he's lying low.'

'Anybody else here?' Pinks' right hand automatically reached for the metal mini-torpedo in his shirt pocket; his left hand checked for his lighter.

'No. Not a soul. Someone might arrive on the plane this afternoon, though.' Graham had decided the more red-herrings the better.

'Oh no they mightn't,' Pinks huffed, clicking open his jet-black DuPont. 'There are two "Hopes" of a plane getting in this afternoon, and one of them's Bob.' After the third pucker of his cigar, Pinks was in danger of relaxing but a ripple ran its way out of his backside, his main course arrived, and the pantomime began again. 'The pilot told me personally there won't be any more flights for the rest of the week,' Pinks gobbled. 'Too cloudy. That's why I've just spent eighteen hours crippling my ring-piece all the way from 'Pindi.'

In between spooning fodder into his gullet, Pinks instinctively reached for his phone.

'What's with the reception up here?'

'There isn't any.' Graham shivered. Now the sun had dropped behind the tops of the mountains the temperature in the café was starting to plummet.

Floyd didn't believe him.

'I'm serious,' Graham stressed. 'The signal's so intermittent nobody bothers with mobiles. This is a strictly landline town.'

'Ridiculous.'

Some of Floyd's spittle rained dangerously close to Graham's notes, so he used it as an excuse to retreat his chair a yard, and return his work to his satchel.

'Guide books are dead, you know,' Floyd chewed, nodding towards Graham's bag.

'Really?' Graham had been getting this a lot lately.

'Yep,' Floyd slurped. 'Dead men walking.'

'Well, in that case, that makes us both "Dead Men".'

'Not me!' Floyd licked his last spoonful, poured himself another drink and relit his cigar, almost in one single action.

Graham hated himself for being sucked in but carried on all the same. 'Why? What makes *Small World* so special all of a sudden?'

'Who's talking about *Small World?*' Floyd's eyebrows did a little dance.

'OK, Pinks, spill the beans.' It was always better to give in early to Floyd.

'I quit! In July. And frankly, Graham, I am disappointed in you for not keeping abreast of such ground-breaking news.'

'I've been away.'

'Humph.' But Pinks was too eager to tell the story to stay in a mood for long. 'So aren't you going to ask me what I'm doing?'

'I did say "spill the beans".' Graham only ever helped Pinks so far.

'I'm going solo.'

Graham grimaced. 'Haven't we heard this somewhere before?'

'No, G, I learn from my mistakes.' Pinks was so earnest he pulled his sock off. 'The Pinks Guide is completely different.'

Memories of 'Out and Proud' protesters in San Francisco brandishing "The Little Pink Book" (aka The Pink Guides' *Shanghai on a Shoestring*) came flooding back in Technicolour. Cerise-hued, but Technicolour all the same.

'It doesn't sound very different.'

'Grow up, Ruff, "The Pinks Guide", not "The Pink Guides". Ain't nobody gonna hijack this bandwagon.' Floyd downed the rest of his glass to prove the point.

'If you say so.' Graham reached for his teacup. 'Hang on, you just said guidebooks are dead.'

'Yep.' Floyd flashed Graham a grin that was Cheshire Cat meets Cheshire Cheese.

'So?' Graham was starting to wish today was a drinking day.

'So, my friend,' Floyd pulled a laptop case from his bag and unzipped his Mac, 'meet the internet.'

'No Internet, either, by the way.' Graham chuckled. 'Not even in the hotels.'

Floyd scanned the room and spotted a blinking computer screen in the corner.

'You're so full of crap, G. For a minute there you almost had me.'

Mr Shah was finally awake and thought this might be an opportune moment to promote his recent addition to the café. He assured Mr Housmann that regarding online facilities in all the other establishments across Gilgit, Mr Ruff was correct.

'So how come you're hooked up?'

Naveed explained he had a cousin in the Ministry of Communications, who, for a very special price, had been able to connect a single dial-up line.

'One line's all I need!' Floyd triumphed.

'But it only works on the café's computer, Sir.' Naveed was at pains to point to the poster above the computer terminal at the far end of the café. Use of 'Computer Corner' came at five dollars an hour. 'We don't yet have what I understand to be called Wi-Fi,' Naveed shook his head. 'And the printer is temporarily unavailable,' he added apologetically.

'Doesn't matter.' Floyd flicked the switch in his laptop. 'Most of it's on here, G. I can show you the dummy version.'

While they waited for Floyd's computer to boot up, Graham dug a selection of guides from in his satchel, and start flicking through at random. 'Don't you think these are called "guide*books*" for a reason?'

'Not anymore.' Floyd span the screen round so it faced Graham.

'"The Pinks Guide",' Graham read, Tahoma font rotating on a transparent globe. 'In Purple?'

'Like I said, no more bandwagons.' Floyd had his serious face on.

'But it doesn't even say where to.'

'And that's the genius.' Floyd chewed on his cigar like it was a bit. 'No more "country by country".'

'So where is it to?'

'Everywhere,' Pinks puffed. 'The Global Village. Headquarters in New York, London office opening as we speak.

'One guide to the whole world? That's a hell of a lot of pages, even for the Internet.' Graham and the rest of Ruff Guide's editorial team were at odds over House Style. Graham believed that for grammatical consistency, the 'Internet' should have a capital 'I'.

'Yes, but this isn't all your backpacker bars, and flea-ridden dives. This is high-end. Boutique Hotels, Bespoke Tours. The Best of the Best.'

'Like your Wild West Safaris?'

Floyd hissed. 'This is a guide for the truly discerning traveller, who wants to see the wonders of the world in style.'

Graham could see that in the strapline. 'Aren't they already doing that at *The Grand Tour*?'

'No,' Pinks countered slightly too defensively. 'This is completely different.'

The bosses over at Grand Tour might not have agreed.

'What do you know about the Internet?' Graham was still deeply suspicious.

'I don't,' Floyd sucked. 'Because I don't need to. I leave all that to my new partner.'

'New *what*?' In Graham's experience Floyd never shared anything with anyone.

'My new, bona-fide, business partner.' Pinks chewed. 'Fifty/fifty.'

'This I've got to see.'

As Floyd's "partner" was currently standing at reception back at the hotel bemoaning the lack of internet access, Graham would have to wait. Floyd pulled his sock and boot back on, and wandered into the kitchen to order more food. Graham couldn't resist having another look over his notes. Context versus padding. It was a difficult dilemma.

Any visitor to The Valley would have to arrive via Pakistan and/or Afghanistan, Graham reasoned. So it was legitimate, made sense even, to include relevant details on these two countries. He rummaged further into his satchel and dug out some of his old guides. The Gilgit entry wasn't exactly his finest work but it would fit nicely and he would hardly have to change a word:

GILGIT

Gilgit is the largest town in The Northern Areas region of Pakistan by quite some distance. Considering it is surrounded by some of the most precipitous mountains in the world, the stretch of land that the town centre has sprouted from is surprisingly flat. There is a large market area, two polo grounds and just enough room for a tiny airstrip. As the 'Capital of the North' it is also home to a large selection of accommodation and eateries.

Perhaps he could include something on China's Xinjiang province, too. Or Tajikistan. Graham had written, or helped write them all, so what was wrong with 'borrowing' a passage here or there? No, he reprimanded himself. Enough short cuts were being taken as it was. Fresh material was paramount. That's what set Ruff Guides apart. He ditched the Gilgit box and looked around for inspiration:

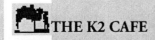

THE K2 CAFE

Naveed Shah has taken a gamble in offering the first, and so far only, Internet service in The Northern Areas. Previously a more traditional café, the K2 opened its Computer Corner in

2001. There may only be one terminal at the moment but more are promised. This despite being in a town which struggles to maintain even a coherent telephone service.

In summer, its open veranda and stunning views of Rakaposhi form a focal point for most visitors. In spring and autumn (when you'll probably want to retreat to the ever-so-slightly warmer inside), don't be surprised if you and your (often somnolent) host have the whole place to yourselves.

Another striking feature is Naveed's idiosyncratic credit policy. He is happy for customers to run a tab and several posters on the wall encourage patrons to do so, offering a ten percent discount. Yet these posters also carry a grammatically-challenged rendition of the old shopkeeper's adage, 'Please do not ask for credit as refusal often offends'. The upshot is that credit can be arranged but you have to wait until it is offered.

Floyd came back with another plateful. 'Don't you ever stop scribbling?'

Graham was desperately trying to think of a way to wipe the smile from Pinks' jowls, when the sound of two roaring propellers announced the existence of a third 'hope' after all. 'Sounds like your pilot friend was misinformed.'

Floyd slammed his fork into the plate in rage.

'Maybe it's Mr Butt?' Graham teased.

Panicked, Floyd sprang to his feet and headed for the door. 'Don't move!'

Graham had no intention. With Floyd gone he wanted to make the most of the peace and quiet. There was plenty of work to do.

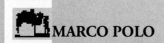

MARCO POLO

Nicolo and Maffeo Polo's first journey to China in the 1250s had made them so much money that, despite the round trip taking nearly ten years, they set out once again in 1269. This time they took Nicolo's son, Marco. His account of their journey gives us an unprecedented insight into the old Silk Road and its inhabitants.

Meant as a practical handbook to assist fellow merchants and catalogue the goods and wares available on route, Marco Polo's natural vivaciousness has left us with an unparalleled picture of the world of thirteenth century exploration (or perhaps it was his boredom at being locked in a Genoese jail, where Polo dictated his account to Rustichiello of Pisa, the famous romantic court-writer). *The Travels* has also left us with one of the earliest written description of Xidakistan: Polo tells how his convoy left Badakshan, where they had been impressed by the speed of the horses and size of the rubies, and made their way through *'many strait and perilous passes, so difficult to force that the people have no fear of invasion ..... on getting up, you find an extensive plain, with great abundance of grass and trees, and copious springs of pure water running down through rocks and ravines. In those brooks are found trout and many other fish of dainty kinds.': Marco Polo, The Travels.*

During times of trouble Xidakistan had been an important safe haven for Silk Road caravans, but the introduction of Kublai Khan's Pax Mongolica brought such stability to the length and breadth of Asia that 'a virgin carrying a pot of gold on her head could walk from the pleasure dome of Xanadu to the shores of the Mediterranean and arrive with both her prizes intact'. This was bad news for Xidakistan, as now traders could stick to the more hospitable terrain of the previously bandit-infested steppes.

The arm of the Silk Road which ran from Balkh via Xidakistan to Yarkand, on the southern fringe of the Taklamakan Desert, was amongst the first to die out. And, as Xidakistan's jade deposits diminished, a journey up to The Valley for its own sake became less and less attractive.

Trade between India and China did, of course, continue, but now it predominantly passed through the Karakoram Pass, over two hundred miles to the east. Indeed, if it hadn't been for the nineteenth century's Great Game (see p000), Xidakistan may have been forgotten about completely.

Feeling the fingers in his right hand starting to ache, Graham laid down his pen and decided to treat himself to some goat's yoghurt and honey, which was duly added it to his tab. Like most customers before him, Graham had been initially suspicious of Mr Shah's credit invitations for fear of falling for a local ruse, but on his third visit he (again like most) had accepted. Perhaps the spirit of The Silk Road lived on, Graham smiled to himself. Maybe that was what Marco Polo had been trying to teach us in his *Travels*. Graham got as far as his second spoonful.

'Good afternoon, Mr Ruff, I hope you slept well.' Zulfiquaar had appeared as if by magic. The fact that Graham had seen Zul less than an hour before made his greeting even more disconcerting.

'Please, call me Graham. And join me for some tea.' Graham was sitting in the same seat but this time Mr Butt took the wicker chair opposite. Graham pushed his bowl to one side.

'Mr Graham,' Zulfiquaar was again dressed in St Michael autumnals from head to toe, but this time in shades of blue rather than grey, and a trained eye would have recognised it as the 1999 collection rather than the 2000. 'I was wondering if I could talk to you about something.'

'Fire away.'

Zul took a deep breath, 'As you know, there have been a few inconveniences in Xidakistan recently.'

'No one's been allowed up there for months.'

'Exactly.' Zulfiquaar shuffled in his seat.

'Apart from you.'

'Indeed.'

'What's causing the problem?' Graham sensed Zul's discomfort. 'Is it the Afghans?'

'No, no, the Afghans are fine.'

'The Chinese?'

'No.'

This was worse than pulling teeth. 'So, who is it?'

'Well, you could say it's the new king's fault.' Zulfiquaar started playing with the handle of his cup. 'But in some ways it's yours and mine.'

'Mine? I've only just got here.'

Zul handed Graham a copy of the invitation for Hat's coronation and explained how, when none of the British, Chinese, Russian or Afghan royals arrived, the prince had flown into a rage, then a sulk and finally a depression (Zul chose not to mention his role as Punjabi Maharaja).

'I tried to make peace on my visit in April, but he refused to let me into The Valley.'

'Refused you entry? But you're the only person who's allowed up there.'

'I know, and I think my higher authorities are now very upset.'

'Which higher authorities?'

'That I cannot say, but they've ordered me to organise a new independence conference, and I'm afraid if it doesn't happen soon the snows will come, the passes will be blocked, and my authorities will lose patience.'

'Perhaps you could try going up there again. Maybe we could go together.'

Zul seemed to brighten at this idea and Graham congratulated himself on his softly-softly approach.

'Maybe we could take him a gift. A sort of peace offering.'

Naveed's new brass bell would have rung loudly at this point if it hadn't been swung clean off its hook by the force of Pinks' bursting entry. The dome and the clapper shot off in different directions across the floor.

'OK, Ruff, no more Mr Nice Guy.' Floyd was on a charge. 'I tried to help. Was happy to do things your way but no, you had to keep all the goodies to yourself. Well, hard bull, mister. You've got to get up pretty early in the morning to catch this old worm and I've just caught you red-handed. Ditch the dessert; you're taking me to meet Butt.'

Pinks pointed to the door. 'Right now.'

Graham didn't budge.

'I said "right now"!' Floyd made a move to force the situation but there was something about Graham that could always make Floyd back off.

'Relax, Floyd.' Graham re-gathered his yoghurt and slowly began to spoon. 'Take a load off.'

Zul could only sit and stare.

'Don't play cute with me, pal. Time is moolah and I ain't wasting. I want Butt, in his office, right now.' It was at times like these that Pinks' Texan roots overran his more polished east-coast accent.

'I don't think he's there "right now".'

As Zul was about the lowest-ranked government official in The Northern Areas, he didn't actually have an office.

'I'm warning you, Ruff.'

'Alright.' Graham made as if to pack up his things. 'But it's going to cost you.'

Floyd's face was turning the purple of his new company fleece. 'How much?'

'Let's just say if Mr Butt does get us up to The Valley, I get to go in first.'

'You toe-ragging son of ....' The implications of this in terms of The Game were not lost on Floyd. 'After all the favours I've done for you.'

'It's not my fault you were so slow getting here.'

The stand-off showed no signs of resolving itself when it suddenly dawned on Zulfiquaar that, despite his innocent role in this charade, he might end up being the one to take the blame.

He stood up. 'Please, Sir, may I introduce myself?'

'Not now, Imran.' Pinks was too busy staring at Graham even to look.

'Deal?' Graham challenged.

Floyd hesitated.

'But my name is Zulfiquaar,' Zul pleaded, poking his head into Pinks' narrow line of vision.

'I said not now, Charlie.' Pinks' insides were itching, but eventually his hand rose to meet Graham's.

'Done?' Graham's face was poker-perfect.

'Done.' Pinks cursed as he spat into his palm and reached.

'Zulfiquaar Al Butt,' Zul frantically raced.

It was too late, the hands had shook. Graham rose from his seat with his 'when will you ever learn?' smile.

'You low down....' Pinks started to growl.

'Now, now.'

'No way, Ruff. I forfeit.' Pinks' nostrils were flaring for all their worth.

Graham almost skipped his way over to the far side of the room and retrieved the broken bell. 'But as you take such great pleasure reminding us,

Floyd, "a Housmann's handshake is his bond".'

Floyd snorted.

'So, introductions time, I think.'

Zul looked scared.

'Mr Butt, I would like you to meet Mr Housmann. Mr Housmann, Mr Butt.'

'Please, call me Zulfiquaar.'

Pinks ignored Zul's outstretched hand and kept his stare fixed on Graham. 'This isn't over.'

Zul waited. Then coughed. Then coughed and waited. Eventually Floyd turned and shook his hand. 'You can call me Mr Floyd.'

Floyd leaned out of the window and bellowed down to the car park. 'George, get in here with those maps. And be careful with the bottles.'

A young Asian-American, dressed in UCLA sweats and bearing an uncanny resemblance to an early Elvis Presley, was still unloading gear from the boot of a taxi. At his feet were a pile of tubes and boxes. Floyd turned back to the room and signalled to Naveed. 'Barkeep, a large cola. Coca Cola. No ice. But make it cold this time.'

Naveed brought Floyd the warmest can of Coke he had.

'Anyone else want a drink?' Floyd didn't want to be sociable but made himself try, for the sake of the bigger prize.

'Some more tea would be very nice,' Zul suggested.

'Yeah, and some more tea, and a Diet Coke for George.' Pinks added. The Elvis look-alike nodded his approval as he bundled his luggage through the door.

'I was only kidding there, Zuley.'

'Please, call me Zulfiquaar.'

'Me and Graham go back a long way, you see, and we always play these kinda games. I knew you were Mr Butt, I was just foolin' around.'

'Of course, Mr Floyd.'

'Of course,' added Graham wryly, as they all sat down.

'This is George, my assist-, sorry, "partner".' Floyd's first-ever dogsbody had been called George, and the name had stuck.

George dumped his load onto the table with a thud.

'The name's Vanh. Vanh Le.' He shot Floyd a glare. 'But you may as well call me "George".' He shook hands with a puzzled Zul and Graham, who gave him a sympathetic smile. 'Nice to meet you.'

'Perhaps, as you have your maps, Mr Floyd, it would be a good idea if I fetched mine,' Zulfiquaar suggested.

'Smart thinking, Zuley. George, go with Zul back to his place and give him a hand. Graham and I will start rolling these out.'

'It might be quicker if we took a car, Mr Floyd. There's quite a lot to carry.'

Naveed's decision to enter the car-rental business hadn't been taken lightly, and, indeed, had proved something of a financial white elephant. But his 1987 Ford Transit was always parked outside, and young Mohammed often used it to double up as a taxi. Zul tried to steer his clients towards the service, as and when he could, in return for the occasional free ride up what was a rather steep hill to his mother's house.

As Naveed appeared with a stool and a screwdriver to fix his broken bell, Floyd poured himself a drink and re-sparked his cigar. The map rolling was left to Graham.

'Alright, Big G, cut the crap.'

'What?'

'I said cut it.'

'Look, I know only what you know – that both of us want to get up to Xidakistan and we both need Butt to help us.'

'OK, Mr Cards-so-close-to-my-chest, let me put it another way. What are you here for? The Game or the guide?'

'As I have told you many times, Floyd, I am, and always have been, a disciple of The Book.' Graham took a self-righteous sip of tea from his cup and withdrew into his cushions.

'Yeah, right.' Pinks huffed. 'You've got twenty-five caps the same as me, and you know it.'

'That I can't deny, but getting out the first ever guidebook to Xidakistan has, and always will, come first.' Graham wasn't even convincing himself. 'To beat *Small World,* if nothing else.' He hoped that might ring truer. 'If what you said before is correct, you should be doing everything in your power to help.'

Pinks considered the situation for a moment. 'I'll believe you. For now.' He took a glug from his glass. 'Don't get me wrong, there's nothing I'd like more than to see Terry's hide whooped. But that's as far as I'm going.'

'That's as far as is needed.' Graham reached over for his satchel. 'If what you said is true.'

'Oh, it's true alright.' Floyd puffed. 'Me and *Small World* are history. With a capital 'H'. I'll be honest with you, Graham, all I care about is winning The Game. And after that? Retirement.' Pinks slowly ran his hand over his knee. 'So I was thinking-'

'Be careful!' Graham joked.

'I was thinking,' Floyd didn't flinch, 'if we can come to some sort of arrangement on that ...,' Floyd pulled a pair of spectacles from his pocket and slowly unfolded them, 'I could be behind you all the way.'

Graham unbuckled the clasps.

'Think about it, G.'

'I'll give it my undivided attention.' Graham emptied the contents of his bag on the table. 'In the meantime, this is me.' In between the guidebooks were a few old photographs of Xidakistan and the surrounding area.

Floyd picked up one of his tubes, pulled out a map and put his glasses on. 'How much do you reckon Butt knows?'

'A bit more than he's letting on, I'd say.' Graham helped him roll it out. 'Sound familiar?'

'Cross my heart, G.' Pinks tossed over an apparently random couple of his pocketbooks as if to prove the point. 'I wouldn't work for *Small World* again if they paid me. And I can assure you there were plenty of times they never did.' Floyd's buckskin boots emerged from under the table, and he plonked his feet on an empty stool. 'Besides, like I said, this might be the last you see of old Pinks out in the field.'

Graham rolled his eyes.

'I'm serious, G. Truth be told, I'm not altogether convinced by this internet business either. Too much money up front. Don't breathe a word to George.' Floyd gave his toes a bit of a wriggle. 'I promise you, G, if I win The Game I'll be happy to hang up these old boots.' His right foot trapped his left, and eased it out of its leather casing. 'For keeps.'

'No more writing?'

'Nope.' The second boot followed.

'Wild West Tours?'

'Finished.' Floyd mellowed. 'Time for some well-earned R and R back at the ranch.'

Graham remembered Floyd talking about inheriting a small hacienda in Patagonia from a great-great-grandfather. 'I'll believe that when I see it.' Graham skimmed through some of Pinks' notes, his tongue worming its way around his top lip. 'You're as hooked as I am.'

'Not anymore.' Floyd tried to tie Graham's eyes down to his. 'All I want's The Game. The rest can go hang.' Floyd allowed himself a larger than usual wetting of the whistle. 'On the level.'

'On the level?' Graham scanned the array of maps and notebooks in front of him. 'That's what I was worried about.'

'Come on, G.' Floyd re-sparked his Cohiba to encourage the thought process. 'Just the two of us? We should be working together.'

'I said I'd think about it.'

'Hey, we could even split it? You know, you get the book, I get The Game.'

'I've already got the book.'

'Yeah, but this way you'll have me on your side. Protection.' Pinks spat into his hand for the second time that day. 'And I'll cover your share of the expenses. Whaddya say, *Disciple?*'

Graham pretended to mull it over.

'OK, we both get The Game. Together.'

This time Graham mulled for real.

'Deal?' Pinks added rather too hastily.

'Maybe.' Graham raised his cup of tea and left Floyd's hand hanging.

'I want your hand.'

'Well, you're not getting it.'

Floyd, eyes closed, was about to let fly, but he checked himself. 'It's OK. I trust you.' He congratulated himself on his cunning.

'You don't have a choice.'

The two men straightened out the rest of the maps across the coffee table, and pretended to involve themselves in cartography. Pinks eventually broke, taking his frustration out on the butt of his cigar.

'OK, you win.' Pinks took another swig and wiped his mouth with the back of his hand. 'You get to go before me when enter The Valley, but first we gotta work out how to play this Zul fella.'

'Like I said,' Graham was conceding nothing, 'he probably knows more than he's letting on, but I doubt he's heard of The Game. And I've not mentioned anything about a guide.'

'Wake up, G. Why else would Ruff Guides be in town. You might as well hand out flyers.'

'Listen, Floyd. You may enjoy announcing your presence in every town in the hope of being slipped a few FOCs, but some of us still have integrity.'

'Integrity crap. You'll pencil in a couple of extra lines for a kickback like all the rest of us. You're just too up your ass to admit it.'

'I have never taken a freebie in my life.'

'Bullshit. What about all your hot-air ballooning in Cappadocia?' Pinks leant forward and stared straight into Graham's pupils.

'I paid like everyone else.' The black dots didn't flicker.

'The suite in The Peninsula for New Year's?'

'The company paid for it as a Christmas bonus.'

'Ha!' Floyd wasn't born yesterday. 'Everest base camp? I know you didn't pay for that.'

Now Graham had to readjust his sitting position. 'Jos did that behind my back and, if you remember, that's why I refused to mention their operation in my book.'

'It was there in the second edition though.' Pinks sucked in the smoke as though it was his last. 'Christ, what am I saying? You wrote that whole *Silk Road by Rail* thing on the back of two free tickets from Moscow to Beijing.'

'That wasn't me.' Graham's hands were beginning to clench.

'It was Ruff Guides.' Pinks pointed with his cigar.

'It was Jos and Antonia.'

Silk Road by Rail, in the summer of '91, had been Jos' first, and last, attempt at writing a guidebook for Ruff Guides. Despite the fact that the Silk Road never went within a thousand miles of Moscow, Jos was determined to make use of his freebie, and Sarah and Graham's concerns were overruled. The result was a messy hash of a dozen other guides, as Jos was too busy buying Fabergé eggs, Bukharan carpets and Ming vases to carry out his own research. Fortunately, within a few months of publication, the breakaway Soviet republics of Central Asia fell out with their former overlord, and the scheme, allowing the whole trip to be completed on one ticket, was abolished. People stopped following the route and the book was quietly relegated to the back catalogue.

'Oh yes, that's right. It's always "Jos". Never Graham. Ever so convenient. Seeing as how Jos's never here.' Floyd was on his feet, boots or no boots.

The tension was broken by the sound of Vanh and Zulfiquaar crunching the gravel leading up to the café steps. Naveed scurried to open the door in an attempt to preserve his newly-repaired bell.

'Let's put it to the test, shall we? Once and for all.'

Vanh had seen this sort of posturing before. He dropped the extra maps on the table and headed for Computer Corner.

'Zuley, I wonder if you'd mind taking a seat.'

Zulfiquaar looked at Graham nervously but sat as instructed.

'Zulfiquaar, do you know who this man is?' Pointing to Graham, Floyd puffed out his chest and straightened his shoulders.

'Of course, it's Mr Graham. Mr Graham Ruff.'

'Aha!' Floyd's eyes flashed to Graham's and Zul's eyes followed. 'And why does everybody know Mr Ruff?'

'Because he is Mr Ruff.' Zulfiquaar hesitated. 'Of Ruff Guides.'

'Thank you. And do you know why Mr Ruff is here?' Floyd sat down on the couch opposite.

'To write the guidebook on Xidakistan.'

'Thank you and good night.' Floyd leant back and puffed gratuitously on his miniature torpedo. 'Oh, and just for the record, do you happen to know where Mr Ruff is staying, Mr Zul?'

Zul began to relax now and replied with a smile. 'In the Madina Guest House, Mr Floyd. Gilgit's premier backpacker's.'

'Call me Pinks, Zuley.' The battle was won. 'You wouldn't happen to know which room Mr Ruff is staying in, would you?'

'The best room.' Zul hesitated again. 'Chalet number one.'

'The best room?' Floyd feigned shock. 'Why is that?'

'Because he's writing his guidebook.' Zulfiquaar could see the disappointment in Graham's face and tried to make amends. 'And the beds in all the other rooms are very hard.'

'Alright, we get the picture.' Graham snorted. 'Let's leave it shall we, Floyd?'

'Thank you, Zuley boy. Remind me to buy you dinner tonight.' Pinks celebrated with a large alcoholic burp.

'Zulfiquaar,' Graham was determined to move on, 'tell Floyd what you were telling me before, about your problem with the new king.'

Zul recapped the situation.

'Back up a minute there, Zuley.' Floyd scratched a fleabite on his left ankle. 'What happened to the old king?'

'He passed away.' Zul nodded before adding as way of explanation. 'During the first conference.'

'What first conference?' Floyd scowled.

'Last year,' Graham thought it might be easier if he took over the explaining, 'Zul organised a preliminary conference for the Xidakis, the Pakistanis, the Afghans, and the Chinese. To discuss the idea of getting Xidakistan's independence recognised by the UN.'

'Wait a minute.' Floyd was catching up fast but there still seemed to be some pieces missing. 'How the hell did you get those guys to sit around a table together? The Taliban and the Chinese hate each other.'

Graham looked back at Zulfiquaar. Pinks had a point.

Mr Butt looked reticent.

'Is there something you're not telling us, Zul?'

'No.' Zul's fingers started fiddling. 'Yes.' He looked down to his lap. 'Mr Pink is right. It was no plain sailing.' He brightened at his idiom. 'The Taliban were very hard, and it took a long time to convince them that if they recognised King Tah's independence he *might* become an ally against the Northern Alliance.'

'Or might not.' Graham commended the ingenuity.

'What about the chop suey brigade?'

Zul looked blank.

'The Chinese.'

'Ah. Yes. I took the liberty of forgetting to mention the Taliban's involvement until the very last moment.' Zul kept his face as straight as he could.

'I bet you did. You crafty old dog,' Floyd was warming to his new found friend.

Zul couldn't help letting out a tiny smirk. 'Once they arrived, I reassured the Chinese delegation that any breakaway by Xidakistan would serve to weaken their Taliban enemies, whom they suspect of running guns to the Uighurs fighting for independence in Xinjiang.'

'Touchdown!' Pinks slammed his palm into his fist.

'And the Pakistanis?' Graham was intrigued.

'It didn't take much to convince them.' Zul mocked. 'Especially when they heard the Chinese were paying.'

Graham laughed. 'So then what?'

'Well.' Zul thought back. 'There we all were up in Sost, and with the provisional treaty signed, Xidakistan was elevated to the position of "autonomous state within the Islamic Emirate of Afghanistan".'

'Good work, Zuley my man, good work.'

'It would have been,' Zul conceded ruefully. 'China had even agreed to act as sponsor for full independence and membership of the UN.' He took a deep breath. 'But that is when news arrived of King Tah's death.'

Graham nodded. 'Which brings us back to the beginning of our story.'

'Unfortunately so.' Zul looked downcast again. 'The Xidaki delegation packed up as soon as they heard, and set off home to bury their king.'

'But they'd already signed the treaty,' Floyd argued.

'Yes, but that was only a provisional treaty. And with King Tah dead it's virtually worthless. We need the new king to sign.'

'And he's refused to meet anyone since the coronation debacle,' Graham thought out loud.

'What coronation debacle?'

Zul explained.

'So this guy,' Pinks surmised, 'is pissed at the Brits, the Chinese, the Afghans and the Ruskies, correct?'

'Correct.'

'Well, in that case, why don't I, as 'Official Representative' of the US of A, go up there and do the do single-handed?'

'I don't think that would be a good idea,' Zulfiquaar squealed, looking to Graham for support.

'Me neither,' Vanh interjected from the corner of the room.

'I am the only foreigner who can speak Xidak, you see, Mr Floyd, Mr Pink.' Zulfiquaar corrected himself, panic-stricken.

'The name's "Pinks".'

'Doesn't anyone up there speak English?' Graham tried.

'Oh, no. Well, only the new king, and only a little,' Zul lied. 'Besides, it's not officially independent yet. The second conference still needs to be held and then permission to go up there needs to be granted.'

'Look, in my book it's independent, and in the Xidakis' book it's independent.' Floyd was back on his feet. 'What more do you want? You guys can sit here with your paperwork 'til you're blue in the face, I say I'm going up.'

Graham was used to such talk but this was one occasion he couldn't afford to call Pinks' bluff.

'Hold on, Floyd. Whatever happens, Zulfiquaar will have to make the introductions. You can't just barge in, unannounced.'

'Why not? I seem to remember that's what your hero Younghusband did.'

Graham could see Pinks was thinking unusually fast, and was struggling to stay a step ahead. 'Come on. We're talking about serious trekking here. And you'll have to go through Afghanistan. Taliban country. They're not going to say "Oh, Pinks Housmann, US citizen, come on in, make yourself at home".'

'I've found a way to get in without going through Afghanistan.'

Graham flinched. 'Where?' he demanded, pouncing on the cartography in front of him.

'The Ishkaman Pass.'

Graham started scouring, but Zulfiquaar put him out of his misery.

'No, there's no way through there, Mr Pink, Sir. That pass brings you out on the south side of The Valley, which is a sheer wall of glaciers. It's impossible to climb.'

'Well done, Zul,' Graham breathed easy. 'You see, Floyd?'

Floyd inspected Zul's superior map and conceded defeat.

'So what *do* we do?'

'Well, Zulfiquaar and I were discussing the possibility of taking the new king a special gift, to get him back on side.'

Zul nodded.

'The question is, what gift?'

'When I was at Cambridge,' Zulfiquaar confided to no one in particular, 'I saw a very clever present. On the box it said 'For the man who has got everything'.'

Zulfiquaar waited for his cue and broke into a smile as Floyd delivered.

'What was inside?'

'A badge which said "I've got everything".' Zulfiquaar began to giggle but Floyd wasn't laughing. He broke away to the window and looked down onto the main road, where a group of goats were narrowly avoiding being run over by an old Enfield.

'I know what'll work.' Pinks looked confident. 'A motorbike.'

'Yeah, a Harley!' Vanh vroomed from the corner. He left the computer screen and made his way over to join the group.

'How are you going to get a Harley Davidson up a twenty-thousand-foot mountain?'

Pinks turned to face Graham and the sea of maps on the table. 'Alright, maybe not a Harley. But how about an off-road bike, a scrambler?'

'But Xidakistan has no fuel,' Zulfiquaar worried.

'We'll take some with us. Once he's won over, who cares?'

'Pinks, you're an idiot but a good idiot.'

Floyd was never comfortable with Graham's backhanded compliments.

'You've just given me the solution. Anything electrical is no good, right Zul?' Zulfiquaar nodded. 'In fact anything that needs anything from the outside world is pretty useless?' Zulfiquaar nodded again. 'So we give him the most hi-tech, lightweight, shock-absorbing mountain bike money can buy.'

'You're not going to win a king over with a push-bike.' Vanh was clearly holding out for the Harley.

'Listen, partner.' Pinks was on board now. 'If it's bright, shiny and no one else in your world has got one, a dollar yo-yo can be the Crown Jewels. Graham, I like it.'

'Thought you might.'

Floyd kicked back in his chair and hauled a socked foot back up onto the table. 'Zuley, where's the best place to get a top of the line bicycle round here?'

'I'm afraid your choices in Gilgit are extremely limited, Mr Pinks. But may I suggest my cousin, Jahanghir, in Karachi. He has an exceptional range of all the latest models. Many of them imported from Europe and America.'

'Excellent. Give him a call, and tell him to send up the best one he's got.'

Zul rubbed his hands. Cousin Jahanghir might pay him a commission.

'And tell him we need it a.s.a.p.'

That could be another 5%.

'Alright, George, it shouldn't take more than a day or two for the bike to get here, so I want us ready to go at any time.'

George nodded wearily.

'All good, G.?'

'All good.' There was no point trying to stop Pinks taking control. Not just yet.

The Wakhan Corridor

The next morning, Graham was revising notes, Vanh conducting his ritual email check, and Pinks lounging at the main table helping himself to poppadoms. Breakfast at The Chinar, like the internet, was not on the menu, so Pinks and Vanh had arrived at the K2 early. Not that the options at the café were particularly lavish: a choice of last night's curry or fruit.

One of George's many unenviable tasks as Floyd's new 'partner' was to screen emails to The Pinks Guide website, and print out those of interest. These Floyd would then peruse at his convenience. '*George, you're the I.T. guy. Division of labour.*'

Vanh handed over the day's missives (he had 'fixed' Mr Shah's printer, by turning it on). It was a fair-sized pile, but Pinks' composure disintegrated on the first page.

'Holy, Jesus, Christ. No! No Way!' Floyd couldn't reach for his hipflask fast enough. 'She wouldn't dare.'

'What is it, George?' Graham mouthed. He felt it safer to leave Floyd alone for a while.

'Looks like Bonnie's coming to town,' Vanh whispered. 'But I only read the first couple of lines.'

'Bonnie? What's she doing here?'

'Apparently she got a tip off and is coming for a story on The Alphabet Game.' Vanh's voice dropped even lower. 'She's told Pinks to book her a room in his hotel.'

'The two-faced, breast-implanted, liposuctioned bitch!' Pinks' second volley shattered what was left of the silence, and Naveed nearly fell off his stool. Rising to his feet, Pinks managed to kick the coffee table so hard all the plates and mugs went flying, but Naveed was still too shocked to pick up the pieces.

'So where is she now, Floyd?' Graham inquired tentatively.

'Get this.' Pinks wasn't listening, preferring to boot a couple of door jambs. 'You're not going to believe her goddam cheek this time.'

Bonnie had decided early on in life that all PR was good PR. Whether it was asking for (and getting) a kiss from the Pope, or pinching the city mayor's behind live on TV during millennium night.

Pinks scanned the document for a final time, and turned to face Graham, clicking his DuPont open out of habit.

'Right,' he double-checked the sheet of paper underneath, just in case there was more. 'You're going to love this, G. Sweet Jesus, you're gonna love it.' Realising he had no cigar, Floyd clicked the lighter shut and began reading aloud.

'"*The Traveler* launches 'The Alphabet Game' and offers all its readers the chance to win a Holiday of a Lifetime - for Two. *The T's* intrepid feature writer Bonnie Fidler has been to many an exotic location to bring you, our readers, some of the most extraordinary stories on the planet. And now it's YOUR turn."' Pinks stopped to drain his glass. 'I can't believe I'm reading this.'

'"I thought of the idea last year while doing a story in Qatar, as a guest of the Sheikh, an incredibly generous host and a true gentleman. Mid-massage at the divine Al-Jarimah Resort, I suddenly realised I was in the only country beginning with Q."'

Floyd skipped down

'"A few spins of the globe later, of course, I discovered the problem was there was no 'X',"'

More skipping.

'"Now my friends in high places tell me the UN is poised to grant Xidakistan independence. Finally, the game can be completed. I'm so excited."'

'Which friends?' Graham pondered out loud. 'In which high places?'

'She'd never even heard of The Game until she met me.' Pinks jumped to the end of the piece in disgust. '"Our fabulous prize – an all-expenses-paid trip for two to anywhere in the world, and a chance to write a review for *The T* – will be awarded to the first reader to collect all twenty six caps."' Floyd threw the whole pile of papers down in front of Graham and poured himself another drink.

'Well, you've got to admire her balls,' Graham desperately tried to joke. He grabbed the papers from the table and scanned through the article for himself. His face fell further. 'It says here that she might even have a go at winning The Game herself.'

'If she goes anywhere near The Valley, I'll give those collagen-injected lips such a crack.' Pinks was back on the prowl.

'Hang on,' Graham continued to read, 'it looks like she's on an FOC from China Tours, and is coming in via Kashgar. If that's the case she won't be here for days.'

'Good work, G.' Pinks came to a stop. 'Too late, bitch!' he crowed, unfastening his shoulder bag. He extracted a mahogany mini-humidor and turned the key. 'Where's Zul? Do you think we can get him to close the border?'

'Wait a minute.' Graham scanned back up. 'She's saying the UN is "poised to grant independence".'

'So?' Pinks was busy choosing cigars.

'*So?*' Graham tingled. 'That means a date for the conference must have been set.' He tingled some more. 'Which means independence is on its way.'

'Which means we're on!' Floyd gave his silver cigar slicer a short sharp press and the end of a Cohiba was gone.

As the ramifications continued to sink in, 'Little Mo', the youngest of Naveed's seven sons, proudly opened the door. Mo junior earned his crust as the latest in a long and prestigious line of Gilgit messenger boys. Giving his father's newly-repaired bell a loud ding, he brandished an envelope. As Floyd and Graham seemed pre-occupied, he decided upon Vanh as the recipient.

'Here's some more good news. The bike's in 'Pindi, bright blue and will be here tonight.'

'Hallelujah! We'll leave tomorrow. What date's that, George?'

'September seventh.'

'And what date was that article written, G?

Graham, immersed in re-reading Bonnie's email, stifled a giggle.

'Come on, G. This is important.'

'I know, Floyd.' Graham couldn't contain it any longer. 'But she says here you're to make it a double room.'

'She ain't sharing with me, if that's what she thinks.'

'No, no,' Graham pressed on. 'She's hooked up with, and I quote, a "Young *Thor Heyerdahl* type", "with a cute ass". It sounds like he's planning on hitting Xidakistan, too.'

'Tough titties, darling, we'll be there and back before you've had chance to pull your panties up.' Floyd's lips were sucking on his cigar like a baby on a pacifier. 'How did I end up marrying that slut?' he managed between shucks.

90

'Don't be too hard on yourself, Pinks. It was only for six months.' Graham winked at Vanh while Pinks had his back turned.

'Yeah, and ten years down the line, I'm still paying for it.'

The blanket blocking off the kitchen was silently drawn to one side and the entrant gave a polite cough.

'Zuley! Just the man I wanted to see. The bike arrives tonight, we're leaving tomorrow.'

'Actually, Mr Floyd, I think it would be wise to leave as soon as the bike arrives. If not before, '*n shallah.*'

'Are you alright, Zulfiquaar?' inquired Graham. Zul was as pale as it's possible for a Punjabi to be, and couldn't stop fidgeting.

'Yes, Mr Graham. Quite fine. It is just I have received instructions from my authorities.'

'They're cool with the trip, right?' Pinks was looking a little nervous now.

'Oh yes. Very cold.'

'So what is it?'

'Do you mind if I sit down, Mr Graham?'

'Of course not.' Graham was genuinely concerned. 'Here, have some tea.'

Zulfiquaar shuffled towards the empty chair next to Floyd and took a blast of his inhaler.

'You see, we must go to The Valley at once. I have received instructions this morning from my authorities that the Independence Conference will meet in Sost very soon. Xidaki independence will then be ratified post haste. I must arrive in Sost with the Xidaki delegation or else…' Zul gulped.

'Or else what, Zul?' Graham was teetering between the confused and the bemused.

'Or else,' Zul shook, '*shhwwuckk.*' He slit his finger across his throat.

'Stop frettin', Zuley boy.' Pinks gave him a playful slap on the back. 'Who are these authorities of yours, the Mafia?'

'I cannot say, but I know that I must not, we must not,' Zul looked around the room for support, 'we must not fail.'

'And we won't.' Pinks gave Zul a firm clench of the shoulders. 'Relax.'

Zul couldn't. 'I have ordered our provisions to be ready for us to leave as soon as the bike arrives. Even if it's in the middle of the night.'

'Don't panic, Zuley.' Pinks' mood had well and truly swung. 'We've still got plenty of time. Young Tah's gonna love the bike and then it's just a case of bringing Mohammed down to the mountain. From the mountain.' Floyd looked at Graham for clarification. 'Or is it the mountain we bring to Mohammed?'

'Please, Mr Pink!' Zul was bordering on the hysterical. 'Don't you see? Last time it was so very complicated.' Graham made Zul take a long sip of his tea. 'When the old King Tah sent his delegation, it wasn't to an independence conference, it was to a party.'

'Uhh-Ernn.' Pinks made his favourite 'wrong answer' buzzer noise. 'It was definitely a conference, you told us so. Didn't he, Graham?'

'Maybe for the Chinese and the Pakistanis,' Zul continued forlornly, 'even the Taliban. For them it was a conference, yes, but if I had told old King Tah it was a conference, an Independence Conference, he never would have agreed.'

'Why not?' Vanh was as confused as everyone else. 'I thought he wanted independence.'

'Yes, but...' Zul stuttered. 'As far as he was concerned he already was independent. He had never been anything but independent. Such a stubborn old man, you know.'

'So what happened?' Graham felt it was time to bring some direction to the conundrum. 'His delegation was there. You brought them.'

'I told the king that there was going to be a big party. To celebrate his jubilee.'

'His what?' Pinks' mouth forgot to shut.

'His Golden Jubilee. Well, that's what I called it. You see, a few days before I had asked the king how long he'd been on the throne. He'd said he wasn't really sure but it must been quite a long time, so I told him about the Queen of England and her golden jubilee next year, how everyone is going to throw parties to celebrate.'

'I still don't get it.'

Graham looked at Floyd to indicate that Zul hadn't finished, and could do without all the interruptions.

'I explained that at this party, all the king's royal cousins would present him with cards to commemorate the occasion.'

'One of which was to be the treaty.' Graham twigged.

'Exactly.' Zul slapped Graham's knee.

'But an independence treaty looks nothing like a birthday card.' Floyd's nose continued to curl.

'Yes, but I pretended that royalty often used over-sized cards with archaic forms of the English language, as a mark of respect. I told him he shouldn't be surprised if some of his guests congratulated him on his 'autonomy' rather than his 'reign'.'

'You sly old devil.' Pinks finally cottoned on.

Graham, however, could tell from Zul's face that there was to be no happy ending.

'But not sly enough?'

'Unfortunately, not.' Zul's head dropped. 'Still he refused to go, saying he was too old to make such a long journey. And instead he sent his brother.'

'So?' Floyd felt he had missed something.

'So, this time my authorities say the king must come in person, and I'm not sure young Tah will be so easily fooled. He's still very upset about his coronation.'

'Don't worry, Zul, old Pinks will think of something.'

Vanh's cough turned into a splutter.

'Alright, Big G will think of something. Let's sleep on it and just make sure we're all set to leave in the morning.'

Pinks signalled to Vanh to fetch his gear, and made for the steps.

'Excuse me, Mr Pink.' Zul ventured, just as Floyd was closing the door. 'About the provisions for the trip.'

'I thought you said they're all set?'

'Oh yes, everything is prepared. It is only that I need to settle the accounts before we leave. Mr Graham said you were taking care of the expenses and that you always preferred to pay up front.'

'I bet he did.' Pinks scowled at Graham but drew out his wallet and counted out five notes. 'These Benjamins should take care of everything for the time being. But I want written receipts when we get back.'

'Of course, Mr Pink, of course.' Zul's eyes were back to their shiniest best.

*   *   *

King Tah's bike duly arrived that night. An hour before dawn Graham, Zul, Floyd, Vanh, a local guide and three porters set out from town on the old Chitral road. It was a long, tough drive, zigzagging in tandem with the banks of the Gilgit River, and Graham was glad he was in the lead Land Rover. Vanh and the porters were in a battered old Hi-Lux behind. Tarmac soon gave way to gravel as they passed one dilapidated farmstead after another, until, late in the morning, they came to the bare village of Gakuch. Here the tributary stream hurtling down from Floyd's Ishkaman Pass meets the main course of the Gilgit River.

Just before lunch they gear-crunched their way into Gupis but it, too, appeared little more than a ghost town. Ghost hamlet, Graham thought to himself. The problem was that all economic activity was now centred on the KKH; no one came this way anymore. From Gilgit everyone headed north to Karimabad and Gulmit, and this old road had all but been abandoned.

THE NORTHERN AREAS

'The Northern Areas' applies to the collection of semi-autonomous states that make up most of northern Pakistan. These states might not mean much to most, and before the 1930s, the only detail The British considered noteworthy of the region was the locals' propensity for tit-for-tat murdering and feuding.

Then came *Lost Horizon*. Almost as soon as it was published, people started to put two and two together, and head here in search of Shangri-La. The Northern Areas, and Hunza Nagar in particular, were suddenly very much on the map, whether the locals liked it or not.

James Hilton's work was inspired by ancient tales of an incredible life force in the region – tales which Marco Polo himself seems to have believed in, making a deliberate detour to Hunza when he took ill on the way down from Xidakistan. The healthiness of current inhabitants is certainly undeniable: on average they live up to twenty years longer than their fellow Pakistanis.

Yet along with worldwide acclaim came a mini-invasion of karma-seeking herbivores, and for a while every wacked-out celeb worth his or her joss-stick came to tune in, buy a Hunza hat, and drop out.

Standing at the head of the Hunza Valley is its main village, Karimabad, previously known as Baltit. At the peak of the village is the old Baltit Fort, for centuries ceremonial home to Hunza's ruling *Mirs*, and now a well-preserved museum.

As their 4x4s coaxed their way up the rough track, Graham kept scribbling. But this last box rankled. Not least because he couldn't work out how to fit in the story about the path he was now on. It was the same route along which, back in 1895, Colonel James Kelly and his 400 Sikh Pioneers had marched, waist-deep in snow, famously to rescue Major Robertson's garrison. Robertson had been helplessly besieged in Chitral's White Fort by tribes of cut-throat Pathans. Gupis was where the river split, and Graham would have liked to have pointed out that it was where his route left that of Colonel Kelly, who had headed south-east via the Shandur Pass. A second helping of flat bread, stewed mutton and rice was little consolation.

Towards the end of the afternoon, the porters' vehicle led them on the final steep stretch north up to Yasin, a scruffy place at the best of times, all adobe walls and corrugated iron. At least the locals were pleased to see Zul and his chocolate supplies.

Graham and Pinks had taken it in turns to nap, as they knew that from here on they would be walking alongside the vehicle as often as riding in it. The next stage, to Darkot, looked straightforward on a map but the cartographers' gravel had yet to materialise. As Graham exhaustedly leant his shoulder against the bumper for the seventh time, he was finally relieved to see a battered group of huts huddled around an inky lake. Darkot is perched at the foot of the more famous pass that bears its name, and although it was still below the snow line, ice lurked in every shaded ravine and the air was becoming thin and scratchy. It was enough to make Pinks reach for his hip-flask.

'You're going to give yourself a heart attack one of these days, Floyd.' Vanh had moved up to help push the Land Rover.

'I made you my partner, George, not my doctor.'

'How many of those things did we bring, Pinks?' Today was one of Graham's drinking days.

'*We*, G, didn't bring any. I, on the other hand, have a limited supply of superior single malt whisky, which you are unlikely to come into contact with unless you can rustle up some mixers.'

'No vodka, Mr Pink?'

'Not when walking, Zuley. Scotch-only sport.'

'Single-malt whisky has propitious medicinal powers,' Graham explained.

'You got it, G. Purely medicinal.' Pinks turned round to gloat. 'But I still ain't sharing.'

'I'm afraid that might not be wise, Mr Floyd.' Zul shook his head. He had watched a napping Floyd dribble down his front for half the journey and wasn't feeling particularly impressed. 'Not sharing in this part of the world is a dangerous habit. You don't want to wake up to find all of your belongings have accidentally fallen off a cliff.'

Graham grinned.

'Who you kidding, Zuley? These guys are Muslims. They can't drink alcohol.'

'I'm sorry, Mr Pinks, but that's not strictly one hundred percent accurate.'

'Well, it was the *last* time I looked in the Koran.'

'Like you ever have.' Vanh had had an uncomfortable ride.

'It is true the Koran and Pakistan both strictly forbid the consumption of alcohol for all Muslims,' Zul conceded. 'Even if the government does run two breweries and sells the beer at extortionate prices,' he sniffed. 'Here, however, we are in The Northern Areas, and each village can decide its own rules.'

'Typical.' Floyd sulked.

'Don't look so disappointed, Mr Pink. Perhaps our hosts will offer you some of their local specialities in exchange. Their mulberry brandy is particularly potent.'

Graham winced.

'And if you water it down it turns pink!' Zul added, quite thrilled at the connection.

'Is that recommended, Big G?' Floyd looked sceptical.

'In a word....'

'I had a feeling you were going to say that.'

As it turned out, Zul's Darkoti friends were still recovering from a rather large birthday celebration three nights before, and only gingerly broached the subject of alcohol, before making their excuses and turning in.

*   *   *

Day two began at 5am with the near-vertical ascent of the Darkot Pass, 5000m high and snow-covered throughout the year. With the vehicles abandoned, local pack horses took the best part of the morning to complete the climb. The most recent snowfall had been deep and the path obliterated. Zul suggested everyone take an extra half hour at the top to recover and they willingly did so, gobbling down their chapattis and jam. Graham, driven to distraction by Pinks' now incessant whistling of Billy Ocean's *When The Going Gets Tough*, took the last of his tea and wandered off in search of a tranquil rock.

From his new-found vantage point a mound of a mountain still obscured views north of the pass, yet southwards the rocks dissolved into a windswept panorama.

'Darkot village lies gloomily in the shadows but the cobalt blue ether seems to stretch forever, pricked here and there by the whites of mountain peaks. At the very back, the bulky cap of Nanga Parbat blazes higher than all its peers.' Even without a pen in his hand, Graham was on automatic pilot. But a fresh wind picked up, whipping into his jacket and hood, and he was forced to retreat.

The next section involved a perilous descent into the shallow valley that separates the Darkot Pass and the, slightly less exhausting, Baroghil Pass. Come winter, snow, ice and crevasses would turn crossing this valley into a deadly marathon. Now, however, still basking in the last of the sun's nurturing warmth, and with cool, fresh water from the small brook babbling its way from east to west, it was difficult to see how anyone could ever come to any harm.

As they crossed the Baroghil, Vanh investigated a small hut, which had been built to serve as a border checkpoint. He needn't have bothered, the last Afghani guards to patrol this crossing left shortly after the overthrow of King Zahir Shah.

Finally, with night drawing in, they swung down into the Wakhan proper, and joined up with the eponymous river. Along its southern side ran a dirt track, which their guide optimistically hailed as 'The Main Road'. The group pitched camp in some empty outhouses on a bend in the river, once marked on maps as Sarhad. Vanh and the two 'Sahib's collapsed into their sleeping bags. The porters, who between them had been struggling with the bike as well as all the usual supplies, finally took the opportunity to consummate the relationship with Pinks' Islay malt.

Next day, the slightly-worse-for-wear porters negotiated a ride with the only mini-truck to pass by, and the final ride up to Bozai Gumbaz began. It started out as a relaxed affair, but the reception at the checkpoint gate, some two miles short of the village proper, was tense. Zul explained that this wasn't uncommon.

It appeared the local chiefs were becoming increasingly nervous amidst rumours that something very big, and very bad, was going to happen. Any day now, though no one knew quite where. They had tolerated Zulfiquaar coming up here over the years, but the presence of white men (this was the first time Vanh had been called white) could only spell trouble. It soon became clear they would not be allowed to proceed any further, under any circumstances.

'Floyd, just stay calm.' Graham was as nervous as the locals who had gathered in the sentry's hut. The Wakhan Corridor was the type of place where people could disappear without the rest of the world hearing a peep for months.

'Hey, I'm calm. Calm as calm can be. But if that hairy jerk-off spits in my direction just one more time, I'm gonna….' One henchman, significantly broader, taller and meaner than the others, hadn't taken his eyes off Floyd since they arrived. He had begun spitting pips, in between scratching his rifle.

Graham, Pinks and Vanh were sitting around planks of wood hammered together into something resembling a table. Inside the hut was dark and smoky, not tobacco smoke (although that was there as well) but wet wood smoke, from the open fire. Zulfiquaar was negotiating with the sentry in the corner but it didn't look good.

'Mr Floyd, I think it might be a good idea to bring out your remaining whisky.'

There was only one bottle left, but by its end the mood seemed to have lifted. Zul broke off to update the others.

'Good news, gentlemen. You can now stay for the night, but they want to know our exact plans.'

'What are our exact plans?' Vanh voiced the question on everybody's minds.

'How far are we from Xidakistan, Zul?'

'Not far, Mr Graham. It's only a few miles from Gumbaz to the foot of the mountains on the north side of The Valley, and there's dirt track most of the way. From there, though, we have to carry all our own supplies, up through a small gorge to the base of 'The Dome', which leads into The Valley itself.'

No one spoke for a good few minutes while the guards began to shuffle and whisper amongst themselves.

'OK,' Graham reasoned. 'What if we tell these guys we're just passing through. Give them some money for letting us stay here the night, and head up to The Valley tomorrow, without entering the village.'

'We must be able to bribe these guys, right Zuley?' Pinks was a firm believer in the 'throw enough money at it until it goes away' solution.

'You could try.'

'Agreed then.' Graham reached over for his pack. 'If they accept, we'll spend the night here, and then see what happens in the morning.' He unzipped the inside pocket for his wallet. 'If they still won't let us in, Zul, you and the mountain bike will have to go it alone.'

'What? Come all this way only to turn back,' Pinks was still eyeing the Tajik with the spitting disposition. 'No way, José.'

'Yes way, Pinks.' Graham had sixty dollars in cash. 'We agreed before we left that it would be too risky to barge in unannounced. It's much more important that Zulfiquaar persuades Tah to attend the conference.'

Floyd didn't look convinced.

'We're still going to be the first ones up there.' Now Graham was trying to convince himself. 'We'll still win The Game.'

'I don't like it, G.'

'Neither do I, but-'

'She'll be in Gilgit by now. Plus her new boyfriend.' Pinks huffed on his cigar. 'And I can't believe Ned Kelly's too far behind, either. I don't like it, Graham, not one little bit.'

Graham knew the dangers as much as anyone, but once Zul and Vanh had added their support, he managed to persuade Pinks grudgingly to agree. The guards relented (in exchange for the crisp dollar bills), and as they all settled in for the night Graham tried to make the best of a bad job:

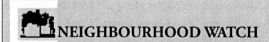

NEIGHBOURHOOD WATCH

Xidakistan's isolation has been greatly assisted by its surroundings. In essence, it sits smack in the centre of what mountaineers often refer to as the 'Pamir Knot'.

The Valley is protected by a huge ring of granite peaks, which in turn are surrounded by the Pamirs, the heart of Asia's mountain ranges. To the north are the Tien Shan ('Heavenly Mountains'), a sheer wall barring China from Central Asia; to the east is the great Tibetan plateau, the largest winter desert outside of Antarctica; to the south are the massifs of the Himalayas ('abode of snow') and the Karakorams ('Black Rock'), which have been gradually ploughing into one another over millions of years to produce the only mountains above 8000m anywhere in the world; and to the west are the Hindu Kush (literally, 'Hindu Killers').

Only the toughest survive at this altitude and Xidakistan's neighbours are no exception. They have each earned their reputation for ferocity and hostility to intruders: be it the Tajik and Kyrgyz shepherds who, despite decades of subjugation, refused to buckle under Moscow's hammer, or the few Sarikol herders who still eke out a living around Tashkurgan under the watchful eye of the Chinese.

Others to have come into contact with The Valley include the Uighur jade miners of the Taklamakan Desert, a wasteland which has repeatedly underlined the meaning of its name 'Desert you enter but never leave'; while the hill-tribesmen of Afghanistan and Pakistan are so volatile their governments have allowed them almost complete provincial autonomy, via the creation of 'Nuristan' and 'The Northern Areas' respectively.

Only the Dards have ever made any real effort to engage with the Xidakis. The Dards have become scattered over the centuries but their heartland is the villages around Bozai Gumbaz, itself an island in the snow at the head of the Wakhan River.

The next morning all hopes of moving on were unceremoniously dashed by the arrival of the village elders. Indeed, it took all Zul's negotiating powers to secure them a second night's rest in the hut. Zulfiquaar was allowed to set out for The Valley with the bike and one of the porters, but the others were turned round and sent back the way they came.

∗   ∗   ∗

Graham wearily climbed out of the Land Rover. Given the time of year, he wasn't too surprised to see Gilgit even emptier than when he had left it. What did puzzle him, however, was the number of shopkeepers and householders who came out onto their porches to stand and stare.

Pinks stayed seated.

'OK, G, I'm going up to my place to run a bath. I've got the porters covered.'

'I should hope so too.' Graham's wallet was empty.

'George, you're going to have to wait your turn.' Their rooms shared an inter-connecting bathroom.

'Gee, thanks.' Vanh had been dreaming of a hot soak all the way from Gakuch. He levered himself out and slammed the door.

Pinks climbed up the wooden steps of the Chinar Inn, and as he opened the door to the small but well-appointed reception, the manager and the cleaning lady went deadly quiet. For a moment everything in the foyer seemed to stop.

'I'm very sorry for you, Mr Housmann,' began Mr Al Huq. 'We are all very sorry.'

'That's alright, Ali. There's always a next time.' Mr Al Huq was slightly taken aback by the equilibrium of this last remark and showed it. 'All I want right now is a hot bath and a whisky. There is hot water isn't there?'

'Oh yes, of course. Nafezah will bring up fresh towels. Is Mr Le with you?'

'Yeah, he'll be up in a minute.' Pinks smirked to himself.

'Of course, Mr Housmann. No problem at all.'

'Oh, Ali. Any messages?'

'Yes, indeed, Mr Housmann. Two days after you left a lady arrived, a Miss Fiddler. She said that as you hadn't organised a room for her, she would be staying at the Serena Lodge up in Jutial. But, of course, in light of what's happened...'

'Do yourself a favour, my friend, it's "Fidler".' Floyd deliberately exaggerated the long 'I' vowel. 'And call her 'Mizz'.'

Mr Al Huq was still at a loss. 'She has come in every day looking for you, and this evening she keeps calling to say you must meet her in the K2 as soon as you return.' Ali paused, a lump welling in his throat. 'As soon as you return.'

Does that woman ever stop?' Pinks groaned to himself, but his thoughts quickly turned to his bath.

Three quarters of an hour later, Floyd was splashing on a last coat of aftershave and tying up his shoelaces. A final look in the mirror reminded him that the shirt he was wearing was one that Bonnie had once said she'd liked, so he changed it. Rather than head to the K2 alone, he called into Graham's room on the way. Standing in the doorway, despite the offer of a seat, Pinks began to vocalise his concerns.

'I'm worried, G. She'll sleep with anyone for a story.'

Pinks was too nervous to smoke. He always was before meeting Bonnie.

'Relax,' Graham urged.

'How can I? Christ, she must have known about the conference before Zul did.' Floyd's stomach was knotting up. 'Who's to say she's not his Higher Authority?'

'Now you're being ridiculous.'

'Am I? If she's not, she's probably sleeping with whoever is.'

Graham pursed his lips. 'Alright, let's just slow down.' He rose up from his seat and suggested they make their way to the café. The streets were now completely deserted except for the gusts of wind blowing down off the mountains. With the sun long gone there was a real bite to the air.

'So,' Graham recapped. 'She knows about the conference, and maybe about Zul. But whatever she knows, she doesn't know he's up there now. Let's not say a word and see what she wants.'

Pinks led the way up the K2's stairs out of habit rather than desire, and opened the door. Vanh was sitting in front of an old box television that hadn't been there when they left, and Bonnie was leaning on the back of his chair.

'Oh Floyd!' Bonnie span round and made a bee-line for him, throwing her arms around his neck 'Thank God you're here.' Her normally immaculate coiffure was in a mess.

'Bonnie?' Every muscle in Floyd's body froze rock solid. It was the one welcome he hadn't prepared for.

'It's all so terrible! How could they, Floyd?'

'Christ almighty!' Graham's line of vision had suddenly landed on the screen. 'What's going on?'

Bonnie withdrew from Pinks' shoulders and stared into his eyes.

'You mean you don't know? You don't know?'

The flickering TV replayed a plane crashing into a skyscraper in slow motion. Pinks was transfixed. The commentary was in Urdu, but the pictures spoke for themselves. 'When did it happen?'

'Around six, our time. Morning rush hour back home.'

The next sequence of images to hit the screen seemed to be showing the crash from a second angle, but as the view widened it became clear that this was actually a second crash into a second tower. The buildings in the background left no doubt as to the location.

'They hit both towers?' Floyd pulled the words up from his stomach.

'Two separate planes. Another's hit The Pentagon, and now they're saying one's gone down near Pittsburgh.' Bonnie's eyes were beginning to stream.

'Jesus, there's guys jumping out of the windows.' Graham's fascination recoiled into nausea.

'Who did it?' Pinks' eyes continued to stare but were strangely blank.

'Al Qaeda.' Vanh hadn't moved since he'd arrived. 'At least they're the ones claiming it. That Bin Laden guy in Afghanistan.'

'How many dead?' Graham reached out for the back rest of Vanh's chair.

'They don't know.' Bonnie's voice was choking up. 'Since the towers collapsed it's been impossible to tell. They're saying five thousand.'

'Christ!' Floyd snapped himself back to life. 'I've gotta call my apartment.'

'I already did. Frank said he heard the second one go in as he was putting out the trash. The whole of your street's been cordoned off.'

'I need a drink.' Pinks was running his sweaty hands through those hairs that were left.

'I thought you'd never ask.' Bonnie attempted a weak smile.

Floyd fumbled through his jacket and pulled out his hipflask.

'Maybe we should all go up to my place. At least it's got CNN.'

Bonnie agreed, and Graham and Vanh promised to catch up once they had checked their emails. Everyone knew it was going to be a long night.

Jos

The problem with Graham is he's got his head in the clouds. You've got to be cruel to be kind, right? That's what mates are for. I'm sure he's already told you, we're more brothers than cousins, but still, all that 'professional layabout' stuff? He's a dreamer. And for the past however many years, it's been my job to bring him back down to earth. Like when Sarah got pregnant. If he had been smart, he would have listened to my advice. But it didn't fit with his 'romantic ideal'.

Sarah had been avoiding Jos for weeks but could put it off no longer. If Graham hadn't been stuck in the middle of some Silk Road desert she would have gone to him. But then again, she smiled ruefully, if Graham hadn't spent the majority of the last five years being stuck in the middle of some Silk Road desert, none of this would have happened in the first place.

Sarah knocked on Jos' door. It was shut, despite the 'my door is always open' sticker on the frosted glass. Inside she could hear Jos regaling one of his friends with his latest exploits, and the tap, tapping of chrome balls swinging on his desk. She opened the door.

'Are you busy?' Sarah just managed to hide her sarcasm.

'Just a sec, Scoops.' Jos covered the handset with his hand.

'You know me, Sarah. Always working.' Jos had a habit of borrowing other people's lines.

Sarah stood with her arms folded.

'Scoops? I've gotta go. Important client.'

Jos swung round so his back was towards Sarah, and bent down into the phone. 'Remind me to finish the story tonight, it's a cracker. Seven o'clock in De Vino's, OK?'

Jos' borrowing habit extended to stories, and he happily told other people's when he ran out of his own. Sarah enjoyed catching him out.

It was the Adventure Travel Show drinks party the year Ruff Guides launched their first African series. Jos was holding court, telling a story about 'a friend' who had been in the Serengeti the year before doing a walking safari. In the middle of the night the camp had been attacked by two lions, and the friend had only managed to escape by jumping up a tree and diverting the animals with some sweets he'd found in his pocket. By the time reinforcements arrived to drive the predators away he was down to his last jelly baby. Sarah was eavesdropping from a nearby conversation circle and, allowing Jos to finish, sidled up to his elbow.

'What was your friend's name, Jos?'

'Err, Paul.'

'That's funny. When I first told you that story, it was about my friend, called Chris.'

Sarah caught hold of the last ball bearing mid-flight and brought the whole game to a stop.

'I was wondering what you were doing for lunch.' Sarah tried to sound friendly.

'Why? Are you offering?'

'No, but I'll let you take me to The Emporium.'

'Can't we go to Oscar's?' The waitresses were prettier at Oscar's.

'Alright, but we'll have to go now, or we'll never get a seat.'

Sarah waited while Jos groomed himself in the mirror behind his desk. Her eye wandered to the mantelpiece and the plaque resting in the middle. She couldn't help but snigger. Once again the Phantom Female had struck, and the smart brass 'JOS THE BOSS' sign now read 'FLETCH THE LETCH'. Jos' eyes followed Sarah's, and he hurriedly moved towards the door.

'Let's take the Porsche.' It was only four hundred metres. 'It's in need of a run.'

Much to Jos' chagrin, the only table still available was at the back, but this suited Sarah perfectly.

The following week was Graham's birthday, yet Graham himself was absent. Again. On this occasion stalking a route through the Caucasus as an alternative path for his Silk Road adventures if Iran's borders were ever to close. Nearly two thousand nights had passed since the infamous Thomas Cook Awards, but Graham had not relented, and Sarah was missing him more, perhaps, than ever.

Sarah ordered a salad, Jos plumped, as always, for the Steak Frites.

'Finally heard from G.' Jos speared an olive, tossed it high into the air and caught it in his mouth.

'Oh.' Sarah fiddled with her napkin.

'Yep, he's finished the Caucasus route, taken a ferry across the Caspian, and now's heading for the Karakum Desert.'

'Right.'

They fell silent.

'He'll probably call me when he gets to Ashgabat.'

Sarah still lived in their flat, and had kept all Graham's things in his room just as he had left them, in the vain hope that one day he would come back. But once 'the office' had moved out of the lounge and into shiny new premises on Upper Street, Graham hadn't even set foot in the place. Technically, he was staying at his mother's 'until he found a new place', but in reality he spent his whole life on the road.

'Antonia's moved in with me,' Jos managed in mid-mastication.

'Congratulations.' Sarah gave it six months.

'Yeah, it's really great.' He stopped to wipe pepper sauce from his chin. 'The boys at Foxton's say a property always benefits from a woman's touch.'

'And that's what counts.' Sarah physically bit her tongue.

By the time Jos' red wine arrived, Sarah decided she too needed a drink.

Desperate not to spend another evening home alone, Sarah had walked the short distance to the office. Everyone had gone except for Jos, busy conference calling the American distributors.

'Look, Jos, I wanted to speak to you about something specific. It looks like there are going to be quite a few changes in my life over the next few months, so I might have to take a back seat in the office for a while.' Despite half a glass of shiraz, Sarah hadn't stopped fiddling.

'And?' As far Jos was concerned Sarah had always been in the back seat.

Sarah began working on the Iceland guide she was editing but couldn't concentrate. She was almost relieved to hear Jos' footsteps cross the production floor to her office, and accepted his offer of catching last orders at The Red Lion.

'I'm three months pregnant.' Sarah didn't pretend she felt great about the whole situation, but consoled herself with the fact that, at least with the baby, she would finally come to know what unconditional love really felt like.

Several (double) vodka, lime and sodas ('to absent friends') found them heading for the late night restaurant at Jos' club. Courvoisier nightcaps took them into a cab and onto Jos' new 'des res' in St George's Square. Sarah wasn't enjoying herself but had long since decided that wasn't the point.

'What's what's-his-name said?' Jos jousted.

With Graham not around, Sarah had begun spending more and more time with Nick, one of the few friends she had made at UCL before dropping out.

'Who?' Sarah was in no mood to dance to Jos' tune.

'Your boyfriend bloke.'

'Nick is not my boyfriend,' Sarah retaliated with a smile as cutting as it was sarcastic.

Jos snorted in triumph. 'So how d'ya know I was talking about what's-his-name, if he's not your boyfriend?'

Sarah stabbed her fork into the tablecloth.

It hadn't lasted long, and Jos was soon snoring and grunting into his silk pillows, as Sarah dressed and fled back to North London. In the office the next day, as Jos couldn't even remember much past the first snog, Sarah chose to lie. The matter was closed.

Jos was glad he hadn't seen much of Sarah since that night. Of course, he was always tempted to gloat, but he knew if word got back to Antonia (or Graham for that matter), his chopper would be chopped. Sarah could still turn heads, though, and as Jos caught a suit eyeing her up from a nearby table, he rewarded himself with a mental pat on the back.

That morning, Sarah had imparted her news to Nick over coffee in his front lounge, and he had been the second man to storm out of a house on her account.

'If I were you I'd get an abortion.'

It was the answer Sarah had expected. As she watched Jos drench the remainder of his fries in ketchup her resolve to never to tell the father of his involvement cemented.

'Ooh,' Jos spluttered through a mouthful of juice and flesh. 'I know what I wanted to say to you.'

Sarah felt revulsion seeping down to her toes.

'I'm going to write another guidebook.'

The revulsion froze.

'Jos, I thought we agreed you would never write another shopping list.'

'That's quite funny, for you.' Jos decided to use it later that evening.

'*Why,*' Sarah shrieked to her inner herself, '*could he never see that everyone thought he was a complete and utter-? Aaaahhhh!*'

'The Raj by Rail I'm going to call it.'

'What?' Sarah screeched.

She hadn't wanted this lunch date to last a moment longer than was strictly necessary, but now felt compelled.

'Do you like it?' Jos trapped an errant *frite*. 'We begin in Calcutta.'

'We?' Sarah choked. For a hideous second she seriously thought he was about to invite her to go with him.

'Yeah, me and Antonia. It's my birthday present to her.'

Sarah didn't know whether to weep or wail.

'We start in Calcutta, take the train up to Delhi and Jodhpur; then Agra for the Taj Mahal, Amritsar for the Golden Temple. You get the picture.'

Sarah knocked back the remainder of her glass, refilled it in one and had to use all her strength not to down it again. Pregnancy or no pregnancy.

'The sleeping cars are pretty swish these days, you know. And they've offered us tonnes of FOCs, so it's Five Stars all the way.' Jos licked his lips.

'That's the most ridiculous idea I've ever heard,' Sarah finally managed.

'No, it's all signed, sealed and delivered. Tour India have even thrown in the flights.'

Sarah glowered in disgust.

'First class,' he added, thinking it would make things better.

'Give them back.'

'Why?'

'For starters, the Raj hasn't ruled India for over half a century.' Sarah slammed down her knife and fork. 'For main course…,' Sarah pushed the table so hard the remnants of Jos' lunch landed in his lap. 'And for dessert,' she didn't need to justify herself a moment longer, 'you are a complete and utter…, aaaahhhh!' Sarah was on her feet and completed the menu with a glassful of shiraz.

For once Jos was left speechless. Sarah calmly gathered her things before making her way through the stunned onlookers.

'Be like that!' Jos finally retaliated, wiping red wine from his chin.

Sarah kept walking.

'I told Graham,' he hollered after Sarah's silhouette. 'And he said I can do what I like.'

Sarah checked her stride at this last boast, hesitated, but refused to turn.

She did me a favour, actually, because Becky was the waitress who helped clean me up. I had to wear her spare T-shirt to get back to the office. Of course, Sarah was already there, furiously dialling deepest, darkest Turkmenistan in search of Graham. But he didn't come back, even after I spoke to him. Like I said: head in the clouds. When it's not stuck up his arse.

Playing the Game

A telegram arrived for Zul, stipulating that Xidakistan's independence, along with sports, air travel and apple pie, had been put on hold until further notice. Little Mo had been determined to wait until he could deliver the message to Mr Butt in person but Floyd's third and final offer, a crisp twenty, persuaded him that corners could sometimes be cut.

'Until further notice' can be a very long time, and it was certainly enough for Bonnie to lose her need for Floyd. Within a few days she returned to bitching about his social skills and Floyd resorted to drinking, and looking for drink. Graham immersed himself in boxed texts and Vanh holed himself up in his room.

All told, Ned Kelly's arrival was almost a welcome relief.

'Pinko!' Phil threw open the door to the K2. 'G'day, mate!' He strutted over towards his old sparring partner, clad in the loudest of loud Balinese shirts.

Floyd quickly hid his hipflask.

'GETTING ANY?' Phil often spoke in capitals.

Floyd was about to bend the truth but remembered Bonnie was over in Computer Corner.

Phil stopped in the middle of the room and flung out his arms to flaunt his shirt's dazzling array of greens, yellows and blues. Just in case anyone had missed them. 'I'll take that as a "No".'

Floyd nodded across the café in Bonnie's direction.

'Strewth. Pinkie *and* Perky. You kids getting back together?' Phil began to half-smooch, half-slide his way across to Bonnie's cubicle.

'Beat it, Ned,' Bonnie gnashed.

Phil held his hands up in mock surrender and skedaddled his way back to Pinks' corner.

As he span a chair round to straddle it in reverse, Graham returned from the kitchen with his lunch. 'No chance, Ned, that's my chair. Hit the couch.'

'Crikey.' By sending his son away to boarding school while he was still in short trousers, Philip Kelly Sr had hoped that junior's Woop Woop twang might one day be refined, if not entirely eliminated. But it was not to be. 'It must be Brownlow Medal night,' Phil marvelled. 'The place is chockers!'

111

'Hit the couch.'

'No worries, G.' Phil removed his over-size bumbag from under Graham's chair. 'But if we're having a party, where's the grog?' Phil looked around the room in vain for a bar.

Graham shoved a bottle of Coke in Phil's hand and gave Floyd the sign. He reluctantly produced his flask and poured a top up .

'That's better.' Phil had downed it in one and was licking his lips. 'So, how is everybody?'

'Not quite *every* body.' Bonnie bristled her way over to the central table.

'What?' Phil did a quick double take around the café before turning to Graham. 'No Sarah?' He was nothing if not predictable.

'No. No Sarah.'

'That's a kick in the guts.'

'I'm sure she's thinking the exact same thing.'

'I'll just have to beat you bunch of tin arses by myself then.' Phil helped himself to some of Graham's chicken. 'Shamoe.'

'Beat us at what exactly?'

'Come on G, it's Grand Final time.' Phil dropped the spoon back onto Graham's plate and grabbed his bumbag, like a football. 'Listen to the crowd, they're on their feet. The 'Pies are down by two. Kelly's got the footie, he slips one tackle, slides another; he's almost at the fifty; he looks up, he kicks. It's up, it's up. Carlton can't get back in time. It's there! Kelly's won The Game.' Phil was now screaming round the sofa. 'He's done it. The Alphabet King. Go on you good thing.'

'Stick a brick in it, Kelly,' Bonnie cranked.

'Jeez. Someone been serving red wine with the fish again?'

Silence.

'You'd think someone had died.'

'That's not funny, Phil,' advised Graham.

'Suit yourselves.' Phil celebrated his defiance with an extravagant Fosbury-flop onto the long settee. 'But when the new king comes down that mountain it's going to be me who's here to meet him.'

'I'd forget about any royal audiences for a while, if I were you, Ned.'

'Tell him he's dreamin', Floyd. The Independence Conference is all set, and I know it.'

Graham was tempted to ask how, but settled for bursting Phil's bubble. 'Was all set.'

'What d'ya mean?' Phil's customary optimism was beginning to evaporate. 'What's happened?'

While Floyd explained how events were not quite turning out as planned, Bonnie made her way over to the long reading table by the window. Naveed, who, as always now, was hovering by the curtained-off kitchen, swiftly grabbed one of the more comfortable chairs and carried it over for her to sit on. Once she was settled, he returned with her green tea.

'Doesn't matter,' Phil re-inflated his chest, 'I'll still cream yers.' He began to rub his hands like a young hustler spying a high roller. 'Beat you straight.'

'I wouldn't go as far as "straight".' Bonnie gave Floyd and Graham 'that' look. 'These two have already done a deal with the one and only go-between.'

'You've what?' Phil sprayed. 'You dirty mongrels. That's cheating.'

'That's what I said.' Bonnie scowled at Pinks who had pointedly reminded her of his advantage three times already that morning. 'In fact, I had just suggested before you came in that, as old friends,' Bonnie flashed Graham an unapologetic smile, 'we should all team up and work together.'

Floyd gave a sharp snort at the phrase 'old friends'.

'Onya, Bonns.' Phil turned to Graham and Floyd in turn with his arms outstretched. Amidst all the greens and the yellows, six monkeys could be seen riding their way across the waves. 'Come on boys, if it's just the four of us,' he bleated. 'Fair go!'

'Actually, there's five of us.' Graham should have said 'six' but in his eyes Floyd and Vanh counted as one. 'Bonnie's got a "cute bit of ass" hiding in her hotel room.'

'Jesus, Mikey!' Bonnie was choking on her drink and much to her embarrassment a mixture of mucus and green tea dribbled down her front. 'Mikey.'

Naveed rushed in with a serviette.

'I forgot all about him.' Bonnie wiped her front.

'That's not like you, dear.'

'Can it, Housmann!' His ex gave Floyd a stare as well-rehearsed as it was understood. 'Christ, he could be anywhere.'

'Have you tried under the bed?' Pinks worked hard to keep a straight face.

'Have you tried-?' Bonnie hissed

'Come on, Bonnie.' Graham panicked. 'Anywhere? This is important.' What if 'Mikey' was a rival Game player? 'When exactly did you last see him?'

'I'm not sure. That's the point.' Bonnie started twisting her thumbs. 'Since we arrived everything's been such a blur. As soon as he found out you'd already left, he tried to work out how he could catch you up. But now I don't even know which day that was.'

'How far could he have got?' Graham grabbed his map. What if 'Mikey' got to The Valley before they did? 'We came back the exact same way we went up and we didn't see anybody. Did we, Floyd?'

'Not a single ass.' Floyd lifted himself up out of his chair and moved to look out of the window. 'Not even a cute one.'

'Did he say which way he was going?' Graham was re-scrutinising the route. This could ruin everything.

'He said something about hitching a lift up to Gakuch and catching you up at the pass.'

'Which pass?'

'The Ishkaman, I think.'

'Forget about it!' Pinks turned in towards the table to celebrate. He suddenly felt a little peckish. 'That way's a dead-'

'Are you sure, Bonnie? Think. Are you sure it was the Ishkaman Pass.'

'That's what he said.' Bonnie flustered. 'He showed me it in his book.'

'But we didn't go through Ishkaman. We went over Darkot.' Graham was worried.

'He's probably hanging off some precipice as we speak.' Pinks not so.

'If anything happens to that boy,' Bonnie threatened, 'I'm holding you personally responsible. '

'Me?' Floyd nearly swallowed his glass.

'It's your fault for going up there in the first place.'

'You're the retard who sent him the wrong way.'

Bonnie's hand sprang. Whaaack. The red mark was still evident across Pinks' face as her fingers recoiled to the side of her tea cup.

Bonnie stared straight into Floyd's eyes. 'I said "Never", remember?'

'Whooaa, Bonnie.' Graham's cheek hurt just looking at it. 'Floyd didn't mean it, did you, Floyd?'

'I warned him before, Ruff.' Bonnie hadn't stopped staring. 'He's not to use that word in my presence.'

Floyd didn't say anything. He looked anything but conciliatory.

Bonnie scared the pants off Phil when she was in one of her moods, but his mouth wouldn't let him stay silent. 'Wait a tick,' he offered as his brain caught up. 'This drongo? Was he blonde, kind of Sheila-looking?'

Bonnie didn't blink.

'Norwegian?'

'Finnish.' Bonnie finally turned her face away from Floyd's.

'I reckon I saw him dropped off in town this morning. Looked like he could do with a hose down and a gutful of tucker but apart from that I'd say he'll be right.'

'I'm going up to the hotel.' Bonnie gathered her handbag from the reading table.

'Why don't you just do that, dear?' Floyd still hadn't moved.

They waited in silence until Bonnie's feet could be heard on the gravel at the bottom of the steps.

'Jeez. Sorry about the whack, mate.' Phil consoled Floyd nervously.

'Don't worry about it, Ned. Comes with the territory,' Pinks massaged his cheek, 'when you marry a retard.'

Phil looked at Graham. 'In that case, Pinks me old digger, I reckon it's your shout.' Phil gave Floyd a playful punch on the arm. 'You still owe me a longneck from last ANZAC day.'

Floyd kept massaging with one hand, and reached into his bag with the other.

'Unless, of course, there's more where this came from?' Phil chanced. 'I've had a shocker with the grog since I got here. A mate of mine in Islamabad traded me a slab of stubbies for a couple of chicks' phone numbers, but it was rotten piss.' Phil's eyes flicked to Graham. 'You'd have liked it though, G. It was warm.'

Pinks took a swig from his flask and passed it over. 'That's all I've got.'

Phil finished it off and signalled to Naveed to bring out another plate of curry. 'Not bad, but I could murder a bourbon.'

'Don't look at me.' Graham held open his satchel. 'Day off.'

'Jeez, G, every day's a day 'off' with you these days.' Phil couldn't believe there wasn't more alcohol. Somewhere.

'You'll have to make do with our intoxicating conversation instead.'

'Yeah, right.'

'Maybe, we could retire to my hotel.' Floyd's face could finally manage a smile. 'I might have another bottle or two.'

Phil looked over to Graham and grinned. 'Now you're talking.'

Graham looked to the heavens.

'*Another bottle or two,*' Pinks indicated that he hadn't quite finished, 'that I might be willing to sell. If the price is right.'

'Pull y' head in, Floyd. You're worse than a bloody Queenslander!' He man-handled some fluorescent lime-green clothing out of his bag, and defiantly tugged it over his surfing monkeys.

'Nice fleece.'

'You're going to have to find some proper clothes if you want to come up to my establishment.' Pinks stood up to go.

'Rack off!' Phil looked anything but hurt.

'Shouldn't we first go and check out Bonnie's Finnish guy?'

'No, we'll go back to mine and wait for the coast to clear.' Pinks was at the door but, as he paused to slice the end of his Montecristo, Phil's food arrived.

Phil gave Floyd a mournful look.

'I thought you said you were thirsty.'

Phil gobbled as much curry as he could in one mouthful, and scooped up the rest in a nan bread. 'No wuccas.'

The next thing Naveed knew the men were bouncing down the café steps ready to set off up the hill.

It was getting late by the time the three men reached The Madina. Graham's day 'off' was reluctantly back 'on'. The back of the hostel was set out in a horseshoe of adjoining chalets, like a holiday camp. The terrace running along Graham's wing was as dark as the communal garden, yet they decided to make do without the main light. Alcohol, as they had been reminded at Floyd's place, was tolerated by hoteliers, but only if guests were discreet. Graham found an old hurricane lamp underneath his patio table, and soon had it hissing out its low glow. He turned it down until the orange cast little more than shadows.

'You see, Ruffo? You just don't get times like that anymore. *That's* why I miss the old days.' Phil and Floyd had been reminiscing about the night in Istanbul when they had chanced upon a hammam with mixed bathing sessions.

'Hey!' Graham pulled his head out from underneath the table. 'Don't include me in your schoolboy fantasies.'

'Come on, G.' Phil gave Graham a playful kick. 'We're the Three Amigos. Remember?'

Graham suggested they make do with two.

'Ignore him, Ned.' Pinks produced a new bottle. 'George can be our third.'

'Elvis?' Phil burped. He had worked with George in Bolivia the previous year, whilst leading one of Floyd's 'In search of Butch and Sundance' tours. 'Where is the little heartbreaker?'

'In the hotel.'

'No!' Phil pouted. 'He should be here.'

'Did you see what I did there?' Floyd beamed to no one in particular. 'Heartbreaker? Hotel? Elvis?'

'Let's go back.' Phil made to stand up and just about succeeded, after an initial wobble. 'I wanna see the Little Fella.'

'Leave him.' Pinks gestured for Phil to sit down. 'He doesn't like drinking, remember? Besides, he's busy.'

Graham returned from inside his room with glasses, ice and some mixers. 'What? Washing your socks?'

'If you must know it's his day off.'

'So what's he doing up in his room?' Phil couldn't work it out. 'Don't tell me,' it suddenly clicked, 'not another new computer game?'

'You got it. Mekong Meltdown, or something, this latest one's called.'

'Alright, lay off the boy.' Graham didn't know George too well, but he didn't want either of these two lording it over him.

'Strewth, G. Who are you? His mother?'

'If he can survive eight days floating on a bamboo boat across the Pacific, he can sure take a piece from an ugly mug like Ned.'

'That's ugly Aussie mug, if you don't mind.'

'Which takes us back to the Turkish baths.' Floyd laughed.

'How many times do we have to go through this?' Phil protested. 'She didn't call me "ugly", her friend mis-translated. Tell him, Graham.'

'Nothing to do with me.'

Phil went quiet for a second. But only a second. 'Who cares what they said?' he bluffed. 'The key is we're still here. Kings of the Road.'

'Kings, indeed.' Floyd's eyes began a mock sweep of his court.

'Unless, of course, one of the kings is planning on hanging up his crown?'

A quick finger across the throat in reply was enough to cut Graham off but Floyd needn't have bothered, Phil was too busy reaching over for the bottle.

Graham's attention turned to something or, more accurately, someone in the shadows. 'I think we've got company.'

A tall young man had emerged from the end chalet. 'Jeez, that looks like Mikey, Bonnie's boy.'

'Mikey' sat down, switched on a dim canopy light, and began reading. He had deliberately chosen the chair at the table where he could be seen by the others, whilst still looking as though he was happy to be on his own.

'We should ask him over.' Graham stood up.

'Like hell we should. If he wants company he can go see Bonnie.' Pinks enjoyed holding grudges. 'What's he doing here anyway?'

'Come on. We could be here for weeks, and I'm not spending the whole time listening to your war stories.' Graham pretended he needed the toilet, which he knew would take him past the newcomer. On his way across he gave a friendly nod and on the return leg stopped for a chat. After a couple of minutes he brought the new guy over.

'OK, boys, this is Miko. Miko, this is Phil and Floyd.' Graham offered Miko a seat, and went to fetch another glass.

'I thought it was Mikey.' Phil looked at the newcomer for clarification.

'Mikey, Miko. It doesn't really matter.'

'Mickey Mouse,' Pinks chipped in, without lifting his head out of a map he wasn't looking at.

'If you like.' Miko's English was fluent, but a northern European rasp still poked through on the 'K'.

Graham returned with a beaker, firmly extracted Floyd's map from his lap, and made him face the rest of the group.

'We thought you were up at The Serena,' Graham began.

'Me?' Miko unzipped his jacket. 'No. A bit out of my price bracket.'

Phil gave Floyd a confused look. 'But we thought Bonnie–'

'Doesn't matter.' Floyd was saving that line of inquiry for later. 'Nice sports uniform.'

Miko was wearing a dark green football shirt.

'Thanks.' He knew Floyd wasn't exactly being friendly, but was happy to play along. 'The Pakistani national team. I picked it up in the market this afternoon.'

'Cricket?' Phil's eyes lit up. He had spent many a Boxing Day drinking VB in Bay 13 at the MCG, and had particularly enjoyed goading Waqar and Wasim.

'Football,' Miko almost apologised. 'I try and buy a shirt from every country I visit. Either the national team or one of the local sides.'

'I take it by "football" you mean "soccer"?' Pinks wasn't letting up.

'"Football" is "soccer", right?' Miko smiled.

Graham was ready to jump in but, knowing what was to come, decided to wait.

'Wrong. Soccer is soccer,' Pinks laboured. 'Football is Gridiron. NFL. The Dallas Cowboys.' Pinks' Texan drawl was getting thicker by the syllable.

'Actually, I'll think you'll find our young friend is right.' Graham dangled the bait.

'Oh yeah, how much?' Pinks spun round as quickly as his chair, and his waistline, would let him.

'How much do you want?'

'A hundred dollars.'

Hook, line and sinker.

'And another hundred, Aussie, from me.' Phil was as sure as Floyd that Graham was wrong. 'And a bottle of something.'

'Fine by me.'

Pinks stretched out his hand. 'You Limeys can call it what you want but-'

Graham's recital had already begun: 'On October 26th 1863, a small group of gentlemen gathered together in the Freemasons' Tavern, Great Queen St, London. They had been summoned to draw up the rules for Association Football, thereby formalising their game, and distinguishing it from "Rugby Football", the sport that may, or may not, have been founded by William Webb Ellis in 1823 at the eponymous boys boarding school.' Graham took breath. 'Association Football soon became known by the shortened form of "Soccer Football", rather than "Assoc Football", which didn't trip so willingly off the tongue.' Graham watched his adversaries' faces drop. 'In the following decades the sport spread but "Down Under" a rival code was being developed, and Australian Rules Football played its first game in Melbourne in 1858. In North America "Soccer Football" and "Rugby football" remained the most popular sports for some time. In 1910 100,000 turned out to watch a game of "soccer" in New York, whereas the game we now refer to as American Football wasn't fully developed until 1912.'

Silence.

'That will be two hundred dollars, please, gentlemen.' Graham squeezed the bottle out from between Phil's fingers. 'Don't worry about the "something".'

Pinks pretended it had never happened and returned to his map. Phil twiddled with the stopper.

'Take no notice of my associates, Miko.' Graham shook his head.

Floyd was suddenly all ears: 'Sorry, G, is that "Assoc-iates" or "Soccer-iates"?' He leant back with a celebratory puff on his cigar.

'Like I said, take no notice.'

Miko felt the safest option was just to nod.

'So, partner?' Floyd gestured towards Miko, all nice as pie. 'Diddums kick you out, did she?'

'Diddums?' Miko stopped nodding.

'Floyd's favourite nickname for Bonnie,' Graham explained wearily.

'Condé Nasty Bitch. That's my favourite.' Phil didn't wait for a response. 'CNB. Cos she used to write for Condé Naste. Geddit?'

Graham shook his head.

'Sorry, mate.' Phil nodded to Miko. 'I forgot you two were…'

'Whoa! Hold on!' Miko looked to Graham for support. 'Me and Bonnie?'

'That's what she said in her email…,' Graham tried hard not to look away. 'Which is why we thought you were at The Serena.'

'Come on, guys. Isn't she a bit old for me?'

'You'd better not let her hear you say that,' Pinks gleefully chided, as he needlessly adjusted his chair.

Graham changed tack. 'So, Miko, you're Finnish?'

'Half Finnish,' Miko nodded. 'On my mother's side. My father's Dutch and I was brought up in Holland.' Miko flashed the orange of a Dutch Football shirt he was wearing underneath. 'But for the last few years I've been living in London. Hence "Mike" or "Mikey".' He flicked a quick glance at Floyd. 'Or Mickey.'

'Well, Mikey, have a drink.' Phil retook control of the bottle, and poured.

'And you're Phil, right?' Miko helped out.

'My friends call me "Crazy".' Phil gave Miko a wink, but over his shoulder Graham was shaking his head and mouthing the name 'Ned'. 'Crazy Philpot. Cos' I'm a bit, you know.'

Miko sipped.

'So you got stuck in Ishkaman, eh Mickey?' Pinks was back on the offensive. 'There's nothing up there, you know.'

'Well, maybe.' Miko was no longer feeling so intimidated. 'But don't believe everything you read in the guidebooks, right?'

'I'll pay that one, Mikey.'

Graham acknowledged the hit as Phil topped up Miko's glass. 'But that path does suddenly stop, right? It's a dead end.' Despite Zul's earlier assurances, Graham didn't want complaints from his readers.

'It's blocked, if that's what you mean. Too many rock falls. But the glaciers are amazing. I had great fun climbing around, and the locals were happy to put me up.'

'OK, cut the crap.' Floyd had heard enough. 'What are you really doing here? What are you up to?'

'I was going to ask you guys the same question,' Miko swigged. 'Graham Ruff and Pinks Housmann in the same town? I feel a new guide coming on.'

Phil gave another chortle.

'About Xidakistan perhaps?' Miko felt comfortable enough to start digging around his person. In the fifth zip pocket below his thigh, he found his quarry – a small bag of grass he had been offered up in the mountains.

'Do you guys mind?'

'Not a bit, mate.'

'If you're looking for books,' Pinks was paying more attention now that it appeared Miko knew who he was, 'I'm afraid that's entirely Graham's department these days. I'm just here for the ride.' He raised his glass and cigar as proof.

'I thought *Small World* were planning one, too.' Miko laid out two cigarette papers on his knee.

Pinks froze momentarily. 'Not that I heard,' he blustered. 'Actually I'm not with Small World anymore. Am I boys?'

'But?' Miko looked up from his papers. 'It doesn't matter.'

Phil began licking his lips as Miko unpicked one of the buds.

'Back to you, then,' Graham probed.

'Me? I'm just….'

'Don't tell me,' Floyd's composure was fully recovered, 'retracing Marco Polo. How many times do we have to tell you kids? It's been done already.'

'It's more Robert Byron, actually,' Miko twitched, spilling some his weed. Phil over-eagerly picked it up.

'But you've just come from Kashgar.' Graham's copy of *Road to Oxiana* never sat on the shelf for long. 'Byron didn't-

'No. But I wanted to have a look at the Sunday market, you know. And that's when I bumped into Bonnie. And she said there was a chance of Xiddy becoming independent, so I thought it was worth coming up here to have a look.'

Despite his cross-examination Miko had managed to roll a perfect trumpet. To buy himself some time he sparked it into action, and took in an unhealthy lungful.

'So you know about Xidakistan, then?' Floyd looked less than impressed.

'Sorry,' Miko paused to release the smoke, 'was it supposed to be a secret?' He offered the spliff around. Phil was the only taker.

'No, no, Mickey. All good. It's common knowledge now, anyway, thanks to Bonnie's article'

'The one about her Alphabet Game?' Miko ventured. Half innocently. 'I thought you guys might be playing.'

'There she goes again, G.' Pinks slammed his glass on the table, making Miko jump. 'The bitch has no shame.'

'Be careful,' Graham meant it for Miko but ended up directing it at Pinks.

'Get one thing straight, kid.' Pinks' free hand reached for an empty cola can and crushed it in one go. 'It is not. NOT. Bonnie's game. Alright?'

'Relax, Floyd. It's not Miko's fault.'

'She's writing a crap story to sell a crap magazine to crapheads in Manhattan,' Floyd continued.

'You mean your neighbours?'

'Not funny.' Pinks was still eyeing Miko suspiciously. 'What exactly has she been saying?'

'Nothing really, she just told me about her, sorry, this game, and we started playing it on the ride up from Kashgar.'

'Look, buddy, if anybody is going to tell you about the Alphabet Game, it's me.' Pinks may have been on the wrong side of sober but he could still reel off the full history of The Game at a drop of a hat, and was about to do so when Graham coughed.

'Or Graham.' Floyd backtracked.

'I see.' Miko wasn't entirely convinced. 'She's still on a lot of countries, though. You can't deny her that.'

'You just watch me,' Pinks bellowed. 'First of all, they're called "caps" not countries, and she's on twenty-four, along with a million other people.'

'Twenty-four?' Phil double-checked.

'The customs guys in Qatar never let her in.'

Miko felt suitably chastised. 'Sorry.'

The group briefly fell silent.

'Forget about it,' Graham offered Miko the bottle. 'You're not the first person Bonnie's tried to impress.'

123

'And that one hundred Aussie dollars I owe you, G, says he won't be the last.'

Graham smiled, and Phil passed the rest of the joint back to Miko.

'So, how many caps are you guys on?' The young man felt he should ask.

'Twenty-Five!' The three men answered as one.

'I had a feeling you were going to say that.'

'What about you, Mikey? You got a score?' Phil was always the first to ask.

'Yeah,' Miko nodded. 'I think I'm on quite a few. I was surprised.'

'How many?' Phil needed to know.

'About twenty, Bonnie said.'

'Are you sure?'

'Where else have you been?' Graham inquired a little more amicably. 'You said you're doing *The Road to Oxiana?*'

'Yeah, and well, you know, most of Europe. And I did the Pan-American top to bottom in '98, with South-East Asia the year before that.'

'And how old did you say you were?' Graham was impressed.

'Twenty-six.'

'So the Pan-Am top to bottom by the age of twenty three? Pretty good, eh Floyd?'

Pinks scowled.

'So about twenty all up?' Phil checked. 'Not bad, not bad at all.' Inside he was just relieved Miko's total didn't rival his.

'Thanks.'

'OK then, smart guy, let's see you in action.' Pinks was still sore. 'A?'

Miko didn't blink. 'Austria.'

Phil took out a pencil from his bumbag, and a small pad he had had specially printed for such occasions. He began to mark score. 'B?'

'Belgium.'

'C?'

'Canada, or Chile.' Miko pronounced the last country the South American way.

'Alright. Don't worry about the semantics.'

Graham decided against correcting Floyd's use of English, and Miko carried on. Denmark, Estonia, Finland and Greece filled the next four slots as he calmly ticked off the mental list constructed earlier. He was confident but didn't rush.

'H?'

'Holland.'

'Nope, doesn't count. It's The Netherlands.' Pinks took a triumphant chew on his cigar. 'Which is an "N".'

Miko didn't seem to be worried. 'OK, Hungary.'

Pinks stopped chewing.

'I?'

'Italy.'

'J.'

Finally, Miko paused. 'Jamaica?' He didn't sound too sure.

'No,' Phil jumped in, 'she came of her own accord. Boom, boom.' Everyone looked at him in shame. 'What? It's my all-time favourite.'

'Jamaica?'

'Well, I haven't actually been there yet,' Miko conceded. 'But I'm planning on going to the Caribbean when I get-.'

'Which doesn't count!' Pinks relished. 'And we'll be checking your passport.' His face confirmed that he actually meant it.

'How about Jordan?' Miko countered.

'K!' Pinks snapped.

'Kyrgyzstan.'

'Nice one,' Phil applauded. Lithuania and Mexico followed like clockwork and Pinks was becoming exasperated.

'Are you sure you're not a player?'

'No. I swear.' To a more sober audience the last comment might have sounded a little too forced.

'Don't worry, Pinks,' Phil consoled. 'This is where it starts to get tough.'

'N?'

'Well that must be the Netherlands, right? Or New Zealand?'

'Or New Holland?' Graham offered.

125

Miko set to thinking. 'New *Holland*?' he scratched his chin. 'Isn't that what we first called Australia?'

'That's right. It was the original name used by Dutch sailors.'

'And it's funny, because New Holland also happens to be the name of the latest publishers to turn down Ned's book.' Floyd tried hard not to giggle.

'If you must know, "New Holland" wasn't the original name,' Phil scowled. 'The earliest European maps called it "Ulimaroa", the old Maori name.' Phil was back in the Game. 'O.'

'O? O,O,O,O,O,O,O.' Miko started scratching his neck.

'Do you want a clue?' Graham offered.

'No clues,' Floyd snarled.

Phil took the opportunity to pour himself some more alcohol.

'Come on.' Floyd sensed weakness.

'OK, I give in.'

'That's because there's only one.' Phil added a fourth tap to the habitual three he gave to the butts of his Camels before smoking them. Ideally he would have asked Miko to roll another spliff, but 'Game' etiquette precluded interruptions.

'Oh, Oman?' Miko was right but he wasn't smiling. 'No, no go. I've never been to The Gulf.'

'Ha! In that case you're toast,' Floyd gloated.

Phil scored a first cross on Miko's card. 'P?'

'Peru,' Miko hit back. 'And I suppose Pakistan now, too.' He had almost forgotten about that one.

'Q is Qatar.' Pinks didn't give Miko the chance to reply. 'Which is also in the Gulf. So you're toast again.'

'Qatar's the only "Q"? Right, I remember.' Bonnie had made him read her article several times on the way up from Kashgar.

'That's right.' Phil hadn't flexed his Game muscles for a while. 'No matter what the bloody Queenslanders say.'

Graham pushed on. 'R?'

'Russia.'

'You have to have been there when it was Russia,' Phil took a long drag on his cigarette, 'not the USSR.'

'I was there last year. Does that count?'

'Certainly does.'

'Alright,' Floyd came again, 'S.'

'Sweden.'

'T?' Phil tagged.

'Turkmenistan.'

'U?'

'U?' Miko looked puzzled.

'U,' Floyd pressed.

'Well, I didn't go to Uruguay.'

'It's easier than you think,' hinted Graham again. Now it was clear Miko wasn't a contender, Graham was rooting for him all the way.

'No helping,' complained Phil.

'Easier than you think?' Miko took a sip of his drink. 'Of course, United Kingdom.'

'United *Keng*dom? United Kengdom?' Pinks imitated the 'eng' sound Miko had made. 'Sorry, don't remember any soccer team called 'The United *Keng*dom'.'

'Think of Floyd.'

'We said "no helping"!' Phil really didn't like it.

'Of course, USA.'

'V?'

'Venezuela.'

'Venezuela's not on the Pan-Am,' Floyd bullied.

'Yeah, but when I flew home I changed planes in Caracas. Or is that against the rules?'

'Rules?' Floyd spat. 'Rules are for field hockey.'

'The Alphabet Game is governed by laws,' Graham explained. 'And Law Nine-'

'Sub-section B,' Phil jumped in, 'states that changing planes counts for zip.'

'You have to go through passport control and get your passport stamped.' Graham verified.

'*Stamped.*' Phil repeated, gratuitously stamping his own hand.

'So unless you've been to Vanuatu or Vietnam, it's tough bull,' Floyd crowed.

'The Vatican City?' Miko hazarded.

'No, no, no, no, no,' Phil rebuffed. 'Not in FIFA. Or the UN.'

'In that case….'

'More toast.'

Miko accepted defeat and offered to surrender.

'You can't give up now,' Phil insisted. 'You haven't got a score yet.'

'Only four to go,' Graham encouraged. 'W.'

'W? I'm sure Bonnie told me of a "W", but I can't think of one.'

'If you can't think of one, you can't go to one,' Phil and Pinks chorused.

'It's very small,' helped Graham.

'Ruff, will you keep your god damn trap shut?'

'Western Samoa?'

'Drongo!' Phil cried out. 'It hasn't existed for four years, you muppet.'

Miko looked slightly taken aback.

'Sorry, mate,' Phil remembered the possibility of a second joint. 'It's just Samoa now.'

'Gareth Edwards?' Graham tried to steer Miko back on track. 'JPR Williams?'

All three men gave Graham a blank stare.

'Wrong sport.' Graham tried an alternative route. 'Ian Rush?'

'Liverpool?' Miko had avidly watched English football from a young age. 'No, but close.'

'Ah. Wales. Yep, I've been to Wales. Always raining.' Miko grinned a 'thank you' to Graham. 'Don't remember getting my passport stamped though.'

'Shit, G, he's got a point. Someone needs to get onto that.'

Graham pulled out his notebook and scribbled himself a reminder.

'OK, Wales,' granted Pinks.

'Which brings us to "X".' Miko pretended to wonder. 'Does Xinjiang count?'

'Come on, dozo. X is why we're all here.'

'Sorry,' Miko laid it on thick.

'Y?'

'Yugoslavia?'

'Not any more, kid.' Floyd was enjoying his cigar again. 'Yemen is your only shot.'

'That's not strictly true,' interrupted Graham. 'I was emailing the committee last month, just to clarify a couple of points, and they confirmed that the current ruling is "any country that has ever entered for the World Cup" counts.'

'What do you mean you were emailing the committee?' Floyd was up on his haunches.

'Nothing important.' Graham gave his wriest of smiles.

'G's right, though.' Phil flicked through to some notes at the back of his pad. 'Law Six, sub-section G. And I quote: "As of the millennium AGM, all FIFA World Cup entrants past and present will be accepted as caps in "The Game"".' Phil scanned down to the bottom of the page. '"So long as the contestant's passport bears a valid stamp for that said country: e.g. Yugoslavia".'

'Nobody told me,' Floyd flounced.

'Is there really a governing body?'

'Is the pope Polish?'

'I'm afraid there needs to be with people like these two around.'

'Don't joke, G.' Floyd was starting to worry. 'That amendment changes everything.' He did a quick calculation. '"Past and Present" could mean two hundred and ten possible caps, two twenty even. "Present Members" are only two seven.'

'You see what I'm saying, Miko.' Graham held up his hands.

'It also means I spent six days on the back of a camel, rode half way across The Empty Quarter, nearly died of thirst and had my ass shot at,' Floyd looked scandalised, 'all for nothing!'

'Get real, Housmann. The only time you went to Yemen, you docked in Aden, took a taxi to the nearest knocking shop, and were back on board before they'd finished fastening the bow rope.'

'They all count for the AAG,' smiled Phil.

Miko was lost again.

'The Alternative Alphabet Game.' Phil spoke in his most reverential tone.

'Floyd and Phil are also playing an *Alternative* Alphabet Game, between themselves.' Graham played the bored teacher. 'But they're finding the caps much harder to come by.'

'Don't knock what you can't afford, Ruff. You're just jealous.'

'Yeah, Ruffo, you'd play, too, given half the chance. The only problem is, you can't get any.'

Miko still didn't understand.

'Let's just say you keep score with notches on your bedpost.' Graham's tone was intended to distance himself from proceedings.

Miko started chuckling.

'You got it, Mikey. And massage parlours don't count!'

'No, no.' Miko was still trying to overcome his own laughter. 'It's not that.'

'So what's so funny?' Pinks instinctively jumped back on the defensive.

Miko found his giggles escalating. 'Nothing', he managed, before coughing in on himself.

'What?' Phil and Pinks demanded together.

'What is it?' Even Graham thought it sounded important.

'Come on, kid. Spit it out!'

Miko slowly pulled himself back together and wiped his eyes. 'It's just.' He took a deep breath and started again. 'It's just Bonnie warned me to keep an eye on you, Floyd.' Miko turned to Graham for support, but Graham was as puzzled as the others.

'She said,' Miko was spluttering again. 'She said she thought you might take a shine to me.' Miko couldn't help himself looking at Floyd. 'And that was why they called you "Pinkie".'

Phil cracked up. 'Pinkie Winkie! Give that man a coldie.'

Even Graham was finding it hard to keep a straight face.

'That's it, G, no more,' Pinks boiled. 'I'm going up there right now, and I'm gonna give her such a sock in the mouche she'll be eating soup for months.'

'You never told me we could count boys, Pinkie.' Phil was embarrassingly happy to see Floyd suffer.

'Graham, tell them.'

'Tell them what?' Graham's face stayed as straight as a dye.

'I mean it, G. Tell Ned to stop acting like a prick and tell *him*', Pinks pointed at an awkward looking Miko, 'that the name's Pinks. P.I.N.K.S.' Pinks went to stand on the other side of the terrace, his arms folded. He was as far away from the other three as possible.

'OK, Phil. Wrap it up.' Graham put his arm on Phil's.

'And the other thing,' Floyd shouted. He couldn't believe Miko hadn't once thought to query Bonnie's assessment.

'Come on, Floyd.' Graham cajoled.

'I'm deadly serious, G.'

'Alright.' Graham recalled his straightest face. 'Miko, I'm afraid Bonnie was having you on. Floyd and her used to be married a long time ago, but now tend to concentrate on giving each other grief.'

'Don't bring me into this. She's the one who starts it. Every God damn time.' Pinks was shaking with anger.

'I'm sorry, Floyd.' Miko declared, as solemnly as he could. 'It's this stuff,' pointing to his bag of grass. 'It's really strong.' Which was half true.

Everyone took some time out, and eye-contact was avoided for a while. Finally, Graham sensed a calm returning and stopped twiddling his empty glass.

'Let's finish The Game, shall we?' he suggested.

'Apology accepted,' Pinks moved over to the group, 'but only so we can all go to bed.' He sat back down. 'Where were we?'

'Yugoslavia.' Phil's Game face was back on. 'When exactly did you go there, Miko?'

'When I was a child, my parents took me to one of the islands off Croatia. But it was still Yugoslavia then.'

'So it still counts.' Phil nodded his approval.

'Not until we see the passport stamp.' Floyd dug his heels in.

'Floyd!' Graham clamoured.

'Alright.' Pinks adjusted his seat. 'Zee?'

'I guess we're looking at Zimbabwe, Zaire and Zambia, right?'

'No points for guessing, boy.' Pinks drained his glass.

Graham nodded that Miko was on the right lines.

'Well, as I haven't been to Africa, that's me gone again. Toast all round.'

'Good. What's his score, Phil?'

Phil had a quick look at his book. 'Well, twenty-two if you include Venezuela.'

'Which we don't, as he has never officially been there, so twenty-one.' Pinks was almost enjoying himself again.

Phil wrote '21' at the bottom of Miko's score sheet and handed it to him. 'Good onya,' he congratulated.

'One more than the Queen,' Graham offered as way of encouragement.

'But still a few short of the big boys.'

'Yeah,' Pinks twisted the knife. 'Twenty-one's a bit of a Mickey Mouse score, I'd say.'

'How many were you on when you were twenty-six, Housmann?'

'Twenty-six?' Pinks feigned uncertainty. 'I'm not quite sure.'

'Can't remember more like,' Phil joked. 'It's so long ago.'

'Watch it, Kelly.'

'Why? Because I don't lie about my age.'

'Not much you don't.'

Phil pulled out a wallet-shaped shoulder holster from under his shirt. 'Here's my passport. Where's yours?'

Floyd looked away.

'June four, nineteen sixty-two.' Phil brandished the photo page for all to see. 'Still in my thirties, and,' he added for good measure, 'still got a full head of hair.'

'That's going so grey you have to shave it.'

'OK, children, that's enough. In fact,' Graham made a quick assessment of the 'drunks' versus 'to be drunks', 'I suggest we all call it a night.' He knew Phil could happily go on 'til dawn.

'But we're just getting started.'

'Not me, Ned.' Graham pulled on his jacket.

'Nor me,' Floyd echoed. 'I've still got to walk home.'

Miko felt it judicious not to rock the boat and said his goodnights, too, but Phil was never one to miss an opportunity.

'Hey, Mikey, looks like you're next door to me. How about one more smokoe, before bed?'

Miko looked at Graham for advice, but it was too late. Phil already had his arm around the young man's shoulder and was guiding the way.

Small World

It was light the next morning, but it would be another three hours before the sun climbed over the wall of mountains to the east of Gilgit. In this illusion of day Pinks, Vanh and Graham were enjoying their slumber, but Miko and Phil had been only too happy to ease the aches and pains that come with sleeping on a cotton-covered washboard. Whilst making their way to the K2, they earnestly rubbed various bones.

'So are you writing a guidebook too, Phil?' Miko's hand was numb from where he had slept on it.

'Me?' Phil looked at Miko with only-slightly-mocking disdain. 'Yer kiddin' aren't yers? Never used a guidebook in my life, mate.' Phil looked particularly pleased with himself.

'What. Never?' Miko was impressed, despite himself.

'Guidebooks are for Poms and Sheilas,' Phil flourished an imaginary book in the air, 'walking around all la-di-da in their pristine Timberlands. "I'm on my year off, don't you know".' Phil's jolly-hockey-sticks accent was surprisingly accurate.

Miko laughed; he had seen enough of them on his travels.

'You know what us proper travellers call *Small World?*' Phil puffed out his chest. 'The Bullshitter's Bible.'

Miko didn't want to guess what Phil called Ruff Guides, but he had a feeling he already knew.

'So how come you spend so much time with Floyd and Graham?' Miko was first up the café steps.

'I don't. Well, only sometimes,' Phil allowed reluctantly, 'when they're not coming out with all that: "I can't tell anyone I'm here writing a guidebook" stuff.' Phil was now half Inspector Clouseau, half Basil Fawlty. '"It's the Guidebook code, don't you know. If I told you I'd have to kill you".' Phil spat down into the car park. 'Crock of shit!'

'Right.'

'Ask them to pull their undies down, if you don't believe me. Not a pair of balls between them.'

134

Miko opened the door.

'Me, you see,' Phil surged, 'I travel not to go anywhere, but to go. That's my mantra.'

Miko could have sworn it was Robert Louis Stevenson's.

'It's all about the journey, the adventure. You gotta put yourself out there, right?'

'If you say so.'

'It's not "my book's bigger than your book", or who's published the most titles. This is life,' Phil was sounding more and more like a cut-price John Wayne. 'No rehearsal.'

Miko took the window seat.

'Brekkie?'

'Sure.' Miko looked for the menu, and realised there wasn't one. 'But isn't the Alphabet Game a bit like "who's got the most titles"?'

'Completely different.' Phil called Naveed over and asked for the curry. 'This is History. And besides if I don't win, they will, and then they'll think *they*'re right.'

Miko chose the same. 'So what do you do. Back home?'

'Back home?' I haven't been home in donkey's. Always travelling, see.'

'Nice work if you can get it.'

'I do do the odd job,' Phil conceded. 'Now and again. Helping out Pinks with his tours, or doing overlanders for the big boys. You know, as expedition leader on their trucks. Asia mostly.' Phil's eyes were on the kitchen. 'They're a bit daggy but it gets me to where I want to go. And then I just chill out while they drive back to pick up the next load. Money for jam.'

As he looked up to the mountains, Miko wondered how many times Phil had told this story.

'Lots of nice little "extras", too, if you know what I mean.' Phil, as usual, couldn't help himself. 'There was this one Sheila on the last ride from Calcutta to Karachi. Danish; nurse. You would have loved her, Miko. Just broke up with her boyfriend. Such a great-'

Miko didn't seem so impressed.

'What about you, young fella? What brings you on walkabout?' Phil produced a bag of beef jerky from his pocket and pulled out a long string. 'Biltong. South African, the best. Mate of mine, Johan, sends it over by the box load. Have a bit while we're waiting.'

'Thanks.' With his other hand Miko was fishing out copies of *Road To Oxiana*, *Lost Horizon*, and some of the other classics he had in his knapsack. 'Well, I'm trying…..'

'I remember.' Phil picked up *The Travels*, and started flicking through. 'You're really into these guys, right?'

Miko nodded.

'Isn't there a place in here where Polo talks about some mob who invite you in for a loosener, hand over their Sheilas and then go bush for a few days while you help yourself?' Phil yanked a strip in half and started to chew.

'Well…' Miko wasn't sure what to say.

'And they don't come back 'til they see ye boots have gone from the top of the tent pole?' Phil went all misty-eyed. 'That's what Xidakistan'll be like, I reckon.'

'I think you're talking about the bit on Hami.'

'Yeah, that's the place.'

'I'm not sure Xidakistan has that much in common with The Hexi Corridor. They're on completely the other side of the Taklamakan Desert.'

Phil looked hurt and disappointed in equal measure.

'Although I suppose the custom of *Kuri bistan* in Afghanistan is pretty similar.' Miko's mind wandered.

'*Curried Bisto?*' Phil bad-joked as the food arrived. 'I thought we ordered the lamb.'

Naveed returned with a giant teapot and two cups.

'So is that why you're here?' Miko asked after a while. 'Have you just finished leading a tour?'

'I'm here for The Game, mate. The Game, and The Game only.'

'So this Alphabet thing's real?'

'Course it's real. Where've you been living? Under a rock?' Phil slurped.

'You've been playing for a while, then?' Miko poured. 'Bonnie didn't just make it up.'

'Bonnie? Wake up! The Game's serious, mate. Like I said, History. People have been playing for over a century.'

'But no one's ever won.'

'Not yet.' Phil flexed his shoulders.

'Right. Because you three are all on twenty-five caps?'

'Yep. Ouch.' Phil felt his left collarbone jar with pain as he nodded.

'Are there many others?'

'Other what?' Phil was rubbing frantically.

'Many other players on twenty-five caps?' The curry was a bit hot for Miko first thing in the morning and he pushed it to one side.

'Well, that depends.'

'On ...?'

'The Laws, of course. Like Pinkie said last night, they do have a habit of changing. But as far as we know there's only about a dozen of us.' Phil opened up a new pack of Camels, removed the foil and turned the cigarette at the right end of the back row upside down. He took another from the front row and lit it.

'There's me, Pinks and Graham,' Phil started counting on his fingers. 'Bonnie.'

'Hang on, I thought Bonnie was on twenty four. Because she was stopped at customs in Oman.'

'Yeah, but somehow she got her passport stamped. So whether Floyd likes it or not she's in.' Phil licked his fingers and used them to tot up his list. 'Then there's Jane and Terry.' He was all earnest now. 'The three Von Tienhoven brothers. And the IBEMs.'

'The computer company?'

Phil had pronounced it the same way.

'No, you goose. The "I've Been Everywhere Man"s, on the web.' Phil belched. 'Out to visit every country, every state, and, knowing that pair of pricks, every bloody Starbucks on the planet.'

Miko had to smile. 'And they're all here now?'

'Bloody hope not.' Phil indicated to Naveed that he could 'go another'. 'You see, Jane and Terry are 'finding themselves'. Which probably means they're hugging trees in some jungle as we speak.'

Naveed took everything back into the kitchen, tipped Miko's largely untouched curry onto Phil's plate, and brought it back out again.

'Boy, will they be spewin'!' Phil took an extra moment to savour the thought. Miko poured some more tea.

'And touch brick,' Phil knocked a particularly bony piece of his shaven skull, 'the others have yet to twig.'

'That's it?'

'Might all change, though, like we said last night,' Phil worried. 'Thanks to Bonnie's bloody article.' He pulled a bandana out of his bumbag and tetchily tied it around his 'brick'. 'May even see The Mad Professor out here.'

'The Mad Professor?'

'Museum of Budapest. He's crook in a wheelchair these days, but who's to say?' Phil had almost finished his second plateful. 'Then there was that rumour a while back about some young gun getting close.' He mopped up the last bits with his finger. 'Never count your chickens.'

'Young Gun?'

'Pinks bets he's an Israeli. You know what they're like when they get out the army. But he could be a Sheila for all we know.'

'Still.' Miko took another sip. 'That's not very many. I thought this game was massive the way Pinks was describing it last night.'

'It is massive!' Phil gave Miko the hard stare. 'The biggest prize in travelling. Bar none.' Eyes wide. 'It's just most people get stuck in the twenties.' Not a blink. 'And with no "X", they give up. Like you.'

Miko fiddled with cup.

'You wait until everyone hears about Xidaki independence.' Phil was riding his high horse as fast as it would carry him. 'There'll be a bloody stampede.'

'Who do you think will win?' Miko thought it best to let Phil charge.

'Me, of course.'

'You're that confident?'

'Too bloody right. That medal is going to guarantee yours truly immortality.' Phil thumped his chest Tarzan style. 'For the rest of my life.'

'I don't think Floyd and Graham would like the sound of that.' Miko decided it wasn't worth pointing out the other, lexical, flaw in Phil's plan.

'That's their lookout. Like I said before, they should stick to their books. Leave the travelling to the professionals.'

'And Bonnie?'

Phil started to gather his things. 'I can handle her.'

Miko finished his tea.

'Say, Mikey.' Phil tried desperately to sound casual. 'Before the others get here, I don't suppose there's any chance you're looking to offload any of your,' his voice was right down to a whisper, 'gear? Ever since this 9/11 thing, everybody's turned real touchy.'

Miko quickly weighed the pros and cons, and decided that as things stood Phil was worth having in his debt.

'Sure. I'll drop some into your room when we go back.' There was no point risking anything in the café.

'I'll return the favour when it calms down, for sure.'

Miko had expected a more solid form of payment but let it pass.

As Phil licked his plate clean for a second time, and made ready to leave, the door opened and Vanh stepped into the room.

'Elvis! You little beauty. I was looking for you.'

Vanh forced a smile.

'Come and meet my new buddy, Mikey.' Phil padded down the cushion next to him on the settee. 'Have a seat.'

Vanh had been heading for Computer Corner.

'No, no. Enough Super Mario Brothers. How about a bit of Super Real Brothers? Human interaction.'

Vanh gave in, slowly.

'Mikey, this is my old mate Elvis. Floyd's new partner.' Phil gave it a bit of razzle-dazzle. 'Also known as George.'

'Also known as Vanh. Nice to meet you.' Vanh offered his hand. 'I'm sorry about Phil.' Vanh spoke as though Phil wasn't there.

'That's alright.' Ditto.

Vanh ordered fruit.

'How's Donkey Kong Seven coming on?' Phil patronisingly squeezed Vanh's shoulder before turning to Miko. 'Elvis is very big in Video Games.'

'Gaming. It's called computer gaming.'

'Writes his own.'

Despite the silence it seemed Phil was no longer going anywhere. He confirmed the fact by attempting to wrestle his fleece off over his head, and pull out his cigarettes, in one go.

'Smokoe?'

Phil was concentrating on the packet in his hand, but Miko and Vanh's eyes were transfixed on a box of Durex that had come out of another zip pocket. Apparently unopened, it was lodged on the headrest just above his left ear.

'What?' Phil laughed nervously. As he leaned forward to turn around, the box slipped down behind the cushion.

Checking all over, Phil spotted the club badge of his footie vest, poking out from underneath another of his Bali monstrosities, this time zebras and mating giraffes. He tugged the embroidered crest into the open for them to get a proper look.

'You mean this?' he cried. 'It's the black-and-white, my boys, the legendary black-and-white.' Phil spoke as though he was divulging The Meaning of Life.

'The mighty Collingwood,' he added in reverential tones. 'Go the 'Pies!' he hollered, bounding up from his seat.

'Good old Collingwood forever,
We know how to play the game.
Side by side we stick together,
To uphold the Magpies name.'

Phil was now marching around the café, punching his fists in the air as he sang..

'Hear the barrackers a shouting,
As all barrackers should.
Oh, the premiership's a cakewalk,
Phil climbed onto the back of the sofa and had his arms aloft.
For the good old Collingwood.'

'Ned, either shut the crap up or get the crap out.' Floyd stood with Graham at the entrance to the K2. Neither was in any mood for football songs.

'Haven't you got a hangover?' Graham nursed his temples.

'Fortunately, Ruffo,' Phil was still balanced on the couch, 'I'm not a Sheila. So I don't get hangovers.'

'Well, isn't there a cliff you should be jumping off?'

'It's called base-jumping, ye gooses.' Phil vaulted down to the floor as if to prove his point to the younger members of his audience.

'Morning, Graham,' Miko nodded, with an appreciative glance.

Phil carried on regardless. 'No wonder no one buys any of your drongo books.'

Graham and Floyd ordered coffee, remembered how bad it was and settled for milky tea.

'With lots of sugar!'

'I don't know,' Phil regaled the room at large. 'One night on the grog and these boys look like a pair of pussies. Maybe it's time you grandpas hung up your boots.'

Graham flashed Pinks a look, and all Floyd's eyes could reply was 'what the hell'.

'Funny you should say that,' Graham began.

Phil's confidence thudded to a halt.

'I am indeed thinking of hanging up the old boots, you see.' Floyd sank into his chair.

'Crock of shit.'

'It's true, Phil,' Graham assured him. 'You're looking at the new Mr Pipe and Slippers.

'Cigar and slippers, if you don't mind.' Pinks puckered his lips on the end of a new Romeo y Julieta. 'But don't worry. I'm still only at the thinking stage.'

Phil staggered to a standstill. 'Strewth.'

'Wait a minute.' Floyd gave himself a shake. 'What am I saying? Even if I do go, I ain't wearing no slippers.' Floyd began checking all his pockets for his lighter. 'You make it sound like I'm dying, G. Or shrivelling up in some Florida retirement home.'

'Can everyone just back up a minute.' Phil was still reeling. 'Quitting Small World was one thing, mate. But stopping altogether.'

'Not altogether. There's still The Pinks Guide.' Floyd nodded Graham's eyes towards Vanh. 'Right, G?'

'Course. Silly me.' Graham raised his eyebrows.

'But, yes, Ned, maybe my real travelling days are over. Maybe it's time to retire.'

Phil theatrically collapsed onto the couch.

'By the way, I hear Intrepid are already sniffing around.' Graham had done a bit of digging.

'Who told you that?'

'Just a little bird.'

'How much they offering?' It didn't take long for Phil to resuscitate.

'None of your damn business.' Pinks refused to remove the cigar as he spoke. 'It's between me and Michael.'

Michael was the old school tie in charge of Intrepid Trekking, and he had made a bid for the 'Wild West' arm of Floyd's business. *The Blue Guides* were also considering a bid for *The Pinks*, but that was a fact less widely known. All in all Floyd was pretty pleased with himself, and as he set his R and J glowing, his hangover began to lift amidst a self-satisfied sigh.

'You know, G, with all this time on my hands, maybe I'll come and stay at your place for a while. Say "hello" to that girlfriend you keep hiding away. I'm sure her sister has the hots for me.'

Two years before, after a travel fair in Istanbul, Floyd had invited himself to stay at Graham's house on the Bosphorus for a few days. A mistake Graham was determined never to let happen again.

'*A* - she is my housekeeper, not my girlfriend.' A pain returned to Graham's head. '*B* - her sister thinks you are a fat slob.'

'Boo Boo said that?'

'And C - her name is Burcu.'

'Touchy.' Smoke spilled from Pinks' nose as he chuckled.

Graham stiffened in the silence.

'You can't chuck it all in now, Pinko.' Phil was worried. 'Even if we win The Game, there's still the AAG.' It would be no fun playing it on his own.

'All good things must come to an end, Ned.'

'Doesn't want to hang around like a bad smell, you see.' Graham was still prickly.

'Lay off him, G.' For once Phil meant it. 'The number of years he's been in the game,' a twinkle returned to Phil's eye, safe in the knowledge he was at least a decade younger, 'old Pinks deserves a medal.'

'Don't you worry about that, Ned. I'm planning on getting a big, gold shiny one, before I'm done.' Reference to The Game brought everyone to attention, much to Floyd's pleasure.

'How many years have you been in the saddle, Floyd? If you don't mind me asking.'

'Well, let's see, Mickey. Next year will mark twenty-five years since *Shoestring* came out, I believe.' *Shanghai on a Shoestring: A route and planning guide to crossing Asia* had been the inaugural imprint for Floyd's earliest venture into publishing, The Pink Guides.

'A Silver Jubilee, no less.'

'Ah, "The Little Pink Book".' Phil sighed in admiration. 'The grandaddy of them all.'

'Shame it didn't sell any,' teased Graham.

Floyd didn't rise.

'Nice title, though.' Graham pressed. 'Who came up with the name again?'

'Listen, that was my title. My idea.' This time Pinks rose to the bait right on cue. '"Shoestring" was my nickname from seventh grade, for Christ's sake.'

'So how come everyone calls you "Pinks"?'

'That's what they called me at Princeton.' Floyd remembered Miko's comments from the previous night. 'Pinks, not Pinkie. But back home they called me Shoestring.'

'I bet they did.'

'Come on, G. No one's going to lie about a thing like that.'

'Do you want to hear the story, or not?' Pinks produced a tiny hipflask from nowhere.

'How many of those things have you got?'

Floyd ignored Graham and carried on. 'It was June 1974, and I was driving from Esfahan to Shiraz. That's when it came to me. From then on I told everyone I met, and one way or another, Jane and Terry must have heard about it. You know as well as I do, the original title for their book was *Asia on Peanuts*.'

Phil eased himself off the sofa and onto the next-door chair. He was now within stretching distance of Floyd, who reluctantly held out the mini-chalice.

'You see, G, *Small World* stole it off him.' Phil handed it back empty. 'Thanks, mate.'

'Stole? I'm sure Terry told me-'

'Look.' Pinks knew Graham knew. But he also knew Phil didn't, and wanted to keep it that way. 'It was all part of the package when I joined. And if there was any justice in this world, the record would also show I gave them Small World as their house name.' Pinks chewed into his cigar wishing it was brandy.

'Gave?' Graham waved an imaginary wad of money.

'Did I say I didn't make a couple of bucks out of the deal?' Tobacco spit was sticking to the corner of Floyd's mouth. 'Cheap at twice the price if you ask me.'

Phil nodded in recognition of Floyd's achievement.

'Terry,' Floyd wasn't finished, 'Terry, if you remember, wanted to go with "The World is Round", after listening to some Beatles track. It took me the best part of six months to talk him out of it.' Floyd realised he was doing a lot of pointing, and reined in his finger.

'*Everyone* knows that bit, G.'

'OK. I'll believe you.' Graham sniffed. 'Thousands wouldn't.'

'But now you've quit *Small World*, right?' Miko checked.

'Again!' Phil snickered.

'Again?'

'It's an old story.' Floyd was refusing to be drawn.

Phil hoped there might be more alcohol. 'It's a touchy subject, Mike.'

Miko looked at Vanh.

'Shit. You tell him, G,' Pinks relented. 'When I do it everyone just accuses me of being biased.' He re-fired his cigar and settled back into his chair.

'You sure?'

'Yeah, go on, G,' encouraged Phil. 'You always do it the best.'

Graham ordered more tea.

'As you correctly surmised, Miko, Pinks quit *Small World* a few months back. But that wasn't the first time. Floyd, you see, in many ways really was instrumental in *Small World's* success. Together with Jane and Terry Noland, the couple that set it up. But it wasn't all plain sailing. Jane and Terry, as Floyd was suggesting, had heard about his *Shanghai on a Shoestring* when they were putting the finishing touches to their first guide. They decided that having two very similar titles at the same time in such a new marketplace was bad for business, so soon after they launched *Peanuts*, they offered to buy Floyd out. In return for a stake in their company, the remaining copies of 'The Little Pink Book' were pulped, and The *Pink Guides* disappeared.

'A tragic loss to the industry.'

'Not that tragic.' Graham pointed out.

'You didn't even make it to Shanghai!' Phil catcalled.

'That wasn't my fault. Blame Mrs Mao.'

'Anyway,' Graham resumed. 'They pooled their resources, and as the call for more guides grew louder, they decided to expand. Floyd concentrated on the Americas, Terry Asia, Jane Europe.'

'Wouldn't give anyone else a look in,' Phil complained, balancing on the back legs of his chair.

'Everything went well for the first few years, more and more titles came out, and they even won awards.' Graham hesitated. 'But then they sort of fell out over what to do next.'

Graham looked to Floyd for approval and it was given.

'Jane is a bit of a control freak, you see, and wanted to go full steam ahead until every country in each continent was accounted for; Terry wanted to stick to regional guides; Floyd just wanted to keep tracking down cowboys.'

'That's not fair,' Pinks interjected. 'I was with Terry.'

'To no one's great surprise, Jane won, so they did a deal. Pinks headed for South America in search of Butch and Sundance, but promised to write new guides as he went.'

'When he wasn't playing the AAG,' Phil cackled.

'Which you heard all about last night.' Graham took another sip of his tea, Floyd shook his head vehemently.

'That was fine for a few of years but then other guides started to appear and Jane began nagging Floyd and Terry to do more unusual titles, something that would grab back some of the headlines.'

'He did that alright.' Phil whooped. Graham wondered if there would ever be a time when Ned would tire of hearing this story.

'It was 1980. Khomeini's Islamic Revolution was in full swing and 52 US hostages were holed up in their embassy in Tehran.'

'And Iraq had just declared war.'

'Yes, there was also the war with Iraq.' Graham's raised eyebrows told Miko that Phil always interrupted. 'So Floyd, having enjoyed his time there in '74, says "OK, he'll do the first ever guide to post-Shah Iran".' Graham shrugged. 'Jane nearly wets herself imagining all the publicity they are going to receive, and off he goes.'

Floyd began fidgeting.

'And this is where the real argument begins.' Graham paused. 'Getting a visa into Iran for an American in '80, as you can imagine, was hardly a walk in the park. So Pinks went to Beirut and tracked down a fixer he had heard of who, for a price, could get anyone who wanted it dual Yugoslavian nationality, together with a Yugo passport. Next Floyd persuaded an old Turkish contact of his to arrange some papers about being a crude oil buyer on his way to Tehran, and the process began.'

Graham broke off for further lubrication; the effects of the night before were finally starting to wear off.

'But all this was taking time and Pinks became bored. He was staying with the Swedish ambassador to Lebanon, whom Jane and Terry knew, and before too long he found himself spending most of his time with their nineteen-year-old daughter. One thing led to another, and another, and so when all the necessary documents did arrive, he pretended they hadn't.'

'That's not quite true,' Floyd interrupted. 'I was still waiting for a letter of recommendation from the Yugoslavian Ambassador.'

Phil was getting excited.

'Like I said,' Graham gave Phil a look telling him to control himself, 'there's more than one side to this story.'

'Anyway, soon the whole summer's gone and it's time for Ingrid to go back to university in Stockholm. Suddenly Pinks announces the arrival of his visa, but instead of hitting the road in search of Persian carpets, he secretly flies off to ABBAland, with Ingrid.'

Miko nodded in deference to Pinks' taste who, in turn, doffed an imaginary hat.

'Now this wouldn't have been so bad, had it stopped there,' Graham continued, 'but in Stockholm Pinks ran into an Iranian exile, who had fled with his family after the revolution. This guy had been a history teacher at Shiraz University and was a keen photographer. To cut a long story short he had enough anecdotes to sink the Straits of Hormuz. And a slideshow to match.'

'Don't forget the stunningly beautiful daughter.' Phil licked his lips.

'Indeed. Rezmi. We must not forget her.' Graham refilled his cup. 'So, Pinks' mind starts tossing and turning, and soon while Ingrid's in the lecture hall, he's reading all the books on Iran Mr Azir has in his library. By the end of the year, he has enough notes, together with Mr Azir's tales and a few stories from other exiles, for a whole guidebook. With photos to boot.'

'Without ever going there?' Miko baulked.

'Precisely.'

'I was there in '74,' countered Pinks. 'And as a kid in the sixties, visiting my Uncle Jed on the oil fields.'

'A guide to POST-revolution Iran,' Graham coughed, 'without ever actually going there. No one else knew this, of course, and nobody was really going to Iran to find out, so his secret was safe. The new guide was front page news in all the travel mags and won that year's 'Thomas Cook'; everyone who was anyone bought a copy.'

Phil nodded enthusiastically. He had two.

'Whichever way you looked at it, it was a great success.' Graham allowed.

'And I would have succeeded,' Floyd declared.

'And he would have *got away with it*,' Graham tutted, 'because the handful of people who did eventually visit Iran, were kind enough to excuse the various discrepancies as par for the course in such a fast-changing society.'

Miko felt something was missing. 'But what about Mr Azir?'

'Exactly,' Graham confirmed. 'Ordinarily, it would have been fine. Pinks was cutting him in on half his royalties, and Mr Azir was doing something he loved for a country he desperately missed, but that was-'

'Until Pinks had had enough of Ingrid, and Mr Azir found him rootin' young Rezmi, in the back of Mr Azir's Volvo.' Phil leant too far back on his chair in celebration and it started to topple. Vanh lunged out to catch him but was too late.

'Ouch,' Miko sympathised with Phil and Floyd simultaneously.

'Indeed.' Graham smiled. 'Suddenly Papa was up for blowing the whistle. And he blew that pea as hard as he could.'

Lying on the floor, Phil eased his pain with images of swapping a Swedish beauty for an Iranian.

'Letters started appearing everywhere and soon the whole story came out. Floyd was kicked out of the Travel Writer's Guild, and rather than be relieved of his position at Small World, he quit.'

'Took a very long vacation.'

'Hence your *Authentic Wild West Experience?*' Miko had done his homework.

'That's "Authentic Wild West Experience: Search For The Men Behind The Movies", if you don't mind.'

'But if you've just quit again, they must have taken you back.' Miko leaned towards Floyd, but was redirected to Graham.

'You see, Miko, Pinks maintained he was innocent. He claims it was meant as a spoof, a deliberate wind-up. In his words,' Graham turned for approval, 'correct me if I'm wrong here, Floyd, it was "a one-fingered salute to all the industry's hypocrisy and arrogance", and "a shot across the bows of Jane and Terry's ever-increasing obsession with their joint bank account".'

'And he still had his stake in the company, don't forget.' Phil managed to pull himself off the floor. 'They couldn't force him to sell that.'

'Damn right they couldn't,' Floyd huffed.

'So, when the outcry eventually died down, some of his fellow writers….'

'Yourself included,' Floyd interjected approvingly.

'Myself included,' accepted Graham. 'A few of us decided that even if Floyd had been "in the wrong", the industry had received a much-needed kick up the backside. Jane was already being accused of taking herself far too seriously, and when it emerged that some of her and Terry's own books had themselves been little more than condensed versions of readers' letters....'

'Neither of them had even stepped foot in Sri Lanka when *that* guide came out!' Floyd banged his fist.

'Thank you, Floyd.'

'Terry's still not been there to this day.' Another bang.

'OK, I think we've got the message.' Graham finished his tea. 'As I was saying, when all these details emerged, the balance of opinion shifted to such an extent that Pinks was welcomed back into the fold.'

'Championed back!' Phil pushed.

'Not championed exactly,' Graham opened his hands to Miko, 'but last year he was finally returned to his position as senior writer at *Small World*.'

'Which is why, this year, I quit.' Floyd banged his fist one last time.

Miko, Phil and even George gave a round of applause, and Pinks once more raised his illusory chapeau skywards.

Ultar Meadow

With the others having gone off to find lunch, Vanh and Miko found they had the café and Computer Corner to themselves. They were soon happily swapping links and websites, as they took it in turns to check their emails. Most of Vanh's offerings were about gaming.

'So what's this about you writing your own?'

'Mekong Marauder?' Vanh looked the other way. 'It's a sort of Vietnam War version of Tomb Raider, I suppose.' Vanh cautiously turned round.

'Nice.' Miko was impressed. 'So what are you doing here?' He couldn't stop himself. 'And what are you doing working for Floyd?'

They both laughed.

'Working with, remember.' Vanh pulled himself straight in his chair. 'I'm a partner.'

'Right.' Miko's eyebrows did a little jig. 'Seriously, though. What are you doing?'

'I know, I know. It doesn't look like the smartest move but it works pretty well. Floyd knows nothing about computers or any technological advance post the moon landing, for that matter. So he gave me half his company to set it all up.'

'What? Wild West Tours?'

'No, the new online guide he's launching. Based in New York.'

'Shouldn't you be in Silicon Valley or somewhere?'

'Maybe, but right now no one's really sure where the internet's heading. So the way I see it, Floyd's paying me to find out.'

Miko accidentally opened one too many windows and, for the fourth time in two days, the screen froze then went blank.

'Damn.' Miko banged the monitor. 'I was right in the middle of an email.'

Vanh wheeled his chair into position. 'Give me two seconds.'

It may have taken a couple more but Vanh soon worked his magic, and Miko's work miraculously reappeared.

'There you go.' Vanh moved back out of the way. 'And I still get time to work on my games. Hopefully this latest one will be good enough to go mainstream.'

'Cool.' Rather than take any more chances, Miko finished his email, sent it and suggested they take a break.

'What about you?' Vanh asked as they headed over to the market.

'Me?' Now it was Miko's turn to look away. 'Oh, you know. Just travelling around. Hey, I was thinking of heading to Karimabad and maybe spending a night at Ultar Meadow. You wanna come?'

'Where is it?'

'Just a couple of hours up the road.' Miko looked Vanh up and down. 'There's a hike at the end, but it's not too hard.'

'Hey! Geeks can walk too, you know.' Vanh's mum made him promise to exercise at least one hour a day. 'What's up there?'

'There's supposed to be a pretty cool icefall and Graham says the shepherds will put us up for the night. It's nearly a full moon so we should get some pretty spacey views.'

'Don't we need a tent?' Vanh didn't have much in the way of gear.

'No, the shepherds have spares.' Miko looked at his new friend and saw the nerves he'd been expecting creeping in. 'And plenty of blankets. We probably won't even need sleeping bags.'

'At this altitude? No thank you.'

As they made their way across town, they passed Graham's room and gave him a wave through the window. He was spread out on his bed, eating samosas while he edited.

GETTING AROUND

Moving up and down the KKH isn't difficult. Virtually every vehicle that passes is happy to act as an impromptu taxi, if the occasion demands. The charge is little more than that of public transport.

Not that a trip on a state omnibus should be eschewed: for most drivers, their bus is their prize possession. Even if they are doomed to spend the rest of their lives in drab poverty, they are not going to give in to the dreary forces of that foe when it comes to their motor.

Every spare can of spray paint seems to have been conscripted into their efforts on the bodywork, and the effect is a true kaleidoscope of brash, uncoordinated colour. Add on a truly eclectic assortment of bells, horns, whistles, baubles, flags, pennants, ribbons, tinsel and paper chains, and you start to get the picture. The tyres are bald, the gears crunching and the seats dilapidated but, as every proud smile behind the wheel will tell you, these babies are happy babies.

After a couple of loops of the old polo ground and a quick visit to the market, the expedition was ready. Vanh figured it was wise to double-check Floyd's emails before they set off.

Graham was back in the café and had installed himself on the couch. 'No Floyd, George?'

'Nope. But we just saw him, and I've got a feeling he'll be here pretty soon.'

Before Vanh had even finished, Floyd's whistling could once again be heard floating up from the car park.

'I'd better warn you. He's pretty pleased with himself.'

'What this time?'

'Some good news from Zul: the king wants another bike.'

'Another? Don't tell me he's broken the first one already.'

'No. King Tah…' Vanh would have finished but was interrupted by a very merry Floyd.

'Big G, pack your bags! It's *Show Time*.'

'"Show time"?' Graham rolled his eyes. 'We're in Gilgit, Floyd, not Vegas.'

'Don't try funny, Ruff. It doesn't suit you.' Floyd pulled an envelope from his pocket and gave its contents a quick double-check. 'And there isn't the time to teach you.'

152

Graham went back to his books.

'I mean it, G. On your feet. Time is money.'

'What's so important?' Graham bristled, but his curiosity had already got the better of him.

'Like I said, "the money". Because "the money" my friend, is what we are in! With a capital "I".' Floyd whooped. 'This is from Zul.' Pinks was waltzing around the café with the telegram as his partner. 'Our new King Tah has fallen hook line and sinker in love! And guess who's in charge of the wedding?'

'Hello *magazine?*'

'Don't try facetious, either.' Floyd couldn't help grinning from ear to ear, but Graham wasn't moving.

'How can Zul, up in The Valley, be sending you telegrams?'

Pinks stumbled, just for a moment. 'His higher authorities? Who cares?' Floyd beamed. 'All that matters is that Tah's getting married. And I,' he coughed, 'sorry we, are in charge of organising it.'

'I heard that.'

'Actually, Zul's in charge,' Floyd stalled, 'but right now that's the same thing. Because Tah wants another bike.'

'So George was about to tell me.' Graham remained far from convinced. 'What on earth for?'

'For his fiancée, dummy. I've already called Jahanghir and the matching 'his and hers' model is on its way. The king has promised Zul that if he gets him the bike he'll attend anything we want. Conference, 'party', call it what you like – he doesn't care.'

Graham had to admit he was impressed.

'So all we have to do,' Pinks dropped his voice to a whisper, 'is keep schtum, wait for the bike and it's "home runs all round. Pass the beer nuts".'

Floyd had been so eager to tell his story he hadn't bothered to look if the high-backed armchair he was about to lean on was occupied. 'Shit, it's you!'

Miko didn't look particularly impressed with the greeting.

'At least you're not Phil, I suppose.'

'Thanks.'

'Alright, kid. I suppose you want in on this?'

'Up to Xidakistan?' Miko chomped.

Floyd looked to Graham, who shrugged his neutrality, and then Vanh, who gave him the thumbs up. 'Alright.' Pinks bent down until he was eyeball to eyeball with Miko. 'But this is the deal. No one must know what we're doing, especially not Bonnie and Phil. If I find out they've found out, you're out. OK?'

'OK.'

'And you pay for your share of the expenses – including the bikes.'

'Sure.' Miko backed into his chair.

'And when it comes to passport stamping time, you're at the back of the queue!'

'Alright, Floyd, I think he's got the message.' Graham was all for getting started there and then. 'So what's the plan?'

'Until the bike arrives we pretend nothing has happened.' Floyd's voice was deadly earnest. 'Zip.' His hand mimed his mouth tight shut. 'On Sunday we leave before everyone's awake and if anyone isn't there on time, tough, we go without them. Zul will be waiting for us in Gumbaz .'

'Hang on Floyd. What about the Taliban?' Graham wanted to regain some sort of control over the plan. 'Since September 11th, if you haven't quite forgotten, they've put a ban on all non-Afghans entering the country.'

'Those flee-scratchers? Their yellow bellies are running for the hills, my friend. Hiding out in caves so deep, they won't see sunlight 'til the next millennium.' Pinks swelled out his chest. 'The Northern Alliance control things now, at least the areas that matter to us. And they're begging every Westerner they know to come over.'

'But that still doesn't get the king his independence.'

'That's the best bit, oh ye of little faith. Zul says his authorities have made it a priority. Tah's been identified as a potential US ally. And what the US President wants…' Pinks' face indicated that if his help was ever needed by said Mr President, it too was there in spades.

'All your president ever gets,' Graham soured, 'is egg on his face. Every time he steps foot outside of Washington.'

'Quit carping.'

'Like when he thought Africa was a country not a continent.'

'I'm not listening.' Pinks had already wrapped his hands around his ears.

'Or inspected Korea's DMZ through binoculars with the lens caps still on.'

'Jesus, Ruff. Whose side are you on?'

'Not yours.'

'Fine.' Pinks swatted Graham's negativity aside. 'The less lily-livered liberals the better. Our boys are going to kick these Arab's butts to kingdom come, and you know it.'

'I'm going to give you the benefit of the doubt that by 'Arab butts' you are referring to the Al Qaeda contingent with the Afghan forces rather than the ethnically Pashtun Taliban themselves.'

Floyd's mouth twitched. And twitched again.

'But let's not change the subject.'

'I ain't changing nothing.'

'Yes you are, Floyd.' Up until this point Graham hadn't actually raised his voice. 'Don't you see, Housmann?' he shouted. 'Your President's "War on Terror" is just another disaster waiting to happen.' Graham threw his hands up. 'How can you go to war with an abstract noun?'

'Bullshit.'

'Sophisticated argument,' Graham fizzed. 'I like it.'

'Thousands of innocent people died on nine eleven and I'm not going to sit here listening to you or anyone else,' Pinks rapidly fired his glare at Vanh then Miko, 'pissing on their graves.'

'You can't agree with terrorism, Graham.' Vanh shook his head.

'Of course not, and that's why I'm not condoning what happened.' Graham didn't welcome the interjection but took it in his stride. 'All I'm saying is: who gave America and, in particular, Floyd's President, all this moral high ground?'

'Leave it with all the Chomsky shit, will you?' Floyd sneered. 'Who gave us the right? I'll tell you who gave us the right. They did, that's who. When they flew into the twin towers.'

Pinks folded his arms in triumph.

'That's ridiculous, Floyd. Unbelievably ridiculous,' Graham's voice cracked under its own weight. '"They" are the same people your country has spent years writing blank cheques for in return for fighting the Russians.'

Graham paused to let Floyd digest the point.

'Graham's right,' Miko nodded.

'Thank you.' Graham stopped shouting. 'And we're Europeans, Floyd. Your closest allies.'

'Alright, Mr Know-it-all.' Floyd snatched a chair from under the table but rammed it back in frustration. 'What would you suggest we do? Let Bin Laden get away with it?'

'No.' Graham stopped to calm himself. 'Just admit that this is not about some "axis of evil" or "war on terror" but, as always, it's Captain America trying to-'

'Talk to the hand, Ruff, talk to the hand,' Pinks grabbed his shoulder bag and made for the exit. 'You can spout your namby-pamby crap as much as you like but take it from me, Bin Laden's toast.'

'And just how do you plan on serving this toast, Top Gun?' Graham blasted after the closing door. 'You haven't the faintest idea where he is.'

Floyd turned round halfway down the steps.

'George, until the bike arrives I'm not leaving the hotel. If Bonnie or Kelly ask for me, tell them I'm ill. If they,' he paused to indicate Miko and Graham, 'still want to come on my trip, tell them they'd better not be late.'

'Whatever, Floyd.' Vanh had seen this routine too many times before.

'I mean it, George. A thousand percent.'

'Alright.' Vanh closed his eyes. 'I'll see to it.'

Graham waited until Floyd could be heard ordering Mohammed to drive him to his hotel.

'Well, at least that gives us a bit of peace and quiet.'

The next morning the two boys decided on some breakfast before setting off on their trip.

'Most important meal of the day, brekkie.' Phil was sat at the dining table, and already half way through his morning curry.

Vanh and Miko took the seats opposite.

'Eat your breakfast alone,' Phil put on his hoarse, old-man-of-the-sea voice, 'share your lunch with friends, and give your dinner to the enemy.'

Vanh and Miko swapped glances as Phil strained forward and speared a stray chunk of mutton.

'An old Russian army saying.'

'But what if the enemy saved the dinner and ate it for their breakfast the next morning?' Vanh's look was genuinely innocent.

'I don't know.' Phil was more defensive now. 'Ask a Ruskie.'

Naveed arrived to apologise that fruit was 'not currently available', so it was jalfrezis all round.

Phil's brain was still whirring. 'You've got a point though, Elvis. I reckon it wouldn't have taken long for the enemy to suss out what the Bolshies were up to. And then it would have been *Dos Vedanya* Vienna.' Phil licked the remaining sauce from his knife and fork. 'Still, it worked well enough against Napoleon and Adolf.' The curry-only diet suddenly took its toll and Phil dashed for the toilet.

Rather than wait for the second half of Phil's history lecture, the young men left some money on the table and scarpered. Phil wasn't stoked to find an empty café on his return, but was soon comforted by the arrival of two more breakfasts. Shits or no shits, he wasn't turning down free curry.

Miko and Vanh set themselves up at the side of the main road and waited. The first engine to announce itself belonged to an old white Datsun van, crammed with rice and squashed faces. Even in these conditions care was taken to separate men and women, so the half-gap at the feet of an octogenarian great-grandmother was off-limits. In fact, Vanh was about to wave the driver on when a human whistle sounded from the roof, and a long muscular arm appeared. Next a grinning moustache, and soon both the young men were being hauled onto the roof rack by the self-appointed porter.

The ride was windy, and a little hair-raising around the bends, but the views over the Hunza Valley and its silvery river were ample compensation. There were none of the famous fruit blossoms, and most of harvest was already in, but the deep, verdant textures still provided spectacular contrast to the arid grey scree scratching up the slopes of the mountains, and the blinding-white glaciers on higher up.

Miko and Vanh dismounted at Karimabad, and marched up the long hill from the main road to the village proper. In the teahouse next to Baltit Fort, they opted for a 'second' breakfast of yoghurt and *chapattis*.

'Do you think Phil will be mad at us for leaving him like that?'

'Ned? Don't worry, Floyd does that to him all the time.'

'So are he and Phil friends, or not?' Miko was still a little confused.

'Let's just say they're "Friendly rivals". Like Graham.'

'Is that because Phil doesn't buy any of their books?'

Vanh half-snorted. 'He gave you that story, did he?'

'What do you mean?'

'The old "I don't use guidebooks" line?' Vanh shook his head.

'He said he's never used a guide in his life.' Even as he spoke, Miko realised he'd been had, and started kicking himself.

'He's got cupboards full of them,' Vanh smiled.

'A backpacker just like all the rest of us.' Miko kicked again.

'Flashpacker, more like. Stands to inherit the largest copper mine in the southern hemisphere, and half the slots in Australia.'

'Slots?'

'Slot machines.' Vanh smiled. 'Or as Phil would call them, Pokies. Throw in the family villa in Bali and a penthouse overlooking the Opera House, and you're beginning to get the picture.'

'You're kidding?' Miko tore off more bread for both of them.

'I wish I was.' Vanh mopped up his bowl and washed it all down with green tea.

'So all that about him doing overland tours?'

'Oh, they're very much for real.' Vanh chuckled. 'It's his only way to meet thirtysomethings having just enough of a mid-life crisis not to care about who they're sleeping with.'

Miko cast his mind back to Kashgar where he had found himself sharing a hotel with one such tour truck. Vanh's description of some of the females was harsh but cruelly accurate. Now he thought about it, Jeff, the tour leader, was Phil all over.

'So all the "I don't need a guidebook" bravado is just part of his chat-up routine?'

'Maybe, maybe not. According to Floyd,' Vanh gave his neck a stretch, 'the real reason, in fact, is that guidebook writing's all he's ever wanted to do. Floyd says Phil was supposed to write *Small World's* first Thailand guide, but him and Jane had some huge falling out. Since then he's tried all the other guys,' Vanh almost started feeling sorry for him, 'but no one will give him a gig.'

158

'Why not?'

'I don't know.' Vanh shrugged. 'I think it's a matter of principle these days.'

'I can't believe I fell for it.'

Vanh laughed. 'Like Pinks says, and I want you to understand how much it loathes me to give him credit for this, but he's right, "there's Truth and there's Travelling Truth".'

'I suppose there is.' Miko lit up his first Lucky Strike of the day.

'Did Phil tell you about his other book?' Vanh carried on with a smile.

'I thought you just said no one would touch him.'

'Oh, this isn't published. But according to Phil it's going to be a "corker". I'm surprised he didn't bore you with it.'

'What's it about?' Miko let the smoke filter through his nose.

'See if you can guess from the title.' Vanh adopted a tone of mock reverence: '*Around the World in Eighty Lays: 'Crazy' Philpot's guide to the hottest pick-up joints on Earth.*'

'Catchy.' Miko sipped the last of his Darjeeling.

'You should read the first chapter.' Vanh signalled for the bill.

'My shout.' For the second time that morning Miko insisted on paying.

They gathered their belongings and headed out into the fresh air. Above the village the path petered out, and the going became steep and tough. They pushed on until the fort was no longer in view, before stopping for a drinks break on some large boulders.

'So how did you get into all of this, Vanh?' Miko tried to sound casual, but it was a question he was eager to know the answer to.

'Same as most people, I guess,' Vanh shrugged. 'Lucky break.'

'Come on,' Miko angled.

'No, seriously. My folks were booked on one of Floyd's tours, but mum broke her leg, so I went with pops instead.'

'I don't get it.'

'Well, it was a tour around Utah, the "Hole in the Wall" gang, that sort of stuff. Secretly, I think mum's leg wasn't broken at all. On about the second day Floyd's laptop crashed, along with all the back-up drives in his office, and he was literally begging for help. After about six hours I was able to fix it. Not a very sophisticated worm. It turns out his IT guy'd quit, and left it as a sort of goodbye present.'

159

'Unlucky.'

'That's what Floyd said. Before I suggested he offer me a job.' Vanh had been pretty pleased with his negotiating skills. 'I started off building a website for his tours, and then, when he decided to launch The Pinks Guide, I persuaded him to make me a partner.'

'Nice one.'

'Not really. It's meant I've had to work with Floyd ever since.'

Miko laughed.

'And the money's lousy,' Vanh lamented. 'But it suits me for now.'

'That still doesn't explain why you're up here.'

'Officially, I'm on holiday. A reward for all my hard work. But honestly…' Vanh looked down the valley.

'Sorry, buddy. None of my business.' Miko made a point of packing up his things, ready to recommence the climb.

'It's no big deal.' Vanh cautiously supped up the last of his juice. 'It's just I think Floyd wants me out of the office for a while. I've got a feeling The Authentic Wild West Experience isn't all he's thinking of selling.'

'So what are you going to do?'

'No worries, mate.' Vanh attempted what could only be described as a pretty lame impression of Phil. 'Seriously, it's not a problem. The Web's a big adventure, right? The great unknown.'

'I wish you luck.'

Vanh gathered his belongings and the two of them set off once more. 'Besides, I've got dirt enough on Floyd.'

By the end of the sweaty climb both young men had stripped down to the basics. Vanh was in a cotton T-shirt, Miko the same electric-orange football top he had been wearing as a vest all week. They could see activity higher up the meadow but their legs demanded rest. Vanh could feel the blood throbbing around his brain in the silence, and wasn't sure if he would ever move again.

Rather than waste energy talking, Miko handed Vanh the first page of notes from Graham.

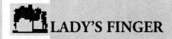LADY'S FINGER

The ascent up to the meadow is as steep as it is high. The slow dribble that is the Ultar rivulet in the cold of early spring, becomes a bursting stream of melted glacier ice cascading down the ravine by autumn. It is impossible to stick to the river path throughout, and at various points you are forced to scramble up dusty moraines as high as ten metres. The narrowness of the gorge gives little indication of your progress and after more than three hours, the lean air burns at your lungs and your calf muscles scream for respite. Allow yourself about four hours.

Following the cramped confines of the gorge, the vastness of the natural amphitheatre and the towering mountains is almost enough to bring on agoraphobia. Suddenly your world, which has been dark and shadowy brown, is bombarded with colour and light. To the right is an enormous icefall and the massive Ultar Glacier. Towering away behind is Ultar II, until recently the highest unclimbed mountain in the world. Facing you is Lady's Finger, a black steeple amongst the other icing-sugared peaks, its faces so sheer no snow can stick.

In early spring and late autumn shepherds will often come out to greet you, and the warmth in their welcome is always genuine. These men are still attached to the nomadic lifestyle and haven't adapted to modern, town dwelling. They are also iron hard, if a touch punch-drunk. When they are well-stocked with Hunza-water, the local jungle juice that scorches every hair it puts on your chest, beware.

You'll probably have some sort of fire in the evening, and in the gloaming, the snowy peaks turn white-chocolate, then mellow yellow. If there's a moon out, one side of the valley blackens into shadows while the other shines silver.

A third guzzle of water gave Miko just enough energy to speak. 'So come on then.'

'What?'

'The dirt on Floyd.'

'No, I shouldn't.' Vanh was struggling, in every sense of the word.

Miko gave him a look.

'OK, OK.' Vanh pulled himself up so he was supported by the grassy bank. For the first time he really appreciated the magnificence of his surroundings. He was tempted to let out a loud 'wow'.

'Apparently, you nearly guessed the other night.'

'The other night?' Miko shifted himself next to Vanh.

'When you said you'd heard Small World were doing a book on Xidakistan.'

'How do you mean?'

'Well, officially, they aren't. But *unofficially*.' Vanh gave a long nod. 'Or to be more precise, we are. Me and Floyd.'

'You're working for *Small World?*' Miko was taken aback.

'Sort of,' Vanh's hand mimed fifty/fifty. 'They didn't think it was worth sending their own team as book sales are likely to be tiny, but Floyd phoned up Terry and offered to do it for free.'

'I thought he quit?'

'He did. And it's not really for free. You see, this way Floyd gets to write one final guide for *Small World*. Which for Floyd is like a final admission from Jane and Terry that they were wrong and he was right over "*Irangate*".'

'And you?'

'I'm chief photographer.' Vanh held up his camera. 'Oh, and I get the joy of typing it up.'

'Some holiday,' Miko laughed, and Vanh felt just about strong enough to laugh back.

'Graham's going to be real, real mad.' Miko whistled.

'Yep.' Vanh pursed his lips.

'Well, I'd better not show you any more of these then.' Miko jokingly packed Graham's notes back into his knapsack.

162

'Do me a favour.' Vanh got his right arm caught in his camera strap as tried to pull his jacket on. 'Don't be the one to tell him.'

'I'm staying well out of it,' Miko promised, pulling on his dark green Pakistan top.

Vanh was keen to change the subject. 'Do you always wear football shirts?'

'You mean this?' Realising Vanh hadn't been there the other evening, Miko recounted his obsession for collecting football jerseys. 'Fifty one and counting. This one's Pakistan, and this one,' he lifted the green to reveal the orange, 'is the '88 shirt from when we won the European championship. Gullit, Rijkaard, Van Basten.'

'I don't think I understood a word of that.' Sweat beads were still calcifying on Vanh's face.

'The legendary Dutch team,' Miko started to explain. 'Don't worry about it.'

Vanh made a meal of packing up his bag.

'Actually, I am worried. Which is why I'm thinking of pulling the pin.'

'On the *Small World* guide?'

Vanh nodded.

'I presume you haven't told Floyd that.'

Silence.

'Can he do it without you?'

'Probably not.' Vanh broke off some chocolate. 'At least, not in the time he's promised.'

'So he's going to be madder than Graham.' Miko laughed.

'Right.' Vanh had to smile too. 'And Jane and Terry. If it had gone well they wanted me to help them on their next Vietnam Guide.'

'Makes sense.'

'Not necessarily.'

Vanh went quiet and again Miko worried it was something he said. 'Sorry.'

'No, no. No problem. My fault really. I was just thinking about Vietnam, and going back.'

'Have you not…?'

'Not yet. They aren't exactly welcoming us Viet Kieu back with open arms.'

163

'Viet Kieu?'

'The Vietnamese that left after the war.'

'Right.' Miko could imagine the potential problems.

'Pops reckons we're better off in the States. But I'm not so sure.'

'"Better to die a poor man in your own country than a King in another's land."' Miko had read Babur's quote in Samarkand.

'You should be doing this job. Not me.'

'And work for Floyd?' Miko mocked. He was too shy to confess the extent of his ambition.

'You could write for Graham,' Vanh volunteered. 'He seems like a good guy.'

Miko smiled, 'I've got a feeling he might not be so keen if he found out I knew what you two are up to.'

'Forget I mentioned it.' Vanh didn't like to think about it. 'Now's probably not a good time to be getting into the guidebook business, anyway.'

'You really think they're on their way out?'

'Well, sales are certainly slipping, and this "War on Terror" won't help.'

'Graham doesn't seem too worried.'

'He's not.' Vanh snapped off some more chocolate and handed a square to Miko. 'But Floyd says Jos is, the guy who runs the show in London.'

'I thought it was Graham's company.'

'Officially, yes, but his partner, Jos, handles all the day to day stuff.' Vanh broke off another square. 'Depending on who you listen to, Graham's either lost control, or doesn't care.'

'Interesting.'

'Not really,' Vanh finished off his snack. 'Not compared to collecting soccer shirts.'

Miko laughed. 'Yes, but it's what pays for the soccer shirts that's the problem.' Rather than explain, he handed over a business card.

'Scooters?' Vanh frowned. 'Is that what you do?'

Miko's name was on the card with a string of job titles.

'ISkoot.com. That's me.'

'You're behind those guys? They like totally rule the entire market.'

'Well, twenty-six point four percent, but further growth is anticipated,' Miko grinned. 'One of the few dot com bubbles that hasn't burst.'

'Yet.'

They both laughed.

'In that case you can buy me dinner.'

'Sounds good.' Miko offered his hand. 'How do you like your goat spit-roasted? Medium or rare?'

They pulled each other up off their rocks and zipped up their jackets. Ahead, a small knot of shepherds had gathered round a camp-fire in the lee of a small bluff.

Phil

The problem with Graham? Well he hasn't given me a job in twenty years, for starters. Probably not his fault, though. More likely the old man, putting on the squeeze. Cos the funny thing is, me and Mr Guidebooks have more in common than he might think. And I'm not just talking travelling.

Like Graham, I'm an only kid from an only parent, although in my case it was mum who did the runner – can't say I blame her. And we both went to Scotland to study History. Hands up how many of youse saw that coming, eh? I've got a feeling Ruffo did a bit better than my ropey Desmond, though; there are some strings not even Kelly Sr can pull.

Phil was growing increasingly suspicious. But he didn't know why. Was it because Floyd was ill? Phil was pretty sure he wasn't sick at all, having lost count of the number of times his old rival had spat the dummy in self-imposed exile. Was it Vanh and Miko's sudden departure? It wasn't the first time. Was it the arrival of another Westerner in town the previous evening? A military man if Phil was not much mistaken.

'G'day, Ruffo.' Phil had headed to the K2 to do some digging. 'What's happening?'

Graham was on his third cup of milky tea. 'The usual.' He sat surrounded by the various components of chapter three of *Silkman on the Silk Road*.

'Right oh.' Phil didn't wait to be invited and sat himself down. 'I've been meaning to have a chat to you.'

Graham rested his pen on the table.

Phil picked up a chunky hardback notebook acting as a paperweight and started flicking. 'You should use Moleskines.'

'I'm not a poser.' Not since Sarah's teasing.

Phil decided to leave his in his bag. 'I'm writing a travelogue, too, you know.'

'Why doesn't that surprise me?' Graham yawned.

'*Kelly's Heroes!*' Phil planned to retrace the expeditions of his favourite explorers in the New World, from Burke and Wills to Lewis and Clarke.

'Sounds like a film.'

'Very funny.'

Graham reclaimed his notebook and stroked the well-thumbed blue linen cover as he would Omar, his mother's Persian Blue.

'How about this for an epitaph?' Phil's mini-sulks never lasted long. 'Ask not when you're going to stop, but who's going to stop you.'

'You mean epigraph, Ned.' On second thoughts, maybe the world without Phil wouldn't be such a bad idea.

Phil ignored him. 'And then for the opening line: "Forget Bill Bryson. He's a dead set goose!".'

'Perfect. Then, when you get Bill to review it, he can write: "Forget Phil Kelly. He's a dead set goose" and you can quote him on the cover.'

'Hey, not bad,' Phil was excited. 'You're not as stupid as you look.'

'Why are you here, Ned?' Graham gave up all hope of achieving anything productive that morning.

'Like I said,' Phil became deadly serious, 'there's something I want to talk to you about.'

'You've got two minutes,' Graham sighed.

'Fair go.' Deep breath. 'Is it me, or is there something weird going in?'

Indeed there was, Graham thought, but no need to tell Kelly that. 'Nope.'

'Well, people have been mighty strange around me, lately. Bonnie was even nice to me yesterday.' Phil had been genuinely shocked.

'Now you come to mention it, she has been behaving rather oddly.'

'Went home without even checking her emails.'

'Maybe she's got a new man.' Graham shuffled all his papers into a neat pile. 'Perhaps it's that guy who arrived last night.'

'That guy?' Phil feigned nonchalance. 'No, he said he was just passing through.'

'Ned, six-foot six Jamaicans don't "just pass through" Gilgit. Least of all driving a shiny gold Chrysler Jeep with blacked-out windows.'

Phil thought he had Graham just where he wanted. 'How do you know he's Jamaican?'

'I saw his passport while he was checking in.'

'Alright then. What do you think he's doing?'

'He told the receptionist he was on holiday.'

'Ha! And you believed that?' Phil jumped in with both feet.

'No, birdbrain.' Graham watched him fall flat on his face. 'That's why I asked you if you knew.'

Without looking round, Graham felt a third presence in the room. 'And why I was just about to ask Bonnie the same question.'

'I'm impressed, Graham.'

The air crackled. It wasn't often Bonnie addressed Graham by his first name. She was standing with one finger lightly on her hip, the other seductively up against her lips. The waves that had wriggled loose in her hair over the last few days had been iron-clamped straight. Tommy Hilfiger had been replaced by Coco Chanel. Bonnie meant business. 'Tell me what you really think is going on. What's he really up to?'

'You mean Pinks?'

Bonnie tutted, but without dropping the pout from her lips.

'Oh, the new guy?' Now it was Graham's turn to feign.

Phil's head was spinning.

'Of course I mean the *frigging* new guy.' Bonnie's façade crashed with a shriek.

Phil panicked. 'Maybe he's the Young Gun.'

'Young? He looked older than Floyd.'

'Whatever his age, he's military.' Bonnie took up a position by the dining table. 'I can smell it.'

'The Jamaican army?' Not for the first time Phil hadn't wanted to speak, it had just happened. 'What are they doing up here?'

'I think we can safely say that the whole Jamaican thing's a front.' Graham reached for his pen and notebook.

'I want answers, G.' Bonnie began drumming her fingers on the wood.

'You're the one with all the Pentagon contacts,' Graham steadied himself. 'B.'

It was enough to bring Bonnie at least part way down off her pedestal.

'Yeah, why don't you ask your Mr Hunky Spunk in high places?' There were some games with Bonnie that even Phil could play.

'I have, actually, Phil, but the reception dish for my satellite phone is not working at the….' Bonnie froze, just as she had on seeing a photograph of herself and the head of New York's finest romping nude around his pool. 'Tell me I'm not justifying myself to Ned,' she wailed. 'Somebody shoot me!'

Graham was tempted.

Re-gathering herself, Bonnie turned on her Prada heel, wrenched open the door, and slammed it shut on her way out. Once again the café doorbell found itself en route to the kitchen, this time with the torn-off hook in tow. Careering down the steps, Bonnie could be heard muttering something about a Kalashnikov.

'Where are you going?' Graham shouted after her through the open window.

'To see Floyd!' For once Naveed's van was previously engaged so Bonnie, cursing, stopped the first car she met in the street and ordered the startled driver to take her up the hill.

'Things must be desperate.' As Phil spoke, a boy striking an uncanny resemblance to Little Mo came in from the veranda, where he had been waiting patiently. He picked up the freshly broken bell and gave it to Naveed.

'Excuse me, Sir, is that lady a Mrs Fidler?'

'That's Ms Fidler to you, little grommet.'

'Where is she going, please?'

The boy had eyes wide enough to charm the devil but Graham wasn't falling for them. 'Why do you want to know?'

'I have a telegram for her.' Despite a heavy accent, his delivery and grammar were pitch perfect. Graham was suitably softened. 'And who might you be?'

'I'm Nasser Nansur.' Young Nasser's chest puffed. 'Of Nasser Nansur Communications Enterprises.'

'A friend of Little Mo's, no doubt?' Graham had a feeling the letter contained something important.

'Oh no, Sir. He is my archest rival.'

'Well, you'd better not let him catch you in here,' Phil warned. 'This is his turf.'

'Tell you what, Mr Nansur,' offered Graham. 'Give me the note and I'll pass it on to Ms Fidler when I see her tonight.'

'Oh no, Sir.' Nasser had a feeling this telegram was going to get him a nice, juicy tip. 'I must give it to her personally. Has she gone back to her hotel?'

'Yes,' lied Graham quickly, trying to think of a new plan.

'No, G,' Phil dunced. 'She said she was going to find Pinks at The Chinar.'

Graham looked at Phil in dismay as the boy darted out of the door. Before they reached the bottom of the stairs he was half way up the hill. They could only give chase.

No doubt they've already told you about Grandad Kelly's mine and Philip Kelly Sr's pokies empire, but what they probably forgot to mention is that for the old man, all that doesn't count for piss. He'd set his sights on becoming the next great Aussie media mogul, you see. So yours truly was sent to the finest schools, 'won' a scholarship to St Andrew's, and was groomed for a long and successful career running newspapers. Only problem was, no one asked muggins here.

I should have brought it to a head after graduation, but rather than burn every bridge we agreed to disagree, and I took a year off 'to think things through'. Of course, I'd already thought everything through, twice, and there was no way I was going back. So in the end he issued the ultimatum: return to stand by his side or kiss the inheritance goodbye. I was written out of his will the very next day.

When word got back that I wanted to be a travel writer, the old fella chucked a wobbler to end all wobblers. You can imagine how long it took him to put the fix in with Small World and all the other publishers. I thought Ruff's mob, especially Sarah, might have been different, but I suppose it's true what they say: shit sticks.

Pinks had been true to his word and not left his hotel once in the two days. He had taken the opportunity to catch up on some bedtime reading, bedtime snacking, and bedtime full stop; so much so that he hadn't yet noticed Vanh's departure.

As Graham panted his way up the hotel drive, peaceful snoring drifted down from his window onto the car park. A copy of 'Innocents Abroad' delicately balanced on a medium-sized plate of cheese and biscuits, which was less-delicately balanced on Floyd's belly. Nasser was stood proffering his telegram, but Bonnie was too busy berating her bewildered driver for taking a detour via his aunt's chicken farm.

170

Nasser saw Phil coming for him and leapt onto the hotel porch. Unfortunately for the young entrepreneur, gymnastics was one of Phil's strengths. He swung up the railings like an orang-utan, grabbed the young boy by his left leg and dangled him upside down over the parapet. Graham tried to prize the telegram from his hand. Nasser's defiant kicking and screaming was soon amplified by Bonnie's hysterical wish to know exactly what was going on, plus her driver's tearful pleas for payment of dues.

Floyd jerked awake, sending the cheese plate spinning under the wardrobe. Normally, he would have eased himself from his slumber, all the while allowing the scene to unfold, but a plague of biscuit crumbs had got under the sheets and the screams were becoming louder. He carefully retrieved his glasses, placed his bookmark between two particularly dog-eared pages, gave his smouldering Don Juan a firm tap and marched out onto his balcony. In his socks and boxer shorts.

'Quiiiiiiet!' Pinks bellowed, cracker crumbs dropping from his chest hair. 'I was trying to read.'

Graham took advantage of the momentary pause to whip the telegram out of Nasser's hands.

'I knew you weren't ill,' Phil stamped, spinning Nasser back the right way.

As Floyd surveyed the battlefield, Bonnie's driver let out a final wail.

'Imran, turn off the engine and get back in the car.'

The driver, surprised that this strange man knew his name, did as he was told.

'Bonnie's got a telegram.' Graham couldn't help noticing an uncanny resemblance between the Floyd looking down at him from the balcony, and Penfold, Dangermouse's bespectacled assistant.

'G reckons it's from her government/Pentagon/high-places guy.'

'Give it to me.' Pinks clicked his fingers.

'Like hell you will.' Bonnie lunged at Graham's arm. 'That's private property.' But Graham had already tossed it up in the air.

Floyd lent over, snatched, snatched again, and smoothed the envelope on the balustrade, before slicing it open with the blade of his cigar cutter. Normally, he wouldn't have so blatantly confronted his ex but the gap was a good ten feet.

'I'm warning you, Housmann.' Bonnie's coiffure had come loose in the scuffle, and blonde strands were beginning to frizz.

Floyd took a step back. 'Come, come, my sweet. As you said just the other day, we should all pool our resources.'

'Sweet nothing. Give me that letter right now, or I'll have a lawsuit on you so fast…'

'You already have a dozen lawsuits against me,' Floyd cut in. 'What difference is another going to make?'

He scanned the contents of the telegram before reading it out aloud.

'It's from the White House, darling. We're moving up in the world.' Pinks gave a small bow.

Phil began to giggle, and Bonnie raised her hand for the second time since she arrived, but he managed to flinch out of the way.

'"Dear Bon-Bons,"' Floyd adopted his most statesman-like pose.

'Very touching,' Graham had already checked the distance between him and Bonnie's hand.

'"Tried email x 3. No reply",' Pinks tutted. 'All that money you're paying at The Serena and still no internet?'

Bonnie redoubled her efforts to tear down the wooden railings.

'"Action any day now. UN told Xidaki independence a must."' Floyd was struggling to control himself as he watched Bonnie suffer. '"Conference + Tah = Sost. SI agent arriving to co-ordinate security. Hugs + Kisses. Ross. PS Everyone loves your",' Floyd looked at Bonnie in disgust, '"Everyone loves your Alphabet Game. Even Larry King Show".'

For a moment Bonnie didn't look quite so righteous.

'"PPS hugs + kisses x2."'

Pinks folded up the telegram and slipped it back into the envelope. He paused, relit his cigar and rested both hands on the wooden bar in front of him.

'Well,' he finally announced, sucking on his torpedo, 'I think that post-scriptum puts us just about quits on the lawsuit front, Bon-Bons.'

'Alright, alright, just give it back.' Bonnie stamped on Graham's toe as she stretched past his head. Floyd let the letter flutter through the air rather than risk physical contact.

'Any sign of an NI agent in town, Graham?'

'SI agent!' Bonnie was still fuming.

'Special Intelligence, No Intelligence,' Floyd larked. 'They're all the same to me.'

'That'll be the Jamaican!' Phil was back in the mix. 'He's staying in our hotel!'

'In which case,' Pinks announced, 'I believe a trip into town is in order. Where's George?' Another of Vanh's duties was taxi-procurement.

'Good question,' muttered Phil.

Graham decided against enlightening them.

'No matter, G, if you would be so kind as to ask Ali over there to wait for me to descend,' Floyd nodded in the direction of Bonnie's now utterly-confused driver, 'I shall be down in two shakes of a goat's cheese tail.'

'Hey, that's my car, get your own.'

'Sorry, Bonnie, is that your car, as in your Alphabet Game?'

'Alright. But I'm in front.'

Phil nodded to the driver as though it all made perfect sense, and climbed into the back.

Bonnie, sensing Nasser was waiting for his tip, pretended to be doing her hair in the rear-view mirror. Graham gave the boy a note and sat down next to Phil. As Nasser pocketed his money Pinks appeared, fully-dressed, and squeezed himself into the back seat, crushing Phil into the other corner in the process. They were off.

Unfortunately, the "Jamaican" wasn't at the hotel and neither was his vehicle, so they were forced to sit and wait in the K2. There they listened over and over again to the Larry King segment that Bonnie, as immediately as Naveed's server would allow, downloaded from the internet.

'Oh come on, boys.' Bonnie's spirits had lifted considerably. 'Just one more time.' She hadn't pleaded this hard since she had wanted (and got) her first pony. 'I just love that bit when he reads the message from the President, urging us all to become "a nation of flyers".'

'At least he's stopped hugging the firemen.' Phil flopped back in his chair.

'"Nation of Flyers". Didn't Goering say that about Nazi Germany?' Graham tapped his pen on his notebook.

'You're so pathetic when you're jealous, Ruff.'

'You mean envious.'

'No, I mean pathetic. Small wonder Sarah-'

Graham never got the chance to hear the insult in full, as the screech from a Jeep's tyres biting into the gravel outside alerted the whole café to the Grand Cherokee's return. To everyone's surprise Vanh and Miko were in the back.

'Where the hell have you been?' Pinks was already down the steps and marching over to Vanh. Two and a half hours of Larry King was enough for any man. Fortunately, Naveed had yet to reattach his bell, so the doorframe merely shuddered.

'Keep your hair on.' Vanh countered coldly, eyes fixed on Floyd's bald pate. 'I've been working.' He held up his camera as proof. 'And JC here gave us a lift back.'

'JC?' Floyd barked. 'You're supposed to be here with me.'

'Why?' Vanh wasn't in the mood either. 'Has Terry given you another book to do?'

Pinks span round to make sure Graham hadn't heard this last comment, but the other three were still at the top on the café steps. Turning back, Floyd glared at Vanh until he muttered an apology. Meanwhile, the vehicle's driver managed to extricate himself from the front seat, and give his new surroundings a once over.

'You must be Floyd Pinks Housmann.' The accent, despite the accompanying red, gold and green wristbands, was definitely more Mid-west than Rastafari. The tone was at best derogatory.

'And you must be *Special Intelligence?*' Floyd scoffed back. 'Don't tell me,' he kept probing, 'let me guess.' Floyd looked his adversary up and down. 'You're agent,' now he looked him straight in the eye, 'agent "Black", per chance?'

The newcomer refused Pinks' hand.

'Agent Brown. John Clayton Brown, *Counter* Intelligence.'

Pinks' eyes remained glued to his adversary's.

'Don't worry about him, JC.' Vanh was too tired to wait for the stand-off to finish.

'Come in and let us buy you a cold drink.' Miko bounded up to the K2 with a 'Morning everybody'.

Agent Brown chose to amble along after, while Floyd caught Vanh's sleeve and pulled him back for one last briefing. Stomping off up the road, Floyd let the world know that he would be retiring to his hotel. For the second time.

'Looks like someone's got his goat.' Phil commented to Graham, as they all made their way back inside. 'Or should I say "goat's cheese"?'

Graham took George to one side as he came through the door. 'What's up with Pinks?'

'Oh, you know,' Vanh bluffed.

'Everything still set for tomorrow?'

'One hundred percent. Just as soon as the bike arrives.'

Miko made the necessary introductions and the group settled into the usual chit-chat. Except for Bonnie, who went back to reviewing (and re-viewing) her download.

'I don't think he likes us Intelligence guys much,' Agent Brown explained when the subject inevitably returned to Pinks. He spoke as if he knew Floyd well.

'That's an understatement,' Bonnie interjected from Computer Corner.

'How come, JC?' Vanh offered his new pal the floor but Bonnie had decided it was her turn.

'He got black-balled by Special Intelligence after Princeton.' Bonnie wheeled herself into the centre of attention. 'They said he wasn't imaginative enough.'

Music to Phil's lugholes.

'True enough,' Agent Brown continued. 'But from what I hear, there's a whole lot more to it than that.'

Now it was Bonnie's ears that were ringing. For the first time since she'd got up that morning she stopped chewing. 'How much more?'

Agent Brown told his story well, beaming the whole way through as though recounting his latest fishing trip on The Great Lakes. Back in the eighties, it transpired, a certain president, on the advice of people who should have known better, decided to launch yet another covert investigation into possible 'Reds under the Bed'. As an SI reject Housmann was already high on the list, but when the computer came up with references to 'Pinks'/'The Little

Pink Book', numerous visits to left-wing Central and South American countries, and the Irangate fiasco….

'Let's just say a young captain got a bit carried away.'

'He never told me this bit.' Bonnie was doing well to not swallow her gum.

Agent Brown's beam didn't waver. The officer had ordered a SWAT team to raid Floyd's apartment in Manhattan for evidence. By mistake, Floyd had returned while they were still there, having cut short a visit to Macy's on account of leaving his wallet at home. In a bout of panic, our not-so-heroic captain decided he was left with no choice but to bind, gag and blindfold Mr Housmann, and helicopter him to the nearest high-security detention centre for further questioning.

Suddenly Phil wasn't laughing.

'He was there for six days,' JC finished off. 'Twenty hours "hard interrogation" a day.'

'Bloody oath!'

'I can't believe he never said anything.' Bonnie sounded genuinely concerned.

'Why didn't he go to the papers?' Graham was trying his hardest to make some sense out of everything he had just been told.

'No can do.' Agent Brown shook his head. 'That's Catch 23.'

'Catch 23?' Vanh was beginning to feel guilty he had been so short with his partner in the car park.

'Well, you're probably guessing this wasn't the first time this kinda shit hit the fan, right? So now there's a contingency plan.' Agent Brown explained that in such circumstances, the powers-that-be immediately enlist the victim as a non-serving officer in some two-bit army corps, and start paying the guy one hundred grand a year.

'No wonder he's always got so much money,' Phil clicked. Graham reprimanded himself severely for having thought the exact same thing.

This way, Agent Brown went on, the victim effectively becomes a serviceman, and as such swears never to divulge information which may be damaging to the State. With the understanding that if he breaks that promise

176

he'll be court-martialled for breaching army regulations, and incarcerated indefinitely.

'What happens if you refuse to swear?' Miko was shocked.

'They court-martial you for not following orders, a breach of army regulations, and you're incarcerated indefinitely.'

'But,' Graham wasn't sure if he was believing what he was hearing. 'Aren't you breaching army regulations by telling us?'

'Yes, I am,' JC straight-faced.

'So how come you're ….?' Phil didn't get it.

'Because it's such a funny story.' Agent Brown whooped as only a two-hundred-and-fifty-pound, former Defensive-End can.

No one else's face moved.

Before Agent Brown could go on, Naveed and his number one son appeared with a large toolbox, step ladder, two industrial-sized wall brackets and an overly-large cast-iron bell. Graham took the opportunity to order pots of tea for everyone.

'So you're up here for the Xidakistan delegation?' Graham thought it polite to let Agent Brown know that they knew.

'Shit-dick-istan?' JC looked around in case it was a joke. 'What's that?'

'Come on, JC. You can tell us.'

'No, seriously, I've never heard of no Dickistan.'

'Dakistan,' Bonnie half-corrected. 'Did you not see this month's *Traveler*?'

''Fraid I must have missed it.' Agent Brown winked to the boys.

'Xidakistan: the new Shangri La. The Larry King Show?' For Bonnie there was definitely no funny side.

'Nope.'

'So why are you here?' Graham tried.

'Well, I'm not really supposed to tell.' Agent Brown paused to look round and this time his focus stopped at the café owner, up his ladder. He lent forward into the table. 'Doing a bit of OTB research.' He motioned for the others to come in close. 'Outside The Box. Looking for Al Qaeda bases,' he whispered.

'But there aren't any Al Qaeda bases up here,' Graham whispered back.

'That I can't comment on.' Brown's tone was deadly serious.

'Wouldn't you be better off looking for Al Qaeda bases in Afghanistan?' Miko asked, forgetting to whisper.

Agent Brown indicated that Afghanistan itself was off-limits for the time being. A case of waiting for the drones.

'But won't they have bombed all the bases by the time you get there?' Vanh could see further flaws in the plan.

Agent Brown shrugged, then gave his arms and neck a stretch, after all that driving.

'So what's your area of expertise, John?' A glimpse of JC's pectorals had suddenly softened Bonnie. Needs must....

'Submarine combat.'

'Very funny.' Graham shook his head.

'I'm serious. The boys in the office were really struggling on this one.' Agent Brown pushed out his bottom lip. 'What you gotta understand is that there isn't actually anyone in the department of Arab or Afghan descent.'

'What about the Middle East team?' Miko was as surprised as the others.

Brown dismissed the idea out of hand. 'Zionists only.'

'So why you? You don't look very Nation of Islam.' Graham was trying to think laterally.

'Hell no.' JC couldn't think of anything worse. 'I've been a good Baptist all my life.'

'Don't tell me you got the job because you're the only blackfella.'

JC swung round to eye-ball Phil in an instant. Graham thought it wise to intervene. 'I think what Phil was trying to say was: surely you're not the only ethnic minority in Counter Intelligence these days.'

'Of course not,' Agent Brown sucked his teeth. 'But I'm the only one who likes Indian food.'

'Are you serious?' Vanh never ceased to be amazed by his adopted nation, but thought he had better check.

'Gee, yeah.' JC door-knocked his belly. 'When it comes to curries, they call me "King of the Ring". I'll eat those bad boys morning, noon and night. Even the ones with chillies.'

Miko looked at Vanh. Vanh at Miko.

'I'd better go and check on Floyd.' Vanh made for the door.

Miko announced that he, too, had to leave. He nodded at Graham and then turned back to JC. 'Thanks again for the lift. Really appreciated it.'

'Yeah, thanks, JC,' echoed Vanh, but with less conviction.

Graham could hear their disgust as they descended the stairs, but turned his attention back to more pressing concerns.

'So you're nothing to do with Xidakistan then?'

'Nope. Unless,' Agent Brown looked alarmed, 'unless you think some of the Al Qaeda boys are up there?'

Phil explained that all the inhabitants of The Valley were 'fair dinkum Buddhists'. 'Probably never even heard of Bin Laden. Or Uncle Sam for that matter.'

'Maybe I should go and take a look anyways.' JC made it sound like driving a couple of blocks to check out a traffic accident.

'It's a six-day round trip trekking across snow-covered mountains.' Graham figured this would be enough to make him rethink. The last thing they needed was Counter Intelligence blundering around the place, just when it seemed everything was starting to click.

'Six days?' Agent Brown felt the initial pangs of hypothermia just imagining. 'And all these guys are Buddhists, right?'

'Every last one of them,' Graham reassured.

JC nodded to himself, and decided such a trip wouldn't be necessary after all. At least he had been thorough. 'Those Buddhists never did like the Islams, did they?' He laughed nervously. 'No Siree. They hate them nearly as much as they hate the.....other ones.'

Bonnie was sick with herself for even appreciating the pectorals. 'It's just we heard that a Special Intelligence agent was heading up here.' She forced herself to smile. 'For the Independence conference.'

'Well, we are quite a large organisation.' Agent Brown looked at Graham as if to ask: WTF?

'I think what Bonnie meant was whether you could do a bit of asking around. You know, amongst the other agents in the area.'

'Ask around?' Now JC was thinking Graham was the one being dumb. 'There are no other agents.'

'You mean you're checking the whole of Pakistan on your own?'

'Gee no, not the whole country.' Some of that earlier positivity returned to Agent Brown's face. 'Just the main towns and cities. The Pakistani government has asked us to stay away from the countryside.'

Graham's back winced. Pointing out that ninety-eight percent of Pakistan was countryside wasn't going to make it any better. He didn't want to know how long JC had allowed for his mission.

'Oh, it's the full five-day tour.' Agent Brown made it sound like a lifetime. 'I'm not driving back to Islamabad until the morning.'

Bonnie looked at Graham. 'I think it's time I got back to my hotel.'

'Lordy. Is that the time?' JC struggled out of his undersized chair as suavely as he could. He had noticed some pretty flirtatious signals earlier on and had a feeling it was time to make his move. 'Those reports won't write themselves.'

The scowl on Bonnie's face as he strolled over to the door prompted a swift rethink. 'Actually, maybe I'll stay and have some dinner. I hear the curry here's got a real kick to it.'

'Now you're talking.' Phil gave Agent Brown a playful jab. 'I hear you Yankees like 'em hot.'

Graham couldn't believe his ears; Phil was usually merciless about vindaloos in America tasting like kormas. Then he spied the two crates of Budweiser strapped into the passenger seat of Brown's Jeep.

So, Kelly Jr, I hear you cry, if you're more bullied than brainless, what's with all the 'Crazy Philpot' dingo, lingo?

Revenge. Plain and simple. If there's one thing that gives the old man the shits, even more than losing to the Poms at cricket, it's being tarred with the 'bogan' brush. Old Grandad Kelly, you see, was Woop Woop born and bred. Lived most of his life in a tin shack next to woolshed. It just so happened underneath that shack was where all the copper was hiding. Even when the money started rolling in, he didn't give two hoots what he or his family looked like or sounded like, and my old fella never forgave him for it. The number of elocution lessons he had for himself, let alone me, must have made the rain in Spain flood the bloody plain. What's it they say about the sins of the father?

OK, maybe that's not quite the whole truth. I have a confession: first stop on the year out was Camden Town (not very original, I know, but at least it wasn't Earl's Court). One night at The Ewe and Roo (affectionately, and not so affectionately, referred to as 'The Woolly Jumper') I chanced upon a not-very-romantic encounter with a not-very-coherent receptionist in a side alley. 'Ocker Aussie' it seemed was what this Sheila wanted and Raw-Prawn was what she got. Not the world's most effective pulling technique, I grant you, but it worked again the following week, and as Grandad Kelly told anyone unlucky enough to be listening: 'If it ain't broke.......'

If Phil had guzzled and gabbled with JC any deeper into the early hours, he would have seen Queen Bea's pink mountain bike being unloaded from the overnight bus when he staggered back from to his room. Nevertheless, he had hardly hit the hay by the time Bonnie came knocking at his chalet door.

'Shift your butt, Ned,' Bonnie hollered. The K2, apart from Naveed's new bell, had been empty, so she had gone looking for company in The Madina. Only Phil seemed to be at home.

'Pronto.' Bonnie was pummelling on his door with her right hand, while her left juggled with a stack of computer print-outs picked up from the café.

Phil pulled his eyelids open and squinted through the crack in the curtain. Normally, Bonnie coming round in itself would have sent Phil trembling, for her to be there before breakfast, devoid of even the faintest daub of makeup, was enough to give him the shakes. He took what he considered to be the only sensible option available, and dived out of the back window, wearing Y-fronts, Collingwood vest, and a single sock. Its match, together with yesterday's zip-off shorts and a pair of trainers was tucked under his arm. This ingenious plan was scuppered by his landing in some of The Northern Areas' thornier specimens of flora, and the subsequent scream of pain was more than enough to give the game away. Bonnie cut him off at the trees.

'Kelly? What the hell are you doing?' It should all have been so different. Bonnie had dashed down to the K2 as soon as reception had given her the message, and the sight of the first sheet to emerge from Naveed's printer had only heightened her state of euphoria. She had almost allowed herself a curtsey. By the hundredth copy, however, the apparent absence of not just Floyd, but

Graham, Miko, Vanh, Phil and Agent Brown had become something of an itch. The reaction of Phil was enough to wear her nerves thinner than her step-aerobics leotard.

Still half-drunk, Phil pieced together what looked like a vindictive descendant of the Spanish Inquisition. 'I surrender!' Halfway embedded into a bush, he held his trainers in front of his face. 'Just don't hit me.'

'Don't be so melodramatic.' Bonnie sounded like Phil's Aunt Sissy. Not a favourable comparison. She ordered him to return to his room, put on his clothes, and meet her in the K2. Preferably in that order.

'And stop dilly-dallying.' Bonnie turned on her least-high heel and left, painstakingly rescuing some of her print-outs from the shrubbery on her way.

'Better late than never, I suppose.' Waiting at the larger of the K2's breakfast tables, Bonnie's mood had swung firmly back into the positive. She had divided her photocopies into three piles and presented one to Phil, with unabashed glee.

'Well, what do you think?' An emergency stick of gum lay ready to be unwrapped, just in case.

Phil's eyes were still smarting from a severe lack of sleep. 'Where's JC?' Two cartons full of empty Budweiser bottles were parked out front but no gold Grand Cherokee.

'No time for that, now.' Bonnie flapped the top sheet of paper in his face. 'Look.'

Phil finally decided on a 'say what you see' approach. 'It's a print out of the front page of The New York Times.'

'And?'

Kelly extended his arms until the photocopy was at a more eye-friendly range, but it wasn't really helping. 'And you're celebrating the fact that Naveed's printer is working again?' Mr Shah's machine had been on the blink once more, and this time it hadn't just been the on/off button. 'By Xeroxing a thousand copies?'

The gargoyle that had assumed the proportions of Bonnie's face implied there was quite a bit more to it than that. Phil looked again. It was a question he really didn't want to ask, but he knew he was going to have to. 'Which bit?'

Bonnie rapped his knuckles hard with a wad of papers but Phil was more relieved it hadn't been the whole pile.

'Bottom right.' Bonnie jabbed, tossing her hair like a movie star. 'The bit about me!'

She didn't wait for Phil to finish reading: 'Isn't it wonderful? Yours truly on the front page of the New York Times.' Bonnie's previous best had been top left, page three.

Phil tried hard to become excited by the small column headlined 'Come Fly With Me!' It appeared that, as part of his 'Fly in the Sky' campaign, the President himself had personally endorsed Bonnie's competition in The Traveler.

'There's no picture.'

'Forget pictures, Ned. This is front page of The New York Times.' Bonnie radiated. 'Just wait 'til I show Floyd.'

Rather than risk another beating, Phil was about to say something about Bonnie's mother being very proud. But then he noticed the silence. 'Where is Floyd?'

Bonnie's paranoia came flooding back. 'I was hoping you would know.'

'You don't think he went with Brown, do you?' Phil's senses were partially coming to.

'Why would he want to go to 'Pindi?' Bonnie was getting a sharp sensation in her left cheek. 'Wait,' she kicked Phil as much out of habit as an attempt to get his brain in gear, 'they couldn't have gone back up to The Valley, could they?'

The pair of them paused to consider the possibility.

'What would be the point?'

A ray of light protractedly dawned inside Phil's sozzled head. 'I'll tell you what would be the point,' he howled. 'They know something we don't. That's the bloody point.'

Phil was up on his feet and leaping round the room. Bonnie tried to calm him but she knew he was right.

'The two-faced mongrels.' Phil spat.

Bonnie desperately tried to click to 'in charge' mode, but all attempts to make Phil sit down were futile.

'Perhaps they've gone to Sost to find out more about the conference.'

'Like hell. They're on their way to see Tah and you know it. The double-crossing pair of-.' Phil began screwing his fist into his palm. Then suddenly relaxed. 'Hang on! We'll follow them.' Everything became clear. It was so simple. 'They can't have got much further than Gakuch. Naveed, I'm borrowing the van.'

Phil snatched the keys from their hook outside the kitchen and made for the exit. Naveed smiled, the car-rental business was picking up.

'If they want to play dirty,' Phil yanked open the door, 'they've come to the right man.'

'No, Ned. Wait!' Bonnie chased Phil down to the car park, and had her hands firmly pressed on the bonnet. She slowly moved round to the driver's side, removed her latest ball of gum and stuck it on the windscreen, slap bang in front of Phil's face. 'If they're going to play hard ball, we need a few tricks of our own before we strike.'

Whilst Phil reluctantly turned off the engine, Bonnie wet her finger, and began outlining a rough map of the area on the bonnet. 'Whatever happens, they can't win The Game until Xidakistan is independent.'

Sticks of gum represented Graham and Floyd up in The Valley.

'And that can't happen until the conference, right?' Bonnie fished in her pocket, pulled out her lip balm and placed it on the other side.

'Maybe.' Phil was by her side but he wasn't convinced.

'Right!' Bonnie corrected.

'So, if they're up there with the king, we stay down here with the UN. We go to Sost.'

Two hair slides took their position next to the lip balm.

'What happens if there's a change of plan?' Phil scratched his leg where a thorn had drawn blood.

'If anything changes, Ross will be the first to know. How long does the trip to The Valley take?'

'Round trip? Six, maybe seven days.' Phil was still itching.

'So, we have plenty of time to organise their welcome home party.' Bonnie released the keys to the van from Phil's grasp. 'I'm going to the hotel to think: you go back to bed, and come up to my place for dinner.'

As Phil walked away, Bonnie took her place in the passenger seat, and signalled to Mohammed that she would be needing a lift back to the hotel.

So, you can take the Jackanories like the one I spun for Miko with a pinch of chicken salt. Larrikin or no larrikin, I do Floyd's tours and the overlanders because I need the money. My exclusive collection of animal-print, finest-silk shirts, hand-tailored by Mr Pandji in Bali? Twenty dollars a dozen, down the Kho San Road.

No need for your heart to bleed like a wuss just yet, though. The old man will probably chuck a U-ey on his deathbed, and I'll be rolling in coin. Which would be handy. Hey, I could even start printing my books myself. Set up my own publishing house. How does 'Get Lost' guides grab you? Call it a tribute to my old man, the miserable codger. Just don't dob me in while he's still alive.

By the middle of the afternoon Phil's unsettled air had refused to dissipate, even after a second plate of goat dopiaza. When had he ever been able to trust Bonnie Fidler? When did she ever invite him to dinner? After several laps of the polo ground he decided to follow his heart. Two minutes later he was back at the K2, doing a deal with Mo to take him up to Gakuch.

After a breakneck two-hour drive, they caught sight of a raggle-taggle pair of Land Rovers taking a rest at the side of the road. Phil roared past Vanh and Miko, lying on a rock.

'Where the hell do you think you're going?' Phil leapt onto Pinks' back like a wrestler, knocking him clean to the ground. Floyd, desperately trying to wrench himself free from Phil's armlock, took a much needed gasp of air.

'Let go, Ned. He can hardly breathe.' Graham got as close as he dared.

Pinks, now pinned against the tyre of his Land Rover, was futilely working to get a grip of something to lever himself up from the floor.

Graham tried to get hold of Phil's right arm. 'I know what you're thinking, Ned, but you're not going to achieve anything tearing around like Mike bloody Tyson.' Once Floyd had been dealt with there was every chance he would be next.

'Don't start, Ruffo, you're next.'

Phil relaxed his grip a fraction, and Graham backed away. He was still hoping to buy some time when Floyd spoke up, his voice strangled from the recent asphyxiation.

'Look, Ned,' Pinks' eyes finally stopped rolling. 'We're only going up there for the king's wedding. Nothing's been decided about independence, and no one is going to win The Game.'

Phil huffed.

'Well, not yet,' Pinks croaked.

'Crock of shit!'

'It's true,' vouched Graham.

'Look, you Pommie prick.' Phil turned his head back to Graham. 'You two have done a deal, and you know it.' He pushed himself up from the grass and wiped his hands on the back of his strides.

'You know it, I know it, the whole world knows it.' Phil didn't actually know it but he hoped this tactic would bluff Graham into a confession. It would have worked but Floyd spotted the ruse just in time.

'Now just what deal would that be, Ned?'

Phil hesitated slightly, hoping to get some sort of indication from one of their faces. None was forthcoming, and Floyd sensed weakness. 'Come on. If you're going to fly up here throwing your weight around, you'd better have good reason.'

'Right oh,' Phil stalled. Then stalled some more. 'Well, it looks pretty clear from where I'm standing.' He took a deep breath and a punt, 'You've given G the all clear for a new guide, and in return you get the go on The Game.' Phil congratulated himself on his logic. 'Yeah, that seems about the size of it.'

Pinks and Graham shared embarrassed glances.

'But that's not why we're going up there *now*,' Graham evaded. 'We're just sussing out the lie of the land.' Graham doubted his explanation would wash.

'So why are Elvis and Mike with you, if it's just a recce?'

'Come on, Crazy,' cajoled Pinks. 'George is my man. Wherever I go, he goes.'

By now, the two junior members of the team had joined them on the small patch of grass. The two drivers and four porters were all crouched on their haunches, enjoying the spectacle.

'And Miko has got nothing to do with The Game,' Graham added. 'We just said he could come along for the ride. Isn't that right, Miko?'

Miko nodded. A better-trained eye might have spotted the Yemeni badge on Miko's yellow shirt.

'OK.' Phil quickly reformulated his plan. 'No worries, I'll just come along for the ride, too.'

'No, no, no, no, no no,' streamed Floyd. 'The king's expecting only the four of us,' he lied. 'It's all been arranged with Zul.' Which was half true. 'Besides, there's no room.' This was a bit more concrete.

'So I'll go with the guides,' Phil countered. 'And one of their boys can ride with Mo back into town. You don't need four porters.'

'Sorry, Phil.' Graham knew there was no use trying to keep up the façade. 'You just can't come. It's as simple as that. You're right, we have done a deal but that's because we got here first.' Graham slowed the pace of his speech right down in the hope of keeping Phil on side. 'You would have done exactly the same.'

Phil hadn't stopped snarling but Graham felt he was over the worst.

'One thing I do promise you, though,' he added, 'we are not going to win The Game on this trip. We need the conference before anything like that can happen.'

'And we'll be back in Gilgit long before that.' Floyd could see Graham's approach was working and warmed to the theme. 'We give you our word.'

Pinks could read on Phil's face just how devalued this currency had become over the years, and looked around for something stronger. 'Don't we, George? Miko?'

Both were reluctant to join in, but for the sake of the trip they nodded agreement.

'I don't believe a cent of it. But if that's the way you want it, that's fine by old Ned,' Phil smarted, backing away towards his van.

His two adversaries breathed a sigh of relief, Graham a little more easily than Floyd, who was still rubbing his windpipe.

'Just don't any of you come to me again askin' for any favours, that's all,' Phil cursed, climbing in. 'Any of you.' He eyeballed each of them in turn.

As the car began its descent, Phil stuck his head out of the window and shouted to the sky without looking round: 'And watch your back, Housmann. Watch your dirty stinking back!'

Everyone's gaze was fixed on Floyd, who shuffled intensely for a good few minutes before shrugging his shoulders. He ordered the drivers back into their vehicles, and they crunched into first gear.

Game Over?

General Martin awkwardly paced his new domain. It was a portable cabin in the perimeter car park, approximately one mile from where the west wing of The Pentagon had once stood. He was fast losing patience with his latest pair of Smith and Jones, and that was before the email began flashing on his screen.

To: '*Classified*'
From: US Secretary of Offence/Defence

Subject: Religious Tolerance

The President would like to reassure the people of Afghanistan that as a mark of respect for the Islamic faith, all food parcels dropped during the month of Ramadan will contain no food, or drink.

'Smith, get me Agent White!' General Martin bawled from behind his laptop. 'I want his ass in Sost. Yesterday!'

Both new lieutenants were squeezed behind a small table at the back of the cabin. The office's other furniture, now pushed to one side, was piled high with pizza boxes.

'We can't find White, Sir. He seems to have disappeared.' Smith ducked as another box of mozzarella, jalapeno, and slightly-putrefied ham came hurtling past his ear.

On the first day following the evacuation of the Pentagon, with the staff canteen temporarily closed, General Martin had decided to treat himself to pizza. The Diablo Supreme duly arrived, but there, scattered prominently amongst the pepperoni and the chillies, were chunks of **PINEAPPLE!** Plain as the silver hairs on his head. Big Tony, of course, denied all knowledge:

'Look pal, don't hustle a hustler. If I had a dime for every time one of you army boys complained about your toppings. You ordered it, we delivered it, you pay for it!'

Once General Clark Mortimer Martin III's full identity was revealed, no-longer-quite-so-Big Tony couldn't backtrack fast enough, and, every day since, a steady stream of savoury-only pizzas had been delivered fresh to the Portakabin door. But it was too late: The Chief had decided to make Tony an offer he couldn't refuse.

'Wrong answer, Smith!' The Chief bawled, swatting a rogue fly that had inadvertently begun nibbling a piece of moulding tomato. 'Jones, who else we got down there?'

The two underlings began furiously searching every database they could find.

'I'm waiting,' The Chief threatened. 'Who's spare?'

'No one, Sir,' Jones reluctantly admitted.

'No one?' General Martin yelled. 'I command four and a half thousand men.'

It looks like Counter Intelligence has an Agent Brown in the vicinity, Sir.'

The Chief didn't trust those cowboys over at Counter. Where were his agents?

'With The Northern Alliance, Sir, waiting for the big push.'

General Martin's blood was boiling. He had given orders to push a week ago.

'It's not our fault,' Jones whimpered. 'We're waiting for airborne, Sir.'

The Chief, rising to his feet, gave Jones a hard stare.

'Well, where the hell are airborne?'

'At base, Sir.'

'So send them out! Christ, if you dumbasses don't smarten up, you'll be selling hotdogs outside Yankee Stadium faster than you can say ketchup.'

The Chief launched another missile.

'They won't fly, Sir.' Jones dodged.

'Won't fly?' General Martin bellowed. 'If they are given an order, they'll do anything they're damn well told.'

'They're refusing, Sir. They say post 9/11 flying's too dangerous.'

Both juniors flinched as The Chief picked up yet another projectile.

'That's Strike One, gentlemen.' General Martin slammed the cardboard box on top of his one remaining filing cabinet

'The team in Tajikistan?' Smith secretly mouthed to his colleague. 'With the death squads.'

'Skiing trip in Kyrgyzstan,' Jones whispered back. 'No radio contact for days.'

General Martin swiped his right paw across the desk, sending a considerable number of Desk-Tidy's rolling across the Portakabin floor. He sought inspiration from his reflection in the varnished wood. As he stared, he felt the warmth of what he could only take to be the Lord's light drawing him up to the heavens.

'Get me Benny Franklin!'

'Who, Sir?' Smith and Jones looked at each other, but drew blanks.

'*Who, Sir?*' The Chief mocked, before raising his voice to a roar. 'Only the finest agent we ever had! That's who!'

General Martin glared at each of them with equal contempt.

'The man who single-handedly opened the road to Nicaragua in '82. That's who! Assassinated Allende, Khomeini and Lennon. That's who.' Martin was on a roll. 'The most decorated undercover officer we've ever had in any theatre of war. Including 'Nam,' he purred.

Jones was wrestling with his computer's hard drive, begging it not to crash; Smith was sifting through the large, chocolate-brown 'F' dossier.

'Got it, Sir!' Smith clutched his prize. 'Benjamin Sherman Franklin, born Boris Siegfried Frentzen, Leipzig, 1944.'

Jones gave Smith a look of pure green.

'Escaped East Germany via Poland in '61. Abandoned mother after she broke leg jumping the Warsaw-Gdansk express.' Smith celebrated.

'That's the man. No job too big for BS.'

'Looks like Grenada was his last action, Sir.' Jones' search engine had finally caught up. 'Left the army with rank of Captain in '84 – honourable discharge – personally presented by the President. Currently living just outside Pawtucket.' Finally, it was his turn to gloat.

'So what are you waiting for? Get him on a plane. Immediately.'

General Martin dismissed his underlings to their adjoining cabin and sank back into his treasured leather armchair. For the first time in a long time he could fantasise about a return to unlimited offence/defence budgets. He was interrupted after only ten minutes by a call from Jones.

'We've found him, Sir.'

'I didn't tell you to phone me when you found him, I told you to tell him to phone me, when he was at JFK.'

'Well, that's it, Sir. That's where we found him: JFK. And he's on the other line.'

'You see, Jones? That's the sort of initiative real soldiers take. Put him through.'

Jones did as he was told.

'Benny!'

'Good afternoon, major-general.'

'Straight "General" now, thank you, Franklin.' General Martin straightened his tie. 'Swell to hear you're still going strong. How's Nancy?'

'Oh, you know her, Sir. Still making the best fried chicken north of Dixie,' Benny schmoozed.

'Good to hear, good to hear. Now I don't know how much Jones has told you, but I need a favour.'

'Well, Sir, I'd love to, but I'm kinda in the middle of doing the government of Equatorial Guinea a few favours, Sir. Right at the minute.'

'Soldier!' General Martin clenched fists and buttocks. 'This is your country calling you. And that's an order.'

'Yes, Sir!' Captain Franklin barked back.

'Excellent.'

The Chief collected his thoughts. 'The situation is this: I know those dumb kids out in the field aren't exactly kickin' much Afghani ass just yet, but trust me, we'll bomb every last inch of that overgrown sand bunker if we have to. Al Qaeda will soon be strictly past tense. Taliban, too, if we play it right. The only chance they've got is if they start running. So our job is to make sure there's nowhere to run to. Understand?'

Franklin understood.

'If we don't, I'm going to be the one who takes the rap. And you know how I hate taking the rap.'

'Yes, Sir!'

'Good. I'm pretty sure no one's gonna touch Osama with a ten-foot pole covered in horse shit, but there's one place which could screw everything up: the Wakhan Corridor.'

'Never heard of it, Sir.'

'A critical strip of territory,' Jones prompted from his end of the line, 'ceded to the Afghan Shah in the nineteenth century, to ensure the colonising British and Russian Empires never touched.'

'Still never heard of it.'

'It's the semi-autonomous mountain province protruding from Afghanistan proper,' Jones clarified.

'A pin-prick on the map next to Talibanland to you and me, Benny.' The Chief knew what kind of language to use with men like Franklin.

'Right, Sir.'

'But a pin-prick surrounded by some of the most impregnable natural fortresses in the world. Just the sort of place Bin "La La" and his cronies might make a dash for.'

Benny had a good idea of what The Chief had in mind. 'And you want me to herd them into this here corridor, lock all the doors and go nuclear.'

'Unfortunately,' General Martin scratched his nose, 'no can do. The Chinese are claiming sphere of influence.'

Benny swore his disappointment. 'Any other options?'

'Well, at the eastern end of this corridor is a valley full of people refusing to recognise the Taliban's authority, and we've got a guy on the inside.' The Chief inscribed 'valley' next to 'Xidakistan' on his blue folder. 'If we can swing some sort of independence deal for that there valley, our man says these guys are ours.'

'Slash and burn, Sir?'

'Not this time, Benny. Should be able to parley it out round the table. I've got The President standing by; just as soon we give the signal.'

'The United Nations standing by, Sir,' Jones butted in.

'Strike Two, Jones,' General Martin boomed.

'Sir, the UN-'

'Shut the hell up, or get the hell off the line.'

Jones didn't risk further comment.

'As I was saying,' General Martin coughed. 'The President will grant independence, but only in return for complete control over the newly created republic's defence strategy, and foreign policy. That, soldier, is your mission.'

'Message understood, Sir.' Benny scanned the check-in lounge to make sure no one was eavesdropping.

'I knew we could rely on you, Agent Franklin. I'm afraid we haven't got much time on this one, so you'll have to come up with your own mission name.'

'Thank you, Sir. A great honour, Sir.' Mission names were the Holy Grail to men like Franklin.

'In the meantime our man on the ground is under strict instructions to let nobody in, nobody out. Not until you're done.'

'Thank you, Sir.'

'I'm giving you triple A clearance on this one, Benny.' Agent Franklin thanked The Chief again. 'Just so long as you complete your mission by November sixteenth.'

'In time for Ramadan,' Jones piped up. 'Good idea, Sir.'

'What?'

'November sixteenth, Sir,' Jones tried again. 'The first day of Ramadan.'

'That's it, Jones, Strike Three. Clear your desk.'

'But, Sir, it's the most important festival in the Muslim calendar. Their holy month.'

'Tell Head of Staff to send up your replacement.'

'Any particular reason for the sixteenth, Sir?' Benny ventured, after a suitable pause. 'It gives me less than a month.'

'No choice, soldier.' The Chief mopped sweat from his brow. 'I've got my mother-in-law coming on the seventeenth for ten days of hell, otherwise known as Thanksgiving.'

'With you one hundred percent, Sir.'

'Good man, Benny, good man.' The Chief's voice dropped to a whisper. 'And remember, if we play this right, Ben, we'll keep those Democrats out of the White House for a generation.'

'Yes, Sir, General, Sir. And amen to that.'

'Amen, indeed.' It was time to wrap things up. 'Officially, of course, you don't exist, so you'll also need a code name. I think I can leave that in your capable hands.'

'Yes, Sir!' Benny's brain was whooping.

'Is that advisable, Sir?' A small voice interjected. 'The Special Intelligence Training Handbook states that "under no circumstances should an agent be allowed to choose his or her code name".'

'*His or HER?*' Benny sniggered to himself. '*Yeah, like that'll ever happen.*'

'Tell me that's not you again, Jones!' General Martin exploded.

'It's Smith, Sir.'

'Smith? Let me decide what's advisable.' The Chief allowed a pregnant pause. 'Strike Three!'

'But General Martin.'

'But nothing.' The Chief was in no mood. He ordered Smith to fill Benny in on the rest of the details, show the new Jones to his desk, and buy a one-way ticket to The House That Ruth Built. General Martin hadn't felt so good for a long time.

'*Choosing my own code name.*' Benny gave himself a pat on the back. '*Wait 'til I tell Nancy.*'

'You still there, Benny?'

'Yes, Sir!'

The Chief had lost track of his thoughts. 'Good luck'.

'Thank you, Sir. One question, Sir.' Benny thought it wise to ask.

'Shoot.'

'Any sign of the Reds on this one, Sir?' In Benny's mind the Chinese didn't count as real 'Reds'.

'Not as yet.' General Martin took a deep breath to underline the gravity of the situation. 'In fact, Moscow is saying it might even be able to assist on this one.' General Martin began picking up his Desk-Tidy's and returning them to their proper positions. To the millimetre. 'But I think we've both been in this game long enough, soldier, to know what to say to that.'

'You betcha, Sir.' Benny saw his flight being called on the big screens. 'Over and out.'

The Chief went to return his telephone to its receiver but jerked it back to his ear at the last moment.

'Smith?'

'Yes, Sir?' '*Of course,*' Smith felt the relief flood through his body, '*The Chief had only been joking.*'

'On your way out, tell the Oval Office we'll be needing an ambassador for Xidakistan. Your replacement can do the rest.'

*   *   *

At higher altitudes, the first snows had fallen since Graham and Floyd's last trip, so progress in the Land Rovers was cold and slow. Yet their welcome in Gakuch and Darkot was warm, even without Zul to smooth the way. Perhaps, Graham thought, with winter approaching this was the 'mountain spirit' he had heard so much about. However, as the porters translated more of the fireside chit-chats, it became evident less altruistic forces were at work. The villagers were anxious to form any new alliances they could, ahead of the predicted power vacuum that would envelope the region as it descended into war. No one, it seemed, was confident just how this latest-in-a-long-line of conflicts would manifest itself, and Pinks' whisky was welcomed with gusto.

The Darkot and Baroghil passes were made more arduous by the deeper snow, but by the time they reached the sentry gate downstream of Gombaz, Graham was quietly satisfied with the time they had made up. Even the burly pip-spitting Tajik guard seemed pleased to see them. Word had preceded them, and a number of local heads poked out to inspect their arrival into the village proper. The children seemed particularly impressed with Queen Bea's shiny bicycle.

Unlike Gilgit and Karimabad, the houses here were built so close together the streets were almost alleys. The porters led them through to the main square, and a largish concrete structure. Inside were the rudiments of a café, on the ground floor, and a communal sleeping area above.

That Zulfiquaar wasn't there to meet them didn't bode well, and matters were made worse by the fact that no one in the hostelry spoke a language that any of the four men understood. As they had been on light rations thus far, they hungrily decided to cheer themselves up with a second lunch for the day. Eventually, after a dramatic mime by Miko, salt tea, curds, cream and hard bread were served, quite a spread by Gumbaz standards.

Graham and Floyd had stopped over in some pretty hairy frontier towns in their day but it was soon obvious Gombaz was in a class of its own. Not only did every male over the age of eight sport an obligatory Kalashnikov, three quarters of the surrounding shops appeared to be some sort of arms-race Cash and Carry. Grenades and dynamite sticks were strung up on the doors like onions and garlic. Crates with Chinese, Russian, Arabic or Farsi lettering were piled high behind each shopkeeper, and every wooden palette had a different red or black stamp, declaring a range of dangers, explosives or poisonous gas.

As they had made their way outside for an evening stroll, the four newcomers received surly looks not only from local Afghans and Tajiks, but also a number of Uzbeks in their sombre red-striped robes and black-and-white box hats. Then there were the yellow-skinned Kyrgyz with their flatter, Mongolian-like features, sporting white felt caps, which Graham couldn't help think made them look like extras from Robin Hood. Not forgetting the Turkmen, whose shaggy black and brown hats were like great frizzy balls of Astrakhan wool scooped onto their heads. Below the waist there was greater uniformity all round with lots of long, soft-leather boots coming up high on short, stumpy legs.

Every group had its own off-road vehicle parked opposite. Most, at first glance, looked like standard, flat-backed Toyota Hi-Luxes, but each one was being carefully drilled, sawn and extended, until it could securely support the tripod of metal piping being welded onto its rear platform. As each stage of the elementary production line was complete, the battle-stations were rolled forward to the next conveyor belt of self-taught engineers. The final team re-checked the previous work, made slight adjustments, and whistled for their colleagues inside to unveil the part they'd all been waiting for. To Miko and Vanh it just looked like another long metal tube, if perhaps fatter than most, but to Floyd and Graham it was unmistakably a Russian 2B9 Vasilek mortar. The next Hi-Lux up was fitted with the same, and a third, but the final two were each given Navarone-sized machine guns, which, by means of a ball and socket joint, could cover a full three-hundred and sixty degrees.

Night fell quickly and as the last of the storekeepers shut up shop there was still no sign of Zulfiquaar. Worse, the porters had disappeared to find horses, leaving the four men feeling distinctly alone. Most of their valuables were safe in Gilgit, but as they turned in for the night, each one double-checked his passport and money-belt. These were bound to their bodies in cat's-cradle-like arrangements, designed to deter the most determined of pickpockets, yet stop short of garrotting the wearer during the night. Suddenly the spectre of conflict seemed very real, and the TV and Radio reports all too close for comfort. This wasn't simulated exercises, it was war. Cold, dirty, stomach-cramping battle, and the lottery of life and death that went with it. That night, for the first time in a long time, Vanh dreamt of his brother, Ko. He hadn't survived the family's escape from Vietnam, in search of the 'Land of the Free'.

They awoke in the morning to near silence and a pale, yellow-grey cotton wool kind of light. An old woman brought them each a washbowl of tepid water and a Chinese-army-surplus-mug of orange tea. Pinks, refusing to relinquish the warmth of his sleeping bag, was about to complain about the temperature of his nose for a second time, when the door opened, and the friendly face they had been praying for appeared.

'Good day, gentlemen.' Zul was dressed in a thick woollen overcoat, a striped scarf large enough to be a poncho, a sleek grey fur hat, which swamped his wizened head, and fur moon-boots the size of waste paper baskets. 'And how are we this fine morning?' He clapped his sheepskin gloves together in appreciation of the new day.

'Zulfiquaar!'

The sense of relief in the room was palpable.

'Where did you spring from?' Pinks spouted from the mouth-hole of his mummy.

'I arrived late last night but was told you had already retired.' Zul was all smiles.

Graham thought this a bit odd but let it pass.

'We have the bike.' Vanh dried his face. 'Bright pink.'

'Excellent, excellent.' Zul took a fidgety puff of his inhaler.

'Is that snow?' Miko inquired of Zul as he shook off his hat and brushed it down.

'Yes, I'm afraid so.' Zul stopped looking quite so cheery, as Graham leaned over to open the wooden shutters. Cloaked in sheepskins, they had proved surprisingly effective against the night's wind and cold. Outside, the view was a moving snowstorm of dirty white.

'This isn't going to…?' Graham was already panicking.

Zul shifted from one foot to the other

'No. No!' Pinks' morning cough was, if anything, made worse by having exhausted his meagre supply of cigars two days back. It sounded as though catarrh that hadn't shifted for twenty years was being wrenched back from the dead. 'No way!'

'Zul, we must get up to The Valley.' Graham was trying to remain calm but sounded as desperate as Floyd. 'We need to be there for the wedding.'

Zulfiquaar looked increasingly forlorn.

Pinks ripped himself out of his sleeping sack and began marching around the room, oblivious to the others' staring at his pink double-layered long-johns, and burgundy bed socks.

'Listen to me, Zul. I've paid a lot of money to get into that valley. Twice. And this time you're damn well going to take me.'

Zul grimaced, and racked his brains for something to counter the increasing hostility. He assured them that if they let him explain there would be nothing to worry about, but no one looked convinced. He retreated to a rickety chair by the fireplace and the group gathered round.

'Owing to circumstances beyond my control,' Zulfiquaar was attempting something he had heard described as sangfroid, but he could feel the jitters bouncing on his diaphragm, 'no one will be able to enter The Valley until the weather improves. And then only after King Tah has ordered the "Clearing of the First Snow".'

Silence.

'There will be no clearing for at least a week,' he clarified.

'So we wait.' Pinks crossed his arms and humphed.

'What about the wedding?' Graham pressed. It was supposed to be the day after next.

'I'm afraid you are going to miss it.' Zul's eyes flicked warily from one inquisitor to the next.

'OK, forget the wedding,' Floyd countered. 'Probably would've been a dud anyhow.' Time to think on his feet. 'We go up a week late, and call it a second honeymoon.' For once Graham approved of Floyd's ingenuity.

'But where will you stay while you wait?' Zul's voice contained more nervousness than concern.

'Right here.' Pinks stamped.

'I'm not sure that will be possible without me.'

Graham stiffened. 'Why? Where are you going?'

'I have to return for the wedding.'

'Hang on. You just said The Valley was blocked off.'

Zulfiquaar began searching the room for inspiration, stood up, took a blast on his inhaler, sat down again, then cracked. He threw himself at Graham and Floyd's feet.

'I'm sorry, Mr Graham. I'm sorry, Mr Floyd,' he began to wail. 'I didn't mean to trick you, truly I didn't, but the wedding takes place the day after tomorrow and you're not allowed to go. No one is. I wanted to take you there, but they won't let me.'

Floyd's fist began to clench.

'Please, please, forgive me,' Zul blubbed.

Graham checked Pinks' raised arm.

'I don't know what to do anymore.' Mr Butt grasped at Floyd's leg. Scalding tears were pouring down his cheeks and glistening off the brighter grey hairs in his moustache. Floyd could only look away in embarrassment.

'Hey, come on, Zul.' Graham bent down and hugged his arm around Zulfiquaar's shoulders, before helping him back to his seat. 'It can't be that bad,' he encouraged. 'King Tah will let us up there before too long.'

Zul strained himself to stop snivelling. After several short gasps, he began: 'There is no way you can go to The Valley.'

'The snow's gotta stop sometime, Zuley.'

'It will stop,' Zul admitted. 'Maybe even today.'

'So where's the problem?' Pinks wasn't ready to be quite so accommodating.

'Snow or no snow, I am under strict instructions not to let anyone into The Valley until after independence has been granted. On pain of schwuck.' Zul repeated the slicing of his throat action from the day of their first meeting. Fear was embedded in his face. 'You cannot enter. They won't let you.'

'Who won't?' Miko tried.

Graham looked up and indicated it was pointless to pursue this line of enquiry. 'It's alright,' he reassured Zul. 'It's all alright. Let's start at the beginning and go through exactly what they've told you. Then we'll see what we can salvage from the situation.'

General Martin's orders had arrived courtesy of the Xidaki herdsman, this time returning yaks to The Valley for the winter. Zul's rendition was not the most coherent but it did the job. Floyd was furious, but Graham saw grounds for quiet optimism.

'When exactly will the big snows come, Zul? The ones that shut off The Valley for good?'

'They say in about two to three weeks, Mr Graham.'

Graham did some quick calculations. As long as Zul could bring the king down to Sost in the next week or so, what with independence all but guaranteed, that would still leave him enough time to race up to The Valley, win The Game (Graham glanced guiltily at Floyd), finish the book, and get out.

'OK, guys.' Graham crouched down, drew them all in close, and explained that he had a proposal. 'Listen up.'

Pinks didn't like it, whatever it was going to be.

'Zulfiquaar returns to The Valley with the bike, OK?' One nod. 'Zulfiquaar celebrates the wedding with the king and his new queen.' Two nods. 'Zulfiquaar suggests the happy couple make a trip to Sost to receive one final present from their "Royal Cousins".' The nods stopped. Graham spelt it out. 'The Independence Treaty! And we and the other delegations are the royal cousins!' Tentative nods returned. 'Zulfiquaar then suggests that, as a token of his gratitude for the bikes, the king should issue a limited number of invitations for his cousins to visit The Valley before the snows arrive. Four to be precise, one for each of us. But none for Phil or Bonnie.' Suddenly nods were breaking out all round. 'We clean up, and Zul gets to keep his authorities happy.'

Despite repeated complaints from Floyd as to the expense of another wasted journey, the motion was passed.

*   *   *

Bonnie was loathed to spend so much time with Phil but with the others away, she had little choice. Phil didn't like it either, but drew comfort from the fact that it opened up plenty of opportunities for secondary scheming. Bonnie, not for the first time, was relying on her feminine wiles, Phil on serendipity, which, he wasn't shy to say, had rarely let him down in the past.

By the seventh day, however, both had become tired of their increasingly stale 'mates', so Bonnie discreetly hired 'some wheels' through her hotel, and took off to get some visuals for her follow up piece in The Traveler (there was a particularly dramatic shot she wanted, of a 4x4 driving over a rickety rope bridge on the Deosai Plains). Phil, guessing that Bonnie was going to try something, paid Little Mo to keep his ear to the ground. When word got back to the K2 Phil set out to track Bonnie incognito, in Naveed's van. It was fortunate for Bonnie that he did, because her 'wheels' broke down before she even reached the bridge, and she was forced to beg for a lift home.

They drove back to town in stony silence, which would have continued all the way to the K2 but for a half-familiar figure silhouetted at the window.

'Slow down.' Bonnie reached for the steering wheel. 'Pull over before he sees us.'

Resting against the café steps was a battered old moped, which earlier had puttered its way to a tired halt on the gravel. The figure had his back to the window now. Phil hopped down from the van and cautiously crept closer, but all he could see for sure was a head of long, straggly hair.

'Is it him?'

'I can't tell from here,' Phil whispered. Night was falling and the lights in the café were dim.

The man turned. If it was who they thought it was, he should have been wearing a black leatherjacket, stonewashed jeans, white T-shirt, and Police sunglasses, preferably sitting on a Harley Davidson – Brick Lane's answer to The Wild One (minus the leather cap). This newcomer was robed in a full-on kaftan.

Phil was almost at the steps. 'It does look like Mannie. Sort of.'

Mannie caught sight of them through the glass, and gave a solemn wave.

Phil hesitantly responded, but Bonnie marched back over to Naveed's van, slammed herself in, and yelled through the passenger window: 'I'm going back to my hotel, Kelly. Tell him if he so much as breathes on me, I'll twist his balls so hard they'll look like spaghetti.'

Young Mohammed appeared from nowhere, ready to deliver Bonnie to her destination. Phil took a deep breath, before entering the café.

'Salam Alaykum.'

Phil stopped in his tracks. Mannie had been fired by more tabloid editors than Phil could remember, and was reduced to winging it on a counterfeit Associated Press pass, but he never let it curb his style. Where was the *'Crazy, me old China. Wazzup?'*?

'Mannie? You alright?'

Mannie nodded.

'What's with the dress?' Phil took a step forward.

'This?' Mannie fingered his grey smock. 'Don't you read the news?'

'Not if you've written it.'

'The time for humour is over, brother.' Mannie picked at a loose thread. 'The revolution has started.'

'What The Revolution of Daggy Dress-ups?'

Mannie shook his head in disappointment. 'The revolution of The Base. Al Qaeda, brother. The War on Terror.'

Again 'brother'. Back in London it had always been 'bro'.

'I'm on my way to join the jihadis.'

'You're a Sikh!' Phil looked at Mannie in disbelief.

'Oppression knows no creed.'

'Jesus, Mannie.'

'Ali. The name's Ali now. Ali Mohammed. If The Devil is declaring a 'Crusade', we must join together, rise up and stand as one.'

'You're kiddin'?'

'No, Phil. It doesn't matter if you're Sikh, Muslim, or Christian. As a believer, it's our duty to protect the weak and the downtrodden. To provide a voice for the disenfranchised. If we don't fight The Holy War, who will?'

'Strewth.'

'Let the scales fall from your eyes, brother. First Iraq, now Afghanistan. Where next? Iran? Egypt? Australia? All that is necessary for evil to triumph is that good men do nothing.'

Crazy didn't know where to look. Maybe he should go out and come back in again. 'Naveed? What's cooking for dinner?'

'Curry.'

'Hallelujah! Thought for a minute I'd been zapped into a parallel universe.'

'No!' Mannie stabbed his finger. Phil nearly fell off his seat. 'The world as we know it, that's the parallel universe. That's the mirage. Conjured by the suits we never see, the invisible powers behind the power. They're the ones keeping us all in chains.' Mannie looked at the clock on the wall. 'Their capitalism, not religion, that's the opium of the people.' He bent his head and started to count out a string of wooden beads with his thumb, intoning what sounded like prayers into a pocket-sized Koran.

Phil lit a cigarette. He looked Mannie over, from head to toe, and back again.

'You're serious?

Mannie continued with his supplications.

'Look, mate, I hate the Yanks as much as the next man, but Al Qaeda? They've not just got a few roos loose in the top paddock, they're bloody crackpots. Bin Laden's no more got the answer than me or you.' Phil stubbed one cigarette out and lit another.

'What are you going to achieve driving into some army convoy, and blowing yourself up?'

Mannie fell silent.

'Do you think Bin "Laid Off" would do the same for you?'

The low humming began again.

'I need a drink.'

203

'Thought you'd never bloody ask!' Mannie's head suddenly bounced up from his lap, his face grinning ear to ear. He tossed the book and the beads into Phil's lap and pulled his hair back into a ponytail. 'Not bad, eh?'

'Strewth. You nearly had me there.'

'Thanks, man.'

'I had visions of you practising suicide-bombs in a Tora Bora training camp.'

'But that's what I am doing. As Ali Mohammed. I'm going undercover.'

'You don't know anything about Islam.'

'Alright, keep your voice down.' Mannie gave the café a quick once-over but they were the only customers. 'I'm a convert, aren't I? There're so many boys from The Lane coming over, what's another one?'

Phil took a long draw on his cigarette. 'Do they all look like pricks?'

'You can talk!' Mannie gestured towards the embroidered-silk Komodo dragon motif Phil had picked out that morning.

'Pull your head in. The girls love it.' The number of women Phil had painstakingly laid the groundwork for, only to have the Brick Lane Bad Boy swoop in and steal, made him lie awake at night.

'Don't tell me you're getting any.' Mannie fell back into the sofa and kicked off his sandals.

What really annoyed Phil was the way everyone always said they were so alike. Ever since they first started bumping into each other during Phil's 'gap year'.

'Shake a leg, then. I'm parched.'

Phil reluctantly produced the last of his supplies from his bag.

'Uncle!' Mannie clicked his fingers towards Naveed. 'Speciality of the house. With a Pepsi Max, ice cold.'

Naveed disappeared into the kitchen, and emerged bearing the leftovers of what he had had for lunch. Beside it on the tray was the only can of local cola he could find not in the fridge.

'Very sorry, Sir. No ice.'

'Typical. OK, run a tab for me. I'll pay you when I leave.'

'Sorry, Sir. Please not ask by credit as refusal often defends.' Naveed did his very best 'poor-Pakistani-who-can't-speak-English-properly' routine, pointing to his equally-grammatically-challenged notices.

'Fuck, Crazy, what sort of place have you got here?' Mannie, forced to rummage in his pockets, pulled out a wad of tatty notes. As always they were not enough. He gave Phil 'the look'.

'What's in it for me?'

'Do me a Quaver,' Mannie scowled. 'I'm always lending you money.'

Phil sidestepped this wishful thinking, demanding a six-pack of beer.

'In your dreams. Where's the bank?'

Phil took great delight in informing The Bad Boy that there wasn't one.

'You're having a Tufnell.' Mannie's mockney accent was already beginning to grate.

'Nope.'

Naveed came forward to indicate that he had a cousin who owned a carpet shop, and that, for a small fee, cash advances could be obtained on certain credit cards, by certain people.

'Yeah right, Unc. Do I look like I came in on the last banana boat?'

Naveed deemed it judicious not to reply.

'Come on, Crazy. Spot me a fifty at least.' Mannie thought he might have more success appealing to Phil's native tongue. 'Fair go!'

Phil laid out the various 'go's whereby he would lend Mannie enough money to cover his board and lodgings for the night. Each one involved alcohol, and Mannie was left with little choice but to 'go fetch' the emergency bottle of Jack Daniels he had hidden under the pillion seat of his scooter.

He surreptitiously poured the first fingers into the glasses of warm cola.

'So where were we?' Mannie took a swig. 'Me? Good. I tell you, Crazy, there are some big, juicy stories over there, all just waiting to be scooped.'

Mannie began tucking into his food and, in between spoonfuls, outlined the 'undercover' plan. Phil helped himself to more JD, with just enough mmms and ahhs as was necessary.

'So how you are going to get over to Afghanistan?' Phil was onto his fourth pour and starting to feel a little merrier. 'Sneak in dressed as a camel?' he burped. 'A camel with no money?'

Mannie pulled himself up and leaned closer to Phil. 'This is the deal, but you gotta swear it goes no further.'

'Scout's honour.'

'I met this guy in 'Pindi, and he's set me up with a Taliban handler. Five big ones, and they've guaranteed safe passage across the border. One of the old salt paths over the Kush.'

'Five K? Where did you get that kind of money?'

'I borrowed it.' Mannie couldn't admit to Phil that he had hocked the Harley.

'This guy you met.' Phil screwed up his nose. 'How d'ya know he's on the level?'

'He works for my Auntie Basran. He's legit.' Mannie had been staying with Auntie Basran to save on hotel bills.

'Still doesn't explain what you're doing in Gilgit, ye boofhead. You're nearly two hundred miles from the border! Heading north.' Phil's right arm pointed the same way Mannie's ride was facing. 'Kabul's that a way!' Phil's left arm unfolded westwards. He looked like a very imaginatively dressed traffic policeman.

'I'm meeting the handler, right?' Mannie reached for his bottle, but both Phil's arms were too quick.

'Steady,' Phil growled. His eyes motioned towards Mannie's measly wad of notes on the table. 'Unless, of course, you've got another bottle.'

Mannie had little option but to pour small. And share.

'That's the way.' Phil signalled politely to Naveed, and asked if he could bring whichever soft drink was most convenient. He was rewarded with an ice-cold Pepsi Max. Mannie did a double-take, but couldn't quite put the two and twos together.

'So where's this handler then?'

'Just north of here, in some Khunda Junta district or other.' Mannie spoke Punjabi well enough, but his Urdu was almost non-existent.

'And what's this guy's name?'

'Mr Khan.' Food finished, Mannie started massaging his stomach.

Phil said nothing as he poured himself a large double, but once a good glug was safely down the hatch, he let fly. 'You dumbass dingo!'

'What?'

'How many Mr Khan's do you think there are in Pakistan?'

'We're not talking about Pakistan, you dumbass dingo, we're talking Khunda Junta district.'

Phil sneered and laid ten cents to the dollar Mannie didn't even know where Kunda-Junda-wherever was.

'Get lost. You don't know noffink.'

'Suit yourself.' Phil sipped some more.

Mannie chewed. Then started inspecting his fingernails. Eventually he conceded defeat.

'Oh, Naveed!' As Phil put his drink to one side, Naveed appeared from behind the blanket. 'I wonder if you would be so kind as to assist my good friend here.' Phil's accent was all afternoon tea and cucumber sandwiches. 'He's looking for a Mr Khan, in the Khunda Junta district. I'm not sure if that is the correct pronunciation.'

'Khuda Janta?' Naveed paused. 'I'm afraid, Mr Philip, that would be a very difficult task indeed.'

'And why would that be, Navo?' Phil grinned. 'Khuda Janta doesn't, by any chance, mean "arse-end-of-nowhere", in whatchamacallit?'

The proprietor gave a small bow, turned on his heel and retired into the kitchen.

'The cheating bastard.' Mannie kicked a chair in disgust.

'As my old mate, Robbo, would say: you're up Jacob's Creek without a corkscrew.' The Australian wine industry's switch to screwcaps had had little impact on Robbo's repertoire. 'Nice try though, Mannie.'

'I'm not trying, right?' Mannie would have sprung to his feet but they were hurting from where his sandals had started to rub. Instead, he ripped the hairband from his ponytail and let his mane loose over his shoulders. 'I'm going.'

'Don't forget to send a postcard.'

'Look, The Bun is offering ten big ones for the first inside-story from the jihadi camps, and those notes have got my name all over them.'

'Let's pretend for a moment that that's true, you're still heading in the wrong direction, you gumnut. You want to get yourself over to Chitral. Or Peshawar.' Phil didn't want to stop drinking just yet. 'Once we've finished this.'

'You reckon?'

'Take a look.' Phil pointed to a large map on the wall, which Mannie unhooked and laid on the main table. With his finger he began tracing the route. As he did so, Phil helped itself to some more JD.

'Right, yeah, I see what you mean.' Mannie patted Phil on the back, trying to regain some of his self-composure. 'Then it's just a hop, skip and I'm in. Nice one, Crazy.'

Mannie went to clink his glass into Phil's, but pulled back at the last minute. 'Hang on,' he frowned. 'If it's so-bleeding-obvious, why aren't you doing it?' To spite the old man, Phil was known to pen the occasional piece of 'colour' when an editor was short.

'Me? You're kidding. Nothing to do with the war.' Phil supped. 'I'm here for something completely different.'

Mannie was all ears. 'Keep talking.'

'Keep pouring.'

Phil's glass filled up again.

'Xidakistan. But that's all I'm telling.'

'Xidakky-what? You're making it up.' Mannie grabbed both of Phil's manbreasts, and gave them a good yank. 'Why you really up here?'

Phil tried to push his aggressor away but no amount of AFL training was going to get him out of this double-nipple-with-a-twist manoeuvre. 'It's true,' he yelped. 'It's a new country. No one's been there before. That's why you haven't heard of it.'

'Do I look like a twat?' Mannie's face was in Phil's ear.

Phil's nipples warned him not to answer. But suggested he did need to do something, quite sharpish. With blood vessels on the brink of bursting, Mannie relented.

'Show me on the map.' Mannie let go with one hand, and pushed Phil's face onto the table.

Phil could hardly get his words out. 'It isn't on the map, yet. That's the whole point.'

'Look, mate.' Mannie was twisting again. 'I saw Nasty Bitch out there with you before. You two are onto a story, and I know it.'

Before Mannie could elaborate, the café door crashed open, embedding itself on the two cast-iron brackets still triumphantly supporting Naveed's new industrial-sized bell.

'Stop that. Immediately!' Bonnie was not normally one to complain if Phil was being tortured, but these were strange times. Driving up to her hotel, she had noticed a new arrival wiping what looked like motor oil off his breeches, and had ordered Mohammed back to the café.

'I mean it, Singh.' Bonnie spat the name out like poison.

'Nasty B-' Mannie bit his lip. 'This has got nothing to do with you, Bonnie.'

'No?' Bonnie scowled. 'Then why were there two of you on that contraption down there when it arrived.'

'Says who?'

'Says my female intuition. Put Kelly down and start talking.'

'Back off, sister. I'm not one of your namby-pamby "Yes Men".' Mannie twisted again, and Phil's face went two shades redder.

'I'm not asking twice.'

Mannie swung Phil round to use him as a human shield. 'If you tell me more about this Xidakistan story, maybe I'll be willing to negotiate.'

'Naveed!' Bonnie's scream made Mannie jump, and Phil scuttled free. Naveed appeared.

Bonnie returned to diplomacy. 'Thank you, Naveed. Some green tea would be wonderful.'

'I haven't told him anything, Bonnie. I swear.'

Bonnie assured Phil that it didn't matter in the slightest, and produced a packet of chewing gum. 'There's nothing to tell.'

Mannie warily took the stick he was offered. 'So how come a Special Intelligence geezer just pay me five hundred smackers to hightail his ass up here for some independence conference?'

The tears that had been welling in Phil's ducts burst their banks. 'You dirty bludger.' Now his nipples were bleeding. 'I knew it. I knew you had money.'

Mannie was fully focused on Bonnie. 'Is this something to do with that Traveler competition I've been hearing about?'

'The Alphabet Game?'

'Yeah, The Alphabet Game, that's it.' Snippets were popping up everywhere. 'Presidential endorsement, not a bad angle.' One thing Mannie could never be faulted on was his bloodhound's nose for a story. 'Getting many inches?'

'Front page of the New York Times.' Bonnie couldn't resist.

'Maybe I'll come back here after Kabul.' Mannie had taken to pronouncing the city's name 'K-Bull'. 'And get myself another scoop.' His mind was off in a flash. 'Wait a minute. The Bun's gonna have its 'Babes Brigade' here next week. I could get them to do the conference, as part of their Bust Some Ass tour.'

Bonnie winced. 'What do you know about the conference?'

'I know enough.' Mannie chewed hard. 'Spice could do her "Happy Birthday, Mr President" number.' He was in the zone. 'This could be massive.'

'The conference, dickbrain.'

'What's it worth?'

'What are your balls worth?' Bonnie rose to her full five-foot-eight-inches-with-heels. The last time they had been in this position, Mannie had ended up with a stiletto-shaped crack in his ribs and a twelve-month boycott from all the broadsheets.

Mannie crumbled. 'Alright. The guy said it was going to be in a place called Sost, and that he was hoping to get there tonight.'

'You see, that wasn't so hard, was it?' Bonnie's attention was suddenly drawn to Mannie's chin. 'What's that?'

Mannie explained he was growing a jihadi beard. So far it consisted of three straggly hairs

'It's disgusting. Get it out of my sight.'

'I thought we were-'

'I said "Out"!'

'Don't be like that, Bonnie.'

Bonnie walked to the door, opened it and dangled the keys to Mannie's moped. 'Time to go.'

The Brick Lane Bad Boy frisked his pockets in disbelief. He had been done like a kipper. Resigning himself to the fact, Mannie decided to employ his only other skill.

'Please let me stay, Bonnie,' he grovelled. 'Pretty please. For tonight at least. The bike's got no lights, and it's getting dark.'

Bonnie chewed her gum, looked away with a bored sigh, and jangled the keys once more.

'The track over to Chitral is open. You'll be there by the morning,' Bonnie stopped chewing. 'You could be in Afghanistan the day after. I'm doing you a favour.'

Mannie's keys flew out onto the gravel by the moped, and Bonnie cooed in her bedside-nurse voice that it really was time to go. But he didn't budge.

'Move it!'

Mannie had his holdall over his shoulder and was away. Not even a 'ciao for now'. Phil's eyes remained glued to the half bottle of Jack D left behind.

Bonnie closed the door, strode over to the coffee table and informed Phil that their chance had finally come.

'How did you know he was going to Chitral?'

'Lucky guess.' Bonnie beckoned Phil closer. 'Floyd and the others are back.'

'But they will have only come from as far as Gakuch,' Phil reasoned. 'How do you know the rest of the road is open?' His mind was still picturing the Chitral route.

'I don't.' Bonnie shook Phil firmly by the shoulders, realised the problem and confiscated the whisky. 'Forget about Singh already.' Why did she always have morons on her team? 'Floyd and Graham are back!'

'Right oh.' Phil still couldn't see the connection.

'And Special Intelligence is in town for the conference.'

'Yeah.' Phil was back in his parallel universe. 'Actually, if that guy was looking to get up to Sost, he's probably left by now.'

Aaah!' Bonnie's fingers tightened round her scarf. 'In-De-Pen-Dence. Do I have to-?'

'Alright, Bonnie. Don't crack the shits.'

She twisted the silk around his knuckles. 'I've just received a message from Ross.'

Nothing.

'It's on. The Game. Don't you see?'

211

Phil may not have been Woop Woop's quickest opening bat but once he was on the board, he didn't need to mark his crease twice.

'Crikey.'

'Exactly. We know it's on, but Floyd and Graham know diddly. At last we've got an edge.'

'We've got an edge.' Phil was on his feet. 'Go on you good thing!' He gave Bonnie such a smack on the chops she forgot to slap him.

'So now what do we do?' Phil's genius had a tendency to be fleeting.

'Now?' Bonnie shook her head. 'Now we make our move.' Bonnie looked into Phil's eyes and checked he was following her. 'Don't worry, I've thought it all through.' Phil looked relieved. 'We pretend to go off on one of my photo-shoots, hook up with this conference guy in Sost, and before you can say "Floyd's a male-chauvinist pig", we're ace in the hole.'

In Bonnie's mind the first person plural would soon become singular, but she had decided to keep Phil close for now.

'So what are we waiting for?' Phil jumped up.

'No.' Bonnie was feeling sneaky. 'Go to bed and don't say anything to anybody. If anybody asks, you know nothing. We wait until tomorrow. Whatever we do, we must make sure no one suspects.'

'Right oh!' Phil punched the air.

'Remember. You know nothing.'

With that Bonnie waltzed out of the K2 and Phil headed to bed. Back at The Madina, he ducked under the lights coming from Graham and Miko's windows, and made straight for his room. He unlocked the door but it would barely open. As he squeezed his head inside, it became clear why: Mannie's not-very-mean machine was leaning against it from the other side, and propped up on his bed was none other than the Brick Lane Bad Boy.

'Oii!' Phil managed to stretch for one of Mannie's shoes on the floor, and throw it at his head.

'Hey, man! Relax.' Mannie unfurled his arms for an embrace but Phil was still trapped outside. Mannie stumbled up to move his moped, wisps of smoke emanating from his nostrils.

'Where d'you get that from?' Phil could smell it wasn't tobacco.

'You're sending out some major negative vibes here.' Mannie tried to look philosophical, as he worked out what needed to be moved first.

'That's not all I'll be sending out in a minute.' Phil shunted his way in and started kicking Mannie's things towards the door.

'I've got more Jack,' Mannie tempted, holding up a brown paper bag.

Phil stopped kicking. 'I knew that five hundred dollars would be burning a hole in your pocket.'

'A big fat hole,' Mannie giggled, reaching over with the joint. 'That Nasty Bitch, man, she's gotta chill out.'

'Grab me a glass. They're in the cupboard.'

Pathfinders

Nothing if not a creature of habit, Phil battled his eyelids open early the next morning. It took a pit-stop or two longer than normal but he was still showered and on his way to the K2 before Mannie had even finished his pee. Passing Graham's room, Phil smiled at the sweetness of the snoring: there was a man celebrating being back in a comfortable bed alright.

'*Sleep tight, Ruffo!*' Phil congratulated himself. '*You snooze, you loose.*'

Judging by the movement in the café, Phil wasn't the only one up. As he opened the door, the back of the woman's head that greeted him was as unexpected as it was familiar. The chestnut shade of the bob left no doubt, and as the hair turned, the soft, wide smile, the tiny gap between the front teeth, the long eye-lashes, all fitted perfectly.

Phil, speechless, dashed in and gave this dreamy vision an enormous, perhaps too enormous, bear hug.

'Sarah Kennedy!' Phil finally managed.

'Philip Kelly.' Sarah toyed in reply.

'Look at you!' Sarah was wearing a plain beige shalwar kameez.

'Look at you!' Phil's iridescent shirt was all palm trees and parrots.

The semi-awkwardness would have lingered a while longer but they were interrupted by the dishevelled appearance of Mannie, tearing across the car park. Phil was tempted to send Sarah to hide, but settled for offering her a seat far away from the door.

'No wonder you were so keen to get up this morning, Philip.' Mannie paused for breath in the doorway. 'You should have told me you had a date.'

'Take a hike, Mannie.'

'And with such a beautiful lady.' Mannie gave Sarah on theatrical bow. 'Are you really with him, or were you just waiting for me?' He seemed to be oblivious of the fact that he had skipped showering, was wearing the same kaftan as the previous day, and had started to smell.

'Ignore the dress, Sarah. Underneath is all prick.'

Before Mannie could cowboy his way over to the large leather armchair where Sarah was sitting, Phil pulled a stool in the way and stuck his foot on it.

'I don't think we've met.' Sarah was polite but no more.

Mannie nudged Phil into action.

'Sarah, this, unfortunately, is Mannie. Associated Press.'

'Mandeep, please,' Mannie smarmed. 'Mandeep Gurcharan Singh.' The full name was usually reserved for dates, mothers and Channel 4 executives.

Sarah forced a smile.

'This is Sarah.' Phil grudgingly divulged. 'Sarah used to run Ruff Guides with …' Phil was trying to usher his nemesis into a distant seat but was being deliberately ignored.

'Ah, Sarah Kennedy? I have heard so much about you from Big G. It's spooky we've never met.'

'You know Graham?' Sarah was beginning to have recollections of being told about a journo guy Graham had been stuck with for weeks on the Trans-Siberian. She had the feeling she was going to hear the story again.

'Know Graham? We used to work together, years ago. Old School me and G. And Phil,' he added, just in case. 'The Three Wise Monkeys.'

'You're in luck. Graham should be here soon.' Sarah hoped this might shorten Mandeep's step somewhat.

Mannie's half-truths had been exposed so many times over the years, he didn't flinch. 'Great, let's have a party. Where you staying?'

'Yeah, where are you staying, Sarah?'

Mannie's eyes lit up as the limit of Phil's relationship with Sarah was exposed.

'Well, I'm supposed to be staying with some friends but at the moment it looks like I'll be stuck in The Madina.' Sarah replied. The rucksack at her side indicated she had not yet committed herself to either plan.

'That's where I'm staying!' Phil struggled to contain his excitement.

'Me, too. I'll help you check in.' On the 'ch', Mannie had clicked his finger and thumb into the shape of a pistol.

'No, thank you.' Sarah didn't like to act the Ice Maiden but had studied the likes of Bonnie long enough. As Phil beamed at Mannie's rebuff, the door opened and Nasser, the messenger boy, marched in. A shiny new BMX lay parked at the bottom of the steps, the first instalment financed by Graham's earlier generosity. Little Mo looked on enviously from the kitchen curtain; the free market wasn't turning out quite how he had expected.

'I've come from Mr Hassan's office,' Nasser explained to Sarah. 'He is going to be inconvenienced for approximately one hour, and has requested me to take you up to his family abode, to be entertained by his wife until his arrival.'

'Better get a move on, then.' Sarah had proved impermeable to the years of London speak. After gathering her belongings she said her goodbyes: curtly to Mandeep, but with an honest smile to Phil. The doorway, however, was occupied.

'Sarah?' The surprise in Bonnie's voice only just managed to disguise the disdain.

'Hi, Bon.'

Bonnie stayed glued beneath the doorbell. Had she not been so thrown by the occasion, she would have noticed Mannie scurrying down the drainpipe outside the kitchen window. 'Fancy seeing you here!'

'Oh, I don't know.' Sarah was determined not to be intimidated. 'I hear it's quite the place to be.' She looked around at the empty café. 'Well, maybe not.'

'What's wrong, Cinders?' Bonnie was back to full speed. 'Prince Charming stood you up again?'

Sarah forced her face back into a smile.

'That's better. She will go to the ball, won't she, Ned?' Phil would have given his right arm to take her. 'But you might have to wait a while for your carriage to arrive.' Bonnie leaned in close to Sarah's ear, as though she was about to divulge the secret of a game-changing wrinkle cream. 'The boys have been playing explorers again, and didn't get home until way past their bedtime.' She sneaked a peak at her coiffure in the wall mirror. Bonnie didn't like other females cramping her style 'on location'.

'He shouldn't be too long,' Phil fibbed. He wished Bonnie hadn't brought up the Graham/Sarah thing quite so quickly, but would take what he could get when it came to buying a bit more Sarah time. 'Everyone usually gets here about this time.' This was truer.

'I didn't come here looking for Graham, actually.' Sarah hesitated. 'But if everyone's on their way, I suppose I might as well stay.' Nasser saw his tip disappearing.

216

Bonnie felt a rival tug on her arm.

'Here are those back copies of the New York Times, you ordered, Mizz Fidler.' Little Mo had emerged from the kitchen with a long fat tube in his hand. 'They came to a little more than I anticipated, I'm afraid. Special delivery.' Little Mo had rung his second cousin in Islamabad, and promised rewards beyond young Inzy's wildest dreams, in return for sneaking as many copies as he could from the various embassy waiting rooms on his way home from school. Sixteen copies had arrived that morning with Inzy's uncle, the driver of the Gilgit Express.

'Little man,' Bonnie gushed. 'You are an angel.' Bonnie handed Mo a crisp fifty dollar note and started emptying the tube.

Nasser went off in a sulk. He knew exactly which bike Little Mo had his eye on, and fifty dollars was enough for two instalments.

Phil had carried Sarah's bags back to her chair, and was rubbing his hands in anticipation. 'We should have a drink to celebrate.'

'It's a bit early for that isn't it?' Sarah knew Phil had a reputation, but for breakfast?

'Oh, I don't know,' Phil winked. 'It depends which way you look at it.' He glanced at the dual-dial Breitling his mum had bought him for his twenty-first. 'Back home, the sun will be well over the yard arm by now.' He reconsidered the time difference. 'Gees, some of the boys down the club will already be on the Bundies.'

'Phil!' Sarah winced. She had thought she'd smelt alcohol on Phil's breath.

'Don't be a pelican, Saz,' Phil rolled his eyes. 'I was only pulling your pinnie.' Sarah blushed. 'A nice cuppa's what I had in mind! And maybe a K2 special.' As Phil sat down he made sure the chunky glass bottle in his bumbag was well-and-truly hidden. He grabbed some cushions, pulled in the coffee table and forgot about the tea. Sarah made herself comfortable.

Soon Phil was gabbling at a mile a minute, creating the exact opposite impression to what he wanted, but Sarah didn't mind. Finally, he remembered about the tea, and came up for air.

'Navo!' Naveed was nowhere to be seen, so Phil set off to the kitchen.

'You are hungry?' Phil darted his head back into view. 'I'm starving,' he offered as way of encouragement.

'I'll just have a green tea, please.' But it was too late; Phil had disappeared back behind the blanket.

'So, Sarah.' Having counted out each copy, Bonnie sat down with all the front pages unfurled in front of her. 'If you're not looking for Graham, what are you doing here?' It rankled all the more that her latest rival was nearly fifteen years younger, understatedly more attractive and, on a number of scales, significantly more successful.

'Don't tell me,' Bonnie squeezed her lips into gear before Sarah could answer, '*Trans-Asia with a Tweenie?*'

'No, no. I'm on my own.' Sarah suddenly felt incredibly guilty for leaving Xavier with his Gran for such a long time. 'Good title though, I'll keep it in mind.'

As the women exchanged more cracked pleasantries, Bonnie noticed Sarah had lost a little weight. She tried to pull her stomach in to match.

'On your own?' Bonnie pressed. 'So you're back freelancing?' That wasn't what Sarah had meant and Bonnie knew it.

'Still with Pathfinders, actually.'

Bonnie consoled herself, as she had done so often before, with the thought that at least the father of Sarah's child had left her. She also reminded herself that Sarah had been unceremoniously shown the door at Ruff Guides. And had blown her chances with Graham. These last two observations, Floyd's ex-wife might reluctantly admit, were exaggerations of varying degree, but no less satisfying because of that. 'In that case, I've got another for you.'

Bonnie paused for a moment, as she had been taught.

'*Round France with a Feminist.*' She only half giggled to show that she was only half joking. Sarah's *Round Britain with a Baby* had instantly shot to number one in the list of Bonnie's all-time Most-Hated-Travel-Books, and was only, finally, knocked off its perch with the publication of *Touring with a Toddler*.

The situation was saved by Phil arriving back with a silver tray, china cups and a Victorian teapot.

'Here we go,' Phil enthused, silver sugar bowl and linen napkins tucked under his arm. 'The curry's on its way. You know, I reckon it's gone a year since we last ......'

'Almost two,' Sarah frowned.

'Crikey.'

Sarah brought Phil up to date on Xavier ('about to turn ten') and her immediate plans ('something different'). It was hard not to like someone who was always so pleased to see you. Bonnie flicked between pretending not to listen, brassily chewing her gum and ostentatiously re-reading The New York Times.

'G will be spewin' he slept in.' Phil was lapping it up. This despite the fact that Sarah held the record for the Woman-to-have-rejected-Crazy-Philpot-the-most-times-(nine!)-without-even-so-much-as-snogging-him, as opposed to those who had repeatedly said no, only to succumb, then spent hours/days/months/years, desperately trying to convince him that it had been a mistake/for a bet/because they had been blind drunk/all of the above.

When the curries arrived, Sarah had to do everything she could to convince Phil that she wasn't hungry. After finally conceding defeat he offered Sarah's bowl to Bonnie, then parked it behind his own. 'I can always go another. And then maybes I can show you around.'

'Thanks, Phil. Let's wait and see, shall we?'

As Phil began to dream, a whirring sound in the distance became louder. And louder. A gear-crunching convoy of lorries, trucks, tractors and diggers was clattering its way up Gilgit's main road, and by the time it reached the café, the noise was deafening. Phil tucked into his second plateful, regardless, but Bonnie and Sarah were all ears.

They cautiously made their way down the café steps and over to what looked like the head of the line: an all-black Land Cruiser with blacked-out windows. As they approached, the driver wheel-span his way off towards the market place. The women decided to follow.

Eventually, Phil ran out of curry. Finding himself abandoned, he jumped out the door and down the stairs, but the road in front was blocked. He was still waiting for a gap in the constant stream of heavy-duty traffic to open up when Graham and Miko appeared.

'Who the hell are these guys, Ned?' Graham hollered.

'Don't know what you're talking about.' Phil had promised to follow Bonnie's instructions to the letter.

'Don't clown, Phil.' Graham had tried to ignore the noise and continue his lie in, but it was impossible. 'I'm not in the mood.'

219

Suddenly the convoy stopped and with it the deafening racket.

'Right oh.' Rather than offer a more helpful analysis, Phil looked down at his feet and started a singsong, 'I know something that you don't know.'

'Yes, we gathered that.'

'Somebody special's arrived.'

'We can see that too, you numbskull.' Graham rubbed more sleep out of his eyes. 'Is it the Intelligence guy?'

'Now let me see,' Phil licked his tongue around the tip of his finger like a schoolgirl. 'No.'

'Someone for the conference?' Miko guessed.

More licking.

'Someone we know?'

'Getting warmer.' Phil was rather enjoying himself.

'Zul?' Miko jumped in.

'Oops, cold again.' Some of the vehicles further up the road began choking themselves back into life.

'Do you want another clue?' Phil teased.

'No,' Graham growled. 'Yes.'

'It's a friend of yours, G.'

'Jos?' What was he doing up here?

Phil shook his head.

'Terry?' Graham couldn't believe he could have made it up there so quickly, but he was running out of options. 'Jane?'

'Close.'

'Sarah?' Graham couldn't think of anyone else.

'Bullseye!' Phil shot an imaginary target in celebration.

'Sarah? What the hell is she doing here?' Graham pointed to the racket ahead. 'And what's she got to do with all this?'

'This?' Phil balked in surprise. 'Haven't a clue.' Suddenly all the wheels fell silent again. 'Naveed reckons they're on their way up to the border, to do some road repairs before winter set in.'

'That's some road repairs,' Miko whistled.

Graham reckoned otherwise, but the thought of Sarah's arrival was of more concern.

'She rocked up this morning. Looking sweet as, if I may add.'

Graham shook his head. 'OK, Phil. That's very nice but....' He suddenly noticed a look in Phil's eye, all too familiar. 'Are you drunk?'

'Rack off.' Phil accidentally let out a belch. 'I might,' he begrudgingly conceded, 'be a touch hungover.'

'Spill the beans, Ned.' Graham had caught more than a whiff. 'Who else is here?'

Phil grimaced. 'Like I said: Sarah.'

'Sarah and Jack Daniels? I don't think so.'

It had been JD and Coke that fateful night at the awards, and Sarah had vowed never to touch another drop since.

'Who else?' Graham huffed. 'Who've you been hiding out with?'

'I'm sworn to secrecy.' Phil folded his arms. 'But I suppose I could give you three guesses.'

'Mandeep Singh.' Graham had never, in fact, had the pleasure of working with Mannie, but he had encountered him often enough, and the Tennessee rye vapours he had woken up to every morning in that Russian train compartment would never be forgotten.

'OK. But it's not what you're thinking, G. Mannie's a changed man.' In exchange for the leftover Jack, Phil had promised he would do what he could not to blow Mannie's cover.

Phil was still working out how Graham had guessed so quickly when Floyd came crashing into view. Vanh was in reluctant pursuit.

'What the sweet Jesus is going on, Kelly?' Pinks bawled.

'I know nothing,' Phil replied proudly.

'Ruff?'

'I've just arrived.'

'Somebody must know something.'

'Sarah's here'

'Your Sarah?' Pinks looked at Graham.

'Yes, but I can't imagine she's anything to do with this.'

'Trust no one, G, trust no one.' Pinks was looking up and down the main road, as though vital evidence might be all around them.

'It's got to be something to do with the conference,' Graham reasoned.

'Or The Game.'

'Sarah doesn't play The Game. She thinks it's stupid.'

'Maybe. Or maybe she's started playing since you last saw her.' Floyd's paranoia was in full flow and he lit up his first torpedo of the day. 'Or maybe she's doing a book.'

Graham hadn't thought of that.

Miko felt an important piece of the puzzle was being ignored. 'There's also a guy called Mandy.'

'Mannie Singh,' Graham explained.

'Why didn't you say? That explains everything. It'll be one of his pathetic cod-hack schemes to get a story.'

'I'm telling you guys, he a changed man.'

'Go back to bed, Ned.'

Phil felt himself being torn between keeping a secret and having a story to tell. Something had to give. 'He's a jihadi!'

'And my grandma's the Ayatollah.' Floyd shook his head. 'Let the big boys do the thinking, eh, cork brain.'

Phil shrugged. If that was how they wanted it, he was happy to play dumb.

Pinks turned round to inspect the calibre of the vehicles on parade. 'When one dumb-ass hack thinks he's smelt a scoop, the rest of those lemmings are sure to follow.'

Graham couldn't help but nod.

'You try telling them they're way out in the left field, but it's no good. They think you're hiding something.'

It had happened to Floyd during the Gulf War. There he was in the Jordanian capital, Amman, doing a nice little piece on Lawrence of Arabia for The Digest, all snug in the comfort of a suite in the Hyatt, when up turned four hundred AP boys, waiting to be smuggled into Iraq. It turned out the 'fixer' was waiting for them in Oman, but would they listen? Room-service went haywire, prices quadrupled and Floyd couldn't so much as beg a cigar.

'It'll be the same all over again. I guarantee you.' Floyd gestured towards a crane-bearing lorry. 'Before you know it, Discovery and CNN will be here, the locals smell the big time, and we can kiss Xidakistan goodbye.'

As if on cue, young Nasser and Little Mo skidded into view.

'You see!' Pinks flung his arms up in despair. 'The kids have got new bikes already.'

Vanh turned to Miko and grinned.

'Wipe that look off your face, George. And get packing. We're moving....,'
A stray one of Bonnie's New York Times, mud-splattered, blew between Floyd's legs.

'Jesus wept!' he screamed. 'Have you seen what the harlot has done now?'

Pinks implored the earth to swallow up his ex-other-half in a whirlpool of fire and lava, while Graham, Miko and Vanh ran through the soiled remains of the article.

'Would have been better with a picture,' Phil critiqued. 'But Bonnie's stoked.'

'You mean you knew about this?' Floyd staggered. He began choking on his cigar, and had to bend double to cough himself right. 'The unholy slut,' he eventually managed.

'I presume by that you are referring to me.' Bonnie had mounted the footplate of a stationary armoured car directly opposite Floyd. She struck the same stance that had despatched Mannie so effectively the previous evening.

'I'm gonna get you for this.' Floyd pulled himself up straight. 'I don't care if I go to the chair, but I'll get you.' Floyd lunged, and Graham and Vanh only just managed to catch his shoulders to drag him back.

'Don't waste your strength, boys.' Bonnie jeered. 'I'd chew his fat ass for breakfast, and he knows it. Besides, I came to see Kelly.'

Floyd jack-knifed his attention to Phil, who stood shivering in the spotlight.

Bonnie kept a straight face. 'Our permit has arrived, so we can go up to the Khunjerab. Tomorrow.'

Phil nodded gingerly.

'Photo-shoot,' Bonnie added, by way of explanation for the others. 'Mohammed's busy so I'm letting Kelly drive.' She finished by reminding Phil they would be staying overnight in Sost.

The vehicle she was standing on restarted its engine, and she let herself be carried away up the road.

'You low-down son-of-a-bitch!' Pinks charged again, this time with Phil in his sights. It was Miko's turn to help Graham cling on for dear life.

'Turncoat! Since when have you been her gofer?'

Phil danced back a couple of paces. 'You don't know what I'm getting in return,' he eventually stammered.

'She's dangling you by your dick, and you're too blind to see it.' Floyd finally quit struggling, and brushed the others' arms away in disdain. 'After all these years and you're still falling for the oldest trick in her book. You make me sick.'

He ordered George to move out.

'Where're we going?' Vanh didn't like the sound of things.

'Anywhere, so long as it's away from her.'

There was only one place Graham was going. He started his hunt in the marketplace and did a loop of the town that ended at his own room. There pinned to his door was a note, the smiley face on the envelope was enough. Sarah didn't say why she was in Gilgit but she did outline her attempts to find him and her plans to stay with Mr Hassan. She also promised to return at eleven o'clock and every hour, on the hour, after that. Unless Graham wanted to suggest another meeting place, in which case he could leave directions on the back of her envelope. Graham chuckled at the cosy reminder of Sarah's conscientiousness. It was nearly eleven so he happily waited for her outside his room, throwing gravel at the opposite wall.

'Hello, handsome.' It was ten fifty-nine.

Sarah was looking as fresh as the hand-picked bouquet of flowers she was carrying. Even the mud on her boots seemed to be clean.

'You shouldn't have,' Graham joked. He had been up on his feet as soon as he had heard Sarah's call.

After dusting off his hands Graham made to lean over for a kiss. But both Sarah's hands were full with the bouquet, and it had been nearly two years, and they were an unmarried couple in public in Pakistan.

'Don't be silly.' Sarah giggled, dropping the flowers at his feet. She pulled Graham in tight and gave him a juicy smack on the lips. Sarah's perfume rushed to his head.

'I should come here more often.'

'Indeed you should.' Sarah still had her arms around her catch, and looked unlikely to let go. 'Where have you been?'

'Oh, you know,' Graham raised an eyebrow, 'playing with monster trucks.'

'Look who's become all coy in his old age.' Sarah began retrieving her flowers. 'I must have been very lucky. Mr Hassan said that all the flowers would be gone by now, but I found these up at the back of the Old Polo Ground.'

Graham was content to watch and take it all in. Her hair was shorter than when they last met. It had returned to what he called her 'Alhambra' cut. The henna highlights of their last meeting had also faded and, despite a decade of motherhood, her figure still cut quite a dash.

As Sarah looked up, he noticed one or two more lines around the eyes, but the pupils were keen, and the irises blue.

'How's Shabby?' Graham took the usual pleasure in his nickname for Sarah's son.

'Xavier's fine.' Sarah pronounced the name with an emphatic 'h', in retaliation. 'Just started Year Seven.'

'Which one's Year Seven?' Graham could never keep track.

'Junior Three to you and me,' Sarah smiled. 'He really liked the hat you sent him from Kyrgyzstan.'

'So you said in your letter.'

For Graham and Sarah there were two sorts of silences, and this was the other one.

'Shall we go somewhere?' Graham suggested. 'I just need to get a couple of things from inside.' More walking less talking; he smiled at his mother's old adage.

Graham grabbed his satchel and was automatically heading towards the K2 when he remembered Phil might still be around. He veered off to a coffee house he had seen at the back of the market. The last of the convoy was gone now, and the silence hung like a cloud. It didn't break until the coffees arrived.

'Thanks a bunch for the reply.' Sarah wasn't cross, but Graham knew she wasn't happy.

'I'm sorry. I thought I was going to be back sooner.' It was a poor excuse. 'I didn't realise I was going to be stuck in Bishkek for eight months.'

'Don't they have paper in Bishkek?'

He should have left it at 'sorry'.

'Or email?'

'But you hate email.' Stop digging.

As Sarah twiddled her coffee spoon, Graham took a sip.

'First decent coffee I've had in weeks.' He offered a weak smile.

Nothing.

'Thanks for the flowers,' Graham tried again. He had asked the café owner for a vase and they were resplendent on the next table.

'You've already said that.'

Graham now saw why his instincts had kept him away from England, and his best friend, for so long.

'I'm sorry, Sarah. It's just ...'

They both began to stir their spoons.

'It's OK.'

Graham knew it wasn't.

'Xav really misses you.'

More silence.

'You know, I worked out you hadn't missed a Christmas since he was born. Even after you bought your place in Turkey.'

'I know.'

Stirring was replaced by sipping.

'Did you spend it with Duncan?' Graham didn't know much about the latest man in Sarah's life, but from what he had heard through mutual friends, he wasn't that sorry.

'No, that didn't last. Wasn't our type.'

Graham tingled at Sarah's use of the plural.

'How's Toad of Toad Hall?' They both loosened some more.

'He's not wrapped his Porsche around anymore lamp posts, you'll be annoyed to hear.' Graham was relieved to see Sarah smiling again. 'But he has taken to calling himself Josh.'

'I want to puke.'

'I almost did.'

Graham's foot accidentally on purpose poked Sarah's calf as he stretched out his legs.

'Antonia's had a second child,' Graham added, hoping to keep the ball rolling. 'A girl this time, Rinnie. They were going to name her Penelope, but when I threatened to call her Penny Lope they switched to Catherine. In case others had the same idea.'

'Antonia,' Sarah semi-lamented. 'I always feel I should be sorry for her, but whenever I see her she makes it impossible.'

'They've asked me to be godfather.'

'I hope you're going to say no.'

The switch was flipped and they were off: teasing, taunting and spinning out ideas like the old days. Before they knew it they had ordered, eaten and finished lunch, and were on to more coffees.

'So what brings you here, Sarah?' After Pinks' suggestion, Graham couldn't help himself.

'To beat you and Pinks to the Alphabet Game, of course.'

'What?' Graham squawked. His coffee only just missed the front of his shirt. 'But you don't even play....'

Graham saw he had been duped.

'Only kidding.' Sarah couldn't wink, so both eyes scrunched up simultaneously, as she passed Graham her packet of tissues. 'Actually.' Sarah tensed. 'I'm here to do a book.' She bit her lip. 'On Xidakistan.'

'Sarah!' Graham erupted all over again.

'What? We all need to make a living you know.'

'But I'm doing a book. We agreed not to tread on each other's territories.'

'You never told me you were doing a book.' Sarah curled up on the defensive, well aware that Graham's plans were common knowledge. 'Perhaps if you'd written…'

They both fell silent.

'You're not working for *Small World* are you?' Graham couldn't forget Miko's earlier remark.

'No.'

'*Pathfinders?*' Graham looked puzzled. They didn't usually do this kind of guide.

Sarah hesitated. 'As a matter of fact I was hoping,' Sarah's eyes blinked again, 'I was hoping it could be *Follow Your Nose's* first title.'

'*Follow Your Nose?*' Graham offered a conciliatory smile. 'It's a bit late for that, isn't it?'

'Why, Graham?' Sarah dug in. She had always supported Graham's original name for the company, and was still bitter that Jos had had the final say. 'Why's it too late?'

Memories of an earlier proposal came flooding back, making Graham's buttocks clamp. 'Come on, Sarah, we've been through all this before.'

'I know but things are different now,' Sarah was determined. 'Your mum told me you're thinking of selling *Xanadu*.' There was no mention of Burcu the housekeeper.

Perhaps encouraging Sarah to keep in touch with his mother wasn't such a good idea.

'Look, Sarah.' He immediately regretted his harsh tone and turned it down a few notches. 'I'm happy where I am, doing what I'm doing. I don't need any new,' Graham fidgeted, 'challenges.' More fidgeting. 'And besides, you shouldn't keep going to my mother behind my back. It's not…'

At first, Sarah's eyes simply contained sadness, but then the colour in her pale cheeks began to rise, and tears began to brim. As she raised herself to look Graham in the eye, her head seemed to spin out of control.

'Well, sod you, Graham Ruff. Bloody sod you. You disappear for nearly two years without a word. I come halfway across the globe to find you, make sure you're OK, perhaps even help you rediscover some of your old spark. And all you can think about is you, you, you.' Sarah gulped some air in through her tears.

It was the first time he had ever heard her swear.

'Graham Ruff, the Professional Layabout. Do you know how ridiculous that makes you sound?'

Graham's face froze.

'Yes, I know all about that too.'

He didn't need to guess who had told her.

'I'm not stupid you know.'

Graham couldn't look.

'In that case, fine!' Sarah cried. 'Fine by me.' She pushed herself to her feet. 'Keep your sodding book.' Sarah planted her fists on the table, and leant in so close that Graham had no choice but to meet her line of sight. 'But you can't divide everything between 'Yours' and 'Mine', you know. It's not fair. Not. Fair.'

As Sarah tore out of the café, Graham rocked back on his chair, shell-shocked. He had seen Sarah lose her temper before, but had never been on the end of anything like that. He continued to gape at the space Sarah had left, until the equally dumb-struck proprietor found enough strength to suggest the bill. Graham left the money, and the flowers.

Hotel Shangri La

Graham had retreated to the anonymity of his room and his notes, but couldn't settle. One of his books seemed to be missing. He was wrestling with the idea of breaking into his 'medicinal' supplies for a pick-me-up (today was supposed to be a 'Day Off'), when there was a knock on the door.

'Hey, Graham, I was thinking of going for a drive. Do you fancy joining me?'

Graham's face fell. He had hoped it was be Sarah.

'You OK?'

'Sure. Sure, Miko. You haven't seen one of my notebooks by any chance?'

'Notebook? No sorry. I just thought it might be fun to see where that convoy was off to.' Miko had asked Vanh, but Floyd had put his foot down.

They headed north in Naveed's van, but after a few miles it was clear the convoy had reached a lot farther than they'd thought. They quickly dropped back into town, and picked up some overnight stuff. Miko was driving, so, as the van wound its way even higher up into the mountains, Graham took the opportunity to review a few entries from his old *Pakistan* guide.

 SOST

Sost is one of those villages where it is hard to get lost. It consists of a single strip of drab hostel-cum-cafés, flanking a general store, and a bus station. This doubles as the Customs and Immigration office for anyone coming in from China. The buildings tend to be square, one-storey affairs, with odd extra rooms perched on top, like a sentry posts.

Sost is the last stop before the Chinese border, but many a visitor has been disappointed by their over-estimation of the impact that the modern world has had in this remote corner.

A couple of army checkpoints later, the two men found themselves parked outside the bus depot's main gate. By the size of the crowds swarming around the entrance, it looked like half of The Northern Areas had beaten them to it.

Graham squeezed his way through the packed car park, towards a giant orange crane that seemed to be orchestrating proceedings. Miko followed and, to their surprise, they saw Bonnie and Phil busy in the machinery's shadow, surrounded by all kinds of crates, sacks and barrels. Perched high up on the enormous caterpillar tracks was a pug-faced colonial type, decked out in all the trappings, short of a pith helmet. The crane's cabin, like almost everything else Graham and Miko could see, was decorated with the American flag, and the safari suit was shouting orders through a megaphone. This wasn't quite as effective as he had hoped, since his orders then had to be translated, and repeated through a second megaphone by his Pashtun assistant. But the most important aim had been achieved: everybody looked busy. Perhaps not surprisingly, given the promise of pay ten times the going rate.

'So,' Graham sidled up, 'Taking pictures of the National Park are we?' For the first time he could remember, Graham thought Phil looked bashful. Bonnie pulled out another stick of gum.

'Tough luck, Ruff. You guys tried it with Butt, so we're just levelling the playing field.' Bonnie gave a second scowl to Miko, to let him know that now he'd teamed up with the other side his 'ass' was no longer considered quite so 'cute'.

'One hell of a playing field. What on earth's going on?'

'Well, you see that guy up there?' Phil pointed.

'Leave the talking to me, Ned.'

'I was only going to say he was a German NGO guy.' Phil looked hurt. 'I wasn't going to tell them he was Intelligence.'

'The flags do sort of give it away.' Graham thought through the ramifications. 'So the conference's definitely on then?' He was getting excited.

'On indeed. Your Mr Butt is escorting the King down here as we speak.' Bonnie was beginning to look smug again. 'And my good friend Boris,' Bonnie pointed to her fellow WASP, 'is going to be here to meet them.'

Graham felt queasy. Bonnie had clearly made her move.

A sharp blast on the whistle from 'Boris' signalled the four of them should stay exactly where they were. The crane arm swung to a halt, and the director of operations dismounted the reinforced vulcanised rubber tracks, hopped his way down a steel platform, and dropped onto the mound of Hershey sacks behind Phil.

'New recruits, Bonnie?' Boris bumped his way down the stack.

'Not exactly, Boris.'

'We're friends of Mr Butt.' Graham would have preferred to have hung on to that piece of information for a little longer, but hoped it might establish some credibility. 'I hope you don't mind.'

'Nein, nein. Zee more zee merrier, yah?' Boris proclaimed, grasping Graham's arm, and switching to his best Bavarian. 'Boris Frentzen, United Nations Development Agency Co-ordinator.'

'Dankeschoen,' Graham bowed. 'Du hast einen wirklich guten englischen akzent.'

'Forget it, Boris,' Bonnie chewed. 'They know already.'

The military moustache frowned. Graham shrugged, as if it had been a lucky guess.

'Well, in that case, I'm sorry, gentlemen,' Benny turned to his shiny gold clipboard, 'but these here crates don't have a habit of shifting themselves. So, if you don't mind,' he pulled out a pen, 'Phil, tell me what you've found in sector F.' Boris's Teutonic glottal stops had been replaced by Benny's southern drawl.

'Right oh,' Phil was pleased with his work thus far. 'Six tarmac machines, with 4000 tonnes of tarmac.' He had been issued with a silver clipboard for his findings. 'A fully-equipped M*A*S*H unit.' He flicked through to some peripheral notes at the back. 'But there's a tag and a telephone number on that one. It says to call if you need any help 'cos there's a piece missing.'

Benny inquired as to which piece.

'Not sure. But they think it might be the roof.'

Graham scanned the bus depot. It had been demarcated into ten sections, eight of which were lettered with what looked like cheerleader tops. Together they spelt out CALIFORN. Two young boys, wearing the missing I and A, could be seen chasing each other around a second, smaller crane.

Phil wasn't finished. 'There're a hundred copies of the Lutheran Bible from the Women's Union of The Emmanuel Episcopal Church of Lynchburg, Virginia. That's one for every adult male.'

Graham rolled his eyes.

'And a hundred copies of the New Lutheran Bible, leather bound, from the Women's Union of The Uniting Episcopal Church of Lynchburg, Virginia. That's one for every female.' Phil looked up for approval and was duly rewarded with a vigorous nod.

'I bet they were pleased with themselves when they thought of having theirs leather bound,' Graham whispered in Miko's ear.

'Oh, and four thousand slabs of sugar-free, caffeine-free, Cherry Coke. Leftover from the Atlanta Olympics, but technically within their use-by dates.'

'Solid work, soldier.' Benny was shivering, his shorts no match for the cold. 'What about you, honey?'

'Three more emails.' Bonnie's adjusted the satellite phone connection to Benny's laptop. 'First one's from Discovery. They promise to donate all the funds necessary to build a school house, in return for exclusive documentary rights.'

'Excellent.'

'Next is from Marlboro: they're offering to fund an entire anti-smoking campaign, in return for exclusive distribution rights in The Valley. And the last one's from that Enron guy: he's on his way.'

'Any progress with Disney?'

'Already sent them a pre-contract,' Bonnie twirled her sunglasses. 'They love the first option on the movie and visitors' centre, and are committing to all marketing and advertising expenditure, up front. They're working off a ballpark family-ticket price of a hundred and twenty.'

'Hold on just one minute.' Sarah had been secretly listening to the entire conversation from the shadows, and chose this moment to step forward. 'What exactly do you think you are doing?'

'The lady's right,' Benny cut in. 'We're talking a unique attraction here. It should be one fifty, minimum.'

'No!' Sarah's scream was enough to halt a dozen nearby workmen, sacks of Hershey's mid-air. 'This is not an amusement park. The people of Xidakistan are not here for you to come and play around with.'

233

'Look, everybody,' Bonnie chewed. 'Isn't Sarah so nice?'

'This is a military operation, Missy.' Agent Franklin dropped all remains of his happy Oktoberfest pretence, and looked Sarah right in the eye. 'So I suggest you keep your pretty little nose out.'

'Graham? Phil?'

The two men shuffled their feet.

'Somebody do something.'

An ear-splitting screech from outside the gates suggested that one person at least was intent on taking matters into their own hands. But as a 50s Enfield, with accompanying side-car, came hurtling into view, the look beneath Pinks' visor suggested he was no knight errant. With a combination of brute force and will power, he shucked his considerable size from the semi-vehicle's shell, as Vanh throttled down the engine.

'Amateurs.' Floyd stared at everyone in turn from inside his silver dome. He hesitated on Benny, but only for a second. 'Did you really think you could beat me that easily?' Off came the helmet. 'Did you?'

'Now listen here, Mister.' Suddenly, it was Benny's turn to double-take. 'Shit my Grandma's knickers!' He reached out to touch Floyd's arm. 'It's Shoestring Housmann!'

Floyd's spine shivered at the reference. Bonnie swallowed her gum

'What in the name of Beelzebub are you doing here, partner?' Benny back-slapped. He still couldn't believe his eyes. Meanwhile, the fog was lifting from Floyd's, and from beneath the tan and wrinkles a pale, skinny German boy was emerging. The same pale, skinny, newly-arrived German boy Floyd had taken great delight in kicking around Austin Junior High's football field, during recess, all those years ago. The smell of hot apple pies bought with the extorted pocket money filled his nostrils.

'Frentzen?' Floyd tested. 'Bull Shit Frentzen?' His former classmate's initials had been abused almost from day one. 'Why, you no good son of a gun. I still owe you a dollar from graduation.'

Pinks was about to deliver his customary boot to Frentzen's backside when Benny indicated the need for an immediate discussion in his office. The two men retired into a stack of crates marked AOL.

'Don't get me wrong, Shoestring, swell to see you and all that,' Benny whispered, 'but now's not a particularly good time.'

On the other side of the crates, Graham and the others pressed closer in to eavesdrop.

'I'm here on official business, you see,' Benny added furtively. 'Undercover.'

'Well whistle Dixie.' Floyd had never considered Frentzen destined for anywhere but Wal-Mart. 'You're here for the conference?'

'Sorry, buddy, I'm not at liberty-'

'Don't tell me they let you into Intelligence.'

Silence.

'Jesus.' Floyd kicked a stray crate.

Without warning, Benny dropped to a squat and motioned Floyd to do likewise. He drew 'OK' in the dust. Then, realising there was too much to say, he pulled out a pen and pad from his top pocket.

'There's something you need to know.' Benny wrote, signalling Pinks should communicate the same way.

'What?' Floyd mouthed, ignoring the pen.

'My name's Boris Frentzen.' Benny scrawled.

'I know.' Pinks scribbled.

'No! That's my code name. No one must know.'

'Don't be stupid!' Pinks gave up being silent. 'That's your real name.' Floyd began to worry that all the butt-kicking might have left permanent damage. Not even Special Intelligence would give a man his real name as a code. Surely.

'Floyd!' Benny pulled him in tight. 'That ain't my real name any more. I changed it to Benny Franklin when I left college. Looked better on the resumé.'

'Hang on. Isn't that the guy who…?' Bells were ringing in Pinks' brain. 'The guy on all the conspiracy websites?' his eyes widened.

'That,' Benny felt some of his old 'Captain Franklin' swagger returning, 'that is strictly off the record.'

Floyd let out a low whistle. 'I'm impressed.' He took a moment to reflect on how the puniest, biggest-eared nerd, with the worst case of halitosis in the whole of Texas, could have become one of the most feared killers on the planet. 'Special Intelligence?'

'Keep your voice down.'

Floyd was still reeling. 'Shouldn't your code name be 'blonde' or 'yellow'?'

'Ordinarily. But officially I'm "unofficial".' Benny let the weight of his comment sink in. 'So I was allowed to choose my own.'

'And you chose your real name,' Floyd sighed. 'Ingenious.' He rose to his feet and made to leave.

'Not so fast, Shoestring. I got a question.'

Benny mentally rechecked his orders from General Martin, and the briefing notes from Lieutenant Smith. He had been told the area would be civilian free; he had been told there would be no Westerners; he had been told it would be hot and humid (Smith, only having access to weather data for Karachi, had gambled Gilgit couldn't be too different).

'Lots of questions.'

Floyd guessed this might take some time, and pulled out two Cohibas. Benny declined.

'Never smoked, never drank. The devil makes no work for these hands, Housmann.'

'Suit yourself.' Floyd pulled out his DuPont.

'OK. First question. Why are you and all these other guys so interested in this here conference?'

'You don't know?'

'No, I do not!'

'Alright,' Floyd calculated. 'But if I tell you, you've got to promise it's "me and you" on this, from here on in. No more giving a leg-up to Bonnie, or any of the others.'

Benny was reluctant, Bonnie's were the hottest pair of legs he had come close to giving a leg-up to in a long while. She'd even called him 'Bozzy'.

Floyd sensed his dilemma.

'Don't worry. You'll get over her,' he consoled. 'I did.'

Graham had heard enough. Before Bonnie had a chance to tear into the intervening crates, he suggested a tactical retreat to the hotel across the road.

The dining room in the Hotel Shangri La was as bare as the rest of the establishment, but Miko and Phil managed to pull a few rickety tables together.

236

Graham coerced the owner into bringing more chairs from the back, along with a big pot of chai.

Bonnie sat at the far end with Phil. Vanh and Miko took one flank, Graham the other. Sarah waited for everyone to be seated, and then pointedly chose the chair furthest away from Graham. They had hardly had time to propose an agenda when Floyd and Benny appeared in the doorway. Bonnie didn't stop cursing either of them as they invited themselves in.

'I suggest we listen to what Boris has got to say,' As no one seemed to know where to start, Floyd had taken it upon himself to open proceedings. 'Since he's leading this operation.'

Benny nodded.

'Objection!' Graham raised his hand. 'Let's make one thing perfectly clear: your long-lost buddy is no leader of mine.'

'Or mine.' Phil chipped in.

Benny pouted.

'And he holds no sway over The Game,' Graham continued.

'I think you'll find, Graham,' Floyd held his hands up, 'that from now on, Boris holds sway over pretty much everything. And can do as he damn well pleases.'

Graham could feel the cards stacking against him. 'Such as?' he bluffed.

'Such as?' Floyd thought quickly. 'Such as, he can have you locked up in Elmore quicker than you could say "tough shit, Amnesty International".' Floyd puckered. 'How's that for size? Right, Boris?'

'That's about the sum of it.' Benny nodded. 'Probably use one of our off-shore facilities, though,' he added nonchalantly. 'Guantanamo most likely. Fewer prying eyes.'

Graham and Phil looked at each other for help, but they both knew they were beaten.

'So perhaps we can scrap the 'pow-wow' idea, people.' Floyd leaned in. 'And let Boris here tell us how it's going to be.'

Benny stood up and rested his fists on the table.

'Thank you, Floyd.' He began with a cough. 'Our man on the inside,' he eyed each participant in turn, but found no friendly faces, 'is due to arrive

237

with the King at 08.00 hours. So the conference will commence nine sharp, and there's no reason why we shouldn't have the whole thing wrapped up by lunchtime.'

'Your man wouldn't happen to be Zulfiquaar Al Butt, would it?' Graham sensed one last chance.

Benny choked, and did well to hold on to the pen he was spinning through his fingers. How come everyone knew so much?

Graham leant back, satisfied.

'What about the other delegations?' Phil spoke more out of something to say than any pressing desire for answers.

'The Chinese and Pakistani officials arrive tonight.' Benny didn't want to divulge any more than was strictly necessary.

'And our guys, Benny?' Floyd prompted.

'Shoestring!' Benny hissed exasperatedly. 'The name's "Boris", remember?'

Floyd looked sheepish. 'And I would appreciate it if you kept on remembering, for the duration of the conference.'

Boris retrained his gaze on the rest of the table and tried to exhibit some outward composure. He explained that The United States was to be represented by its newly-appointed ambassador to Xidakistan.

Graham and Phil sat resigned to their fate, but Bonnie had other ideas.

'Do you actually know who Mr Butt is, Boris?' Bonnie smacked the table as she rose to her feet.

'Of course.'

'Oh really?' Bonnie pouted her lips until they were ready to pop. 'I bet you couldn't pick him out of a crowd of two.'

Boris blustered.

'Just as I thought.' Bonnie felt a lift amongst her companions. 'Because Butt's our man. Isn't he, Graham?'

This was a gamble but Bonnie guessed Graham would allow it. For the moment he did.

'Don't listen to her, Boris, she's bluffing.' Floyd pulled the worst face he could manage at his ex. 'Zul's our man.'

Graham wanted to sound strong yet reasonable. 'Mr Butt has indeed promised me first call on his services,' looking Floyd straight in the eye, he rapidly played a number of possible scenarios in his mind, 'but in the present circumstances I think I could be persuaded to share.' Graham thought about it some more, and figured he would need someone watching his back. His heart said 'Sarah' but his head nodded at Bonnie. 'Or should I say "we could be persuaded"?'

'I can't hear you, Boris.' Bonnie cupped a hand around her ear.

Benny wasn't used to having broads purring up to him one minute and scratching his eyes out the next. 'I'm still calling the shots here, lady. Butt or no Butt.'

'Of course you are, Bozzy.' Bonnie wasn't sitting down either. 'But our demands are not extravagant.' Her eyes again looked to Graham for approval. 'Graham wants his book, and I want my story.' No mention of The Game. 'Zul has arranged for a party of four to accompany the King back up to Xidakistan, right, G?'

Graham would have liked to have known how Bonnie had come across that piece of information, but for the time being nodded.

'Naturally, you, Boris, as our glorious leader will be taking one place, and I presume for protocol's sake, the US ambassador will require the other?'

'Naturally.' Benny hadn't actually thought that far ahead.

'All Graham and I want.' Bonnie broke off just long enough to pull a face back at Floyd. 'Is an assurance that the other two places will be ours.'

'That's ridiculous!' Pinks leapt to his feet.

'What about The Game?' Phil jumped in after him.

The battled raged on but the day was already won.

Sarah

The problem with Graham is he's full of shit. There: I've said it. And I even swore again. As you have probably guessed, I am not in the best of moods just at the moment. But now I've got that off my chest, perhaps I can calm down.

I don't mean Gray's a habitual liar, a Walter Mitty, but before we went any further I wanted you to realise he wasn't whiter than white. All that 'Silkman on the Silk Road' stuff. If he loves Macclesfield so much, why hasn't he lived there for twenty years?

The seventh chapter of *Silkman on The Silk Road* was dedicated to Graham's home town and all things thereof: from the eponymous hillside hamlet outside Adelaide, which Graham visited on his *Return of the Macc* world tour of '99, to every major occasion the town has made an impact on the wider world. These broadly fall into four main categories: **Historical**, as when Lord Savage courageously raised Macclesfield's colours at Bosworth Field to aid victory for Henry Tudor; **Geographical**, around the world there are two Macclesfield Forests, a Macclesfield Canal, a Macclesfield Promontory, and most surprisingly a Macclesfield Bank (as in 'sand', not 'savings'), a low reef in the South China Sea which, along with the Paracel and Spratly Islands, has been the cause of many a sovereignty dispute; **Literary**, at auction the Macclesfield Psalter, a medieval compendium ranging from piety to bawdy poetry, and considered one of the greatest surviving examples of English manuscript illumination, regularly attracts bids in excess of a million pounds, and **Musical**, few record collections would consider themselves complete without Joy Division's *Love Will Tear Us Apart*, although the same cannot always be said for The Macc Lads.

At sixteen years of age Graham spent a lot of time in his local W H Smith's, and it was here he had come across the first ever edition of Small World's *United Kingdom*. Macclesfield warranted a mere one-line entry, as a side-trip from Manchester and a stop-off for the Peak District. Devastated, Graham had run down Mill Street to the library, and ransacked every last reference book.

Macclesfield Street

Curiously, London's historic streets and squares are not named after the towns and cities they seem to indicate, but rather the Dukes, Earls and Lords of the realm who built them.

In the sixteenth and seventeenth centuries, the high-flying Earl of Leicester owned one of the largest estates in the Elizabethan capital. What we now know as Leicester Square was in fact the site of his Earlship's imposing manor. On one side, the Earl looked out on a convent, with its garden, later to be known as 'Covent' Garden. On the other, towards the skittle alley in Pall Mall, lived Robert Baker, a tailor who had made his fortune making high-ruffed collars, known as Piccadills.

Baker's domain was nearly as magnificent as the Earl's, and had been designed to incorporate every luxury money could buy. Then, as now, however, envy didn't take long to rear its emerald-hued head where 'new money' was concerned, and local wags soon reduced the grand edifice to 'Piccadill House' or, even worse, 'Piccadilly'.

To the north of the Earl's manor stretched a long, walled park, and the open area beyond was known as Leicester Fields. Here he would go hunting with his entourage and the area became synonymous with the 'Soe-Hoe' hunting call of his meet.

Following the Restoration, the fortunes of Leicester's earls took a considerable tumble and they found themselves in need of realising some of their assets. Enter Charles Gerard, 1st Earl of Macclesfield, who, having ridden at the head of the King's Life-guards in Charles II's triumphal entry into London, had never sat prettier.

Together with two prominent businessmen, Sir Francis Compton and Richard Frith, Macclesfield offered to purchase a considerable tract of 'Soe-Hoe', with the intention of constructing a small grid of town houses to accommodate London's burgeoning bourgeoisie. This they did, and their model 'new town', centred on King's Square, was quite the place to live for many years.

The thoroughfare bearing The Earl of Macclesfield's name still stands, and Graham tracked it down on his first venture south to The Big Smoke. In fact, he sealed the deal with Ruff Guide's first ever distributor in the street's only pub, which had remained his meeting place of choice ever since.

Today, casual visitors to Chinatown could be forgiven for missing Macclesfield Street altogether as, over the years, the once majestic tribute to the area's prime developer has been whittled down to a mere thirty scruffy yards, and is home to none of the more distinguished eateries in the district. Nevertheless, the name behind this street is still one of the few which can, hand on heart, claim to have changed the country for ever.

In the eighteenth century the earldom of Macclesfield passed to the Parker family. Its head, Thomas, had done much to cultivate his position at court, and was already a member of both the Royal Society and the Privy Council. In 1716 he was appointed Lord Chancellor and, despite the occasional financial irregularity, he was able to bequeath to his son a position of great power.

In 1752 parliament decided to officially change over from the Julian to the Gregorian calendar, in line with the other European monarchies. The Caesars Julius and Augustus may have had courage enough to add months to their years, but only one man, George Parker, now Macclesfield's second Earl and President of the Royal Society, dared to strike off dates from the calendar. And to the tune of eleven days! The loss of nearly two weeks come September provoked a national outcry and Macclesfield was made to carry the can, as fondly depicted in Hogarth's "Give us our eleven days" painting of 1755.

If you find yourself going this way, pop into Dehems, a marvellous Dutch pub serving excellent beer and no gin (Hogarth would be proud!).

Going to watch Macc Town once a season hardly counts, either, by the way. Especially if you suspect, as I do, that 'the match' is little more than an excuse to escape his mum's house over Christmas.

Of course, I don't really care about that. Graham can have Macclesfield, and everything that's in it as far as I'm concerned. What drives me up the wall is that he will scrutinise everyone else's shortcomings to the 'n'th degree, yet sticks his head in the sand when it comes to his own. One rule for one, one rule.... OK, I'm ranting again. I'll give you one example and then I'll shut up.

Graham's usual seat was by the window, upstairs. He had sat there on his hastily rearranged return from Turkmenistan, when Sarah was pregnant. Five years later, a pint of Oranjeboom was once again on the table. This time it was accompanied by a glass of Sav Blanc (rather than mineral water), and an orange squash. On the first occasion Graham had talked Sarah round, but this time he wasn't so sure.

'I can't work with him anymore, Gray. I can't.'

The record certainly hadn't changed.

'I can't, Graham. And I won't.' This time Sarah was not alone. 'Don't do that please, petal.' Xavier, exhilarated from a visit to Hamleys, had just crashed his new monster truck into the wooden skirting boards. The polished floorboards were perfect for races and, as the three of them were the only ones upstairs, he was zooming under the tables to his heart's content.

'Alright,' Graham placated. 'I'll speak to him this afternoon.' Jos' *Woman's Own* reference to Sarah's latest project, *'Touring with a Toddler'*, was still ringing in Graham's ears. 'We'll go over the figures again, I promise.'

'It's got nothing to do with the stupid figures.' Sarah was livid. 'And you know it. Look how many copies *Baby* has sold, and we all know what he said about that.' Sarah flushed, blotches breaking out across her cheeks.

According to Sarah's PA (whom Graham always relied on for the ins and outs), that particular conversation had gone something like this:
Jos: 'Who in their right mind goes backpacking with a baby?'
Sarah: 'I did.'
Jos: 'Precisely.'

Sarah throws Jos' latest executive toy at his head.
Jos ducks and it smashes the mirror behind his desk.

'Yes, but things have changed now,' Graham mediated. 'And we all agreed that as far as finance is concerned, Jos has final say.'

'Graham!' Sarah's shriek brought Xavier to a crawlstill. 'I can't believe you're taking his side.'

'I'm not taking anyone's side.' Graham had been dreading the meeting all week and it was living up to all his worst-case scenarios. 'All I'm saying, Saz, is that I don't want you to leave. And I don't want you, in five years' time, to say I forced you out.'

'You said that five years ago.'

'Exactly.' Graham reached over for Sarah's hand. 'And look how much we've done in the last five years.'

'No, Graham,' Sarah pulled her fingers free. 'Things are different now.' Sarah looked down at Xavier.

'That's right, things are different. Everything's different now. The guidebook world is changing.'

Sarah was back looking at Graham. 'Real guides, on real places, for real people.' It was the mission statement on the title page of the *Ruff Guide To Spain*, and it had appeared in every edition of every book they had published since. 'Has that changed?'

Graham's eyes ducked away.

'Books that *we* would want to buy.' Sarah was back at Ruff Guides' first ever editorial meeting. 'Not ones that break the world down into bite-sized morsels for Jemima and Henry to snack on.' Her cheeks were burning, just as they had been so many years before. '*Toddler* is just the straw that's broken a back which should have been broken long ago.'

More ducking, this time the whole head.

'Graham!'

'I know but-'

'Do you?' Sarah squeezed the stem of her wineglass to breaking point. 'These days, I'm not so sure.'

Graham forced himself to meet her gaze.

'All I see is Mr Ruff Guides, swanning up and down the Silk Road.' Sarah took a long suck on the straw in Xavier's squash. Then a deep breath. 'Look, Graham. I don't want us to fight.' Sarah always found it hard to be angry. 'I came here today because of us. We can start again. Go back to the beginning, and start afresh.' Now it was her turn to reach for her partner's hand. *Follow Your Nose.* Sarah urged.

Graham's throat lumped at the reminder.

'We don't need Jos anymore. He can *drown* in his Free Of Charges for all I care, but you don't have to go down with him.'

'I'm not giving up Ruff Guides.' Graham was adamant. 'It's my company.'

'If it's your company, start running it like it's your company.'

'Come on, Sarah. It's not as easy as that.'

'That's what you said when we first started. But we did it. And we can do it again.' Sarah's mind was back on *Follow Your Nose.* 'Now we know the industry inside out, we'll have a head start no one else could ever have. We can reposition ourselves back on the cutting edge, and *really* write the sort of guidebooks that have never been written before.' Sarah was glowing with exhilaration, but Graham's face soon brought her back to earth.

He wasn't sure where to start. 'I've bought a new place.' Graham hesitated. 'More of a plot of land, really. On the Silk Road,' he added guiltily.

'You've what?'

'You're the one who said I needed to stop living with my mother.' Graham's shoulders tensed. 'It's on the Bosphorus. Next to that restaurant we went to when…'

Anger poured across the table.

'I'll be out there for the next few months at least. I'm,' he stuttered, 'I'm going to build my own *Xanadu.* You know, like I've always wanted.'

'Graham!' Again Xavier's eyes darted up. 'You don't give a-' Sarah hissed rather than swear. 'Do you?' She tried to remain calm. '"I'm alright, Jack" and sod the rest. Is that it?'

Graham made himself look Sarah in the eye, but couldn't produce the words.

'I don't know what I ever saw in you.' Sarah choked back tears as she threw herself up from the table. The legs of her chair screeched across the polished floor, her skirt catching on a protruding nail.

'Saz,' Graham pleaded.

Sarah tended to the rip. For a second time she breathed in deeply. 'No, Graham, no more "Saz". Forget it.'

Graham waited for the inevitable.

'Pathfinders have said they'll publish *Toddler* exactly how I want it.'

Again Graham waited. Tears were rolling on both sides now.

'Stick with Jos and his *Raj by Rail* fiascos, if that's what you want.' Sarah found the bitterness sticking in her throat. 'But don't say I didn't warn you.' She began gathering scattered toys. 'Come on, Xavier, we're going.'

Graham, not for the first time, wished he knew what he should do.

Sarah began to help her son with his coat. 'Say "goodbye" to Graham,' she urged, her eyes firmly fixed on Shabby's toy bag. The small boy reluctantly did as he was told.

Graham gave Xavier the hug meant for his mother. 'See you, Shabby.' Graham squeezed harder. 'Look after your mum.'

Returning to his drink and the window, Graham watched Sarah and Xavier emerge onto the pavement. As he saw them disappearing into Gerard Street, he rushed down the stairs, but by the time he reached the bottom he had changed his mind. Graham's fingers pressed hard into the long oak bar as he ordered another drink.

C

Follow Your Nose

The morning after Bonnie's coup, Graham was sitting on the Shangri La's concrete rooftop, eating his breakfast of fried eggs and toast, a welcome change from curry. He cast a buoyant eye over his notes. Finally, he was on the very last of his boxed texts.

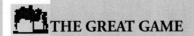 **THE GREAT GAME**

This is the name given to the political wranglings between the British and Russian empires in the second half of the nineteenth century. The map of Central Asia was pretty much a blank in those days, and each of the military heavyweights saw an opportunity to expand. As they jostled for position, their territories came closer and closer together, and the likes of Iran, Afghanistan and Chinese Turkestan were drawn into what the Russians called the 'Tournament of Shadows'. A semi-truce was finally agreed upon with the drawing up of the Durand Lines and the creation of The Wakhan Corridor (see p000).

In 1896, the British encouraged the Emir of Afghanistan to annex the lands of Xidakistan's neighbours, the hill men of Kafiristan ('the land of the non-believers'). This he duly did, converting the inhabitants to Islam as he went. But it was fierce work, and the renaming of the region as Nuristan, the 'land of light', was as superficial as many of the conversions.

Progress with Xidakistan was similarly underwhelming. Despite officially being absorbed into Afghanistan in 1893, it wasn't until 1897 that Kabul sent its first envoy up to the kingdom. Expectations were low. The Shah's man met with King Tah on three separate occasions, but at no point did the monarch indicate any interest in an alliance. Had he broached the idea that The Valley was already part of Afghan territory, the emissary would have been laughed back over the mountains.

As it took nearly six months for any round trip to be completed, there was little enthusiasm in Kabul for any further negotiations. In 1899, it was quietly decided to put the matter on permanent hold.

So Tah and his people simply carried on their daily lives, oblivious to all of the political wrangling taking place in the outside world. They probably would still have been undisturbed today, if it had not been for the building of the Karakoram Highway (see p000).

These final paragraphs read well enough, Graham consoled himself, but the preceding eight and a half pages were pure, unadulterated 'chaff'.

There was almost five pages on Sir George Hayward alone. This particular Georgie Boy certainly enjoyed his fifteen minutes of Imperial fame during the nineteenth century, and was later eulogised in Sir Henry Newbolt's poem, *He Fell Among Thieves*, but, Graham had to admit, few would recognise the name today. Fewer still would consider Hayward's daring attempt on Xidakistan via the Darkot Pass, and the subsequent treachery of his supposed friend Mir Wali of Dardistan, essential reading.

Similarly, if the 'shooting expeditions' and informal 'parleys' of the Great Game were a little obscure, then Lord Rosebury's reference to Xidakistan as 'The Gibraltar of the Hindu Kush' was positively obtuse. Russian travellers would no doubt appreciate mention of General Chernyaev, The Tsar's 'Lion of Tashkent' and French readers might temporarily be diverted by the account of their great explorer, Gabriel Bonvalot (including his first ascent of Mt Xidakistan, at 17,980ft, the country's highest peak), however, as far as Ruff Guides were concerned, it would be ambitious to bestow 'key market' status upon either nation.

Graham sighed. There had to be a way to keep something in on Mount Xidakistan (also known as X1). Its name followed in the great British Survey of

India tradition, which used 'K' for Karakorams (K2), 'P' for Pamirs, and 'X' for Xidaks. Mount Xidakistan's XL nickname may have been a poor cartographer's joke, but it made Graham smile. And what about Younghusband's chance encounter with Captain Yanov? How the two deadly rivals had agreed to shake hands and turn around after sharing a meal and a tent in no-man's land.

Graham paced across the hotel roof in search of inspiration, and stared at the enormous red, white and blue marquee standing where once there had been a bus depot. A pile of wiry Pathans were curled up under the tent's flaps, after a long night's work. Graham was tempted to congratulate Pinks' old school chum on his organisational skills. However, a rendition of *The Rose of Alabama* from the communal shower block, suggested that such a feat may have been achieved precisely because Benny had been tucked up in bed snoring like a gorilla. Graham was beginning to bundle his books into his satchel when Floyd appeared at the top of the stairs.

'You seen BS?' Pinks was still fuming from the night before.

'Try the shower.' Graham could be equally curt.

The emergence of Benny's wrinkled body from the rooftop bunker saved Floyd the bother. The lower half, wrapped in a Donald Duck beach towel, was mounted on two boat-sized flip-flops; the top half was draped in starched, white flannel. Two wiry arms were furiously scrubbing the head with a third piece of cloth.

'Nothing quite like a cold shower in the morning, hey boys?' Benny's gymnasium grin was met with a scowl. 'What's the matter? Couldn't get any sleep?'

Graham was tempted to comment on the previous night's nasal cacophony rasping out of Room Six, but refrained in the interest of brevity. 'If you gentlemen don't mind, I've got some work to do.' He made his way down the steps.

Floyd waited until Graham was out of ear shot. 'BS, you're gonna have to pull some strings here.' He began manoeuvring the pair of them into a more private corner. 'You gotta get me on that trip.'

'Well now, partner. I might just have some good news for you on that score.'

Pinks' ears pricked.

'It seems the White House is having problems coming up with a new ambassador at such short notice. At least one that wants to spend the next four years stuck up in old Xittystan.' Benny chortled. 'So,' his eyes gave a little twinkle, 'they've asked me if I might be able to suggest a suitable stop-gap.'

'Way to go, Bullshit. I knew you'd come through.' Pinks' pulled out his DuPont.

'But,' Boris had not forgotten the beatings he had taken in the junior school playground, 'Houston, we have a problem. They want someone with experience, preferably military.'

Floyd's face fell. But then sparked back up again. 'Wait! That's me, don't you see? Thanks to your department's blunderbuss back in '85, I've been Captain of the North Dakota Light Cavalry for over fifteen years.'

'Of course. Of course you have.' Boris would have to wait for another occasion to make Floyd grovel. 'Yes, sorry about that. Complete misunderstanding. I didn't find out until afterwards, you understand, otherwise I would have....'

'Boris,' Floyd wrapped his arm round his compatriot and gave him a big hug, 'not another word.' Benny looked relieved. 'All water off a duck's back for old Pinks Housmann. Who you have just made a very happy man.'

'What are friends for?' Benny shook his partner's hand. 'Something's rotten in Denmark if you can't assist an old school buddy, right?'

'That's right.' Floyd sucked his cigar to life. 'So how much is this job paying?'

By ten o'clock, the whole village had converged on the new big top, and Boris had taken up his position inside. He sat at an overly-large desk on a platform, at the head of a central ring of trestle tables, covered in white cloth. In the four corners of the tented room, booths had been set up, one for each delegation. The Chinese and Pakistani stands were full of officials (they had been waiting there since before nine, as instructed) but the American and Xidaki booths remained empty. At the back, a few chairs had been laid out, on which Sost's Police Chief, the Head of Customs and Excise, young Nasser, and Little Mo had been invited to sit.

Nasser and Mo were looking particularly happy. Earlier that morning they had decided to abandon the economic principles of capitalism in favour of forming a co-operative. The monopoly this joining of forces serendipitously created was more than a pleasant surprise. The two boys had been able to charge double their normal rate for climbing the big top's central pole and hanging the enormous American flag, plus a few other errands, and the money earned had not only paid off the remaining instalments on their bicycles, but also bought enough chocolate bars to last the winter.

Graham, Phil, Bonnie and Miko stood behind. Sarah, arriving last of all, squeezed in next to Miko. 'Where's Floyd?'

'We don't know.'

Dazzled by Miko's bright blue and green top, Sarah was about to ask what is was with all the football shirts, but then she caught sight of something even more strange, further down the line. Phil was sporting a large, homemade badge, proclaiming him to be the official delegate of MIXUP. Sarah nudged Miko and pointed.

'Graham says we're not to ask.'

At the far end, the Chinese and Pakistani delegations sat in stony silence. Suddenly, Zulfiquaar appeared at a side entrance, dressed in an immaculate, light-grey, St Michael three-piece suit, but also wearing a shaken demeanour. With him were five Xidakis, including a wizened, but happy-looking, elder. The old man was wrapped in an enormous cloak, made of snow leopard fur. Zul fussed him into the Xidakistan booth, and sat down at his side.

As Boris brought the meeting to order, Vanh sneaked through a flap, and took a seat to one side. He was carrying his Nikon SLR, with large telephoto lens. Boris signalled for each party to send their delegate and translator to the inner circle. As the Chinese, Pakistani and Xidaki contingents moved forward, Boris gave a second nod. Floyd appeared from behind a curtain in the American corner, crossed over the room, and took a seat at the negotiating table.

Graham and Bonnie exchanged nervous glances.

'Dear delegates,' Boris' High German accent had returned. 'Dankeschoen to all of you for attending this meeting today, at such short notice. And my special thanks to the United States' newly-appointed, acting ambassador to Xidakistan.'

252

Floyd couldn't help himself, and got up to take a bow. As he sat back down, he blew a kiss to Bonnie, and a raspberry at Graham.

'The Afghan delegation has, unfortunately, not been able to attend today.'

'Not been invited more like,' Graham muttered.

'Nevertheless, together with the delegations from Xidakistan, China, the USA and Pakistan, I, on behalf of the United Nations, will ratify any outcome of today's conference.'

Unable to wait any longer, Phil pushed his way to the front. 'Your honour.'

Floyd's face froze.

'As the representative of MIXUP,' Phil cleared his throat, 'the Movement for an Independent Xidakistan and Upper Pakistan, I consider it only fair that I, too, am invited to sit in on this conference.'

'This,' Benny was flummoxed, 'this is highly irregular.'

'Back off, Kelly.' Pinks was more forthright.

'Hear the man out!' Miko heckled.

Before Phil could continue, one of the non-executive members of the Pakistani delegation approached his colleagues at the main table, and whispered something into their ears. As they fell deeper and deeper into their *sotto voce* discussion, the remaining delegates played with their plastic national emblems, super-glued onto small brass paperweights. Presently, a junior Pakistani official approached the head table with a hurriedly scrawled note, attached to an official-looking document. Boris scanned both documents, nodded his agreement, and felt it appropriate to rise to his feet.

'My apologies, ladies and gentlemen. As our friends from Pakistan have rightly pointed out, this is a meeting to determine Xidaki independence, and as such has no bearing on the status of Upper Pakistan. Any discussions regarding that region's independence, therefore, must be reserved for another, more appropriate occasion. Indeed, the Pakistani officials, on behalf of the Pakistani government, would like the following to go on record:'

Benny motioned for the Pakistani delegate to take the floor.

'"In accordance with the United Nations ceasefire agreement of January 1949,"' the young man droned, '"*The Northern Areas* and *Azadi Jammu and Kashmir* regions, which together constitute *Upper Pakistan,* are already recognised as autonomous states by the government of Pakistan. This is pending a referendum of their inhabitants, together with the inhabitants of *Occupied Kashmir*, as called for by the said UN agreement.

The government of Pakistan would also like to point out that, in light of India's persistent refusal to allow such a referendum (in direct contradiction of the treaty they themselves signed), Pakistan has been left no other choice but to assist in the administration and government of both these regions."'

The delegate breathed a sigh of relief, folded up his notes and turned to Phil.

'We would, therefore, welcome any private discussion with the MIXUP representative, once the conference has drawn to a close.'

Phil slumped into an empty seat. The whole Pakistani delegation flashed a simultaneous smile.

'If there are no further objections,' Boris scanned his audience menacingly, 'I would like to call upon Mr Butt to deliver the opening speech.'

All eyes turned to Zulfiquaar, but Graham was more interested in the old man sat at Zul's side. Certainly the Xidaki delegate looked very stately in his native ceremonial dress, but wasn't the new king supposed to be in his early thirties?

Zulfiquaar remained seated and refused to stop fiddling with the freshly designed Xidakistan flag in front of him. Eventually, he darted a look up at Boris, but his eyes fell back to the horizontal blue, white and green stripes, with Buddhist Sun roundel and Royal Trout naiant.

The Chinese looked on impassively, but others began to cough and whisper. When Boris himself coughed, three times, Zul had no choice but to rise. Squirming, he made to sit back down again, but then took three quick blasts of his inhaler and began. Zul raced through his speech without drawing breath, leaving the translators no option but to paraphrase. The old man at Zul's side was indeed not King Tah. He was his uncle, and had been sent in the king's stead.

Zul then distributed a letter from King Tah to each delegate, and returned to fingering his flag. Boris opened up his letter and scanned down to the nitty-gritty:

My wife and I wish to thank our royal cousins for the beautiful pair of bicycles they have given us. We apologise for not being able to come in person, but we have been sent flying over our handle bars, after crashing into a boulder. Uncle Mas, as our formal representative, has been given full authority to accept any other gifts you might wish to present, including the card of congratulations on Xidakistan's independence. The Maharaja of Punjab has explained such cards are customary on these occasions.

We are still slightly bemused by this practice of congratulating each other on things that happened so long ago, and would like to know more. For instance, when one of our royal cousins next celebrates their birthday, should we congratulate them on all the other birthdays they have had before as well?

The king ended the letter with a request for a new front wheel.

Boris was not amused. Summoning Zulfiquaar to the empty US booth, he whipped the curtain closed. Wild yelps and repeated crashing could be heard for several minutes, but after a final almighty smash, peace reigned. The two men returned to the table, Boris red in the face, Zul very much down at heel.

Boris now proposed that in the interests of time, two identical treaties should be drawn up and signed. One could go straight to the United Nations for immediate approval, and the other would be taken up to The Valley for King Tah to counter-sign. Boris put the motion to a vote and, after some initial hesitation from the Chinese delegation, the motion was carried.

'Right. Down to business.' Benny clicked open his Special Intelligence-issue briefcase and pulled out a red, white and blue clipboard. 'To save time I think it will be easier if I read out the treaty:

1. The United States of America (hereinafter to be referred to as 'we') undertakes to build a new highway from Sost to Xidakistan, cutting a tunnel underneath the Ishkaman Pass.

2. The People's Republic of China (hereinafter to be referred to as 'they') undertakes to build a new highway from Tashkurgan to Xidakistan, cutting tunnels underneath the Wakhjir Pass and the Mintaka Pass.

3. *We*, in association with Cable and Wireless, will build a new communications network for Xidakistan, and will provide King Tah with a satellite telephone. This will give him unlimited talk-time, until new phone lines are connected.

4. *They* will build a new school with enough capacity for all Xidaki children under the age of sixteen. Free Mandarin lessons will be provided for all Xidakis, regardless of age.

5. *We*, in association with Enron, will supply Xidakistan with gas and electricity, and explore for minerals and natural resources, in return for a percentage of all revenues.

6. *They* will supply every citizen in Xidakistan with a bicycle.

7. *We*, in association with McDonalds, will ensure that each Xidaki child receives the United Nations' 'recommended daily food allowance', or Happy Meal equivalent.

8. *They* will issue every Xidaki child with a CCP jacket and cap.

9. *We* will assist Xidakistan in outlawing all cultivation, production and sale of opium, and other narcotics, within its borders.

10. *They* will assist Xidakistan in monitoring all internet usage within its borders.

'And finally,' Boris looked up, flushed with success, 'finally, ladies and gentlemen,'

11. *We* and *they* will jointly guide Xidakistan on foreign policy.

12. *We*, on *their* approval, will be allowed to use Xidaki territory as a strategic base from which to launch operations, as part of the War on Terror.

Boris shuffled his papers into a neat rectangle.

'I think that just about covers everything. Does anyone have anything else to say?' Boris didn't wait for a reply. 'No? Good. Right, who's got a pen?' Boris laughed, as his father used to, at his own bad joke. 'Floyd, I wonder if you could ask your cameraman to come up and take a few pictures of us signing the treaty?'

Vanh was duly summoned.

'Graham, do something.' Sarah sounded doubly frustrated, as she had earlier decided that she wasn't speaking to her former partner. 'They can't sign a treaty like that.'

'What can I do?'

'Do *something*,' she pleaded. 'Anything.'

Graham didn't move.

Sarah's blood was boiling. 'Graham!' Her nails dug into the skin on her forearms. 'What's happened to you?'

Still nothing.

Determined not to make a fool of herself, Sarah vanished through one of the flaps. Phil, Bonnie and Miko took it in turns to stare at Graham, and there was nowhere to hide. He was almost pleased to see Floyd waltzing over to gloat.

'Good afternoon, everyone.'

'Alright, Floyd, congratulations.'

Bonnie and Phil weren't feeling quite so generous.

'Yes, it was rather well played, wasn't it? Even if I do say so myself.' Floyd drew everyone's attention to the US government tie pin he had been presented with that morning.

'It suits you.' Miko tried to keep a straight face.

'Don't knock it, kid.' Floyd inspected the latest football shirt Miko was wearing. Large Arabic script spelt out Qatar on the front. 'Especially when you're dressed like that. Who's it this time? Al Qaeda?'

*   *   *

Graham had lunch on his own. Sarah and Phil were sulking, Floyd and Vanh were 'packing', Miko had taken off up a nearby glacier, and Bonnie had disappeared. Bonnie's absence was the one that really mattered. Graham was hoping to use the laptop with satellite phone connection she had 'borrowed' from Boris. Sost had less internet access than Gilgit, and Graham couldn't wait to let rival players of The Game know that 'X' was back on the table.

Finishing off his meal with some of the Shangri La's milky tea, which was even worse than the coffee at breakfast, Graham could wait no longer. He headed over to the ever-so-slightly more salubrious hotel across the road. Having mounted the outside steps, which led to the 'penthouse', he knocked on Bonnie's door.

'Go away!' Bonnie groaned. She sent an empty champagne bottle rolling across the floor as she reached over for the light. 'Do not disturb!'

Indicating he wasn't the hotel maid, Graham outlined his needs.

'Come on, Bonnie. It'll only take a couple of minutes. I'm expecting some really important stuff for my book.' Graham suspected that this would carry more weight than admitting he was itching to brag.

'I said: "get lost". And besides, it's Boris'. You'll have to ask him.'

'But Bon, we're supposed to be partners.'

'Not this afternoon, we're not.'

Graham slumped down outside the door. 'Alright, you win,' he announced to the concrete wall opposite. 'My book will have to undergo yet another delay, but as long as you're happy.'

'Christ, enough with the whining.' Bonnie checked the exhausted body next to her to make sure he was still asleep. 'I'll meet you at your hotel in ten.'

Graham was about to walk away, a job well done, when he felt sure he heard a snore emanating from inside. 'Bonnie?'

'I said ten!'

Graham tried to peer through a hole in the curtain. 'Is that you, Boris?' He heard a familiar slap, but it was the head Pakistani delegate's hands that had started to wander.

'Don't panic, B,' he laughed, 'your secret's safe with me. I'll see you over the road.'

At the top of the stairs, he called over his shoulder, 'Make it fifteen. If he's up to it.'

Back at The Shangri La, Graham tried to sit patiently in the courtyard out front, but he was too excited about The Game. Finally, it was happening. As if to prove the point, Pinks came bounding down from the rooms beaming a huge smile. Graham could have sworn he had never seen Pinks so happy without the aid of alcohol. Sporting his favourite   sweater and smoking what looked like the largest cigar outside Havana, he plonked himself down next to Graham. The cerise of the lamb's wool was almost fluorescent.

'OK, Ruff, time to negotiate.' Floyd was rubbing his hands with panto-like glee. 'We've got some history to make.'

Behind him Vanh could be seen struggling his way down the steps with Floyd's bags.

'I'm assuming you want to go back to your original deal?' Graham proffered.

'Sounds good to me,' Pinks beamed.

'OK.' Graham brokered. 'Let's just say I wanted to give you The Game. What about Bonnie?'

The beam broke. 'We could leave before she gets here?'

'I'm waiting to send some emails,' Graham stonewalled.

'Emails, sheemails.' Pinks was full of himself. 'Zul will be waiting. Time to go!'

'I'm not going anywhere,' Bonnie snarled from the courtyard archway. 'Not without lunch!' The look on her face settled the argument.

She gave Graham a tart glare but handed over the computer and satellite equipment all the same.

'So soon?' Graham indicated the eight minutes elapsed on his watch..

While Bonnie ate, Graham logged on and Pinks puffed.

The moment was shattered by Graham's first email. Ostensibly, it was a standard update from Jos, but the final sentence contained a bombshell. Graham reread each word to double-check, before letting out an ear-splitting reference to the legitimacy of Jos' birth certificate.

'Oh no you don't, pal. No one messes with my books.' He spun round from facing the screen. 'Bonnie, I need that satellite phone.'

'You're already using it.'

'OK, nobody move.'

Graham yanked the sat-phone connection out of the laptop, and started dialling.

Jos' mobile transferred straight to voicemail, and he wasn't in the office, or the Surrey mansion. Antonia's voice suggested Graham try the Chelsea flat. Finally, on the eighteenth attempt, the receiver picked up before the answering machine clicked in. The muffled voice sounded tired and unfriendly.

'This had better be a joke. Or I'm on the next plane home ready to smash your face in.'

'Graham? Is that you?'

'Of course it's me.'

'But it's half past three in the morning.'

'I don't give a flying monkey's what the time is. I've just read your email?'

Jos stalled. 'Which one?'

'Don't start, Jos. I swear.'

Graham was out of the courtyard and on the main street, searching for the best reception. A host of locals, having never seen a man frantically waving a satellite phone in the air before, had gathered to spectate.

'Look, G,' Jos sat up in bed. 'I won't bore you with the details but basically we're going to have to can the book.'

The naked girl beside him drowsily began to fondle his chest hair.

'Not now, sugar. Go back to sleep.' Jos reluctantly clambered out of bed and took the phone into the en-suite.

'Can you repeat that, G?' he gambled. 'You're breaking up.'

'Don't you dare! ' Graham's fury brought an 'ooo' from the crowd. 'This is my company. No one tells me which books I can and cannot do.'

'Look, G, the accountants came round this week. After 9/11 we've had to re-forecast all the figures.' Jos' voice dropped to a whisper, out of habit. 'Next year's 25% growth is now a big black hole of minuses. Take it from me, this is a purely economic decision.'

Graham wasn't taking anything, but he was too wound up to speak.

'We can't afford to bring a book out that only thirty people will ever buy.' Jos felt the figures spoke for themselves.

Graham's top blew. 'I've bust my balls for fifteen years for this.'

'Look, mate, I know you're upset, but look at it from the company's point of view. I'm not saying we'll never do it. Just not right now.'

'I don't think you quite understand, you…' Graham battled for the right word. 'Dickhead! I've been working my whole life for this. And it's coming out. Out before *Small World,* or any of the others, gets theirs out. I don't care if I have to come back and print the thing myself.'

'We haven't got the money, Graham.'

'Sell your bloody Porsche.'

'Come on, now you're being stupid.' Josh laughed nervously at the thought that Graham might not be joking.

'Either this book comes out, Jos, or cousin or no cousin, I'll …..'

Jos was beginning to lose his patience. 'You'll what? You seem to be forgetting that I'm in control now.' Graham had refused to buy Sarah's stake when she left the company, in an attempt to persuade her to stay. Jos hadn't been so scrupulous.

'Like hell you are.' Graham screwed his face up into the mouthpiece. 'You own sixty six point three three percent; your original thirty three plus Sarah's third. You gave me your point three three recurring, remember?'

'So?'

'So? All decisions over the commissioning and decommissioning of a Ruff Guide need a two-thirds majority.'

'Don't be ridiculous.'

'I'll show you ridiculous.' Graham smashed the handset on the floor and began grinding it into the dust. 'Get it?' he screamed at the disintegrated plastic.

'Without me Ruff Guides would still be four tatty exercise books, and a picture map of Spain,' Jos hollered back. 'You hear me?'

He too threw his handset to the ground, and stomped back into bed.

'That wasn't Antonia, was it?' Becky rubbed the sleep from her eyes.

'No, no. Just someone at work.' Jos stroked Becky's long blonde hair as she nuzzled her nose into his neck. 'Forget about it.'

By the time Graham caught up with the others, they were at the bus station. He threw down his pack and handed Bonnie the remainders of Boris' sat-phone 'Don't ask.'

For once, Bonnie heeded the advice.

'Everything alright?' Pinks grinned, still puffing away on his cruise missile.

'No, it's not *alright*,' Graham strained. 'Jos has had the accountants in, and he wants to pull the plug on the book.'

'Ouch.' Floyd was lapping it up.

A sharp look from Graham straightened Floyd's face. 'I'm still doing it. He can go and whistle if he thinks he's overruling me.'

'You tell him, G. He's nothing but a glorified tea boy.'

'It's not funny, Floyd.' Graham slowly calmed down and took stock of the situation. 'Where's Boris?'

Floyd stopped sucking. 'Just missed him.'

'What?' Too many ideas were flying around Graham's brain.

'Change of plan. Can't make it. Kabul's finally about to fall, and he's been called in for the final push.'

All around them boxes were being packed back into trucks.

'What about the treaty?'

'As acting US ambassador,' Pinks showboated, 'you'll be delighted to hear, he has left yours truly in charge.'

Graham glowered. 'What about his place on the trip?'

'Well, as Mikey's the only one here, I said he can come. So long as he covers his share of the expenses.'

Graham looked at Miko, fresh from his glacial exertions. 'What about George?'

'George's gotta get back to Gilgit to tie up some loose ends.'

Vanh looked away but was saved further discomfort by the arrival of Sarah, racing through the gate.

'Sarah,' Graham looked startled. 'Where have you been?'

'What's happening to Boris' place?'

News travelled fast.

'It's only fair to let someone else go,' Sarah panted.

'Anyone apart from Kelly,' Floyd snickered.

'Where is Phil?' Bonnie wasn't quite as relaxed.

Finally, Sarah looked Graham in the eye.

'I knocked on his door,' Miko offered. 'But there was no answer.'

'Must have got Mixed Up in something,' Pinks chuckled.

No one laughed.

'I want that last place on the trip.' Sarah jabbed her hands onto her hips.

'Too late, honey. Mikey here just bought the last ticket.'

'Graham?' Sarah was determined not to beg.

To Graham's relief Zul appeared from behind the half-dismantled big top, and signalled for them all to come. He had gathered the Xidaki delegation, plus half-a-dozen Pakistani porters, a truck full of packhorses, and all the mountain-bike wheels money could buy: which in Sost was seven.

'Good afternoon, my friends. Everybody ready?' Zulfiquaar was in charcoal grey trousers, fawn-coloured shirt and dark brown V-neck jumper. Setting off the M&S look was a brand-new, army-issue, Gore-Tex wind-cheater, and a thick fur hat. Each Xidaki wore similar gear.

'Slight change of plan, Zul.' Floyd raised his hand. 'Miko is going to come instead of Boris.'

'If that's OK?' Miko hadn't stopped smiling since the decision.

'Fine, fine.' Nothing could dampen Zul's spirits now the treaty had been successfully negotiated, and his authorities had given him the all clear. As each side lined up to greet their fellow travellers, he quickly began the introductions. However, when Uncle Mas reached Bonnie, the old man suddenly stopped, and backed away with a small bow. His response was copied by the others. Zulfiquaar launched apologies at Bonnie, and scuttled over to where the Xidakis had gathered in a huddle. After a brief conflab he returned.

'I sincerely beg your pardon, Mizz Fidler, but would you mind if I asked you if you have any children?' Zulfiquaar had taken care to stand well away from her sharp claws.

'Yes I would mind.'

'Don't worry, Zuley,' Floyd jumped in, 'I'll answer that.'

Bonnie flashed the back of her hand and Pinks bit his tongue.

'Not that it's any of your concern, Mr Butt,' Bonnie recomposed herself. 'But no, I don't have any children.'

'In that case,' Zul hesitated. 'I'm afraid you can't come.'

'I beg your pardon.'

'I'm sorry Mizz....'

Bonnie cut him dead. 'You can "I'm sorry" all you like. I'm going to The Valley, and that's final.' Bonnie's jaws were chewing at Mach three.

'Of course, Mizz Bonnie, but Uncle Mas has just explained that no childless women are allowed,' Zul managed to blurt out.

'Do you know how much coverage I've been promised for this story?' Bonnie snapped. 'Two front covers, four spreads and a commemorative insert. Signed, sealed and delivered.'

'But now the king is married,' Zul countered, 'no childless women are allowed into his house. Not until his first child is born. It's bad luck.'

'So I don't go inside the house. Big deal.'

'But you couldn't go to The Valley and not visit King Tah. It would bring shame on him and all his family.'

'Listen, buster, you can tell Uncle Mas, and all the other little Masses...' Bonnie took a deep breath. 'Better still, I'll tell them myself. You translate, and don't change a damn letter.'

'Mr Graham, Mr Floyd.' Zul shook. 'Help me, please, my hands are tied.'

'Nothing to do with me.' Pinks was keeping well out of range.

As Zul turned to Graham, Bonnie's claws extended. 'Please, Mr Graham. If she doesn't remove herself from the party, none of you will be able to enter The Valley.'

The back of Bonnie's right hand rose up. 'I'd think very carefully before you answer that, Ruff.'

'Come on, B.' Graham trod warily. 'We haven't really got much choice.'

Bonnie's skin was breaking out in a sweat. As her body heat mixed with the cold air, she was literally fuming. 'There's no point none of us going,' Graham ventured. 'Is there?'

Bonnie wasn't biting.

'Think about it,' Graham pressed. 'Think if you were in our position.'

Pinks made himself chew on his cigar to conceal his delight.

'You're going to pay for this, Housmann,' Bonnie shrieked as she marched back to her room. 'Every last cent.'

Graham turned to his partner. 'You didn't....?'

'Me?' Pinks faked incredulity. 'How could I have anything to do with this?' He held his hands out empty. 'But then again it would seem ungrateful not to reward old Uncle Mas with a little something. George, bring me my humidor.'

As Floyd was giving the old man the pick of his prize cigars, Bonnie marched back into view and over to the pack animals. Before they could work out what she was doing, the long silver tube containing the treaty had been torn from the lead pony.

'Everyone stay exactly where they are.' Bonnie was cutting swathes in the air. 'There's no way that smug lump is having it all his own way.' She couldn't bring herself to even look at Floyd.

'Too late, love of my life.'

'You can't come on the trip, Bonnie,' Graham reiterated. 'The king won't let you in. Waving a silver lightsaber around isn't going to change that.'

'Maybe not, but it'll sure make sure you listen to my demands.'

'Which are?'

Bonnie began cackling. 'I'm giving my place to Phil.'

Graham racked his brains but in the end he gave up. 'Phil?'

'Yeah, Phil.' Bonnie scowled at Floyd. 'I don't care who wins The Game, as long as it's not him.' Another scowl. 'I'm giving my place to Phil.'

'Forget it.' Pinks nonchalantly sliced the end of Uncle Mas' cigar. 'This train is ready to depart.'

Graham took a few tentative steps towards the tube.

'I mean it.' Bonnie gripped onto the treaty extra tight, her mane was tossing wildly from side to side as she swiped.

'The king *is* expecting four visitors.' Zul nodded, in the hope of diffusing the situation.

'You see,' Bonnie salivated. 'So either Ned goes, or-'

'Or what?' Pinks had had enough.

'Or else,' Bonnie ripped the top off the tube. 'Or else, I tear up the treaty.'

Miko was sent to fetch Phil.

But came back empty-handed. 'He's gone.'

'Gone? Gone where?'

'Went as soon as the conference finished by the sounds of things. The hotel guys say he just packed his bag and left.'

'He could be halfway to Darkot by now,' Floyd panicked.

Vanh no longer cared. 'He'll probably have wangled himself Xidaki citizenship, and a harem full of beauties, by the time you guys get there.'

Bonnie couldn't hide her delight, and began twirling her tube like a majorette's baton. Graham looked at Floyd in horror.

'We have to stop him.' Floyd was straw-clutching. 'There must be something we can do.'

'No, we'll never catch him.' Graham cursed. 'There's no way we'll beat him with all these animals.'

'But we'll be in The Valley tomorrow evening,' Zul reassured.

Bonnie stopped twirling. 'What do you mean, "tomorrow"?'

Graham and Floyd were similarly confused. They had allowed up to a week.

'We'll be there by late tomorrow, it only takes a couple of days on the old route,' Zul gushed.

'What "old" route?' Graham spoke for everyone.

'The route through the Wakhjir Pass.' Zul looked surprised. 'The route the Chinese road-builders took in '76, remember.'

'So why have we been spending half our lives tramping over the Darkot Pass?' Pinks stormed.

'Because the Wakhjir is in Chinese territory, and for years they had it blocked off. They were only prepared to reopen it once the treaty was signed.'

'Of course,' Graham whispered to himself. 'The Wakhjir. His tongue started tingling in excitement.

'I don't believe it,' Bonnie screamed, dropping the tube to the floor in despair.

'Poor old Ned.' Pinks clicked his lighter and set Uncle Mas' torpedo ablaze. 'Last again.'

'Hold it, Housmann.' Bonnie had frantically started gum-chewing again. 'You've not won yet,' Bonnie turned to Vanh. 'George, if I give you my place, will you take the photos for my stories?'

George shook his head.

'I'll split all the fees. 50/50,' Bonnie bribed.

'No thanks.' Vanh wore an impassive smile.

'OK. 60/40.'

'You're asking the wrong guy.'

'Well said that man,' Pinks rejoiced. 'Forget it, Bonnie, he works for me.'

'75/25.' Bonnie was too desperate to haggle properly.

'It doesn't matter what you offer me.' Vanh shook his head. 'I'm not doing it.'

'George!' Bonnie pleaded.

'The name's Vanh. And besides, I'm not in the travel writing business anymore.' He turned to a gaping Floyd. 'I quit.'

'But, what…?' Pinks came over all weak. 'What about The Pinks Guide? What about our book?' He tried to whisper the last two words so Graham wouldn't hear.

'Time to move on,' Vanh replied flatly.

'But, but,' Floyd stammered.

'No "buts", Floyd. It's time.'

Vanh looked to Miko for moral support, and received a discreet pump of the fist. Floyd's cigar almost toppled out of his mouth.

'Wait a second,' Graham shook his head, 'what book?'

Pinks froze.

'A new Butch and Sundance book,' Floyd improvised. 'It's something I was trying to get done before the sale.' He gave Vanh a Grade A hard stare.

'Don't worry, Geo…, Vanh.' Pinks quickly corrected himself. 'We can talk about it later.'

'No, Floyd.' Vanh dropped Pinks' bags and pulled out a collection of pocketbooks. 'Let's talk about it now. Here. In front of Graham.'

Miko sucked in a sharp blast of air.

'Floyd?' Graham could see it all now. 'Is there something you want to tell me?'

Floyd bit hard into his tobacco leaves. 'Alright. Alright. So maybe I said to Terry that I'd do one last book for *Small World.*'

'On Xidakistan?' Graham stared down the two of them in turn. 'That's why you were sending Vanh back to Gilgit.'

'I was going to let you get your book out first, cross my heart.'

Bonnie would have gladly stabbed him through it.

'Cross your heart, eh?' Graham gave Vanh several nods of thanks, and walked over to where Bonnie had tossed the treaty. He picked it up, carefully, and began to dust it down.

'Don't be mad.'

'I'm not mad,' Graham shrugged. 'But let's make one thing clear.' He turned to look Floyd straight in the eye. 'From now on, no more deals. It's every man for himself.'

'Fine,' Floyd fired back. 'And let the best man win!'

'Or woman.' Sarah had been watching patiently.

Floyd, about to spit in his palm, span round.

'I'll take Bonnie's place.'

'But,' Graham hurried back on to the defensive. 'We agreed….'

'Yes, we did.' Some of Sarah's old Alhambra spark was coming back. 'But like you just said, "no more deals". All bets are off.' Sarah felt a surge of adrenalin rush to her head. 'And as I have a full range of stretch marks induced by thirteen hours of excruciating labour, I am pretty sure King Tah will be pleased to see me.'

'Ah, yes,' Zul enthused. 'And a baby boy, if I'm not mistaken. A very good omen.'

'Don't worry, Bonnie, I'll get the pictures for your stories.' Sarah felt a second surge. 'And you can keep the fees.' Sarah smiled to herself. Why was she always so god, damn, NICE?

The Valley

The journey up to the Wakhjir Pass is a hard one, whichever way you go, and vegetation soon peters. Above 4000m, with no more track, and snow and ice thick on the ground, the group was restricted to little over a mile an hour

The Pakistani porters led the horses on foot, and the Xidakis seemed happy to carry anything and everything they were given, but the four explorers were struggling just to keep one boot in front of the other. As the last light faded, they fumbled their way up to a flattish area just short of the saddle and pitched camp.

After dinner, Miko, and Zul, along with the Xidakis and the porters, turned in early. Graham, Floyd and Sarah kept watch, Pinks worrying how to finish his book, Sarah whether to start hers, Graham how to stay one step ahead. At least he knew what he was going to do with Jos, and it was this thought that drifted him off to sleep.

Graham woke stiffly the next morning, to find his copy of *Lost Horizon* neatly folded into his hiking socks. A postcard to his mother was still saving his place, but attached to the makeshift bookmark was a newspaper cutting: one of the first interviews Graham had given after launching Ruff Guides.

> *'We set out to do something new when we published the first Ruff Guide. We had just returned from Spain and felt let down by the various guides we'd used.'*

Scrawled underneath it in red pen was:

Read it Graham. That was you when we first met.

I never thought you'd change.

Sarah

An hour after breakfast, the group reached a *chorten*, decorated with two small prayer wheels, and a string of tattered prayer flags. At 5200m this marked the last-but-one bit of 'up', and they duly stopped to celebrate. The pass is known as that of 'a Thousand Ibex' but on this day there were none to be seen so, whilst the porters changed the tired ponies, the Xidakis made do with trapping a brace of snow partridges, which seemed to have made the one of the prayer wheels their home.

To the north-east, two jagged peaks, wearing wisps of snow cloud, indicated the Mintaka Pass and, beyond, China. Down to the west was a small plain. On the far side, the rocky zigzag of the old jade traders' trail led up again. Up to what Zul indicated was the eastern entrance to The Valley, refulgent in the first sun of the day.

A few hours from now, Graham reminded himself, his lifetime ambition would be realised. His years of intangible dreams were about to become very, very real. He sneaked up behind Sarah, and playfully surprised her with a hug. 'I got your note.'

'Good.' Sarah unwrapped Graham's arms, and deliberately removed herself from his grip.

'And I agree with you.' Graham turned Sarah around. 'I really do.'

'Good.'

'It's just…'

Sarah glowered as fiercely as she could and made to go. Graham grabbed her hand.

'OK, OK. No more "justs".'

'Very good.'

'I haven't changed that much.' Graham's field of vision was fixed. 'I promise.'

The two of them stood looking into each other's eyes, until they both truly believed what he had said.

'Excellent.'

Graham put his arms around Sarah again, and gave her a small kiss. This time she didn't pull away.

'It's alright, though.' Sarah added honestly. 'I know how much Ruff Guides means to you.'

'Actually .....' Graham reached for Sarah's hands.

'No, G, you were right. I was just dreaming.'

'You wrote that mission statement too, you know.'

'Maybe, but a lot's...,' Sarah checked herself. 'Let's not go down that road.'

'Alright. But I just wanted to let you know that I've had an idea.'

'This hasn't got anything to do with Jos wanting to pull the plug, has it?'

News did travel fast.

'I won't ask you how you heard about that but, no, that has nothing to do with it.'

Sarah looked unconvinced.

'Alright. It may have given me the kick start I needed.'

'Come on then, spill the beans on your great idea.'

'Not yet!' Graham laughed as he skipped off up the slope. 'You'll have to wait and see.'

Four hours of *crevasses, ablation valleys and bergschrunds* later (Graham had noted the new words for his guidebook), the small party reached the crest of the eastern fissure in The Valley's protective ring of rock.

'Wow!' Miko exhaled coming up behind Graham, and looking down.

'Bingo!' Pinks celebrated.

'All we need now's a Blue Moon.' Graham grinned, thinking back to his *Lost Horizon*. He rubbed his gloves in glee.

The craterlike valley below them was about five miles wide, and fifteen miles long, east to west, with X1 and X2 standing proudly at opposite ends. Graham's altimeter indicated just over 4500m, but the jutting peaks must have been another fifteen hundred metres up at least, and the drop to the valley floor was five hundred metres if it was a centimetre.

Down in the basin, the ground sloped away to the western end, where the various streams gathered into a small lake, below a sheer cliff face. Next to the lake, stood a group of yurts and broch-like structures: the 'capital'. Although the valley floor was itself largely free of snow, the slopes were covered, particularly on the south side. Each compass point in the surrounding ring had its own small crack, just as mythology had described. The gap to the north, Graham presumed, was the route which led to Bozai Gumbaz.

The Xidaki contingent climbed up to join them, and as they did so, each one laid a small stone on a short dyke of rocks about two metres high. The *mani* was topped and sided with flattish stones, on some of which words were carved.

'Om-mani-pad-mi-hum.' Graham couldn't read the Xidak characters, but he remembered the chant. 'I saw something similar in Tibet. The stones are commemorative offerings to Angel Khujidal. On Judgement Day he will appear and read the name of anyone who has placed a stone on the *mani*, and grant them salvation.'

Sarah gave Graham an indulgent smile, and he shut up.

'Hey guys. Look over here.' Miko was perched on a large flat rock next to a small cairn. It soon became apparent that he was standing above the departure point for a kind of home-made bob sleigh track. A snaking channel swooshed left, then right, down the slope before spilling into a large pudding bowl of a finish. Zul explained that over the centuries, every stone and rock had been removed from this 'run' and every hump flattened, until it was perfect. The Pakistani porters had returned to Sost that morning with the horses, so Uncle Mas' retinue were carrying everything in their enormous backpacks. From one there now came a pile of what looked like giant-sized thick, leather pouffes, with all their stuffing taken out. They beckoned their visitors to the ledge of flattened ice at the head of the descent, and indicated their intentions.

The first Xidaki, like his companions, was pocket-sized. He looked the wrong side of fifty but, according to Zul, was not even forty. His grin revealed a half empty set of teeth, and his big furry hat threatened to engulf his wizened head, but this didn't stop him disappearing over the edge with a loud whoop, leaving the four newcomers agog. The second daredevil was more deliberate, and this gave them all a chance to study the technique. Up close, they saw that each 'pouffe' had two pockets at the front, into which the rider could slip his feet, and rope handles on the side to maintain balance. Down the second man sped, getting smaller and smaller, until he slid into the bowl, where his running mate dived on top of him and acted as a brake. A third followed, with the seven mountain bike wheels tied onto a second pouffe behind him, and then Uncle Mas indicated that it was their turn. He seemed particularly keen to see Pinks

273

plunge headlong down the ice face, but it was Miko who volunteered to go first. As the young man prepared himself for take-off, he unzipped his jacket and kissed the Muscat FC badge on his dark-red football shirt. Sarah gave a wry smile.

After a hair-raising sixty seconds the Flying Dutchman safely landed at the bottom. As the two catchers helped him to his feet, he let out a victory cry so loud it set off mini-avalanches down the slope. He turned to his teammates high above, and gave a big thumbs-up.

Graham followed, slowly but surely, and then Floyd. His attempt was less successful. Nervous from the beginning, he had been reluctant to let go of the starting shelf. Halfway down, going too fast and losing control, Floyd put his feet out to slow himself, but only succeeded in sending himself into a spin. As he desperately tried to right himself with his gloved hands, he flipped out and was sent somersaulting into a crash-landing. At the top, Sarah remained deadly silent, but everyone else burst out laughing.

'Don't worry,' reassured Zul. 'You can come down the steps with me and Uncle Mas. Just send your packs down.'

A short bout of blustering followed, as Sarah protested her ability to match the boys in any pursuit, but she was more than relieved to descend the chipped out staircase at the track's edge. The last of the Xidakis flew past.

As they regrouped on the valley floor, Pinks was still being teased mercilessly by Miko and Graham. They were about to turn their attention to Sarah when Uncle Mas indicated they needed to get going for the village before it became dark. As the group duly strode onwards, Zulfiquaar began pointing out some of the wildlife on offer.

'Some of the rarest horses in the world.' Zul had spotted a few horses gathered across the plain.

'Przewalski's, right, Zuley?' Pinks was desperate to save a bit of face.

'No, they're Lokai from Tajikistan. They're bigger than Przewalski's, and have more meat.'

Pinks sulked.

'There are Przewalski's here though, down by the lake. The ones with the shorter legs.'

'They're the ones I was talking about.'

As Zul moved on to the Bactrian camels, Marco Polo sheep, and Tibetan antelope Graham sensed his *Flora and Fauna* chapter taking shape. From underneath the feet of a nearby Yak, a woolly hare bounded out into the open as if to prove the point.

'They used to have brown bears and wolves here too, but raiders hunted them into extinction,' Zul lamented. 'And then, of course, there is the Hodi.'

'Hodi?'

'It's a Xidak word. What the Tibetans call a Yeti. And you call the Abominable Snowman.' Zul's tongue tripped up on the repetitive 'b's and 'm's.

'Pull the other one, Zuley. It's got bells on it.'

'Footprints have been found. And a few years ago an old shepherd came across an enormous set of bones buried under a huge stone.'

'A huge stone like that?' Graham pointed to a gigantic rock over to their right, its angles too rectangular to have been formed by an avalanche.

*   *   *

THE STONE TOWER

The exact location of the legendary *Tash Kurgan* or Stone Tower, famed throughout the world as the site of the civilisation's first ever dumb-bartering exchanges, has always been shrouded in mystery. However, the remains of a great monolith still rest on the floor of Xidakistan's valley, and many believe this to be the true site.

If so, this supports The Valley's other claim, that of being home to the Garden of Eden, as celebrated in Sir John Mandeville's *The Way to Paradise: 'As I have herd seye of wyse men bezonde, I schalle telle zou with gode Wille. Paradys terrestre, as wise men seyn, is the highest place of Erthe, that is in alle the World: and it is so highe, that it touchethe nyghe to the cercle of the Mone. For sche*

275

> *is so highe, that the flode of Noe ne might not come to hire. And*
> *this Paradys is enclosed alle aboute with a Walle; and men wyte not*
> *whereof it is. And it semethe not that the Walle is Ston of Nature. And*
> *that Walle streccethe fro the Southe to the Northe; and it hathe not*
> *but on entrée, that is closed with Fyre brennynge; so that no man, that*
> *is mortalle, ne dar not entren.'*

'Jeez Louise, Ruffo, you do write some piss.' Phil couldn't help but let out a whistle. 'No one's gonna read all that. Not in a million years.'

Phil spooned in some more curry.

'Thanks, Nav.'

Naveed had found Graham's lost notebook down the back of one of the sofas, the morning after everyone had headed up to Sost. In the interests of sport, if not fair play, he had decided Phil should look after it until Graham returned.

'Not in a million years.' Phil flattened the pages of the notebook to give them a second look. 'Don't get me wrong, I like a nice historical quote as much as the next man. But half the bloody box?'

Phil washed breakfast down with the last of Naveed's cola, and headed over to Computer Corner.

'Who's this John Mandeville, anyway? Another of Graham's Pommie mates no doubt.' Phil started up the computer and turned on the screen. 'No, you've got to be able do better than that, Ruffo. Got to. Maybe it's time I dusted off the old typing skills.'

*　　　　　　　　*　　　　　　　　*

The light was fading now, and the thin air becoming distinctly chilly, so Zul suggested they pick up the pace. As they approached the village, Graham made more mental notes for his guide. All the homes were low affairs with central pillars supporting animal hide roofs. The bases of the walls were stone, but they soon gave way to mud brick, The Valley's distance above the tree line making timber construction almost unviable. At their rear were small *dungten*: pyramids of rocks, inside which were the bones of ancestors, pecked clean courtesy of their sky burials.

It seemed all of Xidakistan's two hundred or so inhabitants had gathered to greet them at the ceremonial *kani*, but it was the children who were the first to dash through the gateway, and break rank. After a few nervous giggles, they began to pull at their new toys with delight. They were particularly impressed with Pinks' spectacles, and Miko's blonde hair. For the moment they seemed reluctant to approach Sarah, and the mothers liked it that way.

'Do any of them speak English?' Pinks was struggling to keep control of his glasses.

'I'm afraid not. Only King Tah and a few of his family. Hopefully that will all change though, with the new school.'

'How fluent is the King?'

'Good, very good.' Zul looked a little embarrassed. 'Although there are a few things I think I ought to explain before you meet him.' Zul ushered them towards some seats that had been specially brought out.

Zul began to recount how, during the early research period, not every word translated successfully from Xidak to English, and vice versa; a situation made worse by Prince Hat's regular refusal to admit an error on his part. Zulfiquaar had been reluctant to upset the proceedings at such a delicate stage, and therefore had let most of the slips pass without correction, in the hope of repairing the damage at a later date. Over time, the majority had indeed been rectified, but Hat (now Tah) had remained stubborn on a few, pet words. Thus an eagle was still called an igloo, and a spoon a sponge.

'The most important thing is not to call the king "King Tah",' Zul concluded. 'Just call him "Tah".'

'That's a bit informal isn't it?' Graham was no monarchist but...

'No, no. It's just another example of the earlier misunderstandings. "Tah", you see, means "King".'

'But you call him King Tah.'

'Yes, because by the time I found out it was too late. So I pretended that very special friends often repeat each other's names as a sign of affection.' Zul went about as red-faced as is possible for a Pakistani. 'Don't be surprised if he calls me "Zulfiquaar Zulfiquaar".'

'I get it.' Graham grinned. 'So "Hat" means "prince"?'

'Exactly.'

Graham rummaged in his bag and pulled out his copy of the invitation sent out the previous year. He quickly scanned it for a phrase that had been bugging him.

'So when Hat said they were going to "celebrate" Tah's death, did he really mean "mourn"?'

'Oh no, Mr Graham. Here death is a cause for celebration. It's part of their Buddhist beliefs. They truly believe in the cycle of reincarnation, which will ultimately lead them to the Western Paradise. Death is an important achievement.'

It was hard to fault the logic.

'What about all the old King Tahs being one-hundred and forty-one when they died?'

'Well, forty really means "many"....'

'A bit like our forty winks?'

'Exactly. So one-hundred and forty means "many, many", and one-hundred and forty-one means "one *too* many".'

Graham couldn't help but smile.

'These are simple people, Mr Graham.' Zulfiquaar raised an eyebrow towards Floyd. 'And simple things please simple minds.'

Zul led them to a large yurt, which was to be their home during the stay. He let them unpack and went off to arrange the official welcome. It was now pitch black and the four were reliant on torches and some precarious oil lamps. A small meal appeared from nowhere, happily rounded off with chocolate and Glenmorangie from Pinks' supplies. On hearing that the reception would not take place until the morning, they were all more than happy to turn in.

The floor was covered in animal skins, furs and woollen carpets. Special blankets had been laid out in a row for them to sleep on. Graham took one middle berth and, as Pinks took the other, Sarah began unpacking at Graham's side, like the old days. Graham blew out the last of the lamps and sneaked a kiss under the cover of darkness.

'Hey,' Floyd whispered. 'I've been thinking.'

Graham wanted to ignore him, but his mind was racing too. 'Again?'

'G, I'm serious.' Pinks hunched himself up on one elbow. 'It's like I'm worried.'

'Worried about what?'

'Well.' Unable to see a thing, Pinks began feeling around for Graham's arm. 'I can't stop thinking someone's gonna suddenly jump out of nowhere, and steal The Game.'

'Relax.' Graham removed Floyd's hand from his shoulder. 'There's no way Phil can get here in time.'

'Yeah, maybe.' Floyd cogitated. 'But what about that young gun you were talking about? The lone wolf.'

Miko pretended to be asleep.

'I'm more worried about Terry. And Jane.'

'No, those two are deep in the African jungle.' Floyd had double-checked. 'I don't know where we are, but it sure as hell ain't Africa.'

'So we're safe.'

'I hope so, buddy,' Pinks yawned. 'I really do.'

Game, Set and Match

All four could hardly contain their excitement as they woke up the next morning, and breakfast was long finished by the time Zul arrived to escort them to the king. Zulfiquaar, wearing his best M&S pinstripe, was accompanied by Uncle Mas, who insisted on giving his guests a tour of The Valley before proceedings got underway.

His pride and joy was the lake, which, on closer inspection, proved to be two separate bodies of water. The higher was a man-made reservoir, which collected The Valley's water supplies, and was home to Xidakistan's now-infamous trout. Lower down, a patchwork of milky pools glistened, fed by hot springs. It was these springs that ensured the temperature of the water never dropped much below twenty degrees Celsius, which in turn gave the valley a micro-climate just warm enough to sustain life. On their journey up to The Valley, a westerly wind had blown remorselessly all morning and afternoon, only dying off in the evening, but here the air was pleasantly calm, with just the occasional draft of cold running down off the slopes. Around the edges of the reservoir, vegetation seemed to thrive, including rows of rhubarb, bushes of straggly wormwood, which supplemented peat on the fire, and grasses for the animals. Marco Polo's memory, Uncle Mas sadly explained, seems to have been as confused about the trees as it was about the purity of the spring water.

The sulphurous pools came together to form a stream, which poured into the mouth of a giant cave. This cave, Uncle Mas beamed, was where the first jade had been found. Over the years a series of further underground caverns had been discovered, stretching all the way under the mountains to where the stream eventually emerged as the headwaters of the River Wakhan. Once, when he was a young boy, the waters had dropped low enough for him to swim through the potholes until a tiny shaft of light could be seen sparkling at the other end. He had discovered more jade deposits in some of the deeper chambers, along with the odd nugget washed up in the stream. However, it was never enough for him to become king, Uncle Mas laughed.

With the old man tiring, Zulfiquaar led the group across what acted as the village square, past another *mani*. This one was some twenty feet long, with inscriptions in several alphabets. Graham stopped for a closer look. Then it was on to The Valley's largest building, which Zul explained was the king's palace. He lifted the entrance flap and guided them through. Graham and Floyd were dressed in Chinos and button-down shirts, while Sarah wore another of her *shalwar kameez*, but this was considerably more decorative, and accompanied by a woollen shawl. Miko was wearing the same football shirt as the day before.

From the front, the palace had looked remarkably like all the other huts, but as they entered, a warren of rooms, halls and ante-chambers was revealed, stretching out like a honeycomb. The roofs were even half-beamed in places. Graham could only wonder at the effort that must have been exerted transporting the timber up from the valleys below. As they got closer to the inner sanctum, rammed earth was replaced by dry-stone walls.

At the end of the main corridor, Zulfiquaar instructed them to wait while he went ahead. To their left a small opening gave way to what appeared to be a granary, with grain, apricots, currants and saffron laid out on a raised platform. To their right was a shrine adorned with faded cloth hangings, miniature silver *manis*, wooden-backed books containing The Valley's most sacred texts, and a carved-stone Buddha. The figure was accompanied by a wooden trout, and a threaded net. As Graham and Floyd began inspecting more jade and silver ornaments, protruding from the shrine's alcoves, Sarah took the opportunity to coax Miko into the food store.

'You haven't been trying to tell us something with all these football shirts by any chance have you, Miko?'

'How do you mean?'

'This latest top, for example. That's Oman, right?'

Miko grinned. 'I thought no one was ever going to notice.'

'So you are a Game player,' Sarah couldn't help but shake his hand. 'I thought as much.'

Miko's face suddenly fell, and he began twiddling his fingers. 'You don't mind, do you?'

'Me? Not at all. In fact, I can't wait to see the look on their faces.'

The two returned to find Floyd sitting on a leather-covered stool, massaging his feet.

'Come on, Zuley. Hurry up.'

Graham quietly making the last of his notes.

At last Zul appeared and they were led into the final ante-room before the throne room. Zul went to pull back the large silk curtain that hung across the entrance, and as he did so Floyd slipped on one of his cerise Pinks Tours ties.

'Nice touch.'

'First impressions, G. First impressions.' Floyd glance round at Miko. 'And a bit more appropriate than a soccer shirt.'

'Maybe I should put a jumper on.' Miko started rummaging through his bag.

Pinks scowled.

'You haven't got it, have you?' Sarah taunted.

'Got what?' Floyd scrunched his shoulders dismissively.

'The soccer shirts.' Sarah mimicked Floyd's Americanism.

'What about them?'

'The Arabic writing on the front?' Sarah was only too happy to draw this one out.

'OK,' Pinks huffed, 'he's seen some two cents Arab team play. Whoopee!' To no one's great surprise, Floyd pronounced it "A-rab".

Miko pulled on his top, the front of which was a stylised picture of an African waterfall.

'Victoria Falls!' Graham's penny dropped.

Floyd's was still hanging.

Sarah put on her mother-to-child voice. 'That's Victoria Falls, Zimbabwe, Pinks. With a capital "Z".'

Slowly, Floyd's face dawned with realisation. He flashed a look at the shirt underneath. 'Oman?' he panicked.

Miko nodded.

Graham thought back to some of the others. 'Qatar, too?'

Miko nodded again. 'I did a whistle-stop tour of The Gulf last year.

'Which puts him on twenty-five the same as you two.'

'He's the kid!' Pinks squawked. 'The young gun.'

Now everyone was nodding.

'You low down dirty....,' Floyd's fists clenched tight. 'I told you he was a rat, G. The moment I saw him.'

Graham looked to the heavens, but Floyd's brain was still whirring.

'Ah-ha!' His whole demeanour leapt as he replayed their first meeting over in his head. 'What about Venezuela?'

Graham's thoughts were in hot pursuit. 'That's right. You said you only changed planes there. That doesn't count.'

Miko shook his head. 'Do you really think I would have gone all that way, and not stopped off long enough to get my passport stamped?'

Graham was surprised to see Sarah so amused by the intricacies of The Game. 'Be that as it may, Miko,' he steadied himself, 'Zulfiquaar is under strict instructions to stamp our passports first. You do understand that.'

'Damn right!' Floyd glared.

Inside the large throne room, hundreds of oil wicks burned, and various incense sticks smoked. The central 'chimney' hole was uncovered, in an attempt to let in some fresh air and extra light, but it couldn't compete with the sickly smell of roasting yak fat, frankincense, and the sweet fumes of an enormous peat fire. On the walls, traced with different colours, were inscriptions in what looked to Graham like Tibetan and Sanskrit scripts. An ancient painting of a game of polo decorated one corner, and carved figures, once bright yellow, blue and red, but now dulled by fumes and yak grease, sat in the other. Sarah and Miko hung back and covered their mouths, in an attempt to avoid the smoke.

King Tah sat in front of the fire on a stone throne, his bald head resplendently crowned by the royal burgundy turban. He was cloaked in the ceremonial lace fishing net and although his bulk was not immense, he would have privately admitted to gaining a few pounds since the coronation. His face was round, his skin taut and waxy. He considered his nose his best feature but to others it might have appeared too flat, especially when his nostrils flared. All in all, he was neither handsome nor ugly. Unlike his wife, Floyd sniggered. Queen Bea, sitting on one of six picnic chairs Zul had presented as a wedding gift, was nothing short of pug-faced. With enormous ears. Her skin was mud-brown, her face fleshy, and her red and blue make-up in shades that could only be described as 'an acquired taste'. But her eyes were bright and kind, and in the king's mind she was the most beautiful woman in the world, as elegant and graceful as the snow leopard, whose skin lay at the royal couple's feet.

Fishing nets aside, Graham was taken aback by the finery of the king and queen's clothes. Their robes and tunics were made of *pashm*, the finest of ibex hair, dyed a glorious indigo. Their slippers glittered gold and their sashes sparkled silver. The whole ensemble was so lavish, it could have come straight out of a Maharajah's wardrobe, which in fact it had: the last ever Maharajah of Kashmir's to be precise, via some Punjabi bandits, an Afghan warlord, and the Bozai Gumbaz weapons bazaar.

Queen Bea gave the king a firm nudge to indicate it was time to start. If there had been any trousers on view it was pretty clear who would have been wearing them.

'Zulfiquaar, Zulfiquaar,' pronounced the king. 'Please introduce our royal guests.'

Zulfiquaar brought them forward one by one: 'Mr Graham Ruff', 'Ambassador Floyd Housmann', 'Miko Gundersen' and 'Madam Sarah Kennedy'.

'Ah,' nodded the king in approval. 'Madam Kennedy, what a pleasure. I understand you have a very healthy son?'

'That's right, your highness.' Sarah bowed respectfully. 'I've got some pictures if you'd like.'

The king invited his guests to sit on the remaining picnic chairs, and for the next hour he questioned each in turn as to his or her homeland. Zul assisted with any necessary translations. During the conversations, plates of rhubarb were brought for everyone to nibble, washed down with a pungent brew of fermented barley and millet, but Graham and Floyd were too preoccupied to relax. At last Tah raised the topic they had all been waiting for.

'Later, the Queen and I wish to show you around our humble abode but first, I understand you have a congratulations card for me to sign.'

'That's right, your majesty.' Floyd extracted the treaty from its silver tube, and handed it to over. Zul brought forward the picnic table that completed the set, and spread the treaty across it.

'Zulfiquaar, Zulfiquaar,' Tah commanded. 'If you would be so kind as to fetch my pen.'

Floyd turned to whisper in Graham's ear. 'You know, G.' He was trembling with delight. 'I almost wish that bitch was here just so I could see the look on her face.'

'That's very magnanimous of you, Floyd.'

'Jack shit "magnanimous". I've been waiting for this day for over half my life, and I'm going to enjoy it.'

They were interrupted by a small cough from Zul to signal the arrival of the pen. Both men willed out the ink. King Tah etched a very precise 'X' on the dotted line, and Pinks gave a little yelp of delight.

'Now Zulfiquaar Zulfiquaar also tells me you have a custom of stamping what you call passports when you visit a friend's country.' The king was also excited.

'Indeed, your majesty,' Pinks crawled. 'And if I may be so bold, I would like to present you with your very own Xidakistan stamp on behalf of the United States government.'

From one pocket Floyd produced a rubber stamp he had been given by Boris, and from the other an ink pad.

'You sure you don't want to go back to our original deal, G?' Pinks gloated.

'Let's wait and see.' Graham crossed his fingers.

Zul removed the treaty, and made ready for the stamping.

'Shall we begin?' he grinned.

King Tah clapped with joy, and everyone became standing.

Floyd gave his glasses a quick polish.

'On behalf of King Tah and his wife, Queen Bea,' Zul announced. 'I would like to welcome you, and formally admit you to the kingdom of Xidakistan.'

Graham and Floyd took a deep breath.

'Firstly,' Zul paused, 'Mr Graham Ruff.'

'What?' Pinks was already taking his step forward and nearly fell into the throne. 'No, no, no.' He gave Zul a scowl. 'Hold on there a minute. I think you'll find my name is at the top of that list, your highness.'

King Tah looked to Zulfiquaar.

'I paid you good money,' Floyd hissed under his breath. That morning Zulfiquaar had woken to find in the front pocket of his knapsack a hundred-dollar bill, with a *Pinks Authentic Wild West Experience* business card attached.

'You did indeed, Mr Floyd.' Rather than collude, Zul addressed the whole group loud and clear. 'But I presumed that was for your visa.'

'Visa?'

285

'All visitors to Xidakistan must have a visa.' Zul gave Graham a surreptitious wink. 'And as Xidaki Secretary of State, I was only too happy to oblige.'

'One hundred dollars for a visa?' Floyd gaped.

'The fee for a standard visa, of course, is only forty dollars, but I assumed, under the circumstances, the usual two-week turnaround would not be advantageous to your position. I therefore nominated you for our fast-track service.' Zul twinkled. 'The cost of which is a supplementary sixty dollars.'

Graham and Miko would have been in stitches if Sarah had not alerted them to the lost look on King Tah's face.

'What about these guys?' Floyd looked at the others.

For a moment Zul looked panicked, but just as quickly his outer calm returned.

'My cousin Jahanghir forwarded payment for their visas many weeks ago.' Zul winked at Graham a second time. 'As a token of his gratitude, and the gratitude of all the staff at the Karachi International Guesthouse.'

Floyd thought for a second. 'OK, Zuley, good job. You got me. But,' now it was Floyd's turn to pause, ' as acting US ambassador I have two words to say to you.' Zul looked worried. 'Higher authorities.' Floyd drew a finger across his throat for good measure.

'Come on, Floyd. That's not fair.'

'No, no, Miss Sarah. Mr Floyd is right. He must do what he must do. Unfortunately, I must, too. And I promised Mr Graham his wish was my command.'

Zulfiquaar bit his lip, face to the floor.

'My wish.' Graham savoured the moment.

'Will you two schoolboys cut it out. This is Zulfiquaar's livelihood we're talking about.'

Pinks started muttering. 'Alright, G. What's it worth?' He looked Graham straight in the eye.

'What do you mean?' Graham asked.

'Don't be disingenuous.'

'*Disingenuous?*' Graham rubbed his tongue along his teeth. 'Swallowing dictionaries again, eh, Floyd?'

'Just tell me what you want, Ruff, and let's get on with it.'

'I see.' Graham began strumming his chin with his fingers. 'So I can have anything?'

Pinks glowered. 'Within reason.'

'OK. No guide for *Small World*.'

'Done.'

Graham darted a quick glance at his companions. 'What was it you said earlier about paying the expenses for this trip?'

Floyd had hoped Graham had forgotten.

'Tell you what, let's make it all of our expenses.' Now he knew about Floyd's US army income, Graham didn't feel half as bad.

Floyd bristled. 'OK. Done.'

'And last but not least.' Graham weighed up his options. 'The Pinks Guide.'

'No way,' Floyd frothed. 'I've only just set it up. It's my baby.'

'You're going to sell it to the boys in Blue, and you know it.'

'Zulfiquaar Zulfiquaar.' The king summoned Zul to his side. 'Is there a problem?'

Zulfiquaar took a quick blast of his inhaler. 'No, no, your highness. All part of the ceremony.'

'But G,' Floyd pleaded. 'That's my pension. It's all I've got.'

Graham grinned. 'Alright, you can keep it. Or sell it, it's up to you. But I want the London offices. And all the equipment that's in them. I've had enough of sharing offices with Jos.'

Floyd tried to do the maths but it didn't make any sense. 'Just the offices?' He inched out his hand. 'Not the website?'

'The offices. For as long as what's left on the lease.' Graham held out his palm. He guessed Floyd had paid for at least the first six months up front.

Pinks tried desperately to work out the catch.

Graham's hand grabbed hold of Floyd's. 'Done?'

Pinks hesitated.

'Done?' Graham flexed.

'Done.' Floyd gripped Graham's knuckles so hard they nearly broke.

'Zulfiquaar.' Graham turned back to the assembly. 'Would you be so kind as to see to my friend, Mr Housmann, first?'

Zulfiquaar gave King Tah a statesmanlike nod.

'If I can have your passport, please, Mr Housmann.'

'Certainly, *Mr Secretary.*' Floyd reached down to his bag, unzipped the top pocket, but came up empty-handed. He looked as though he'd seen a ghost. 'Just one minute.' Floyd rummaged inside his shirt, unclipping the shoulder holster. Nothing. Frantically he tore back to the bag and ripped everything out.

'Aaaaahhhhhhh!'

The king and queen leaped back three paces.

Pinks suddenly stopped searching. 'Very funny, Ruff,' he panted. 'Give me back my passport.' Floyd's face tightened. 'The joke's over.'

'I haven't got it, Floyd. I swear.' Suddenly a terrible thought struck Graham. He too grabbed the top of his pack and began scrimmaging, but, likewise, no passport. 'Phil?'

'Not smart enough.'

'Bonnie?' Graham agonised.

'I don't know how she did it but .....'

'Mine's gone, too.' Miko cursed.

'And mine,' Sarah fumed. 'After all I've done for her!'

'Wait a second,' Miko beamed. 'All might not be lost.'

To Queen Bea's delight he rolled up his left trouser leg and began retrieving some kind of security pouch.

'She may have taken my Dutch passport,' Miko grinned, 'but I've still got my old Finnish one.' He brandished his dark blue documentation in celebration.

'Jesus, no,' Pinks wailed. 'No way. The kid can't win. Graham do something.'

Graham could only hold up his hands.

'Wait!' Pinks' brain was working overtime. 'Of course,' he cried. 'Why didn't I think of that before?' Floyd did a little jig of celebration. 'Nobody even think about moving a muscle until I get back.'

Pinks was off. Down the corridor, out of the palace and back to the yurt. He ransacked his overnight bag until finally he found it, tucked inside the last pocket-within-a-pocket. He raced back to the ceremony, clutching the treasure in both hands, and almost fell into Zulfiquaar's arms.

'My second passport!' he panted. 'The one the Yugoslavs gave me to get into Iran. I knew it would come in handy,' he rejoiced. 'This is it! I've won!'

The look on Zul's face was enough to tell him that 'this' was not 'it'.

'I'm afraid this passport has expired.'

It was too much. Floyd's head fell onto Zulfiquaar's shoulder. As his arms went limp, his passport fell to the floor. In the end Graham had to lead him to his chair, while Miko searched Floyd's pack for some whisky.

After a series of strong glugs Floyd managed to pull himself into some sort of shape, but he still took a while to make any sense. 'Alright,' he eventually moaned. 'Let the kid have it.'

Miko pumped his fist. 'Yes!'.

Zul re-pressed the stamp and ink pad, and the now-bewildered king and queen reassumed their positions. Floyd and Graham formed a guard of honour and Miko stepped up to the table, shaking with anticipation.

'Sorry, Miko,' Sarah blithely interrupted. 'Shouldn't it be ladies first?'

'But, of course.' Miko backed away. 'I only thought you said your passport had gone too.'

'Come on, Saz. Let us finish The Game, and then you can do your bit.'

'Oh, but I was talking about The Game.' Sarah tossed her hair back nonchalantly.

'Sarah.' Graham rolled his eyes.

'*Graham.*'

'But you're not a Game player.'

Sarah arched her eyebrows, and suddenly realisation dawned.

'Don't look so surprised.'

'You always said you hated The Game.'

'Maybe I did. Or maybe you don't know me quite as well as you'd like to think.' Sarah gave her shoulders a playful shrug. From the inside pocket of her bum-bag she extracted a crimson book, with the United Kingdom of Great Britain and Northern Ireland embossed in the gold lettering.

'But you said she took yours,' Pinks snapped.

'She did.'

'So?' Floyd growled. 'You can't have two British passports!'

'Why not?' Sarah countered, opening her documentation to a blank page. 'Blair's got two. And Becks.'

'Of course.' Graham had read an article about it in the paper. 'She's right, Floyd. If you travel a lot on business and there's a chance you might need to visit, say, Israel one week and Syria the next, the UK government lets you have two passports, to avoid diplomatic embarrassment. They introduced it in the 70s for apartheid South Africa-'

'OK, G. We get the message.' Floyd reached for his hip-flask.

Graham re-focussed on Sarah. 'Are you serious?'

'I made up my mind to start playing while I was waiting for my waters to break. Pregnancy can have an unusual effect on a woman.'

Graham kicked himself for not seeing it before. Who, after all, had told him about The Game in the first place? 'Hence "Xavier"?'

'X marks the spot.'

Graham thought back to his similar thought process behind Xanadu. 'Congratulations.'

Floyd drank his whisky, Miko sucked on his teeth and Graham couldn't help but shake his head.

Sarah let them suffer, but not for long. 'Don't look so glum.' She withdrew her passport from Zul's fingers. 'Just because I can win, doesn't mean I'm going to.'

'What?' Pinks was gone.

'I'm not going to claim the prize.'

'Cool, calm and collected,' Sarah reminded herself. She had been planning this moment for a very long time.

'Part of me may secretly enjoy playing The Game. But most of me still thinks it's as stupid as it was all those years ago at The Alhambra.'

Graham blushed.

'So it wouldn't be fair to claim a prize I didn't believe in. I just needed to prove to,' Sarah took a breath, 'to prove that I could.'

Graham blushed again but this time so did Sarah.

'Which means?' Zulfiquaar, like his rubber stamp, was in a confused limbo.

'Which means,' Sarah collected herself, 'these are my terms.'

'Wait a second, Saz.' In Graham's mental rehearsals, he had been the one making the noble gestures. He took a step forward. 'There was something I was hoping to discuss with you first.'

'No, Gray.' Sarah's look was enough. 'This is my turn.'

As the five men drew in closer, Queen Bea gave up and reached for the rhubarb.

'Zul will stamp three pieces of paper, which you will each put into your passports when you get them back.'

The three players nodded. This seemed a little easy.

'Which means you can jointly claim the prize, together, at the Reform Club.' Sarah breathed deeply.

'That's it?'

They were all looking to Sarah.

'Well, there are a couple of conditions.' Sarah bit the tip of her tongue between her teeth.

'Go on.'

'Firstly, you give the gold medal to Xavier.'

'No problem.'

'And secondly, no one is to bring out any book.'

'What do you mean?' Miko scratched his head.

'I mean, no *Ruff Guide*, no *Small World*, no Pinks, no Blue. The last thing this place needs is troops of tourists coming in every day.'

Graham suddenly felt very warm. 'There may be one minor hitch.'

'No, Gray, I mean it.'

'Oh, I know.' Graham adopted his solemn face. 'I know you do.' He took a step towards Sarah. 'And I wholeheartedly agree with you.' Another step. 'It's just that that means our new company's going to have to find another destination for its first title.'

Sarah looked at him askew. *'Our* new company?'

'I take it the deal for your offices is still on, Floyd.' Graham kept his eyes fixed on Sarah.

'Hang on.'

'"Hang on" what? You're still getting to win The Game.' Now he did look at Floyd. 'And a "Housmann's handshake is his bond".'

Floyd downed the remaining drops. 'Alright. But I get the Life Membership of the Reform Club!'

Graham couldn't care less. 'Miko, is that OK with you?'

'Sure, why not?' Miko was just happy to be there.

'Right, so there we are. *Follow Your Nose* ....' Graham watched Sarah's eyes light up, '....has officially begun trading.'

'How can you afford....?' Sarah wondered aloud.

'Easy. I'm selling my stake in Ruff Guides,' Graham responded almost matter-of-factly. 'That was going to be my terms.'

Sarah flung her arms around Graham, and gave him a kiss that had been fermenting for a long, long time.

'The market's saturated, you know.' Pinks was determined to rain at least a little something on the parade.

'Very true,' G hit back. 'Which is why we'll be doing something a little bit different.' He pulled Sarah's arms down and held them tight. For the first time in a long time, he could feel himself becoming excited. 'Rather than go country by country, I thought we could concentrate on popular routes. Starting with a full-on guide to the Silk Road to bury Jos' disaster, once and for all.'

'So you'll still be going out on the road then?' Sarah's hurt was loud and clear.

'Point taken.' Graham turned round. 'Miko?' Both men were tingling. 'How do you fancy getting into the travel writing business?' Sarah backed the proposition with wide-eyed approval.

'I thought you'd never ask,' Miko hooted.

After a long bout of backslapping and handshaking *Follow Your Nose* had its first lead writer.

*   *   *

To: 'Classified'
From: Agent Brown

Subject: Missing Link

Field Intelligence: Mandeep Singh, Taliban handler
Source: Ali Mohammed, undercover jihadi
Access: Al Qaeda command/possibly Geronimo
Requisition: $10,000 + $10,000
Action: Immediate

Agent Brown's request had been authorised by the time the triumphant party of four arrived back in Gilgit. They were met by the sight of Phil lugging an enormous sack of melons across the K2 car park.

'We're home.' Graham's opened the car door nervously, but Phil's face was a veritable moonbeam.

'G'day, mate. You right?' Phil stuffed the last of a pile of black-and-white shirts into a second bag. 'G'day, Saz.'

'We made it up to The Valley,' Sarah replied, a little bewildered.

'Shame it won't count for The Game, eh?'

'Give it up, Ned.' Pinks was the last to clamber out of the share-taxi. He hadn't set out to rub it in but... 'we won fair and square. And there ain't nothing you can do but whistle.'

Phil's smile refused to wane. 'Wanna bet on that, sport?' Phil wiped his palm on his guernsey; Graham was puzzled to see the magpies of Newcastle United had replaced their Collingwood cousins. 'I think youse'll find your trip has just been one big waste of ammo. That's why I came back here.'

Graham and Floyd gave each other a pitying look.

'Xidakistan still doesn't count for squat, see. Not yet. Not 'til it's officially on the list.'

'Bullshit!' Pinks was in need of a soft bed. 'The treaty's been signed, and we've all got the stamps to prove it.'

293

'You're not pretending we have to wait for UN ratification, are you?'

'Nope.' Phil was still grinning like a madman.

'So quit whining and admit we've won!' Floyd marched over to his opponent.

'UN has nothing to do with it.' Phil pulled the drawstrings on his sack tight and swung the load over his shoulder, biffing Pinks' bonce on the way. 'Law Six, mate,' rather than melons, Floyd's head had felt the impact of a dozen fully-pumped footballs, 'Law Six states that FIFA's the one to dictate who's on the list. Remember?'

Graham began to panic.

'Which means Xidakistan needs a soccer, sorry "footie", team.' Phil started to cackle as he opened the door to Naveed's van. 'And guess who's just been appointed their first ever coach.'

'I think, for once, he might be serious.' Sarah smiled.

'Bloody oath.' Phil kissed the badge on his new shirt. 'Registered on the FIFA website this morning.'

'What do you know about soccer?' Pinks slapped a firm hand on Phil's shoulder and span him round. 'You're Aussie Rules.'

'Used to be. Now, I think you'll find, Crazy Philpot is a fully paid up member of the Toon Army! Go the Mags!' Phil had hardly believed his luck when he discovered there was a soccer team that wore the same black and white as Collingwood, and shared the same nickname. 'Might even get an AAG cap, while I'm at it.'

'Bonnie!!' Pinks roared. He was sure she was behind this somehow.

'That sook?' Phil hit back defensively. 'She's halfway to Kabul already; some series on Afghan women for Discovery.' He climbed into the driver's seat and wound down the window. 'Old Phil did this one all by himself.'

Graham didn't know what to believe.

'She did leave you these though.' Phil pulled four dog-eared passports out of his shirt pocket. 'Losers!'

Floyd snatched them from his hand.

'And Naveed gave me this, Ruffo.' Phil tossed Graham's missing notebook out of the window. 'Start again, if I was you.'

With a wheel-spin of gravel he was off.
"We've still won, right, G?' Floyd gawped.
'Course we have.'

*   *   *

Sarah boarded the plane to London next to Graham. As they taxied down the runway she grabbed hold of his hand.

'Before we leave, I've got one more secret.'

'Good secret or bad secret?'

'Good. Well, maybe bad. I sneaked a peak at your travelogue while we were up in The Valley.'

'No?' Graham pretended to wince. 'Alright, give it to me straight.'

'Actually, as glorifications of not very interesting ego-trips go, it's better than average.'

'Thanks!'

'I've made a few changes though.'

'Well, of course.'

'And I scrapped the title.'

'Why?' G was very proud of *Silkman on the Silk Road*.

'Don't worry, I've thought of a new one.'

'It had better be good.'

'Actually,' Sarah raised her eyebrows, 'it was obvious.' She shook her head. '"*Smooth as Silk*", dummy.'

Now Graham was the one gripping tight. 'I knew you wouldn't let me down.'

Sarah's lips opened with his.

'Although,' Graham had pecked a quick kiss on the nose and pulled back, '*Men and the Art of Low Maintenance* isn't such a flash title either.'

Sarah was gob-smacked.

'Two can play at that game, you know.' Graham poked his tongue out.

'That notepad is private property!'

'Unlucky.' Graham squeezed Sarah's hand tighter, and this time he gave her a proper kiss. 'Thank you.'

'What for?'

'For waking me up.'

Sarah stretched her legs as far as the seat in front would allow, and let out a satisfied sigh.

Graham fidgeted. 'I'm going to need somewhere to stay, you know. At least for the first six months, while we set things up.'

'Mmmm.' Sarah sucked her finger. 'Who do we know who has a spare room?'

'No.' Graham pretended to dismiss the idea. 'I can't see Jos letting me…'

Sarah's face warned Graham that this wasn't a time to play games.

'Are you sure?'

'More than I've ever been about anything in my life,' Sarah pledged.

Graham looked Sarah straight in the eyes. 'I'll never let you down again.' He moved her hair back from her face and kissed her. Again.

'I know.'

They sat hand-in-hand, faces forward, for a while. Neither of them wanting or feeling the need to move.

'What about Xavier?' Graham finally broached. 'Shouldn't we ask him first?'

'Are you kidding? Xavier has wanted you to be his father since the day he was born.' Sarah felt her eyes about to sting.

Graham squeezed her fingers.

'Gray, about Xavier…,' Sarah stuttered, 'Xavier's father. I think it's important you…'

'It's alright,' Graham tried to help. 'I know.'

'No, Gray, it's more complicated than that.' Sarah sniffed back a tear. 'Much more.'

Graham turned to face her. 'Sarah, *I know.*' For the first time, he felt no sadness and his shoulders relaxed.

Sarah blinked.

'I've always…' Graham began again, but Sarah put her finger to his lips.

'I know.'

Xavier

I don't have a problem with Graham. Unlike everyone else, by the sounds of it. Not that there have never been any problems, you understand. But for a 'dad-who-is-not-my-dad', I don't think I could have asked for more.

You see, I was born at 5.36 on a Friday morning and Graham kept vigil outside the delivery room all night, only leaving when the midwife pronounced 'two arms and two legs'. Uncle Jos came round at the weekend and told me, while we were playing footie in the garden. Graham doesn't know I know, and mum doesn't know a thing,

They are both in the other room at the moment, watching their friend Bonnie on TV. It's funny, really. Mum says this Bonnie isn't a proper friend, more of a pain in the proverbial, but she's on TV and they're watching, so she must be kind of cool.

'Six months on and Afghanistan is free.' Presenter, Bonnie Fidler, looked hard into the camera, and shared the moment. The camera pulled out to reveal a sprawling Afghan refugee camp behind her. 'The Taliban have been defeated.'

*　　　　　　*　　　　　　*

Well, that was General Martin's line and he was sticking to it. The world's attention had switched westwards to Iraq, and everything else could now be conveniently forgotten. None of Xidakistan's roads would be built, none of the schools, and none of the infrastructure needed to turn The Valley into anything resembling a fully-fledged nation. But the inhabitants didn't mind, they were still happy enjoying the peace and quiet.

'What about the monthly stipend for Butt, Sir?' The latest Jones was tidying up loose ends in the file.

'What would you do if you were me, Lieutenant?' General Martin was pleased to be back in his old Pentagon office.

'Well, Sir. I was thinking it might be an idea to keep paying him. That way if we ever need him again, we've got leverage.'

'What about you, Smith?' It was like The Chief had never been away.

'Ordinarily, Sir, I would agree. But now the mission's over, you know what Treasury will be like. Pretty hard to justify.'

'We could put him in for a 'transfer', Sir.'

'Keep talking, Jones.'

'Well, I was looking through Butt's record, and noticed the anthropology angle. Turns out we used to employ an expert anthropologist for intelligence work. But when he retired, they couldn't find a suitable replacement.

'You know, soldier,' General Martin gave his new recruit the once over, 'I think you might just have a long and successful career ahead of you.'

'The only problem is, he never got his qualifications.'

*   *   *

They've asked me to go in and watch it with them but, to be honest, I'm not really into all their Discovery Channel stuff. I'm happier here, playing 'FIFA World Cup' on the computer. I know mum's right about it being important to know what's going on in the outside world, and everything, but I'm only ten, right? I'm with Graham - long live professional layabouts! But I've got a feeling the rules might change now he's going to be my 'Dad' dad.

'I've seen so much on my journey through Afghanistan.' *Bonnie started* **walking towards camera, Afghan women going about their daily lives in the background. 'So much hardship, yet so much joy. Because the lasting impression I'll always take with me from this journey, is the people. And, in particular, the women. Forget what you've read in your newspapers, these ladies are the beating heart of their society. And proud of it.'**

Graham and Sarah rolled their eyes in unison. Was there any cliché Bonnie wouldn't use?

'If she's "seen so much", how come she didn't see that woman being dragged off by her husband, with a frying pan in his hand?'

'Or get a speck of dirt on her Dior sunglasses?'

As Graham reached over for the remote, the phone rang.

'Are you watching this, Big G?' Floyd's DuPont could be heard clicking in the background.

'Unfortunately.' Graham switched the phone to loudspeaker so Sarah could listen in.

'Has that woman no shame?'

'*You were the one that married her,*' Graham felt like saying. 'Nice outfit, though.'

'Yeah. Maybe the Taliban will think her worth kidnapping, and do us all a favour.'

'Floyd!' Sarah whacked the phone with a cushion.

'I know. Kidnapping's too good for her. And besides, who'd pay the ransom?' Pinks fired up his cigar.

'It's Sunday, Floyd, so I'm guessing you didn't call to speak about Bonnie,' Graham cajoled. 'Have you thought any more about our offer?'

Sarah pulled a face. She didn't want to make this any easier for Floyd. Graham had said they needed someone with experience on the writing team; Sarah had argued for new blood. They had compromised on sounding Pinks out.

'Yes, I have, G. And as much as I am honoured that you thought of me, I'm afraid my mind's made up. I'm staying retired.' With Vanh gone Floyd had decided to cut his losses and sell The Pinks Guide to the highest bidder.

Sarah punched the air in delight. Graham's look reminded her of the hole they were left in.

'I've spoken to Miko, though, and promised to help where I can.' As a follow-up to *Follow Your Silk Road,* Miko had set his sights on *Follow Your Pan-American Highway.*

'Thanks, Floyd. Let us know if you ever change your mind.' Graham could smell the roast lamb in the oven. 'Better go, buddy, it's Sunday dinner time.'

'No problem, G.' Pinks held his hand over the receiver to block out the giggling behind him. Everything was going according to plan. 'Make sure he doesn't burn those Yorkshire Puddings, Sarah.'

'Bye, Floyd.' Sarah signalled to kill the call.

'Oh, one last thing.' Floyd pretended to remember.

'It had better be quick.'

'It's just I got a call from Ned the other day. Saying he was at a loose end.'

Graham frowned. 'So?'

'So,' Floyd trod carefully. 'I was looking at Miko's map. This Pan-Am guide is going to be a really big job.'

'Are you suggesting what I think you're suggesting?' Sarah sparkled.

'But we'd be the laughing stock of the industry.'

'Well, that's exactly what I said, G. At first.' Floyd let the thought sink in some more. 'But then again...'

Sarah pulled back her cushion for another whack. 'Will you two stop it! He's as much a traveller as either of you, and just as dedicated to the cause.' Sarah reined herself in. This was Phil they were talking about. 'In his own inimitable way.'

'Alright.' Graham held up his hands. 'Tell him he can have a month's trial.'

'Graham!'

'OK, OK. Tell him he's got the gig.'

'You little ripper!' Phil yelled, grabbing the phone from Floyd's grasp. 'Good onya, Saz. Knew you wouldn't let me down! I've already made a start on some of the boxed texts.' He was away. 'The thing is, G, this internet caper is going gangbusters. There's talk of e-books, e-guides, e-everything.' Unlike Floyd, Phil was genuinely excited about the potential of the World Wide Web. 'Miko reckons we should be doing some sort of virtual guide, to run in tandem the book.'

Miko was standing right beside him.

'Great idea,' Sarah enthused. 'Got to keep ahead of the curve if we're going to beat Jos. Let alone Jane and Terry.'

'Sounds expensive.' Graham applied the brakes. 'And none of us knows anything about the Internet, let alone e-guides.'

'Damn right we don't.' Phil knew that would be Graham's answer. 'But that's why me and Miko were thinking we could ask...'

'George!' Sarah cried. 'I mean Vanh.'

Graham conceded defeat, and proposed putting out some feelers.

'Already done. Here, let me put Miko on.'

Miko explained that, despite a few of the usual pleasantries, Mekong Marauder would not be hitting the shelves. The computer games business, it turned out, was not quite what Vanh had envisaged. He was 'in'.

*   *   *

Zul looked around his new office and smiled the broadest of smiles. In front of him, on top of a designer desk, his state-of-the-art screensaver was flashing across the monitor. 'Xidakistan – The Land that Time Forgot?' This was it. His life's work, finally rewarded. And front cover of *The Anthropologist*, to boot. For a second time, he spell-checked his article.

Now he had his own office, maybe he should get his own place. Move out from his mother's. Certainly he could afford it. Maybe, if he had his own apartment, he could ask Aunt Ta Ta down for the weekend. With his position now confirmed, the possibilities were endless.

He gave himself a spin in his new executive chair, stopping to look up at the framed certificate on the wall:

'Harvard University, The Department of Anthropology: Honorary Degree – For Services in The Field.'

Cambridge, Massachusetts, but it was a start. And there was talk of a doctorate down the line.

Finally, he would be able to walk into Marks and Spencer's, and purchase their new collection at the counter, like everyone else. With his head held high.

*   *   *

Graham says I can have a go at travel writing when I'm older, and has bought me a leather-bound notebook so I can start practising. Mum says I have to get a proper job. I don't think sales of 'Smooth As Silk' have been quite what either of them had expected. All I really want, though, is to be a sports reporter. Maybe I can go and work for Uncle Jos. He said he's going to sell Ruff Guides and move into magazines. Apparently that's where the real money is, because of the advertising. Maybe he can get me a job doing the football.

THE GAME IS UP

Last night was a real 'Night of Nights' for sky-high Xidakistan, and sports fans everywhere. It was the time The Beautiful Game finally came to town, or in this case, The Valley.

Coach, Phil 'Crazy' Kelly, had been training his Xidaki boys hard all month, but this match, against a FIFA Select XI, was always going to be a giant step up in class.

In the first half, it looked like all Kelly's Heroes were going to fluff their lines. The All-Stars raced away to a 5-0 lead, which became 8-0 by the turnaround. The Xidakis were completely outclassed and the look on the coach's face couldn't hide his disappointment. But then a different sort of disaster struck: altitude sickness.

Xidakistan's home ground is the highest in the world, and physical exertion this far above sea level was always likely to take its toll. Yet no one expected the visiting players to actually collapse. First Kruger, the tall striker from Germany, next the two centre-backs, then the All-Stars goalkeeper. With three substitutes already used, the All-Stars were down to ten men. That quickly became seven with the withdrawal of the Danish winger, Christiansen, and the two replacement centre-backs, from Argentina. The Xidakis rallied and scored their first-ever international goal with half an hour remaining. Cue scenes of wild jubilation, not least from the coach. Could this be the greatest comeback in history?

The Laws of the Game
Law 3 of the FIFA code states that both teams must have a minimum of seven players on the field at all times. When English left-back, Price, went down clutching his chest, the referee was left with no choice but to stop the game.

Match abandoned. Result: null and void. Xidakistan's FIFA ranking? Watch this space!

UN motions for Xidaki independence, like plans for a guidebook, are currently on hold. The Alphabet Game remains a corner-piece short of its puzzle. Occasionally, an intrepid player makes his (or her!) way up to The Valley, just in case, but for the moment the gold medal continues to gather dust, sitting in its commemorative glass cabinet on the Reform Club's first-floor balcony.

Paul Wilson has been travelling and writing for over twenty years. He is a leading light on The Silk Road, past and present. His other works includes *The Silk Roads* and a play, *Shakespeare Tonight*. If it is raining in Macclesfield, Paul can be found in Sydney, with his wife and family

Acknowledgements: Marat, Aleksandra and everyone at Hertfordshire Press for their help and patience. Graham Wilson for countless words of wisdom and encouragement. Jim Manthorpe for an eagle eye. Tim Ferguson for his comedy advice. Bryn Thomas for all things *Silk Roads*, including permission to use the camel icon. Wicksy for setting the Alphabet ball rolling many moons ago – 'Win with Wicks!'. Arlene and Bobby for always keeping a smile on the author's face

~~~~~~ Hertfordshire Press Title List ~~~~~~

FRIENDLY STEPPES: A SILK ROAD JOURNEY
by Nick Rowan

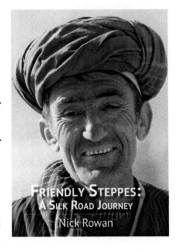

This is the chronicle of an extraordinary adventure that led Nick Rowan to some of the world's most incredible and hidden places. Intertwined with the magic of 2,000 years of Silk Road history, he recounts his experiences coupled with a remarkable realisation of just what an impact this trade route has had on our society as we know it today. Containing colourful stories, beautiful photography and vivid characters, and wrapped in the local myths and legends told by the people Nick met and who live along the route, this is both a travelogue and an education of a part of the world that has remained hidden for hundreds of years.

Friendly Steppes: A Silk Road Journey reveals just how rich the region was both culturally and economically and uncovers countless new friends as Nick travels from Venice through Eastern Europe, Iran, the ancient and modern Central Asia of places like Samarkand, Bishkek and Turkmenbashi, and on to China, along the Silk Roads of today.

RRP: £14.95
ISBN: 978-0-9557549-4-4

THE GODS OF THE MIDDLE WORLD
by Galina Dolgaya

The Gods of the Middle World, the new novel by Galina Dolgaya, tells the story of Sima, a student of archaeology for whom the old lore and ways of the Central Asian steppe peoples are as vivid as the present. When she joints a group of archaeologists in southern Kazakhstan, asking all the time whether it is really possible to 'commune with the spirits', she soon discovers the answer first hand, setting in motion events in the spirit worlds that have been frozen for centuries. Meanwhile three millennia earlier, on the same spot, a young woman and her companion struggle to survive and amend wrongs that have caused the neighbouring tribe to avenge for them. The two narratives mirror one another, while Sima finds her destiny intertwined with the struggle between the forces of good and evil. Drawing richly on the historical and mythical backgrounds of the southern Kazakh steppe, the novel ultimately addresses the responsibilities of each generation for those that follow and the central importance of love and forgiveness.

Based in Tashkent and with a lifetime of first-hand knowledge of the region in which the story is set, Galina Dolgaya has published a number of novels and poems in Russian. The Gods of the Middle World won first prize at the 2012 Open Central Asia Literature Festival and is her first work to be available in English, published by Hertfordshire Press.

ISBN: 978-0957480797
RRP: £14.95

"THIRTEEN STEPS TOWARDS THE FATE OF ERIKA KLAUS"

by the National Writer of Kyrgyzstan, Kazat Akmatov

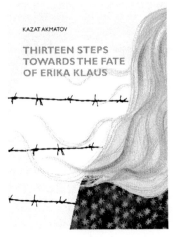

KAZAT AKMATOV

THIRTEEN STEPS
TOWARDS THE FATE
OF ERIKA KLAUS

Is set in a remote outpost governed by a fascist regime, based on real events in a mountain village in Kyrgyzstan ten years ago. It narrates challenges faced by a young, naïve Norwegian woman who has volunteered to teach English. Immersed in the local community, her outlook is excitable and romantic until she experiences the brutal enforcement of the political situation on both her own life and the livelihood of those around her. Events become increasingly violent, made all the more shocking by Akmatov's sensitive descriptions of the magnificent landscape, the simple yet proud people and their traditional customs.

Born in 1941 in the Kyrgyz Republic under the Soviet Union, Akmatov has first -hand experience of extreme political reactions to his work which deemed anti-Russian and anti-communist, resulted in censorship. Determined to fight for basic human rights in oppressed countries, he was active in the establishment of the Democratic Movement of Kyrgyzstan and through his writing, continues to highlight problems faced by other central Asian countries.

RRP: £12.95
ISBN: 978-0955754951

100 EXPERIENCES OF KYRGYZSTAN
Text by Ian Claytor

You would be forgiven for missing the tiny landlocked country of Kyrgyzstan on the map. Meshed into Central Asia's inter-locking web of former Soviet Union boundaries, this mountainous country still has more horses than cars. It never fails to surprise and delight all who visit. Proud of its nomadic traditions, dating back to the days of the Silk Road, be prepared for Kyrgyzstan's overwhelming welcome of hospitality, received, perhaps, in a shepherd's yurt out on the summer pastures. Drink bowls of freshly fermented mare's milk with newfound friends and let the country's traditions take you into their heart. Marvel at the country's icy glaciers, crystal clear lakes and dramatic gorges set beneath the pearly white Tien Shan mountains that shimmer, heaven-like, in the summer haze as the last of the winter snows caps their dominating peaks. Immerse yourself in Central Asia's jewel with its unique experiences and you will leave with a renewed zest for life and an unforgettable sense of just how man and nature can interact in harmony.

ISBN: 978-0-9574807-4-2
RRP: £14.95

100 EXPERIENCES OF KAZAKHSTAN

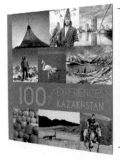 

The original land of the nomads, landlocked Kazakhstan and its expansive steppes present an intriguing border between Europe and Asia. Dispel the notion of oil barons and Borat and be prepared for a warm welcome into a land full of contrasts. A visit to this newly independent country will transport you to a bygone era and discover a country full of wonders and legends. Whether you are searching for the descendants of Genghis Khan who left his mark on this country seven hundred years ago or are looking to discover the futuristic architecture of its capital Astana, visitors cannot fail but be impressed by what they experience. For those seeking adventure, the formidable Altai and Tian Shan mountains provide challenges at all levels. Alternatively, really go off the beaten track and visit Kazakhstan's industrial legacy at Aktau, the Aral Sea or the space launch centre at Baikonur. Bird and animal lovers will gloat over the diversity of species that can be seen from antelopes to flamingos. Above all, whether you are in cosmopolitan Almaty or out in the wilds of Western Kazakstan, you will come across a warm people, proud of the heritage and keen to show you a traditional country that is at the forefront of the region's economic development.

Discovery Magazine's colourful new title, exploring the 100 essential experiences of Kazakhstan covers everything from its cities to culture, horse games to holidays and authors to yurts. Told through personal experiences written by locals, each vignette brings the reader closer to understanding and interacting with one of Central Asia's most intriguing cultures, often missed by transiting travellers keen to reach Uzbekistan and Kyrgyzstan. This publication, filled with stunning photography, brings out the exhilarating flavours of the country's foods, spectacular scenery and warm-hearted people and deservedly leaves you with the urge to return again and visit the next 100 experiences that await you.

RRP: £19.95
ISBN: 978-0-9927873-5-6

Lightning Source UK Ltd.
Milton Keynes UK
UKOW03f0708090514

231359UK00002B/29/P